The Strength of Tradition

The Strength of Tradition

*Stories of the Immigrant Presence
in Australia, 1970–81*

edited by R.F. Holt

University of Queensland Press
St Lucia • London • New York

Typeset by University of Queensland Press
Printed and bound by Warren Printing Co. Ltd,
Hong Kong

Distributed in the United Kingdom, Europe, the Middle East, Africa, and the Caribbean by Prentice-Hall International, International Book Distributors Ltd, 66 Wood Lane End, Hemel Hempstead, Herts., England

Published with the assistance of the Literature Board of the Australia Council

National Library of Australia Cataloguing-in-Publication data

The Strength of Tradition

    ISBN 0 7022 1691 7.
    ISBN 0 7022 1701 8 (pbk.).

    1. Short stories, Australian — Foreign authors.
    I. Holt, R. F. (Ronald Frederick), 1939—.
    (Series: Paperback prose).

A823'.0108

Library of Congress Cataloging in Publication Data
Main entry under title:

The Strength of Tradition

    (Paperback prose, ISSN 0156-6628)
    1. Short stories, Australian. 2. Australian fiction—
20th century. 3. Australia—Emigration and immigration
—Fiction. 4. Emigration and immigration—Fiction.
I. Holt, R. F. (Ronald F.)
PR9617.32.N48 1982   823'.01'08994   82-10874
ISBN 0-7022-1701-8
ISBN 0-7022-1691-7 (hard)

Dedicated to David Martin who wrote:

Roots

Some men can only love
The country of their birth,
But some are not like that,
Their hearts have wider girth.

All trees have but one stem,
Yet some have many roots;
Don't judge them by their bark,
But judge them by their fruits.

Contents

Acknowledgments

Acknowledgments for stories in this anthology are due to the authors and to the following periodicals and publishers:

Dezsery Ethnic Publications for "They, too, were able to go" by Leonid Trett and "Dictionary" by Maria Novak, published in *English and other than English. Anthology in Community Languages* (1979) edited by András Dezsery, and for "Show me the Palm of your Hand" and "A Handful of Earth from Home" by András Dezsery, in *Neighbours* (1979) by András Dezsery; *Southerly* for "The Factory" by Irmgard Duhs and "The Strength of Tradition" by Judah Waten (also published by Readers Digest under the title "End, Tradition" in *Great Short Stories of Australia and New Zealand*); Edward Arnold and John Cochrane for "The Naked Walls" by Heinz Nonveiller, in *Modern Australian Short Stories* (1971), edited by Mary Lord; Kurundu Publications for "One's Land" and "Volcano" by Pino Bosi, in *The Checkmate and Other Short Stories* (1973) by Pino Bosi; Fremantle Arts Centre Press for "Mademoiselle" and "The Pensioners" by Vasso Kalamaras, in *Other Earth. Four Greek-Australian Stories* (1977) by Vasso Kalamaras; *Westerly* for "To Discuss the Possibility of . . . " by Ugo Rotellini and "Wong Chu and the Queen's Letterbox" by Tom Hungerford; *Overland* for "Giovanni's Courtship" by Vic Caruso and "Smoko" by Ray Wood; *Age* (Melbourne) for "The Economies of Mourning" by Zeny Giles; *inprint* for "But Your Ways are Strange to Me" by Zeny Giles, "Jim Christos — the Cuckold" and "Kapetan Nikola" by Nicholas Athanasou, and "'The Black'", by Michael George Smith; Penguin for "Bobbeh" by Morris Lurie, in *Dirty Friends* (1981) by Morris Lurie; "A Beacon in the Night" appeared in *Inside the Wardrobe* by Morris Lurie (Outback Press, 1976); University of Queensland Press for "Barbecue" and "The Boxer and the Grocer" by Angelo Loukakis, in *For the Patriarch* (1981) by Angelo Loukakis; *Hemisphere* for "The Street" by Gwen Kelly; the Australian Association for the Teaching of English for "Indira" by Joe Wright, in *The Blindfold Horse* (1975); Angus & Robertson for "Second Growth" by Helen Wilson, in *The Skedule and Other Australian Short Stories* (1979) by Helen Wilson, "Hostages" by Fay Zwicky, in *Coast to Coast* (1973) edited by Frank Moorehouse, "Before the Day Goes" by Peter Goldsworthy, in *Archipelagoes* (1982) by Peter Goldsworthy; Collins for "Middle Eastern Questions" by Nancy Keesing, in *Shalom. A Collection of Australian Jewish Stories* (1978), edited by Nancy Keesing; Thomas Nelson for "A Slipper for Adriana" by Joan M. Bean, in *Australian New Writing* (1973), edited by O. Mendelson and H. Marks.

Acknowledgment is also made to Jacaranda Wiley Ltd for permission to reprint the poem on the dedication page, from *I Rhyme My Time* (1980).

Every effort has been made to contact copyright holders, but in a few cases this has not proved possible. The University of Queensland Press would be interested to hear from any copyright holders who have not been acknowledged.

Foreword

The purpose of this anthology is to give readers convenient access to an important theme in modern Australian literature: our growing multiculturalism. As a thematic collection, the book does not pretend to be thoroughly representative from this particular point of view, although quite a wide range of cultural backgrounds is included. The sub-title of the collection, for example, indicates that the important area of writing by and about Aboriginal Australians has been excluded; this, to be sure, has not been due to any lack of excellence or quantity in the literary treatment of that important dimension to our multiculturalism, but rather has resulted from considerations such as space, the "immigrant" perspective and the appropriateness of a more exclusive or adequate treatment of the Aboriginal experience in our modern national literature.

Behind this general purpose of the collector have been two aims: first, to provide readers with a resource which, as literature (in contradistinction to the more detached, or even metaphysical, style in which this theme might be typically treated by, say, the social sciences), gives some sort of view "from the inside", as it were, of the rich bubbling mixture which is, or might increasingly be, our culture and society; second, to focus on genuinely Australian writing and writers whose theme has tended to be overlooked.

Only one other collection of this sort has been published, prior to the 1980s: *Two Ways Meet. Stories of Migrants in Australia*, edited by Louise E. Rorabacher, first published in Melbourne in 1963. It was perhaps symptomatic of the times that this was a work which had to be initiated by an American, and in which all but four of the contributing authors came from English-speaking backgrounds.[1]

Since the 1950s and very early 1960s a lot has happened

to the cultural composition of Australian society. The first great immigrant wave, consisting of stateless or displaced persons (the so-called DP's) gave way in the mid-sixties to a still strong, but purely voluntary influx of European, and especially British, immigrants — many of whom treated the exercise as a sort of poor man's *Bildungsreise* and returned home after a few years. By the early 1970s, of course, European migration was less active and Australia's net tended to swing Southeast, towards the Middle East and the Pacific. By the late seventies too another great wave had begun, from Southeast Asia.

With one exception, this collection of short stories consists entirely of materials written and/or published between 1970 and 1980. Its main focus is European immigration, from three points of view: the first generation European's, the second generation European's and the traditional or Anglo-Celtic Australian's. These represent the three basic divisions in the book's contents.[2]

Standard Australian short story anthologies of the 1960s and 1970s seemed almost impervious to what, in per capita terms, might be called one of the greatest population transplants of modern history.[3] Except for gifted, sympathetic, first generation writers like Judah Waten and David Martin or second generation writers like Mena Abdullah or older favourites such as O. E. Schlunke, the overriding impression of Australian prose literature was one of cultural homogeneity. True, even at that time the odd story like Polish June Factor's "The Wedding" gave evidence of the cultural percolations that were going on; the same is true at a more distant level of recollection in a Colin Thiele novel, *The Labourers in the Vineyard*. But it would seem that it was not until the 1970s that the literary exploration of our experience of multiculturalism had begun in earnest.

The stories published here evidence a progression which the social scientists have described as an ideological development from Anglo-conformism to Integration; many of the younger generation's stories reflect that maturity and comfort with the complexities of bi- and multi-culturalism which saw, in the later seventies, the gradual disappearance of the term "New Australian". As such, they might be said to represent something of a considerable achievement in cultural-anthropological terms. From this vantage point the stories by the (predominantly) Anglo-Celts (Part 3) are of particular significance. Gwen Kelly's "The Street" has been included for its depiction of what might be called a picture representative of pre-immigrant postwar Australia . . . the *tabula rasa* sort of condition that the first generation Europeans came across. Its gentle reference to religious bigotry and Scottish traits is a reminder too of the recency of origin of so many of the so-called traditional, British Australians of the 1930s. Tom Hungerford's "Wong Chu and the Queen's Letterbox", on the other hand, reminds one of the signs of the much earlier and considerable cultural heterogeneity which persisted into the present.

The acts of empathy which these writings by "the hosts" incorporate are evidence, of course, for the fact that multiculturalism is a dynamic process, influencing newcomer and host alike. Other stories also show the dynamics of *inter-immigrant* experience. Many writers in evaluating their original cultural values in the new environment have become aware of other ethnic groups' values and experiences, in a way that did not seem possible even when they were intact, geographical neighbours in Europe. (Judah Waten's contribution in this collection is a salutary example of this.)

The present stories are, compared to the realities of the continuing two-way process which is assimilation, merely the tiny tip of a giant iceberg. In a more qualitative sense, however, they can provide us with an insight into those processses "beneath the surface", as it were, which with gathering momentum are forging a new Australian identity.

Bathurst, 1981.

NOTES

1. Only one other collection, to the present editor's knowledge, has been published since then, in 1981: *Ethnic Australia*, ed. Manfred Jurgensen (Brisbane: Phoenix Publications, 1981). It includes writing by twenty four authors (one of Aboriginal, twenty-one of European, one of Mexican and one of Sri Lankan

background) and concentrates on poetry; twenty-two stories and sixty-two poems make up the contents.

2. This classification, of course, is not without its problems of definition. For example, an author like Judah Waten could just as easily be placed in Part 3 and conversely a much younger writer like Michael Smith could easily be placed in Part 2, or even Part 1. (See "Brief Notes on the Authors".)

3. Such as: *Short Stories of Australia. The Moderns,* ed. Beatrice Davis (Sydney: Angus and Robertson, 1967); *Classic Australian Short Stories,* ed. Judah Waten and Stephen Murray-Smith (Melbourne: Wren, 1974); *The Penguin Book of Australian Short Stories,* ed. Harry Heseltine (Melbourne: Penguin, 1976).

PART 1

The First Generation

They, too, were able to go

Leonid Trett

It happens sometimes in our life that in some occasional —
sometimes even not particularly promising — circumstances
we suddenly witness something we can never forget. We
witness a scene in which some striking human quality
suddenly reveals itself to a degree we could not imagine, and
it impresses and teaches us more than outstanding works of
art or philosophy.

It was a few weeks before the end of World War II.
Germany was on the verge of collapse. Following massive and
endless bombing by the Allied airforces the whole system of
public order was thrown out of balance and began gradually
to disintegrate, so that nothing functioned in an orderly
manner anymore.

I travelled in a railway carriage with broken windows from
Augsburg through Munich to Murnau to catch a train there
to Oberammergau. Icy wind mercilessly blew through the
unheated, cold compartments, throwing shots of hard, sharp
snowflakes at the faces of shuddering passengers. I sat in the
corner of a half empty carriage and thought of the distress
and misery brought about by the senseless war. And, while
doing so, I could not help thinking especially of the people
in the next carriage. I saw them when, looking for a seat, I
went through their carriage in Munich, where I had to change
trains. It was not a Red Cross carriage, but just an ordinary
third-class one. It was full of wounded soldiers. They represented all kinds of injuries a savage war can bring about. Two
soldiers there had caught my eyes more than anybody else.
One was without both legs — a fully legless body of a baby-
faced youth in the soldier's uniform, funnily standing, like
a kind of big bottle, on the seat. Beside him sat an armless
giant who was also totally blind. Instead of eyes he had two
deep, empty caves.

Yes, they were there, in the next carriage, one blind and armless, the other with eyes and arms, but without legs, and from where I was sitting I not only was unable to avoid thinking of them, but could even not help actually feeling their tragic nearness.

I usually travelled that way at the same time of evening once a week and I knew well where all these cripples were going to.

Near a station along that railway, not far away from Weilheim, there was a big military hospital, and always, when I drove that way, a crowd of wounded soldiers would alight from the train at that station. Ambulances with big red crosses on the sides and tops were always parked near the station. At the arrival of the train, strong medical orderlies with stretchers and friendly young nurses in white uniforms always awaited them on the platform. The train would stop at this station for a good while and there was always plenty of time to make observations.

Now the train again was approaching that station and the familiar contours of the hospital buildings had emerged on the horizon in the dusk of the cold early spring evening. I looked from the window. There were no ambulances in sight that night, neither were there nurses waiting on the platform. The disintegration of the previously so immaculate German order was that far.

The train stopped and the crowd of wounded men in green uniforms (quickly and eagerly, as the injured soldiers always used to do at that station) alighted from the train and dispersed over the platform. I noticed how the sense of disappointment and indignation overtook them and how strongly it reflected in their faces and even in their bodies when they realized that nobody was meeting them, and even more so when they found out that nobody was supposed to meet them either.

I saw how they lingered for a while on the platform, uncertain and hurt in their feelings, then picked up, with desperate determination, their suitcases and rucksacks from the ground, and began to move along the platform in a solid pack towards the road leading towards the dark contours of camouflaged hospital buildings in the distance.

They went — a sad, miserable collection of young men

with multilated, crippled bodies, bowed under the weight of their rucksacks, energetically moving their sticks and crutches, some without one leg, some without one arm, some with heads in bandages. They went in a hurry you would not expect from them, and soon disappeared behind the high hedge growing along the railway line.

Only two of them remained on the platform. I recognized them at once.

One was the blind armless giant and the other the legless baby-faced youth I saw in Munich and of whom I was thinking all the way. They stood there, (the legless youth with his trunk straight on the ground) both helpless and lost, with their faces and bodies turned in the direction where their more fortunate comrades had gone. The trunk of the legless soldier looking as if it were a strange, manlike plant in a soldier's uniform growing from the platform.

I looked at my neighbours, but nobody was willing to meet my eyes. All sat silently and grimly gazed aside. All were Germans and were ashamed of what they had seen and afraid of their future.

No, something must be done. They cannot stay there forever, but what? What could be done in the prevailing circumstances?

Then the train suddenly began to move, not in the forward, but in the backward direction, and went far past the platform, leaving the two crippled soldiers out of sight. Soon it stopped for a short time and then started moving forward again, and drove without stopping any more past the platform — at first slowly, then at full speed.

And it was then that I saw a picture I shall never forget. The young legless soldier, two big rucksacks, one upon the other on his back, hung on the broad back of the armless and blind giant, with his arms around his neck, and this pathetic couple of helpless cripples, making together two arms, two legs and two eyes, marched on their own, like one ablebodied human being, towards the warmth of the distant hospital.

It was the most touching form of human cooperation, mutual help and ingenuity I had ever seen, and I wished that everybody could see it and think of it in the days of grief and despair as well as luck and happiness.

Show me the Palm of your Hand

András Dezsery

There we were, nurturing big hopes in our hostel room, lounging on our beds, fanning ourselves in the stifling heat, and waiting for the loudspeaker to call us. We waited — but waited in vain — for the first job to come our way. This was Christmas, and while the holiday season stretched out endlessly, nothing happened, nor did we get any mail, nor even newspapers. Rumours were our only link with the outside world. But some of us showed more gumption than the others in finding ways to kill time. They simply stepped over the low fence of our camp and let themselves drift into neighbouring gardens, making friends with the inmates. It was they who brought us the first eyewitness accounts, colourful if incoherent information.

The streets were almost deserted, but all the time we felt we were being watched from behind the white lace curtains. Whenever they talk to us, they tend to be kind, we noted, and as doors opened themselves to us, we met kindness but also many — to us — new customs. We passed them in review: women smoke in public, but special space is reserved for them in tramcars. Restaurants, in the sense we knew them, just didn't exist. Movie tickets were cheap. Bars, where people drank standing up, closed at 6.00 P.M.

At long last, one fine afternoon, the loudspeaker gave tongue: all to assemble in front of the camp office. Jobs will be assigned.

I had no worries concerning my food. As for physical love . . . well, the stupidity of administration had long ago taken care of that, compelling us to leave our womenfolk behind in another State of the Commonwealth. And the summer had marked my face with a stamp of weariness on top of my basically introvert nature.

In other words, I didn't show great eagerness as I tried to approach the loudspeaker through the throng.

All it said was that today three big corporations would take on workers from among us. Holden, Chrysler, Phillips — those were the three names we'd been hearing in the camp, over and over again. They were on all lips, like magic formulae. For if any of those took you on, your life would change at once.

You'd live out of a camp, be reunited with your family, maybe even buy a car. Who knows . . .?

Well, there we stood in the stifling heat, each one of us adopting a posture of prowess, all of us smiling meaningfully, as if conscious that this large group of differing nationalities must present a friendly family picture — how different from the habitual scramble for breakfast or the often rude jostling for the unemployment benefits. This time there was hardly a word spoken and all stood almost motionless.

The envoys of the "three big powers" seemed to be doing their selecting more or less at random. They would point their finger at somebody in the crowd, and if the right chap pricked up his ears, beckon to him to join them.

I wasn't wanted by any of them. So back I went to my tiny room and lay down on my bed, on my fine Australian woollen blanket and let my mind wander back into the past. Why, indeed, has I chosen to come to Australia from Germany?

It had happened a few months before, while I was waiting in a barber's shop. Suddenly a loud voice, speaking with a rasping Prussian accent, had woken me from my day-dreaming.

While his face was being lathered he was holding forth to the entire barber's shop. He was remonstrating about those bloody foreigners who were playing havoc everywhere. Quite recently they had arrested a con man when he appeared with his fifteenth fiancee at the Registrar's office. They'd fought a pitched battle with the nuns, trying to rob them of the potatoes they were harvesting. "They are stealing the fruit from our trees," he continued, "and right now I have been reading a Report by the Ministry of Justice which states that in criminal cases the go-between is usually a foreigner. Just think of it, in Bayreuth alone eighty-nine Hungarians have already acquired individual apartments."

I stepped up to him and said: "Excuse me sir, I happen to be a Hungarian. We are one of the proudest nations in the world. Including our ethnic Germans we account for about two per cent of today's population in Bavaria. I feel like a phantom, an extinct bird, strictly speaking — neither refugee nor a DP. So, please, advise me: where should I emigrate to?"

"Go to Australia," he retorted haughtily. And, perhaps he felt a little conscience stricken, so he laid his head back on the head-guard on the top of the barber's armchair as if to signify that he considered the argument closed.

"But why precisely to Australia," I insisted, although the barber was already working on his lathered jowls.

I had to wait a little while till the barber finished his job and wiped the remaining traces of lather from the man's face. That being done, he planted himself squarely opposite me and said:

"I fought hand to hand against Australian soldiers in the Libyan Desert. They were well fed, well dressed and unfussy. That's why."

Well, now I lay on my bed in Australia.

I didn't like that selection procedure in the camp yard today; no more than I had liked it when during our long voyage I had to show the palms of my hands and my muscles and my teeth, and when they took blood samples from me and had me x-rayed. They turned me into a mere number with the result that I had no desire left in me to step out of line. I did as I was bid and even did it with a smile.

And that last night in Naples, before leaving Europe! By the time we got there I felt as if I had approached my goal painfully, step by step, and was ready to collapse. All I could remember was the whimpering of small children, the cursing of the men, the crying of the women, and oh, that Italian cloudburst sending cataracts of water down my collar. Amid wooden huts and army tents, they drove us from fatigue to fatigue — now to peel potatoes, now to line up at the medical officer's surgery for some inoculation, or again to wash down your bed with disinfectant. The cooks were big and burly, working stripped to the waist among flies big as butterflies. And then the washing and the washing up, always in cold water, and the endless standing in queues for those seatless lavatories. The dread of diseases. The children kept hidden in their beds till departure and frightening each other with the fearful word of illness.

And those English lessons spiked with local place names — Capua, Aversa, San Antonio. The soup kitchen, where five hundred of us were fed and where with each portion issued a small tin number was hung upon a board studded with nails. And, then, the repeated customs examinations and questionings, and the classification of those suitable for light, medium or heavy physical work. And all the black market dealings in blankets, sugar, jewellery, footwear, and so on. Luckiest are the craftsmen among us; they make wooden clogs or cut hair or whatever else their learned craft enables them to do. It's all a turmoil of bargaining.

How much do you charge? How much do you want? What's the price of that?

At long last I am on board ship. The milling of the crowds is the same on the decks and amid those coming up the gangway as dusk is falling. We are about to start, to lift anchor. My nerves are taut like those of a sprinter waiting for the starter's pistol.

My mother's letter which miraculously reached me is in my pocket. She wrote:

"I can imagine how much you must have fought, in body and soul, before you came to this decision. I know how much homesickness is welling up in you right now; but this is how it had to be . . . When from your ship you are looking at the coastline of Italy receding, search the crowds ashore with your eyes; perhaps among those waving goodbye you'll find me."

I can see the waterside where our train deposited us, guarded by policemen. They reminded me of all those different guards who accompanied the first phase of my emigration.

The heavy gangway is just being pulled in; now it lies parallel with the terminal of the railway line.

I am getting more and more excited, looking at those standing ashore, searching for my mother's eyes among them.

Indeed there is a woman, about her height, wearing a red dress and white shoes. Whom may she have seen off? There aren't so many people standing on the seafront, except for the odd dockers, customs officials and policemen. So she's naturally rather conspicuous.

Some people are throwing letters from the ship. The woman collects them as they fall ashore. One of them hits a steel pillar and slides into the dark waters of the Thyrrenian Sea. There will be someone waiting for it in vain.

It's still there, floating, that white oblong, slowly getting heavier with the moisture that begins to permeate it . . . Perhaps it still could be fished out . . .

All of a sudden I'm gripped by fear; I feel, looking into the dark, that the end is close, too close. What's going to happen to me? What am I to become?

It is nine o'clock now and as if at a secret signal we all begin to wave and those on the shore wave back to us.

From among the people standing about on the waterfront a man wearing a black mackintosh is suddenly seen to step out of the crowd, and like the red-coated woman, accompany our ship as it gets moving.

One of our fellow travellers cracks a joke: "They must have been hired as sort of funeral attendants — the man for our womenfolk, the woman for us men!"

But nobody laughs.

I have often recalled, since, our goodbye to Europe.

And now let me turn my hands, my palms upwards and ask myself: What kind of work shall I begin to do with them? And when?

A Handful of Earth from Home

András Dezsery

One fine day, the rumour went round by word of mouth that you could buy earth from home. In the market place, on board the buses, at a number of street corners and Hungarian restaurants, an address was being circulated.

At that time I had delighted in collecting everything with a Hungarian slant: books, gramophone records, cushions, rugs, dolls, ashtrays; gradually assembling everything needed for furnishing a room. I called it my Hungarian room.

Its walls I decorated with Hungarian pottery and homespun fabrics. In a glass cabinet I displayed the best known statuettes coming from Herend, our world-famous porcelain manufacturer: Mrs Dery, the celebrated nineteenth-century actress; Csikos, the typical horse-herdsman, and others. In peasant pottery jugs I placed fresh flowers; Hungarian oil paintings hung on the walls that were daubed in green, and from which the windowsills jutted out painted a vivid cherry-red.

I was in love with that room.

On my next Saturday afternoon off, I set out to get my Hungarian soil.

At the address I had been given I found a house, the type of house that has thousands of exact replicas. My knocking was answered by a slightly-built, surly man, obviously keen on getting rid of me.

"I had some Hungarian earth, you're quite right. But I sold it all." And with that he banged the door in my face.

A few weeks later, curiosity and a sense of dissatisfaction at having been refused impelled me to return to the charge and knock once again at the door of that "two cents-a-dozen" house.

But this time I formulated my request differently.

"Could you help me," I asked, "to get at least a handful

of Hungarian earth; I want it so badly. Even a small handful would be enough, if it's genuine."

"I've just received a limited consignment," said he beckoning me indoors. I saw on his face that he realized I'd been there before. We were strangers no longer. In other words, the business could be discussed.

"I have available earth from different regions; which is your home county?" he inquired.

"I should like to have some earth from the capital; from the bank of the Danube, if possible," I replied, "from the Buda side, you know." And I added with a sigh, "More precisely from that quaint little residential district called the Tabán."

"Kindly wait a little while."

"Can I be of any help?"

"No, no. Just wait a few moments."

The deal done, I was ambling home with my little bit of earth. He'd packed it in a small, white plastic bag, tied round with a red-white-green ribbon in our national colours. I had to haggle with him to accept some money for it, because at first he sternly refused. I implored him to accept at least the refund of his out-of-pocket expenses. And I also bought from him a bottle of paprika sauce of his own concoction, as well as a bottle of genuine Kecskemét apricot brandy, which it appeared had been smuggled out of Hungary together with the sacred soil.

I showed my acquisition to a few friends, took it to my place of work, and finally transferred the earth with great care into a flower pot, making quite sure I didn't lose a particle of it.

Thanks to its presence the Hungarian room became even more pronouncedly a piece of my native land. No wonder I considered that potful of home soil a true treasure to be tended with utmost care.

I didn't want to plant anything in it. But I kept it damp like the other green plants around it. I loved it more like that

— alive with moisture — than I would have if it had all dried up.

My joy became even greater when, one day, I saw a tiny green promise, the tender shoot of a seedling, piercing the top of my good Tabán soil.

Today, I am a man in distress, a man deeply offended. With my arms and legs limp, I sit here, and I just don't know if I should laugh or cry. For the unexpected, tiny plant turned out to be the seedling of an Australian wattle.

The Factory

Irmgard Duhs

She stood in the middle of the street waiting for the tram. The heat gathered over the asphalt. The heat was a new experience for her, all dominant and physical. She felt imprisoned in her body, weighed down, somehow isolated from herself, as if her only existence lay in a thin line of disconnected thoughts and vague desires floating at the edge of consciousness.

The iron stand of the stop sign was too hot to lean against. She moved two steps to the side, closed her eyes to a narrow slit and surrendered. The street scene in front of her was almost as hard to bear as the heat: the line of mean little· shops, shop windows hidden behind a clutter of awnings of all shapes and sizes, topped with great garish signs, as if these alone ought to give them reality. Nothing was real any more, she thought. There was an air of desolate magic over the whole place. In the hard light, streets and buildings looked lifeless and stark. The light wooden constructions of the houses which overspread the hill and the plain beyond gave out a ghostly effect. Even the row of waiting women, dressed up for town in neatly starched pink and light blue dresses, seemed too pink, somehow clown-like.

Gerhild felt caught in a mirage, an imaginary fata morgana, from which she wanted to escape and couldn't. And the only measure she knew was to cling bravely to the surface, to ignore the dregs of fear and desolation in her soul and to summon up determination, or, as her mother would have expressed it, to "become a bit more realistic". But even that helped little here as she had soon found out. Situations vacant and timetables were hard facts in the mornings but usually dissolved over the day into nothing, or into polite evasions of sympathy and regret. And there was always somebody ready to help who — with emphasis and conviction in his voice — supposed something, or had heard of it, and somebody who had been in Munich last year. And then the mutual goodwill could flow along the lines liked best. It was always the same answers to the same questions received with great satisfaction, and strangest of all — in complete serious- ness. She remembered the groups of Italians who in the evenings gathered on the big Platz in front of the railway stations, and who in the winter cold looked like a flock of lost birds. She would have thought it naive to ask them how they liked Germany, let alone to put her whole soul into such a question. This almost religious Australian belief in generali- zation and truism, this too had something unreal.

Sometime later the tram came noiselessly out of the glare, a high rattling machine. Nobody looked up. One after the other the queue of women climbed up with unthinking assur- ance as if it was a hired car for a ladies' outing, *their* car.

Gerhild climbed into the back compartment. In the morning you couldn't do that because then only men sat there. And for two days at her appearance embarrassed male faces had disappeared behind their newspapers until she had discovered that "ladies" sat in the front. She would write that in her next letter home. That was one of the few advantages of immigrant life, you always knew what to write in your next letter. She sat down and took out of her hand- bag the one that had just arrived this morning. "Now it is already Christmas," her mother wrote, "how quickly time passes. Last week we had two days snow . . . It is Sunday morning" . . . Christmas and Sunday, she thought with a feel- ing of envious longing. It sounded as if it came from a fairy story; Germany itself seemed now a country out of time past.

At the same time she kept an eye out for the conductor. From the bus depot it was only ten cents and she desperately wanted to save the other five. At least they didn't make you pay a penalty here and nobody shouted at you. She would act helpless and surprised and the inspectors were as neutral as the Queen's bodyguard. She loved this English custom of hearing no evil and seeing no evil. "Where do you want to go lady? Grey Street Bridge? That's fifteen cents. Hot day today isn't it?" In this way you always carried on two conver- sations, one you could hear and one you couldn't.

Then she saw Tania's black head appear and livened up. Tania was a piece of the old European order which in Germany even in the country was fading out. For Gerhild, Tania had something sparkling, something alive, like a mirror in a dull room, something hard also.

"Hel-oh, you aare air-le today," she said, rolling her heavy Russian r's and her green eyes smiled shyly and mockingly. She too was glad to see the other. Tania was small and solidly built with a narrow waist. She wore a pale green, well-fitting dress whose pattern was as old-fashioned as the bun on the back of her neck and which made her white skin appear even more delicate.

"Here! Try my bread," she said pleased with herself. She reached into her bag and passed Gerhild a carefully wrapped sandwich. "I have baked it this morning," she said still smiling. "This Australian bread is no good."

"I know. But yours is!"

"Sometimes I bake it on Sunday but then my mother-in-law gets so upset because of the church you know. But you can't go every Sunday to church when you go to work."

No, thought Gerhild, practical intelligence was hardly ever found with religious fervour, nor did it question the religious basis.

"What church you go?" Tania asked.

Gerhild shrugged her shoulders, then she saw the other's sincere, wholly concerned glance, and hesitated, swaying between laughter and consideration.

"No church no good," said the Russian girl softly and shook her head.

Gerhild leaned her head against the window and looked outside. The street went into a sharp downgrade. The rows and rows of front gardens and wooden houses seeped into her consciousness like nausea. The whole world had become one spread-out monotonous ugliness of straight-lined and cross-lined streets and house fronts, as monotonous and endless as the bush, as the heat. She wondered why the suburbs still had names, why not like the schoolhouse system, Blocks A, B, C, which in fact they really were, parts of one huge spread-out residential area around the city. At least Annerley lies on top of a hill she thought. Despite that she always counted the tramstops when she went back at midnight. That was a surer way.

"You look much better today," Tania said.

"Do I?"

"Yes, yesterday when we packed the tins I could see how difficult the work was for you and I thought she must be sick." She spoke in a neutral tone like a teacher about a poor student and her smile was tinged with a mixture of curiosity and contempt. Gerhild nodded tiredly. Suddenly she felt weak beside the alert intelligence of this girl who had grown up in the same eastern tradition of perseverance and exactness but was its true product. She would be a good technical assistant Gerhild thought. No, probably Tania would master nearly every job and she knew it. But Brisbane had no prospects for a young Russian woman who spoke broken English.

"Why do you do night shift?" she asked.

"Because of my son," Tania smiled happily. "My husband minds him in the evenings and I in the morning. I was so tired yesterday, and in the night he woke up and cried and I gave him a little smack but my husband said 'Don't hit him!' You know he loves him so."

"Then why don't you give a few Russian lessons?"

"Oh no." She lifted both hands expressively. "I'm not an educated woman and I don't speak good English."

"You understand English better than I do," said Gerhild.

"I know some Russians who do this. They advertise in the paper but they are educated people," Tania repeated with conviction. Suddenly she looked at her curiously. "Do you teach German?"

"No, I was a typist in Germany," Gerhild lied. She saw the thoughtful weighing glance of the other. At Siemens' I got the same glances she thought. They only needed to look at your lame helpless smile with which you apologized all the time for having an "education" and filing Müller under Myer. "Yes the ABC isn't as simple as some people think, not even for Uni students," somebody would say with great satisfaction, and she had felt back again as mummy's darling amongst shouting kids at the infants' school. Here, all was different. For the girls in the factory she was just another girl, thank God. The only real social barrier in this country was money, and "education" was nothing but a degree, a special licence for making money, and as such admired, but then so was winning the casket or owning a block of flats. If Karl Marx would climb out of his grave tomorrow and add a nought to all the factory wages, the whole nation would queue up before the factory gates. She suppressed a smile, Tania looked at her expectantly. How young she looks Gerhild thought. Fancy that in her head of all people the old world's social barriers should survive. Bildung, culture — for this Russian girl education was still the other thing, the mysterious power that mightn't make you successful but would make you different. Yes, Tania lived in a no-man's-land. She had a conception of a society which didn't exist any more in Russia and which had never touched Australia.

Gerhild looked over to her. But she seemed absorbed in her own thoughts. Gerhild liked her a lot but sometimes she dreaded those quick mocking eyes — more than Lorraine's cold blue ones. I want to live, she thought defiantly.

They got off the tram before the bridge. Gerhild stared at the broad river and the spreading red poinciana trees on the other bank and wished she could spend the afternoon there. Exactly opposite was the factory and each evening at six o'clock when the work slackened off she looked over to the chain of lights above the river.

"Not here," Tania's voice broke in, "they don't want us to go through the front entrance."

"Don't they?"

"No, we are not fine enough," Tania said and her ironic smile shimmered in her voice.

They climbed up the small dark staircase. Gerhild tugged nervously at the neck of her dress. The next seconds were always unpleasant. The sudden fluorescent lighting, women in blue work dresses running to and fro and Tania's sudden disappearance. She went over to the wall where the work cards stuck out. Hers wasn't there. She bit on her nails and tried to think. The day before yesterday the time had been missing and she couldn't remember anything. "You might not get paid for the day," some of the women had said, as if the place was a high school and she had forgotten her exercise book and might miss out on marks. Yesterday her card had been hidden behind somebody else's. Helplessly she looked around. "They've changed the boards," a woman said passing by. Gerhild went around the corner. 552. The card stuck. She took it out and held it in the slit of the time clock. The apparatus gave a bright singing sound. Carefully she replaced the card. Then she went into the changing room. A group of younger women were sitting around the wash-basins smoking. She went straight through to the back. The room was big and windowless and the dull light of yellow bulbs hung around the ceiling. A narrow passageway cut through the rows of lockers that filled the room and on the wooden benches between them, women were sitting, the young ones chattering and giggling, the older ones knitting in silence. She nodded to Judy and unlocked her locker. Tania was just changing. In her blue shift and her white bonnet she looked gay and rustic.

"Four minutes left," a thin blonde said.

"Not quite." The girls beside her checked their watches. Gerhild knew they wouldn't go upstairs a minute too soon. It was a game they played every day. They sat their minutes away as if they wanted to demonstrate the rights of the worker and gain a second or two if possible.

Exactly four minutes later she lined up at the end of the long queue of women for the night shift. At the top of the staircase by the entrance to the packing room Lorraine stood with one of the other superiors and each of the girls passing them smiled and said "Excuse me". Gerhild took Tania's arm. "What nonsense is this? The queens are taking the parade I suppose."

"They want us to be polite."

"Ridiculous," hissed Gerhild, pressing her lips together and staring at the floor.

The smell of hot flour dust and the pounding of machines filled the hall and through it came a few shrill voices and the clanking sound of shunting trolleys. A group of new day-shift girls stood by the sorting machine. You could recognize them immediately by their Dutch look: the sticking-out ends of their white caps. In a few days like all the other girls they would shorten their uniforms and pin their bonnets back coquettishly with lots of pleats, reducing them to half the size. Lorraine came sailing through the room, her head exalted. Maria Meneghini, black hair, black eyes and a Roman nose. She bore an amazing resemblance to Callas and Gerhild wondered why nobody had remarked upon it yet. Her elegant figure, her moods and theatrical gestures fitted strangely in a factory. Even amongst the slim, well mannered Australian women of her age Lorraine contrived to look like a peacock in a chicken run.

"Gert-ie! You go over to section four for fifteen minutes. The girls there will show you what to do." With each sentence her pronunciation became more distinctive and stressed. "Then go to the reject section and relieve Jill."

Section four, what on earth was that? And who was Jill? Gerhild knew them all by sight but she found it difficult to fit names like Jill, Jean or Kim to faces of forty-five year old women. "Do you know where section four is?" she asked Tania nervously and thought that they had actually started on the same day.

"Over there." She pointed to the right towards the line of windows.

She knew there was no help to be expected from Tania anymore. Tania followed the call of authority now and from her eastern experience "they" had a watchful eye to sift out those who could cope and those who lagged behind.

Jill, who was Jill? Was it the big blonde? And how many minutes did she say for? When she turned around she saw Tania already disappear behind the first conveyor belt. She started to hurry after her.

"Gertie!!" A domineering cry, and Lorraine's long manicured forefinger danced up and down in front of Gerhild's nose. "You must not run! Do you understand? You must never run in a factory! You might fall and cause an accident! Do-you-understand?" Gerhild nodded contritely. "Now go over there. Can you see the tall dark girl? Yes-ss? Ask her for Marion."

Gerhild took a deep breath as she went. There was no need to ask. Marion was the English girl, in figure and character the most similar to Lorraine. You saw them together often but you could tell they didn't like each other very much.

Then she saw Tania's round face with the high cheekbones appear over three empty tins. "Gerda," Marion called, "could you please bring some more empty tins over?"

"Where shall I put them?"

"It doesn't matter." She shrugged her shoulders nonchalantly. "Everyone's falling over them anyhow." Her long slim fingers seized a stack of biscuits from one conveyor and placed it on the narrow band with the metal walls that led to the packing machine; an upward lift from left to right. Left, right, left, right, full seven hours long. I could never do it, thought Gerhild in a mixture of horror and admiration. How can a human being stand that? And she's slimmer and more delicate than I am. "That's enough tins Gerda. Now tear the package open and put the good ones on the band."

All of a sudden Vivian appeared, a stout middle-aged figure. "Come on," she said to her, "I need a girl for a job." Gerhild crept through under the belt and hurried after her. "Go over to . . . " she just managed to catch, the rest was lost in a mixture of machine noise and broad Australian. For an instant she longed again for Lorraine's affected English and kindergarten tones. Seeing the stout woman standing in a group of women and girls giving directions, she was reluctant to ask. "Excuse me please," she finally said in her best English, "I couldn't . . ."

"Come on girl!" bellowed the supervisor, "don't stand around and do nothing. I told you to go over to section six and unload tins."

"Come I'll show you," said a voice beside her. Gerhild looked up. It was one of the women she had tea with in the canteen at half-past six. "Take it easy, she doesn't know you are German. I can imagine it's hard for you to understand her. See that girl there?" A well-set girl was standing, arms akimbo, in front of two stacks of tins. She didn't look Australian. "Put them on the band," she said briefly. The tins were packed full and heavy. Gerhild lifted one after the other on to a short conveyor belt that disappeared into the wall and the girl stood beside her and gave each one a little push. After ten minutes she stretched her back and brushed the hair out of her face. The girl turned round waiting for her.

"Could you lift them over for a while now and I take your job?" she asked hesitantly.

"No," the other said resolutely, "I did the other ones." She pointed behind her. There was nothing to see but a fully loaded carrier and the one she had half unloaded herself. She looked into the impudent, provocative eyes and resigned herself. It was no use complaining and after all perhaps it was true, she didn't know, did she?

When she looked up again she saw Lorraine's black eyes on her. "You are supposed to be at section four doing rejects," she said huffily.

"But . . . but . . . Vivian told me . . ."

"Nobody else has to tell you anything," Lorraine shouted, beside herself. "Hurry up the girls want to go to tea."

Gerhild hastened back forcing herself not to run. She trembled all over and had trouble holding back her tears. Jill was waiting with her teacup in her hand. It was the big friendly blonde she had expected. "Thank you dear; don't lose my knife. Slice the packet open at both ends and put the tins on the trolley, will you?" she called as she walked away.

"Rejects, box please!" called three voices on the conveyor belt above her. Something seemed to be wrong with the packing machine. Gerhild pulled at the wooden box overflowing with packets. The rolls of biscuits jammed. It was too heavy for her. One tug and the box crashed to the floor. Boxes, there were no other boxes. While she was putting one of the tins up instead she could already hear the new packets clatter in. "Box please, box please, rejects!" She ran to and fro changing tins, got a stack of empty ones from the trolley, tripped over the full ones she had hurriedly put down wherever there was room. Then the machine stopped.

"My God!" said Jill when she came back.

"Shall I stay and help you?"

"No dear I'll manage. Thank you dear. You can go up to the girls now." She smiled brightly. Gerhild liked her a lot.

She looked up at the big conveyor. It was the only high construction in the hall: about nine feet altogether. From beneath the whole thing looked like a giant toy out of Disneyland. A crazy elephant for example which leaned, sloping, in the room and at whose legs shining colourful packets of biscuits rolled up. High up at the end of each leg a woman in a blue apron and white bonnet stood and packed them all into big and small cartons which then sailed along the elephant's back. And in his head two young girls stood who laughed and waved down to her, then they took each carton twirled it round and let it drive on. The cartons now all lined up properly for a right angle turn. After that they drove quickly along the outstretched trunk and disappeared, as in Aladdin's wonderworld, in the wall. Something of that flashed through her mind each time she went up the narrow staircase, and it was almost as if the only thing that was missing was the fun-fair music and the coloured balloons. Today everything was different. Everything was quiet. The cartons hung in the room like ships in the harbour; at least it seemed like this to her after the shaking thirty minutes she had just put behind her. She squeezed past a young worker in white overalls who stood in the middle of the staircase. Gail's black head bent down to him and they whispered silently. From the opposite stand Nancy's bright eyes signalled to her. "Hey Gerda, come a bit closer. That boy there just asked Gail to go out with him but Gail said no because of her boy-friend and . . . " But Gerhild wasn't in the right mood for teenage talk. She was still battling the turmoil within, furious with herself. One unfriendly word was enough for the whole automatic process to set in, she thought. It's like the instinct of an animal, a second nature I have no control over. Absent-mindedly she watched Judy's quick sure hands unfold the carton and put the packets in: along, across, the top layer flat. And Michael is just as mimosa-like as I am. No wonder we have all those difficulties.

"What's wrong Gerda?"

We are both children: over-sensitive children we are, run away from home to free ourselves, but it seems the real problem lies within.

"Gerda, wake up, are you sick?"

She turned around. Two pairs of eyes stared at her. She smiled. Only young eyes could look so attentive and searching. "It's nothing much," she said. "Vivian sends me to unload tins and Lorraine sends me to open rejects, everything at the same time and both yell at me. I can't split up in two, can I?"

"Go to Robin, Gerda," Gail said and Nancy nodded approvingly. "Yes go to Robin, Gerda and tell her." Gerhild shook her head. They were young girls, seventeen dollars a week, and besides Gail was very competent and worked overtime. She herself, however, was so easy to replace wasn't she? For almost every job she had applied for, dozens of married women had lined up, and besides she was not Australian. "Oh she's a German girl, she doesn't understand what you say to her. We have that trouble every day." She imagined Lorraine's high-pitched voice and the manager downstairs would smile understandingly and the talk would go on to something else. "Yes Gerda do go to Robin and tell her." Gail pointed to the back of the room. "She's the head supervisor and very nice. Yesterday she came over to me and said the new girl seems to have a bit of trouble, show her how to do it."

Oh my God, thought Gerhild. "Well can you show me then?"

"Yes, now look Gerda. Measure the tape and press the ends on, like this." Gail was tall, a head taller than Gerhild, pale and curvy with the soft heart-shaped face of Australian women. Her movements were round and fluent. Whatever she did she did easily, never seeming to exert herself. "Take it easy Gerda," Gail continued in her sing-song, while her rounded hands taped the cartons as if she was caressing them. "No, don't lift the cartons just turn them with your hands. You're doing all right," she said as if encouraging a child.

"Yes she's doing quite well," Nancy echoed. Gerhild burst into laughter.

"See you Gerda," Nancy called out taking her cup. Gail handed her the roller. A moment later the bell for the day-shift girls rang and they both clattered down the steps.

She worked now as fast as she could and avoided looking at the endless train of small cartons that approached from the left. Fear of a stoppage like the last one ran in her mind. After all a minute's interruption was enough to set all hell loose; and from now on she was by herself. Till eleven nobody but Lorraine's furious hands would come to her aid. Roller, turn, tape . . . the next carton, the next and the next. But she was able to pace herself better now. I will manage she thought, with a sudden rush of joy. Greg looked up at her. He took the carton and put it on the trolley. She would have liked to swap places with him. For exactly ten movements she made, he made one. And nobody shouted at him. She leaned back again and shifted her weight on to one foot. Eight hours standing was really too much, but as long as they were packing the *big* cartons it was all right with her. The work itself was almost pleasant. After all what was this sequence of manual movements other than a sport, another form of swimming or skiing? And the monotony didn't worry her; rather it helped her relax and left time for thoughts and dreams. The next carton hovered nearer. Gerhild yawned. I could do with a cup of coffee, she thought shaking herself out of her lethargy and seizing the roller. A turn, the pressing of a button, a push and the sleepiness came back. Absently she picked at the crust of glue on her hands. Judy gave her a side glance. Gerhild wondered if she was going to say something. None of the packers spoke much. Perhaps because they were separated by conveyors. But then their work hardly gave them any breathing space.

An hour later the machines stopped and the four packers hurried downstairs like ballet dancers to their places. Gerhild looked around. There in the middle of the hall stood Lorraine and Vivian surrounded by a circle of women. Reluctantly she started to go down too. "Gert-ie," Lorraine called up, "you stay there till I call you."

At the back of the hall the light went out. On the staircases beside her the mechanics hung over the conveyors, and beneath, women with buckets and brooms ran to and fro. She started to get nervous. At least I ought to look as if . . . but what? For about a quarter of an hour she waited by the idle band, bitting her nails and hoping that something would happen. At last she turned around and took up the glue bottle but it was too late. Vivian's bird's eyes had already spied her out.

"I told you girl . . ."

Gerhild interrupted her. "Lorraine wants me to stay up here," she said firmly and prepared herself for the outburst that would follow now. But surprisingly nothing came.

"I'm here now, not Lorraine," grunted the stout figure.

"Get a bucket and clean your place up." Gerhild grabbed a wet grey rag hanging over the iron railing. Upstairs she found a piece of metal and started to scrape away at the glue stains. She smiled inwardly. That was the way out. She would stay here standing and scraping till eleven if necessary.

"Gerhild Kestner?" She turned around. Two men stood there. "Don't lose it," one smiled and gave her a brown envelope. Then they went on. She tore it open and studied the white strip. "We are getting more because of the night shift," somebody said from downstairs. Gerhild looked about. All around women stood, eagerly counting their money.

"Let's go to tea," Tania called up. Gerhild rolled her blouse sleeves down and stretched her back. She didn't mind so much the work, it was the long hours that tired her.

The canteen itself was large and bare, light green walls, three double rows of laminex tables and chromium chairs. It was the usual look of Australian snack bars and beer gardens and every time she sat down here she was surprised to find neither coffee nor beer stains nor dirty dishes in front of her.

"There aren't many here tonight," she said while she pulled a chair out for herself.

"No," said Judy, chewing, "not at this time."

Marion sat at the next table, the paper spread out in front of her. Listen to this she said. "Rich widower, forty-eight, with a child, house, car, bank account . . ." She angled for a sandwich.

"What do you want a rich widower for?" Judy and her neighbour called out at the same time.

"Well," Marion said, "what life am I leading anyway? I work all day and on weekends I clean the house. My husband gets up at seven, then he makes his breakfast and reads the sports, takes his bag and says 'see you', and when I come home he's fast asleep."

"That's the morals of these girls," Tania said as they left. "And she's a married woman!" Gerhild nodded lamely. She liked the English girl's rebellious spirit and good natured laissez-faire.

There was a rush, a slamming of doors. They looked around. Behind them stood Lorraine, bolt upright as usual, arm outstretched. "Take a broom girls," she said pointedly, "and sweep all along the floor between the conveyors." Gerhild took a straw broom and tried hard to rake the masses of biscuit dust from under the machines. But she didn't get far. The frames were set too low. Carefully she swept the free space between the bands and looked around for a dust pan. "Take a piece of carton," Marion called out interrupting her chattering to a group of women. She bent down and fished in one of the big plastic bins. "Here! There are some dust pans around but you can never manage to get one."

Gerhild was still trying to transfer the last traces of fine dust on to the cardboard when Lorraine appeared. "Empty the trays!" She looked at her surprised. "These trays here!" the other screamed uncontrolled, pulled out one of the huge trays from under the conveyors and emptied it on the floor. Gerhild stared horrified at the pile of dust and broken biscuits in front of her. She bent down and pulled her piece of carton out. "Empty them all," said Lorraine uppishly in her usual pert manner and walked up to the platform.

Marion came over. "She does that every Friday," she said slowly munching a biscuit. "As soon as you are finished the second sweeping she comes and tells you to dust the bands and then sweep again." She helped Gerhild pull out the trays. "You can't get the dust out of the machines anyhow." "That's true," said another woman eagerly. "That's why they've got rats here."

"Why does she do that?" Gerhild asked.

Marion let the last three trays crash to the floor. "Well it takes a long time to overhaul the machines and I guess there isn't enough work for all of us to do."

Gerhild thought of Michael who was sitting now at home. How happy he would be if she came right now. Each night when she opened the door she found a little piece of paper pinned on the wall with the day's news and a funny drawing: Dear Mouse, Sweet dreams . . . "They should send us home instead of wasting our time here," she said angrily.

"That's what I always say," Marion called out.

"They can't pay you for going home," Tania interposed drily and finished her second sweeping with a big red dust pan.

Half an hour later the area around the entrance was crowded with small groups who stood laughing and chattering behind the laden trolleys or were sweeping biscuit dust from one side to the other. She smiled. It was the same picture each night: the women with their cups and cardigans standing like a school class eagerly watching the minute hand. "Come on," Tania whispered, "or we will miss the tram." Together with a few others they stole away towards the entrance and crept downstairs.

They stepped into the half dark of Brisbane's side streets, making their way through the colourful swarming Friday night crowd: girls in flared culottes and glamorous hairstyles and well-dressed men. At the entrance of Lennon's a young woman in a pink evening dress stood on the lower step with a wine glass in her hand. Two men in dinner suits leaned against the wall.

"I would love a dress like that," Judy said when they had hurried past.

"Lucky people," said another woman, "dancing, drinking, laughing. And what have we got?"

Gerhild took the scene in with one glance and dismissed it. She turned to her own thoughts. A feeling of well-being and contentment rested in her. Unknown to herself the factory had opened up a breach, the long hours of rhythmic work, the contact with the women had released a new quality, a new strength in her. Michael would be up now, waiting for her, she thought. Tomorrow they would take the train together down to their block of overgrown land, which to him was a garden of Eden where thousands of unknown and strangely scented things grew, and where she would admire the rows of bricks he had laid during the week. A sudden rush of joy went through her.

Dictionary

Maria Novak

I woke up with a bad conscience, with a sense of not having done my stint. Yesterday my awakening had been quite different — the sun was shining, it was good to live. Sydney seemed beautiful, the sky luminous, the sea blue. I somehow felt it shouldn't be too difficult to pull through till the end of the day, getting about in these heavenly hues till nightfall.

The afternoon, however, proved already depressing. I visited a sick Hungarian who has been lying in hospital — or rather sitting up, paralyzed — for years. Nobody comes to visit him, apart from his kith and kin, although he had had many friends once upon a time. I took the opportunity for looking up another patient as well who no longer has either relatives or even acquaintances . . . although he had plenty while things were going well for him. Since he's been hospitalized, nobody came to see him. Sick not only in body, his mind also begins to falter. Oh, he recognizes me, all right, but then also thanks me . . . "for having come all the way from Budapest" to call on him. His words hurt me, no less than the regret of never having seen Budapest.

While ambling home, man's destiny was haunting my thoughts.

I am a Hungarian who has been living in foreign parts for thirty years. And I wonder why I am here. A whole generation has already gone before me; soon it's going to be our turn. And what about the next one? Have we left them any legacy at all? They're not aware even of their own fate. No comprehensive history book has been written by us from which they could form themselves an idea of what's happened to those millions of Hungarians who have been forced to flee abroad. And if there had been something published to provide only just a hint, have we taken care to make it available to them? Be it in Hungarian or any other language they can understand. For there will be a few score thousand still to speak Hungarian, and a few thousand resolute young people who may even be able to read textbooks written in their native tongue. But don't ask me how many, nor how many there will be capable of reading fiction. There are, of course, parents and well-intentioned teachers galore who are busying themselves with the upkeep of Hungarian schools, doing overtime gratuitously. There are also the boy scouts and girl guides — shock troopers of courage and tenacity. But over and above those, what happens to the uncounted hundreds of thousands?

Our native tongue is indeed a precious heirloom, albeit we haven't been able to preserve it in its pristine purity. Its roots which yield life-like sensations to us are derived from cuttings transplanted into alien soil. The sap that feeds them is far removed from the ancient roots of origin. Which leads us to the question whether those archetypal roots which were allowed to remain in the soil of the homeland fared any better? This is a thing which it could be long and painful to discuss.

However, the tasks which are incumbent upon us are located where we live.

What saves the language from decay? The writing, the reading, the meticulously correct speaking thereof.

On arriving home I found letters from my younger sister and a tenacious friend who lives in Zalaegerszeg.

My sister's letter proved entrancing. Having read two sentences already makes me feel at home, among the hills of County Zala. They take me back to streets and meadows my feet haven't trodden for a long time; they make me meet familiar faces and tell me everything that's happened. She still has the mastery of good letter writing: her letter talks, as it should be, and I'm no longer reading it. I listen to it.

My friend's letter, too, has this quality of immediacy. His handwriting is beautiful and clean. Like the man himself. Not one comma is misplaced, not one word precipitately chosen. He, too, tells me about Zala, the banks of the Valicka river, Mount Kemend and the villages of the Gcsej region, about people I had known. My conscience begins to bother me. My sister's frostbitten foot comes to my mind. It had happened while she was shovelling snow, clearing away ruins of a vanquished country. I had no longer been there at that time; I'd gone abroad. Not that I'd been living in splendour: I'd been working for some rich Italians, earning one dollar a month, in Genoa. At the end of the month I used to cry because I didn't have enough money left to write a letter home.

The fact remains that I wasn't there when my brothers, sisters and kinfolk reconstructed our country from its ruins. Never mind the excuses I bring up — alien powers forced an alien system upon my country, and I just couldn't stand it. But ten million other Hungarians could. They stayed put, and the country with them. It was they who gave the world an uplift in 1956.

Should I pronounce the remission of my sin? I had a right, after all, to leave and preserve my freedom, as everybody else had. Hundreds of thousands came after me who had tried to stick it and couldn't.

The result of it is: I am here. But what have I done for my native country since I arrived? Time passes fast. Today's again trickled away like water between my fingers which I dipped into the sea.

Late tonight I answer the letters from home. Words are buzzing around me like a swarm of bees. Ancient verbs, nimble epithets, savoury roots, oblique sentences fill the hive. Highlights reflect from golden drops of honey; the perfume of lime-blossoms is wafting through my room.

I ought to sleep. It is late. But it's difficult to fall asleep with a sore conscience. A game comes to my mind which I used to play with Hungarian words, prior to falling asleep. Let's try it once more. Water, rain, dew, source, brook, river, fog, etc. Right down to perspiration, anything that's akin to water and related ideas. Then again: stone, pebble, rock, sand, etc. The names of villages or fields, such as: Pakod, Turje, Apati, Hervadtfa, Ukk, Pokafa, Tormas, Bodonkut . . . Flowers, like: forget-me-not, tulips, briar roses, foxglove, yarrow, woodbine, and so on, and so forth. And let us also say the Lord's prayer, for he who prays in his mother tongue shall not forget it.

That's how I used to go to sleep once upon a time. Later

on I left it off. And now I might try as much as I wish, it just won't work. In vain do I bring the clouds down right above the water, scanning it white and fluffy, they don't bring drowsiness to my eyes. I am a good sleeper, though. At the end of a heavy day's work or a long, rambling walk I used to fall asleep all of a sudden, like a log, sometimes in the middle of the Lord's prayer. But it's no go this time. I'm trying to read a book, but it's too heavy for my hands. What about a periodical? "Notions of Physics" — that may be just the thing I need . . . "Electrons shall escape from the hollow of a potential as soon as they have acquired sufficient impetus." Electrons maintain a reciprocal relationship with both the nuclei of atoms and one another; they "collide" while swapping energy . . . "as between ions and electrons . . ."

Through a gap between two curtains the sun casts a shaft of light on my face.

At long last I succeeded — in falling asleep, of course. As for science, that's as far as it affected me. The scientific magazine slipped down to the floor while cryptic powers took me back to where I had been born.

In my dream I found myself at home once more. But it wasn't like the dreams of old. Things were not in their usual places. I was talking to an old friend I hadn't seen for thirty years — in English! — and he was just staring back at me, till I understood what I'd done. Soon the pictures began rotating vertiginously; first I stood on a bridge, then suddenly the bridge was gone, and my friend was looking at me from the opposite bank of the river, vacantly, like a stranger. I called out to him, but my voice didn't reach him any more.

I woke up — with a troubled conscience.

I picked up my dictionary and opened it at random. "Continuation" was the first word which hit my eye. It seemed encouraging. One mustn't stop. We have to continue what we began, somewhere, at home.

I'm thumbing through the pages. "Poetic license" is a phrase pregnant with significance.[1] I am taking it seriously, but as I do it begins to worry me. Should it be possible that out of thousands of words those few should have sprung into my field of vision by pure hazard. What have I done to deserve this chastisement?

I shut the dictionary and open it again. This time the word which my finger touches is "book".

There's no escape. Orders must be obeyed.

A minute ago I had still been reaching out for my dictionary in desperation, for it occurred to me that the language you speak in your dream is the one in which your feelings also take shape. Now should this be possible? In my case who writes in Hungarian? Let's go back to the dictionary and see what words have dropped out of my memory and which are the magic verbs that have lost their spell over me.

That's how it began.

And now I am standing here, holding my dictionary, like someone who has received a message from immensely far away, in ancient runic script, and has suddenly understood the cryptogram.

NOTE

1. The words "poetic license" have been used in translation. However, the author would have preferred the word "poetic freedom".

The Naked Walls

Heinz Nonveiller

In a new land like Australia you have to build for yourself a past in a short time. I know. I know because I came from Austria six years ago. What are six years in which to build a past? I came to this land like many others, young and ready to conquer. I came and found I had only just been born. I found that coming to a new land like this was like being born. That it was hard and that most of the other life had stayed behind forever.

My father was a painter. When he died the house had to be sold and there was some money. I was twenty years old and there was also a girl. She did not like me. Now I am twenty-six years old. I speak two languages so-so, but it is like sitting between two chairs. That is because I have not come to terms in which of my two pasts to live. Or perhaps these six years are not enough past to sit on, and the rest has got lost when I crossed the equator. Who knows.

Making a past. Yes. When my father died and when the house was sold, and the many paintings on the walls were sold too, the house changed. I can still remember how it changed. First went the furniture. That was not so bad. But next went the many pictures. I must explain that there were many paintings in my father's house. The walls were completely covered by paintings, sketches and etchings. Portraits of famous people also. Or landscapes and still-lifes. When these pictures were taken away from the walls my father went with them. It was his second death. It was the death of his soul on this earth. You could still see the pale squares on the walls where the pictures had once hung. But when the walls were finally naked and still, I could not even remember what the pictures had looked like. The walls were moving together and the large rooms were growing smaller and smaller until there was no air left to breathe and I had to run out into the street with anguish in my heart. Finally I understood that I was alone: that both father and mother were now lying side by side in the old graveyard, in the old family grave. It was the sudden presence of the walls which brought this truth home to me. Until then I hadn't even known that there were walls. To walk through my father's rooms was to walk through riches. Was to walk past landscapes and famous people and sudden moments of stillness hidden away between a jug and three oranges. To walk through my father's house was to walk with the eyes of many great painters and see all sorts of things. There were no walls. You could see far far into fields and faces and oranges. Now there were the naked walls. I understood and wept because my father was dead.

In this new land and young, I forgot for a while. The young have great power over memories. But sadness was only bearable when I began to search for the moments in which everything had been alive to me most preciously. I remembered the richness of the walls.

What did I not do in those first years of my new-born life. I worked with my hands. I served behind bar counters, drove cars and finally hastened through a series of office jobs.

And in the offices there would be time for memories. In the offices was much loneliness. I asked where had I got? True, I was learning to speak English, but there were few people to speak to and the loneliness remained. I could stand it no longer in the offices in the big city and I went to the country.

I worked in the country, first on a dairy farm and that was hard work after the city. Then I bought a camera and took photographs of people and sold the photographs to the people. That was easier but after a year of this there came a big flood so that only the highest roofs of the country town showed. My camera was lost. I had spent a year in the country, finding loneliness in the dusty streets, in the locked faces of the country people who would not admit a stranger quickly and in the scraggy bush not far away, over the river. I returned to the city.

Friends, you ask me — what about friends? I made friends, yes. But it is not the same when there are so many differences.

Friendships with Australians were easy things like clouds passing over the sky. My own countrymen were trying as hard as I to make a living here, so they had not much time, except some who had given up trying to find a place. And those were too depressing for me who was young and still full of hope that suddenly everything would be all right.

The city was as lonely as ever. Loneliness does not help in making a past. A past has to be built like a house to live in. I fashioned such a house out of memories that came to me slowly from my years before I had left the country of my birth. In the memory of my father's room I understood about life. It is like such a room. Life is a prison, I said to myself. You must decorate this prison with pictures, so that you can forget about the walls until you die and the walls go away forever.

But to my horror I found the walls of my memory dissolving. I was not old enough to remember a past so far away that oceans were between. A past so far away that it took two languages to cross. The walls melted away and other walls came up. The present was stronger. I found myself surrounded by the walls of the present. And they were naked walls, and closing in on me. They were like the walls in my father's house after the pictures had been taken off. I was a prisoner in a room without memories.

I tried to hang pictures in the room which I had rented. It was a small room and the light had an ugly quality as it swam through the window. It was a smutty, cheap room. I brought pictures home after work and hung them on the walls. But there was something wrong with them. I realized, stepping back, and looking at them that they were prints of pictures which had hung in my father's house. I could not successfully hang them in a room in this new land. They did not belong and it was no use. I understood that I had crossed a border. A border that led from past to present, from youth to maturity. I could not cross that border.

So you see why I am so sure that to make a past is an important thing for a man in a new land. It is terribly important. How many years, did I ask myself, would it take me to defeat the close walls?

Then I got a job with a recording company. I had good

looks and a friendly smile and this is why they employed me to assist in public relations' matters. I would be required to drop in on radio stations and record shops and tell everybody about the latest records which we were releasing. It was easy work and no trouble to me. I met people. When they asked me how I liked Australia I sometimes tried to tell them about the walls and the paintings but they did not understand because it was not something that could be said aloud just like that.

Then one day the manager told me that my job was changed. I would interview singers and rock 'n roll stars under contract and write advertising matter about them on record covers and for the stations. I was not in publicity.

I thanked the manager for the promotion but he did not mention anything about a rise. Well, so what. I went and made myself interested in singers and artists and show business. It was all very crazy and empty. I began to feel that the world was very busy in one direction and that it wasn't the direction in which I was going. Everybody told me I was doing a good job, but it was only so because nobody there had ever done advertising. My English was lacking and so was my enthusiasm when it came to praising a singer who had no voice, no talent and no nothing.

But one day a couple of new singers were put on a contract with the firm and they came to my office so that I could find out their story and make it interesting for disc jockeys to tell about on the radio.

They sat on one side of the old desk and I sat on the other. The man was bony and rugged, with pale blue eyes and a shy, friendly smile. The woman had the same smile and a fairly prominent nose. They belonged to each other. They were husband and wife in everything. It was easy to see. They sat and I asked them what could they tell me about themselves.

They looked at each other and wetted their lips with quick dry tongues. He opened his mouth and she whispered something to him and they turned their heads and faced me again. They were in their early thirties, and I was surprised to see them here in my office. They did not look like singers but as if they could work hard and still be cheerful.

"We had a sheep farm," the woman said for both of them.

And I glanced at them more closely. Behind my back was a window and through the window fell the weak city light. It fell over my shoulder and straight into their pale, open faces and into their pale blue eyes. Their skin was very dry. It was a silent dryness. There was something in their silence which I understood beyond words. Do not ask me what. It was a wonderful silence.

But suddenly I understood and knew their story. I did not even have to ask them. Of course, officially I asked them to make sure, prompting them gently with words.

"Well?" asked the manager when I saw him later in the day. "What did you get out of them?"

"They had a sheep farm," I said dutifully. "It was a bad year. There had been several bad years. They had to sell the farm and went together through country towns, singing duets. Singing all sorts of songs country people like. They had always been good at it. They like doing all this very much."

The manager looked at me blankly.

"But," he said. "That's no good. Isn't there anything *interesting* in their lives? Can't you invent something? Give them a past?"

"No," I said calmly. "There is nothing to invent. It is all right for me to invent stories for city boys who sing rock 'n roll. But there is no need for me to invent anything for these two people."

"But it's a terrible story," the manager shouted. "Can't you see — it's uninteresting? Can't you track down something exciting? What about their parents? Did they have show business in their blood? Can't you say that their farm went up in fire or something? Brush it up man, brush it up! Nobody is interested in a couple of farmers. You've got to add glamour."

That was his favourite saying. Add glamour. I suddenly understood that it was a big, big lie. There is no glamour of this kind. Even if it makes money.

I wanted very much to say to him that truth is silent like two country people. I said it.

He did not understand, of course. A vein began to throb on his forehead. He wasn't a man who liked to be disagreed with. He was angry now.

"Do as I tell you," he said. "Write something interesting."
"I am sorry, sir," I said, "This is very interesting already."
"Is that so?"
"I am tired of lying, sir," I said.
They gave me holiday pay and some said they were sorry
to see me leave. I wasn't. I had my hands in my pockets and
walked down the street and got into a bus. I did not worry
about the creases in my trousers, nor whether my hair was
combed back smoothly. I felt strangely confident in myself.

It was evening. The sun was sinking down into the harbour
and a few sky scrapers were struck by the last rays and
burned with a red fire against the dark blue sky. The bus was
crowded with pale people, and I suddenly realized that I too
must be pale.

The two people who had sold the sheep farm and gone
singing, came into my mind. A strange series of evocations
followed in the wake of their lives as I had observed them.
The wind blowing the dust into the Jacaranda trees from the
deserted streets of the country town where I had spent one
year. Desolation and myself taking photographs. Again the
wind and the dust, and parched faces. The still faces. The
great silence in them, that had seeped out of the bush and
into them. Poor houses with corrugated iron roofs. The sun,
the flood. A year in the country.

Getting off the bus I was in a dream. I kept seeing the
whole year as if it were yesterday, kept seeing it as I went
into the house where I lived.

They sold the farm and went singing, I thought. Simple.
How simple. And I had defended their right to such a simplicity. Glamour and simplicity are two different things. In
the hallway I stopped and listened to my thoughts. It
occurred to me that my father and I were different persons.
He was an artist, I was not. That was still another border
which I could no longer cross. I was becoming myself more
and more. I could feel myself as I grew into something solid.
What I had missed was glamour, not life. To my father it was
life. That was as should be. But it did not have anything to
do with me. A longing rose within me. It had been awakened
by the two silent faces this afternoon.

I met my landlady on the stairs and gave her a week's

notice. Then I entered my room. It was quite dark now and I couldn't see the walls. There were no walls at all but only long stretches of deep, dark bush, and the silence and the hot sun and the dust. The big loneliness also. The things I could not stand when I came to this land. But now I stood them, knowing that loneliness is life, and dust and sun, and a friendly face here and there. Knowing that my father had not been able to live without walls, that his paintings had been his walls, but that I was able to live without walls. Yes, I was able to. I would go back to the land and work, and be able to live in this large room without walls, Australia. Do not ask me to elaborate on something which I myself will never completely understand. I think it is enough if I say that there were no more walls.

One's Land

Pino Bosi

"Uncle Antonio," cried the young woman hidden in her black scarf, stretching out her arms for support. "I'm fainting!"

As the coffin was lowered into the fresh grave, amid twelve white crosses and three gumtrees, the man supported the young woman with one arm while he made the Sign of the Cross with the other.

Down at the bottom of the valley stood the wall of the dam where the accident had happened.

"Pietro! Pietro! Good-bye," cried the young woman, falling to her knees and breaking into sobs.

Her uncle gave her a handful of fresh earth as other hands dipped into the heap and threw soil onto the coffin. Each handful of earth landed with a hard thud.

The bearded Italian priest read from his prayer book and spoke a few words. "We weep as we bid farewell to such a young life, but Pietro has not left us. We carried him all the way up this steep side of the mountain so that he could be closer to the sky and watch over the honest and holy work which you are all going to carry on. God be with you."

Some of the men remained behind to fill the grave. The others, in a single line, went back to the camp, saying "Goodbye" in a whisper or giving a respectful touch of the hat or a glance to the young woman supported by her uncle and the priest.

When they reached the huts, the uncle said to the priest: "If you take her to the canteen I'll bring the suitcases out."

The young woman pressed her uncle's arm. "May I go with you and see where he used to sleep?"

He glanced at the priest for counsel, but the priest himself seemed unable to decide. The woman pressed the arms of both. "Please . . ."

The priest and the uncle looked at each other again. Then, in silent accord, they took her along the corridor of a hut to a small room. The young woman looked at the small wardrobe, the postcards of Italian and Australian cities stuck to the wall, her framed photograph on the bedside cabinet — and then fell on the bed breaking into sobs again. Her uncle and the priest leant over her, trying to comfort her.

"No matter how deeply and unbearably you feel your agony," said the priest, "you must rely upon God's will."

"Why?" she cried, lifting her head. "Why would God want me to travel thousands and thousands of miles to find, instead of my husband, whom I hadn't even known as such, a wooden cross? Why?"

The priest bent his head in sorrow because, though accustomed to the tears of the bereaved, there were times and circumstances when it wasn't easy to ask someone to carry their cross with fortitude.

"It's not for me to say why, and I am not condemning your tears, most unfortunate sister," he said. "But you must not feel as if God had forsaken you, another of His beloved creatures. He holds for you, too, a future peace of mind and heart which you cannot perhaps foresee."

"He came up here for me," she said, as though she hadn't heard, "to save enough money to buy me a house. Oh, you don't know what he wrote to me! You don't know what he was like!"

She paused and almost smiled recalling a happy memory. Then she began to weep again as she repeated what he had written in his last letter to her, a mumble no one but she could understand. "I've shaved my head and let my beard grow so that I'll never fall to the temptation of going into town over the free weekends. Not that I would look at the other girls, for I have you, beloved Lucia, but there are other ways of squandering the money I have saved up here. The wall of the dam keeps on growing, and I work right on the top where even the birds get dizzy . . . But I like it: the air is fresh and the money is good . . ."

The young woman broke down. "Why, Padre, why did that wall have to grow higher and higher? Why? Why? . . ."

Her uncle helped her up and took her out of the room.

"We mustn't miss our train back home. The truck that is taking us to the station will soon be leaving."

The train was blowing its whistle when the priest said goodbye. They boarded the train. As it started to move, they entered a compartment occupied by a man with glasses who was reading a newspaper, a girl with a boy's haircut, busily chewing some gum, and a man with a bored expression who gave them a quick glance and then went back to looking out the window.

The train was moving fast when the young woman spoke to her uncle in Italian: "Uncle Antonio, I would have died without you. I must thank you for all you've done."

Her uncle put his arm around her. "I knew you both when you were children. Then you grew up and, as I had promised, I did what I could to get him the papers to come here." He remained silent for a few moments, then added with a broken voice: "I helped him come to his death . . . That's what I did!"

"Uncle Antonio, please!" the young woman said, grabbing his arm. "Please . . . We're already all too sad to talk of faults, true or not. What I know is that when they first told me, I hated this country. Oh, how I hated it! Now I feel I don't want to leave it because it almost belongs to me, because he rests here."

The passenger who was looking out of the window cleared his throat ostentatiously. "Why don't you speak English, the two of you," he said, glaring at them.

The two other passengers seemed as surprised by the remark as Uncle Antonio, who lifted his eyebrows.

"Well, why don't you?" the man repeated.

"Because we talk about our things," replied the Italian, trying to hide his feelings.

"This is our country," said the man. "If it's good enough to stay in, then you can speak our language!"

The Italian had a voice that could be heard even if he stayed seated, but tears were trying to break through and he thought that perhaps they might go back if he stood up.

"What we speak not interest you, but I tell you we not want thanks for our work because we do for ourself, but leave in peace the men that die in a dam that brings water to this country! This is your country, this is your land, but the grave where today they put this woman's husband, he pay with blood and she pay with tears! That is her land, not yours!"

The passenger who had spoken stood up, looked around and left the compartment. The other man patted the Italian on the back. "I am sorry," he said, cleaning his glasses with a handkerchief. "Accept my apologies for him. This is also my country . . . this girl's country, I suppose . . . We are awfully sorry . . ."

The Australian girl, who had stopped chewing during the scene, cast her eyes on Antonio's niece who had started to weep. She looked at her uncertainly, then broke a new packet of gum with her red fingernail.

"Take once," she said, showing a kind of sympathy. "It'll help you feel better."

The young Italian woman, without understanding the words, took a piece of gum so as not to show disregard for the offer. Then she started to chew it, swallowing sweet mint mixed with the sour taste of the tears that were running down her cheeks.

Volcano

Pino Bosi

Pasquale went to the races to prove a point. He was a sensible middle-aged father of three to whom life had taught that money was like one's own teeth: painful to get and just as painful to part with. It had all started over a pint of beer at Sydney's Marconi Club when Domenico, his younger brother, admitted to losing a week's wages at the races.

"You are dumb!" said Pasquale, to which his brother replied with a long speech on how migrants who wanted to make the best of their lives in a foreign country must become interested in all the various aspects of its social and sporting life and not just work.

"But you can go to the races and enjoy yourself as you do at the soccer match without betting your shirt away . . ." reasoned Pasquale.

"No you can't. Have you ever been to the races?"

And Pasquale was stumped: he hadn't.

It was a glorious Saturday afternoon and Randwick was a hive of buzzing enthusiasm. Pasquale was impressed. He felt a bit like a fish on dry land but not unpleasantly so. There must be something in what Domenico said, he thought.

"They're gonna come 'ere wearin' flamin' swimsuits next . . ." said a voice behind Pasquale, obviously referring to four lasses sporting minis which revealed more than they covered.

Pasquale, who understood enough English not to really understand all that, turned around to see who had spoken and to make sure it wasn't someone complaining about him obstructing the view.

He saw an old man with a grin.

"You can't see the horses?" Pasquale asked.

"They ain't lined up yet . . ." said the old man. "There . . . They're comin' now. See that blackie? It's a kiwi. Got itchy 'oofs that 'orse, I tell ya. I reckon he knows he can beat the score. He don't even show it, does he? You can take me word for it: as soon as the barriers go up he'll spring like a rocket and never give way. You can take it from me."

The old man's eyes were moist with excitement but Pasquale didn't seem too impressed and acted as if he hadn't heard a single word.

"It won't be long before they start," said the old man wistfully. "Not placin' a bet on that 'orse's plain murder." And he drew closer to Pasquale.

Pasquale, who up to that moment had based his suspicions on instinct, now thought he had positive proof that the old chap was trying to sponge him for a drink. He decided to play goofy, touched his hat and pulled a face that clearly stated 'No understand.'

"Wait!" begged the old man grabbing him by the sleeve. "You're me only chance!"

Pasquale didn't want to make much fuss around himself, being already uneasy in a place where everybody seemed more excited than normally, and contented himself with shaking the old man off. He moved away muttering that he had a wife and children to provide for, pay their fares to Australia, pay off the house and even if all these things were settled, he could still think of other ways to get rid of any surplus money. He was also going to add a few commendable things about work, saving, etcetera but the old man interrupted him.

"Fair go!" he said. "I's not tryin' to touch you for a few bob! All I want you to do is bet for me. D'you understand?"

Pasquale looked puzzled.

"You mean you not want my money?"

The old chap pulled a bundle of notes out of a pocket.

"Look," he said. "You go to that window and put them all on Volcano for a win. Understand? Better hurry now, and then I'll tell ya me story. D'you get it?"

There was no doubt about it: the man didn't want any money. What Pasquale couldn't make out, however, was why a man who had money wanted him to place a bet on his behalf.

He was standing there with the money in his hands uncertain of what to do: was the money stolen?

"Please!" the old man begged. "Be a sport."

Pasquale shrugged.

"Orright," he said making up his mind. "All on Volcano."

"Make it a win," explained the old man, and Pasquale repeated: "All on Volcano, make it a win."

Pasquale had just placed his bet when the barriers went up and Volcano shot through just as the old chap has predicted. As soon as the horse was in front of all the others, his jockey went for the rails where he stayed all the way.

It was a fast race but it didn't provide much excitement because Volcano looked a winner all the way.

In the last furlong he even outdistanced the second horse by an extra couple of lengths, flying past the winning post with ten lengths to spare.

The crowd roared because Volcano wasn't the hot favourite and the old man tapped Pasquale on the back. "Didn't I tell ya? I haven't seen one alike in fifty years of racing." He then added with a wink: "Ya can go and collect now. To place this bet I've cleaned windows for a week . . ."

Pasquale, who felt as empty as the drum of the brass band playing somewhere on the course, was going to say that work was a matter of pride, not shame, but inexplicably it all sounded so silly. So he said nothing and collected the winnings.

"I'm gonna tell you what it's all about now," said the old man when Pasquale came back. "You've got a right to know. You see, you can go without food for a week but you gotta pay a bookie: he'll stand no foolin' around, and if you don't pay 'im he won't take your bets no more. I was a hundred dollars short, a black day, the worst I'd seen in the whole of me life, and the bloke in the same boardin' 'ouse copped a cheque for fifty in 'is letter box. I said to meself I'd give 'em back to 'im, I swear I did, but got caught. I told the judge why I'd taken it, an' he said he understood me problem and wasn't going to send me to gaol if I paid the other chap back, which I'm doin' mind ya, but said that if I got caught placin' another bet for twelve months I'd be paying even for me first offence. That's tough, my oath it is . . ."

Pasquale was listening with a mixed feeling of curiosity and diffidence although he didn't know why he should distrust the man: someone wanting to con you wouldn't start by telling you he had got a suspended sentence for taking someone else's money. Quite a reasonable thought, reckoned Pasquale, so the man must be honest in his own way.

"The second race will soon be on," said the old man, interrupting Pasquale's reasoning. "Here, put the money on Rainbow. He's not much of a horse himself, but all the others are asses."

Rainbow won. A very surprised Pasquale couldn't find words to express his amazement and gradually seemed to become intoxicated with horses, bets and the old man's words.

As the races progressed he felt more and more uncomfortable when confronted with the little man's winnings that were the result of a cautious betting on placing and "each way's" when the race offered some doubts and straight out wins, the certainty of which the old man seemed to sense almost scientifically. It must be one of those days, Pasquale reckoned. Hadn't the old man been put in gaol for stealing to pay for his gambling debts?

At the fifth race Pasquale caught his own hand slipping into his hip-pocket.

"Holy Mother of God!" he stuttered in a daze. "Make me think of Rosa and the children!"

The horses went off and Pasquale became so excited as the race proceeded that he felt embarrassed when he cooled off enough to realize it.

"I almost had a bet on it, that's why," he thought with a shrug.

When the horse backed by the old man went past the winning post Pasquale clutched his fists, then wrenched the wallet from his hip-pocket and excitedly placed some notes in the old man's hands.

"On the next!" he exclaimed as determined as he could be.

The old man laughed.

"You've been doin' all the bettin' for me. Whaddya give me your money for?"

Pasquale felt embarrassed and glanced around pulling his hat down over his eyes.

"I not trust myself. I not bet if I start to think . . ."

"Go on," the old man incited him. "There's a first time for everybody."

So Pasquale bet and the race earned him ten dollars which he collected in a pool of perspiration and his hat back to front.

"See? said the old man as Pasquale put the money in his wallet. "The races are a pretty easy game."

Pasquale assumed an expression appropriate to the situation, then quipped: "Yes but to win there is just one way: stop when you win!"

Yet the excitement of the win gave way to a strange desire to win some more.

"What horse next?" he asked when he just couldn't hold it any longer.

"Archibald."

"He win?"

"Dunno. But he'll end up placed. Put everything ya have on Archibald for a place."

Pasquale didn't feel too confident and only invested half his win.

The horse got beaten by a couple of lengths and Pasquale shouted: "Place! Place!"

The old man smiled.

From then on Pasquale completely lost his head and bet with blindfolded confidence asking questions for the sake of information but never to be reassured.

At the end of the ninth race Pasquale counted the money he had won: it was close to one hundred dollars.

"You are a genius!" he exclaimed, wiping the sweat that was running down his cheeks in little streams. "How you are not millionaire?"

The old man shrugged.

"I love them beasts too much."

The reply was a bit of a shock to Pasquale.

"But that why you win!"

The little man shook his head.

"Knack and memory make you win, with a little luck. Hey, do you know who's in the last race? Volcano."

Pasquale looked down on the turf and saw the black stallion with his shiny hide and polished hoofs.

"He race again?"

The old man shrugged.

"He's a champ all right. How much have I made up to now? Two hundred and seventy-five dollars. Put them all on Volcano. But you'd better stay outa this."

"Why?" asked Pasquale. "He not win?"

"He's a great 'orse," replied the old man. "But it's his second race and Flying Saucer's no ass."

"We bet place?" suggested Pasquale.

"No. I back him to win. You can do what you like!"

Pasquale went to the window he'd come to know so well and pulled out all the money he had, his own as well as the old man's. When he left the window he looked down at the black stallion as he was coming to the barriers. When they were all lined up, Volcano was as still as a statue yet all his muscles seemed to be working up full pressure to spring as the barriers went up.

"Go!"

Volcano immediately placed himself among the first five but it was number 13 that took the lead after about one hundred yards.

"It's his second race," explained the old man. "The jockey wants him to save his wind."

At the first bend Pasquale was already shaking his fists in the air with the veins of his neck near bursting point.

"Pipe down!" the old man told him. "You don't have to worry about Number 13: the 'orse you've got to watch is Number 7, Flying Saucer."

Suddenly a horse came out of the group and challenged the leader: it was Volcano.

"It's murder!" shouted the old man getting excited for the first time in the whole afternoon. "You'll kill him before the finish!"

With a terrific burst Volcano caught up with No. 13 and passed him without effort. Flying Saucer was still in the group a couple of lengths back while all the other horses were helplessly trailing behind.

"He win! He win!" Pasquale was screaming. "Like the first race!"

"That's the bloody trouble!" replied the old man. "It ain't the first."

The black stallion was still leading when No. 13, still in second position, came up with a wonderful sprint.

"Let 'im pass!" yelled the old man with renewed hopes. "Let 'im pass!"

But as soon as No. 13 levelled with Volcano, the black horse literally jumped forward leaving the challenger behind.

"It's not the jockey . . ." commented sadly the old man. "The thundering horse just can't stay behind as long as he's got enough breath to keep going!"

But the sad-looking old man was now talking to himself because Pasquale was screaming his head off.

"Go on! Go on, Volcano! Beat 'em all! Beat 'em all!"

All of a sudden, from the group that was trailing the leader, sprang out No. 1 which began to challenge No. 13's position several lengths in front.

"Look out!" shouted Pasquale gesticulating like a windmill. "Number one, he come up!"

Near him the old man shook his head despondently. "He's a goner . . ."

There were three furlongs to go and in first position was now No. 1 followed by No. 13. Volcano had been swallowed by the group led by No. 7, Flying Saucer, who was now starting to tackle No. 13 for the second position.

After passing No. 13 without much effort, Flying Saucer closed to the rail and began to gain on No. 1 whose jockey had begun to use the whip.

At two furlongs from the finish Flying Saucer gained the lead and there seemed to be no doubt left when an unexpected burst from Volcano put him in front of the group a good ten lengths from Flying Saucer.

"Too late . . ." muttered unhappily the old man. "A miracle's not enough . . ."

But the excitement in the crowd was mounting because

Volcano, which in the last furlong had caught up with No. 13 and No. 1, was now challenging Flying Saucer.

The black stallion seemed electrified in the furious chase: the five lengths became four, then three as the old man mumbled to himself: "Impossible . . . Impossible."

Under the astonished eyes of the spectators Volcano gained another length but the finish was too near to hope for a miracle to happen.

With a terrific burst Volcano almost touched Flying Saucer's tail and kept on reducing the distance. Pasquale's and the old man's inciting voices seemed to drown those of the crowd when the two horses raced past the post.

It was a photo finish: and Volcano had lost.

The little old man was sitting on a lawn with tears in his eyes; Pasquale had reduced his hat to a useless rag.

"But why?" splattered Pasquale completely disheartened. "Why he not win? Why the jockey not try before?"

"That's the chance of the game," replied the old man.

"We lost all our money," said Pasquale ruefully. "Why win all races to lose the last?"

"I told you you could do what you wanted with your money. I reckon it was worth it. Nothin' could have made Volcano win, yet he almost did. Best race I've seen in me life . . . It was worth it, every cent . . ."

"But they got our money, the bookies," objected Pasquale throwing what was left of his hat into a litter can, "not the horse."

The old man really looked at Pasquale for the first time and shrugged. "He's a great 'orse, you know, a real champ. See the fight he put up? Tell you what, it was worth it all, to the last cent."

To Pasquale's last cent too because he didn't have one left when he walked away from the racecourse.

Pasquale never discussed betting with his brother again ·for fear of giving himself away and revealing that in the excitement of the last race he'd even chewed up his railway ticket so that he had to walk ten miles to get home.

Mademoiselle

Vasso Kalamaras

The tall, dull-coloured buildings of the big city stood out, severe and ugly, silhouetted against the cold grey sky. People hurried with a desperate sad urgency along the footpaths. A general heaviness, together with their everyday worries, was mirrored in their faces. Today! — always today! They must hurry — to pass the man in front — the business colleague — the competitor — today — and then bring the whole thing back full circle, meaninglessly to the beginning again — an end with no result.

Mud had collected along the edges of the dirty asphalt street, lying there with no escape. Unheedingly the passers-by dragged their weary feet along, splashing their neighbours in their haste. Unbearable cold, dirt, dampness, and dejection.

Mademoiselle Katerinoula ran to get to her last lesson on time. Her pupils' homes were separated by great distances, but goodness, with fares so expensive, how could she ever afford to use the tram or the buses fecklessly, or as often as she wished? She was always working out arrangements that involved her strength, her money, and the length of her journey. She came up with strange solutions, and often made brave walks to save the pennies.

Life was hard for Mademoiselle Katerinoula living with her aged mother. For thirty-five years she had had no father or any male protection. Poor little thing, she seemed so tired that afternoon as she hurried down Hermes Street towards Monastyraki. Her patched-up shoes with their dilapidated wooden heels clicked noisily as she hurried along. She was very conscious of them, and ashamed to be wearing the same pair again this year — but there was no alternative.

Passing the little church in the square, she made the sign of the cross and pushed on uphill into some narrow street in the Plaka, hastening her steps.

"Goodness me, I'll be late!" she kept thinking.

Finally she arrived. As she tapped on the bronze knocker of the front door, her little nose, very red from influenza, started dripping. Her gloves were worn and a few still undarned holes betrayed her to the cold and to the eyes of the world. Nervously she gave her ringlets a hurried once over. Fussily pinned with countless hairclips, they had remained obediently in place.

As the front door opened, the lively heads of five little boys could be seen at the top of the staircase. They noisily greeted her arrival.

"Mother, mother, it's the French teacher, mother!" They could all be heard shouting together as they ran to hide inside the house. From the long dark hall the untidy head of Mrs Evanthia, the confectioner's wife, appeared. Her husband had a big sweets shop with all kinds of goodies. The family was in very fair circumstances. Personal extravagance, however, didn't interest Mrs Evanthia. She had no time for that sort of thing, with all the little children and such a big house. She did find time, however, for a certain amount of leisure. There was always a young servant girl. It wasn't such a great expense to employ a maid. A few worn and faded cast-offs for clothing — and of course, her food. And quite enough too! The food she ate, the little devil! It never failed to amaze Mrs Evanthia. She always found time to voice her complaints to the schoolmistress.

She saw her now and ran to welcome her. She took her into the dining room with the big walnut table with its dark-red velvet tablecloth.

"Sit down, Mamouasel, sit down. You must be freezing in such frosty weather!"

She gave her a chair and called loudly, "Thymioula! Where are you, my bright girl? Put some more coal in the stove. You know Mamouasel Katerinoula always comes at this time. Go and get the children."

The maid emptied the whole bucket of coal into the huge square belly of the stove. Bright red flames, strong and friendly, could be seen through its glass window.

Mademoiselle Katerinoula came closer, and holding out her gloved hands, numb with cold, warmed them at the fire.

Then one by one she began to take off her things — the scarf, gloves, bonnet, overcoat. She waited for Mrs Evanthia to start up as usual on her complaints and gossip concerning family quarrels, news of her husband's relatives, and all about people whom the poor schoolmistress had never seen and would never be likely to know — it was as if it were some clause in her teaching contract. She endured it all — she had got used to it.

From the other room the peevish shouts of the children could be heard, abuse and loud noises. The frightened little voice of Thymioula was repeating over and over. "Your mother told me to, your mother. Go to Mamousella to learn your French. Oh, oh! It's not my fault! Your mother told me . . . Oh, oh!"

Mademoiselle Katerinoula was surprised that Mrs Evanthia had waited so long to begin her chatter. She turned to look at her, and found the woman observing her closely as if she had never seen her before. She blushed, pretended not to notice, and again remarked, "My goodness! what freezing weather, but what a lovely fire." She wanted to be the first to speak, but Mrs Evanthia was serious, very serious. She seemed altogether different, more square and flabby, and even more foolish than usual.

The children rushed into the dining room in cheeky disorder. They quarrelled about who should have the red chair, and who the high leather one, and who the others.

Mrs. Evanthia drew near Mademoiselle Katerinoula and whispered to her hurriedly, "Please Mamouasel, don't leave when the lesson is over. We have something to discuss between us."

She left the room quickly, closing the door so that the noise wouldn't worry her.

The little schoolmistress took a ruler from her worn black leather handbag and threatened the children, "*silence! Bon soir mes enfants.*"

"*Bon soir Mamouasel,*" shouted the five youngsters in unison.

"*Oh pauvre! non Mamousel! Mademoiselle, s'il vous plait,*" she sighed with disappointment.

The lesson commenced, but the poor little schoolmistress's

mind had become very unsettled by Mrs Evanthia's last words. Whatever would the two of them have to talk about? What meaning could the presence of an insignificant school-mistress have in the life of this noisy, well-to-do family? Surely they didn't want to lower her salary again? Only the other day one of her pupils had done that. It was not as if it were some princely sum — a few meagre drachmas, so very few! My goodness! She became pale with fear, and began to tremble secretly. Her eyes filled with tears. Her head began to ache.

In the middle of all this, towards the end of the lesson, someone knocked timidly on the door. Thymioula entered shyly, and left a silver tray with coffee, two small fresh biscuits, and a crystal jug of water on the table near the teacher. Her expression was abject, full of awe, with such a truly deep respect for this very learned schoolteacher! She even trembled slightly — it became ludicrous. One of the children sneaked up and pulled at her untidy plaits from behind. Another stuck out his tongue in front of her. The little maid blushed. She became terribly embarrassed and rushed away precipitously.

It was past seven by the big clock on the wall, and there was still no sign of Mrs Evanthia. The schoolmistress was fearful and impatient. The lesson was over. Everything in the room remained in disorder. The stove no longer burned brightly as at first, but now emitted a quiet and pleasing warmth. The room seemed so very quiet without the children. Unconsciously she realized that this was giving her some confidence. She scratched at the velvet tablecloth with her fingers and gazed at the plaster decorations on the ceiling. When she heard the footsteps of Mrs Evanthia in the passage her heart began to beat. She came in very changed — for the better, carefully groomed and powdered.

"Oh!" the schoolmistress opened her eyes wide in surprise, but she tried not to show it. She smiled as agreeably as she could, and assumed an air of pleasant nonchalance.

"How beautiful you have become, dear Mrs Evanthia, like a young girl! You must surely be getting ready to go out somewhere . . . and me so late! Goodness, my poor mother will be worried!"

The fat hand of the confectioner's wife enveloped the

delicate refined little fingers of the schoolmistress in their plump palms, as she implored her with much tenderness, "Please sit down Mamouasel Katerinoula. Sit down for a little while. I want to tell you something — very seriously!" Her voice seemed to tremble a little as if she were frightened and as if beseeching her from the depths of her soul.

"It is, er, it is about my brother. My dear brother who lives abroad. Ah, if only I could do something for him! He is always my secret sorrow. He is the only one who remains of my father's house. Do you follow me, Mamouasel Katerinoula? You're such a well educated girl, with so many languages . . . and you are so very worthy . . . you must understand me . . ."

Two blurred and heavy tears, oozing from the large colourless eyes, hung on her fat and swollen cheeks, glistening like silver sequins.

The luckless little schoolmistress in her confusion was deeply moved. She fluttered her eyelashes very amusingly, half opening her mouth as she nodded her head up and down. "Yes, yes!" reassuring her companion, as if she already knew and understood everything. But the ill-fated girl understood nothing. Neither on that particular evening, nor weeks and whole months later, did the poor thing realize what had happened.

What is the meaning of "Fate"?

It was as if she had lost her speech, as if her reason had been blotted out. You might say her advancing age was to blame; perhaps a weariness in waiting for her future lot. She seemed so sympathetic, so soft; or perhaps, better to say she was so hard on herself; or so improvident. She left her mother behind her, deserted and without any other company. The afflicted old woman threw her many and varied hopes into the hands of the Virgin Mary — and the good graces of Mrs Evanthia. How deeply earnest were her private entreaties!

"Oh sweet Virgin, let a bright day dawn for my Katerinoula. Let her know the sweet . . . light of life. Let the day dawn for her, my beloved little daughter . . ." Yes, it was necessary for the girl to get married. She was already well on in years. But how would the old woman fare, left all on her own? Well, it would only be for a little while. Katerinoula would send for her as soon as she had exchanged wreaths with Panagiotys, the brother of Mrs Evanthia. The man had a shop in Melbourne, one of the most important big cities in Australia! In her reveries the poor old mother used to imagine all sorts of good fortune for her grown-up daughter, the poor orphan who had suffered for so many years, going from door to door for her living!

Her Rinoula had been the first girl student at the Academy. She was proud of her. She deserved such good fortune. She deserved to see all the best things in the world, all the riches and luxuries which foreigners enjoyed. For this the mother was prepared to turn her heart to stone. She tied her handkerchief in knots so she wouldn't cry too much; so she wouldn't worry her beloved Katerinoula.

Ah, what sorrow was in store for the poor soul! Whom would she wait for at the window in the evenings of the days to come? For whom would she prepare warm food? Whose little hands would enfold her old palms and bless them with their warmth? And at night, who was there to see that she was covered up again when the blankets slipped away?

"But now my Katerinoula will have a fine husband at her side. He will look after her. He will shoulder the worries of making a living. She will be so fortunate and so happy with him. It must be so, it couldn't be otherwise. Lucky girl!"

The old woman would think about herself. What did she have to fear? She only had to arrange for her own meagre requirements. Besides, how many times had her son-in-law written, "As soon as we can, we will bring you to us . . . so you won't be lonely, so your daughter will have you for company, and won't have to worry . . ."

Katerinoula was so sure that they would send for her mother after two or three months, that in order not to weary the old woman, she collected all her belongings privately, and arranged everything for the long journey. She took only two suitcases, with only the really indispensable things. The rest her mother could bring — it was all the same.

"Hey! where are you, you stupid bitch, blast you!" the heavy angry voice of her husband bellowed from the shop. His tongue dripped venom and betrayed his irritation.

Only seven months married, and now all this had happened to darken and weigh down her life. The nightmare was choking her. "Oh my God," the unhappy woman whispered, starting up from the bedclothes which reeked of male breath and cigarette smoke.

"I'm coming, I'm coming," she called out half in her sleep, groping for the switch to turn on the light. It was still pitch dark, as you could imagine in the middle of winter. She looked at the tablecloth and shivered in the chilly dampness. How had she possibly overslept? It was past six o'clock! She rushed to put on her calico dress, and her kitchen apron. This was becoming more difficult to manage these days, now the little one was beginning to hamper her movements. She could feel the tiny creature very much alive, growing and demanding more and more room under her cheap dress. Her hands instinctively caressed the swelling in her belly with a special tenderness. She always seemed to be on the verge of tears, and now her eyes moistened and shone sadly. Going to the dressing-table she cast a disinterested glance into the mirror. She stuck a couple of clips into her neglected hair, and fastened it back in an ungraceful pony tail.

Panagiotys was working in the kitchen. The hot stove, smeared with fat, reeked of beef and fish. "Welcome to our studious one," was his ironical early morning greeting. "Useless bloody thing, you've been looking at those un-nailed boxes since yesterday, and you still haven't put any oranges or lemons in the window. Do you expect me to do everything, Mrs Schoolteacher?"

His wife lowered her head in silence, and with tearful eyes started in on the work — which really called for more endurance and stronger arms than even those of her husband Mr Panagiotys. She tried not to think or reflect on anything. She had extinguished her past; she trembled for her future. Her husband was in one of his fearful moods. He had been playing cards the night before till 2:30 in the morning, and had obviously lost.

"I expected to get a woman who would be a standby in the shop, but instead of that up comes a half-dead cat. Bah! talk about touchy! . . . 'I'd rather not, if you please . . . I can't do it . . . I don't think I can manage' . . . ph! — to hell with such a woman! Ha! look at her, sleeping in till six in the morning like a duchess! And who, I'd like to know, is going to clean the potatoes? Who's going to fillet the fish? I'm asking you. Have you been struck dumb?"

"Dear God, have pity on me," sighed the afflicted girl, unable to restrain her tears. They fell, salting the endless stream of potatoes passing through her chapped and dirty hands. She experienced queer fits of dizziness. An unbearable dullness continually clouded her thought and her will to react. If she could only defend herself, even slightly, even on one single occasion!

It only maddened her husband to see the decline into which she had fallen. He raged from the depths of his soul, and despised her more and more. He provoked quarrels one after another.

"I feel I could rip you in two, you dumb clot! Do you think I don't know that you want to send money to that wretched old mother of yours? Hgh? You won't get a bad penny out of me! I'm not going to roast and fry in this kitchen here for the sake of you and her ladyship. Just for you to sit around and do nothing. Not a bad penny – do you understand? Come on, if you've got the guts ask me for it and find out who's the boss around this place!"

His wife had heard the words so many times that you'd think they would have lost their power to worry her any more. But what would you wish? That she had never been born? That no one had reared her with a fine and gentle nature, in poor circumstances it's true, but with such love, so full of solicitude and devotion?

"Oh mother dearest, what will become of you, my darling?" She whispered in a sort of feverish delirium. She felt tired out, unimaginably exhausted. The fate of her lonely mother in her advanced age, with no hope of assistance from anywhere and no close relations, was all an unsolved and tragic problem for the unhappy girl, on top of all her own troubles with this intractable husband of hers.

His hostile malicious words were a burning knife thrust into the depths of her heart. They drove her mad. She stood up in an attempt to react. She could bear it no longer.

"Let me breathe, Blessed Virgin," she shouted in desperation.

What darkness, what icy frigidity! "Mother, dearest Mother, hurry I am lost! Your ill-starred daughter is lost. Run my dearest." She shrieked like a mad woman, and fell in a heap on to the dirty lino of the kitchen floor.

"Hysterical bitch!" shouted her now infuriated husband. Snatching up a slop bucket, he threw out the mop and emptied the filthy water over his wife's head. He rushed madly out into the yard making straight for the garage. He started up the utility and set off for the vegetable market. He was very late.

Ah, what an eternity all those months seemed to her! Entire months with their immeasurable days; and nights that seemed to know no dawn, strung like a black rosary, repeated endlessly over and over, as they had been since the first day she disembarked.

What bitterness! How could such a fate have been in store for her, this girl who from her childhood had always been so diffident and so reserved? Her timid existence would have been lost and annihilated in the face of some much less dangerous male. Believe it or not she was a girl who had grown up untouched, undefiled and unmolested. Perhaps some deep fear or perhaps from some unusual mental sensitivity and perception, she had lived to that time an almost unbelievably chaste life. Her character was as delicate, fragile, and transparent as fine clear crystal!

She awoke, confused from chloroform, and aware of an extraordinary pleasant numbness in her body. If it were possible, she felt she would like to spend the rest of her life sunk in this half-drugged state, without pain, indifferent to her misfortunes. She tried to collect her thoughts; to remember where she was.

"Mother dearest, mother dearest!" she whispered, reaching out in the darkness for her mother's hand. They always slept with their beds side by side. They had done so since she was a little child. How else could her mother be near to cover her again if the blankets slipped from her?

"How poorly you are sleeping, Katerinoula dear," her mother complained tenderly. "You are all uncovered again, you'll catch a cold."

"Mother, have you put out the lamp?" Katerinoula asked loudly.

The beam of a torch fell on her face. Someone approached, stood at her side, and put the light on at the bed. A beautiful young girl in a white cap bent over her. She asked quietly and sweetly in English, "Did you call me, Mrs Georgiou?" The woman came to her senses. It all returned to her. Her time had arrived, she had become a mother! She had had a child, her own baby child! She should be so proud, so happy . . . But no! that was strange she had lost the sweet drugged feeling. Fear and misery crept into her soul once more. The disillusionment of harsh reality rose up and suffocated her. Ah, so she was not back in her home after all, close to her dear mother. The dream had been so sweet! Reality became a nightmare for her. She looked at the nurse with an uneasy pained expression.

"Don't worry, Mrs Georgiou. She is so pretty; such a lovely little girl!"

"Girl, girl? *Koritsaki*, ah yes, I know," whispered the woman wearily. She closed her eyes, but not in sleep.

The lightly-tapping heels of the nurse faded away into the darkness, leaving her on her own again with all her scattered thoughts, and a bitter taste in her mouth. Her tongue was dry. She was burning all over with fever. What despair she felt! Ah! was this the fruit of that hideous marital experience? Perhaps on that very first night — the very evening that she disembarked. What a frightful recollection! How could she ever forget it? . . . The humiliation . . . the coarseness . . . the violence . . .

"A little girl! I've got a little girl . . . Ah my God, what we will have to suffer together!" For the first time she was thinking in the plural.

"What we will have to go through! Ah, my child . . . Where is my child? No, no, my little daughter . . ."

Her sobs shattered the silence of the hospital. Worried nurses ran and turned on the light. She was crying; loud, poignant sobs. Her breast was bare and her hands tore at her clothing and anything they encountered. She was transferred to another room on her own, with a nurse to watch over her. She had become very sick, dangerously so, but she would be cured. Modern science had such powerful and sophisticated drugs! How could they fail to cure her?

Her husband came next day. He sat in a chair looking at her seriously, absent-mindedly, with colourless eyes. He resembled very much his sister, Mrs Evanthia. The sick woman with the pallor of death on her weak and sunken cheeks slept uneasily, breathing with difficulty. From time to time she whimpered and raved in her sleep in indistinguishable words. Some time passed and Mr Georgiou lost his patience. It was very busy at the shop. Just the time the bulk of his customers were arriving. He couldn't remain here stuck in a chair with his wife asleep. What about the shop? Who knows what would go on there without the boss?

"Katerinoula, come on, it's time to wake up. You've had enough sleep. I've waited long enough." He pushed her shoulder.

Startled, the woman opened her eyes and looked at him wearily. He turned away to avoid her gaze. He snorted, but restraining himself said curtly, "I expected as much; I expected it would all be a ridiculous mess. You never were what I wanted. How can it ever be any better now? We could well have done without being overrun like this with females. The business will go to pot. It will be ruined. Ask me what good you've been in all this. It's the finish of us!"

Her pillow was soaked with dumb tears. As she listened to him, she felt their burning drops wetting her cheeks and running from her ears into the roots of her hair. Her eyes were smarting and her breasts hurt her with an unbearable pressure. His malicious tongue went on and on, exuding its poison drop by drop. You would think he was experiencing some unnatural pleasure, some blind, wild joy. He realized her torture and it stirred him up even more.

"Hm, where in hell did Evanthia dig you up? You know my cousin Michael? He's only three years younger than me, just turned forty-two, and he's got himself a real blossom for a wife, only twenty-two years old! And what a girl she is! Something like a woman. Stretch out your hands and you can grab arms worth cuddling. The thighs she's got . . . the buttocks . . . breasts like mountains! You call yourself a woman and you deal me out another female like this. It gives me a pain in the guts. I told you I wanted a boy. I'll never forget this . . . A dirty black snake can eat the two of you.

Besides . . ."

In the doorway appeared the sweet face of a nurse with bright carefree eyes, and cheeks pink and white like a spring rose. Light chestnut curls hung artfully down from her starched white cap. She entered, gracefully smiling, and holding in her tender arms a tiny babe; a red-faced mite with black hair and a big half-open mouth like a newborn sparrow.

"Mr Georgiou, look how lovely she is! What a charming little girl you have!" She held the child out in her arms towards the father.

"Oh my God, don't," the sick mother screamed wildly. Mad with fear she jumped up and snatched the baby into her embrace.

"No, no, not my child! Dear God protect my little daughter! Ah! where can I hide my little one?" she screamed despairingly. Barefooted, clasping the tiny newborn creature to her breast, she made one confused circuit round the bare room before rushing into the passage. There she began to run with all her might.

She had only one thought, to escape, to get away from this tyrant; from her loneliness; from this foreign country with its strange language; from her fate. Where, dear Virgin, could she allay her fear? How could she even admit to this torture of her soul, her hatred for this entire foreign world, and above all for her husband?

"She's gone mad, the crazy bitch," grumbled Panagiotys, the brother of Mrs. Evanthia. "That sister of mine really caught me out with this bookworm for a present. They tell you to go and get married . . . hgh, and at a busy time like this! I'll lose all my customers! How did I ever come to get mixed up with a thing like her? Bugger me dead! A man ought to be pitied!"

The Pensioners

Vasso Kalamaras

The old woman was not in the habit of waking early in the morning. You see she fretted all night trying to get to sleep, and sleep doesn't come easily simply because you desire it. The crippled old soul used to curse her destiny, and the fate which had finally deprived her of the use of her legs, and had pinned her to this dilapidated bed. It was all she could do nowadays just to shuffle along the floor. On top of that, these last months she had suffered a further embarrassment which she could hardly admit even to herself. She was indeed in a sorry state. When the old man was away it was too much for words.

"To hell with his beer and the wretched pub! As if there aren't enough things to worry about without him gobbling up the few pennies we still have left in our misery." The old woman was mumbling loudly to herself, and squirming in her need. "We're plagued with this god-damned place where the old wretch goes grogging-on day and night." She shouted again to her husband, "Manolio, hey! Manolio!"

But how was Manolio to hear, cooped up there in the bar of the local pub, where he was pouring his savings, gulp by gulp, down his throat, hoping to drown his sorrows and his gloomy thoughts in the amber contents of each foaming glass. "Curse this foreign existence," he muttered. He was peering into his glass as if into the dull eye of some solicitous friend. "Curse it, eh? What do you say? Don't you say so too?" The glass emptied without giving an answer.

Back in the lonely house the old woman went on howling away to herself. "Manolio! Come quickly! Where are you, Manolio? I'll wet the bed! I can't wait, Manolio. Oh Mother of God! I'll do it again and you'll curse and hit me like a mad dog, you old wretch! Where are you man? Damn you, Manolio!" Finally the pain of straining and trying to hold herself in became too great. She could contain herself no longer. As she felt the warm trickle, the old woman gradually ceased yelling. With an almost stupid expression on her face, she waited stoically for her husband's return. In her loneliness the old woman started thinking and murmuring quietly to herself, "I suppose I can only expect such calamities; but how mad can a man get when he can't even take one step to return to his native land . . . not even in old age, for pity's sake!"

He had always wanted to die far from poverty-stricken Greece, with all her miseries and deprivations. He hated everyone back there, and kept saying to his wife, "Don't drive me mad with that tongue of yours, old woman, because I'm not going to budge from here whatever you say!"

He yelled angrily at the poor old thing, cutting her off short whenever she made any objection to his ranting. For years these thoughts had eaten into her. They had tortured her daily until she felt now that she had reached the black and bitter dregs of her existence. She was terrified by old age and the thought of them both alone, all alone, here in a foreign land. They hadn't had any decent food for years now. How could they ever expect to taste any in old age? Then too, she knew Manolio's weaknesses and they cut her like a knife.

They had not saved much. There was only this wreck of a house, and if that were sold to pay the fare home, who knew if it would be sufficient, or if anything more than a few pence would be left over. "Back there in Greece old woman, it's hard enough even for schoolteachers and educated people to get the pension, let alone a poor worker like me." Manolio kept telling her this maliciously, over and over. You'd think it was her fault that workers couldn't get the pension. "Your own husband, woman, slaved for years, navvying on the railways, working all his life with pick and shovel. He didn't push a pen for a living! Pull yourself together then, or you'll find we've even lost the small pension we get here." Oddly enough, Manolio felt in his heart that people back in Greece were somehow responsible for all he had suffered and was suffering in this foreign land. How or why his compatriots were to blame he could never explain, even to himself. It was only in these last more trying years that he was finding himself increasingly involved with drink and the pub.

The ill-fated woman went on cursing, "Oh God, if you would only send a thunder-bolt and blast the place to ashes! Then perhaps the old fellow would pull himself together and return to his own humble cottage." She sighed and sniffed as she always did when she had a cold, or when she was trying to hold back the tears before they ran down her wrinkled cheeks.

"Manolio!" she shouted as usual, as soon as she opened her eyes that morning. Opposite her on the stained and cob-webbed wall hung an old clock, framed in blackened wood. Its hands showed ten minutes past ten. The room was flooded with light. The curtains hung undisturbed from the previous evening. With an effort the old woman tried to get up, pulling at the filthy ragged blankets. "Oh God!" Again she tried to rise and fell back heavily. Her pillow was a mass of holes from which the stuffing half protruded. From long use with no pillowcase it had become like faded greasy hide.

She screamed again, making the sign of the cross. "Jesus and Mary! Manolio, hey Manolio! What's wrong, are you still asleep?" She became anxious. Turning towards his side of the bed she pushed with all her strength. "What's the matter with you, man? Manolio, what's the matter?" The man was facing towards the door. She always slept between him and the wall. His untidy head with its uncut hair hung slightly outwards as if about to fall to the floor. "God protect us, God protect us," the old woman murmured in terror, when she found she got no answer. She tried to reach over and grasp his head to bring it closer. With a great effort she sat up. The poor thing was paralyzed with fear when his flesh felt cold in her grasp.

"God protect us, God protect us! Oh my God," she screamed again madly. This was no trifling matter, finding him suddenly like this, a lifeless corpse. He had such a dread-ful appearance; all unshaven, with rough white hairs from chin to neck, and with his mouth looking like a deep hole, without his false teeth. These were now useless, having been broken for a year or so, and thrown into the corner of a cup-board. "Old people don't need ornaments," he used to say to her ironically, "besides, beer doesn't need chewing, so teeth are useless things."

The old woman felt that she was on the verge of fainting with fear. "What's happening to me?" she thought. Such a foolish expression came into her staring eyes, you would think she had lost her wits. Her toothless mouth opened in surprise, and she was unable to control her trembling chin. She remained looking at him and dribbling. How could she dare to touch again that stiffened body, lying there unmoving in the bedclothes at her side? "Oh mother, mother, what has happened to me?" she stammered over and over again.

Then after a time she began to scream. "Oh, oh, oh, mother, oh my goodness!" The screaming revived her, and brought her back from the stupor which was clouding her mind. Nervously and hurriedly she crossed herself over and over in desperation. "Goodness me, oh goodness me!" This was a relief. She felt her wits returning, and she kept on screaming even louder and more piercingly, trying to find in the howls that issued from her tortured throat some form of protection and forgetfulness. She no longer bothered to make any distinction between what she was saying and what she wanted to say.

This hysterical lamentation lasted for hours, until the evening came. The rays of light which warmed the room grew fainter. The old woman's crippled body, chilled by terror and illness, trembled with cold. The bedclothes which had remained wet all day, stuck to her shrivelled flesh when she tried to turn a little in the blankets. Their smell didn't worry her much, because she had got used to that long ago.

She had eaten nothing and was beginning to suffer from hunger. She was weak from fatigue and exhaustion, from all the screaming to which she had received no answer, and from the lamentations which had issued from her tortured soul like some fearful never-ending dirge. How could she fail to mourn the passing of her old mate; he had for so many years, for good or ill, been her companion through life, and when they were young, her lover. Besides, she had looked after him and had cared for him for so long. She had suffered his rude habits and his rough behaviour, because she believed a woman's role in life was to suffer and put up with tribulations. The poor soul had never known what it was to be pampered, even in childhood. Too tired to think, she lay there staring languidly until, as in some clouded dream that darkness slowly covers, she sank into a heavy deathlike lethargy. She forgot the frightful death of her old companion who lay there cold and unmoving at her side.

The tormented woman woke again next day. Much as she wished to sleep, she woke, a living body once again. She turned to the clock on the wall to see the time, as she was in the habit of doing since rheumatism had stiffened her legs.

While their savings lasted, the old man kept taking her to doctors; sometimes with good grace, but mostly grumbling and cursing. The years dragged on until finally they both became pensioners. That brought an end to the coming and going to doctors with all the expenses involved. She had received no benefit from them after so many years. She was tired of all the traipsing around, and fed up with doctors and their medicaments. Confined now to the house, the old woman had nothing to do but wait and see what fate might next have in store for her.

The months dragged into years this way. Sometimes whimpering with pain, sometimes a little improved, she would go out onto the landing and sit there in the sunshine, gazing at the grass as it changed colour with the seasons. She was thinking of that other country she had left behind, for which she yearned continually, and desired with more passion and heartache than an ardent young lover could feel for his beloved. She was always comparing the new land with the old, forgetting all the blemishes and sorrows of her own country in the process. She thought of it blindly, with love and pain, and the more she yearned, the greater she felt her loss to be. Further bitter years ensued! Much against her will she became an invalid, confined completely to her wretched bed.

She was listening to the sound of the clock's pendulum as it swung back and forth. Tick-tock, tick-tock . . . It was almost breaking day. Unaccustomed to waking at this hour, she remained for a long time motionless, watching the hands of the clock as they slowly changed places. When she moved a little, trying to rise, she felt the pressure of the hard, unmoving body of her husband at her side. Locked in the depression made by the ruined springs of the bed, the two of them had passed the entire night together. A draft of morning air streaming from the open skylight in the kitchen, caressed her forehead and cooled her pale cheeks. These had been reduced to two deep holes, exaggerated by her cheekbones, which seemed as if they were about to tear the darkened skin they covered.

She felt better today. The first impression of fear and terror had subsided. She turned and gazed sadly at the pitiful sight of the old man's corpse. Three times she made the sign of the cross with deep devotion. "God rest your soul Manolio. You tired yourself out for us all. Now you can rest for ever. Now there is only me, poor wretch. What will become of me now? Who will there be to give me a mouthful of water when my soul burns? Who will clean up the messes I make? . . . You had troubles enough caring for me, poor old chap, but what's going to happen now in the desolation of this foreign land? I have no one to attend your corpse Manolio. Who will conduct your requiem and see to the death notices? Who will come to your grave to light the candles? Who will give out the memorial wheat for your poor soul? . . . What a stubborn wretch you were! You never did want us to return to our country, our own sacred land, to find there the gentle soil of a friendly cemetery. It touched your pride and you were ashamed that you hadn't made enough money. 'Donkeys don't breed dollars,' I used to say to you. Now the bad times have found us out! Oh God, forgive us . . . "

The old woman began to wail again in a piteous and desolate monologue which went on and on. She made the sign of the cross. "Oh Jesus and Mary, save me!" she implored with all the strength of her tormented soul, turning her head to the corner where two or three old moth-eaten icons hung, covered with dust and dirt. A broken lamp stood beside them, unlit, with some burnt dry oil at its base. "Who knows when we last lit your lamp, dear Christ? Your sacred image stands there in pitch darkness. And there's your mother too, without light, with you in agony in her arms. Forgive me, oh Mother of God!" The simple old woman started crying again, grieved because she could not light the lamps and the icons had to remain in darkness. Her sobs were extraordinary as if they proceeded from some other person. Suddenly she felt her clouded and tormented brain begin to clear. For the first time, she faced the bare plain truth. She felt an agonizing twinge as she realized the tragic situation. She suddenly understood that Manolio's death was also her own, and a violent trembling shook her body. Her soul froze. For the suffering old woman it was something more unbearable than any of the other trials in her cruel life.

"Take this cup from me." She remembered the phrase from the Passion of Christ in the gospels. She whispered it full of entreaty and with a suppliant and fevered expression. It was the same as that on the face of the bedraggled and exhausted Christ in her icon "The Crowning with Thorns".

"Such martyrdom and death are too much for my tormented body," the poor woman continued, loudly praying.

Later, feeling the pain in her stomach and the craving for bread becoming greater and greater, she decided to call for help. She used the English words, "Help, help, help, please!" But who could hear her? The place was well out of town, with a wide area all round it; any neighbours were a long way off. It was impossible to be heard! She knew this from other occasions. All the screams, curses, and shouts that she had directed at the old man over the years had bothered no one. No one had ever worried, or come to knock on her door to ask what was happening to her, or what the shouting was all about. The old woman thought that Mrs Mathews, the mother of the local gardener, might come to ask how she was getting on. She used to do this sometimes, but now, like her, she had one foot in the grave. She just couldn't manage the journey any more.

Then there was that other curse they had, the language problem. "What? Doesn't Manolio's old woman speak English?" "Only one or two broken words." To make herself understood she used a lot of gestures which covered the most necessary and indispensable things. Among the Australians she had very few acquaintances. They were typically cold, and usually talked ironically and with bitterness. So the old woman carried on for years as if she were dumb. When she had the strength, which was seldom enough, she went to the Greek church and there chattered with her compatriots. She had no relatives, and after losing her eldest child, she cut herself off completely. The old woman was continually cursing her fate, and she had no incentive to show kindness to others.

Death had come close to her on two occasions. Once when it took Spirakis from her as a child no more than two and a half years old. He was stricken down by diphtheria, that unspeakable disease which swept away like a broom so many little children throughout the world. But it was Stamatis who caused her the greatest pain which was still unhealed in her soul. Cruel fate had presented her with his mangled body when some train carriages had crushed the poor boy as he was working. He went to an untimely death before he had any opportunity for happiness or a family. He was only nineteen years of age.

She thought about all these things in those tragic moments, but she found she could no longer weep as she had at other times. With all these fresh sorrows it was as if her tears had run dry and the edges of her eyes had become seared and hot. She was burned up with agony! She had no need to grieve for the old man, the obstinate old wretch. He persistently wanted to die in solitude rather than back home, so that they should never know that he had failed after so many years in a foreign land. He remained continually very poor, with nothing but his meagre pension.

Once she said to him, "Let us go, Manolio, before we use up the little we have saved for the fare. Let us go, man, back to our own country, to breathe again our own air before we are completely ruined. Poor here or poor there, at least we'll get a kindly 'good-day' in a place that has been blessed by God. Here I have been driven mad for so many years, despised by people, drowning in a dumb world."

Old Manolio would get angry and become furiously stirred up. He cursed and blasphemed, and put the matter off. He exuded ill-will and bitterness, because secretly in the depths of his heart he wanted and yearned for the same thing. When he had wept on a few occasions, he had done so secretly and silently in case any of the "bosses" saw him! — or so that his

old wife would not suspect him, and start grumbling more
than ever. "No! No one back there cares a hoot for us. No
one even knows we exist. They are only interested in what
we can send them! Ha, ha, woman. So you were expecting a
happy old age? Don't be stupid! Who would give us anything
to eat back in that poverty-stricken village of yours? The
government? Ha! What government, you old fool? The one
that kicked us in the backside and turned us down without a
thought? Surely you can see that? At the other end of the
world we will be searching for bread. Do you hear? For a bit
of dry bread! Have you forgotten how you lacked even the
roughest food, and how you used to gulp down crusts as if
they were cake?" The old woman shrank back in terror. Perhaps more than anything else the thought quietened her that
he carried within him the same pain, the same incurable
longing as she did. She sympathized with him more than she
had power to show, and she bent her head in patient endurance mumbling some indistinguishable words . . .

It was an unbearably hot day at the end of November, such
as are usual at that time of the year in West Australia. The
place was sweltering, and outside, a hot, uncomfortable wind
was blowing. The unfortunate woman now had little strength
left. She was thirsty, unbearably thirsty. Her throat had
become so parched that it hurt. She tried over and over to
think of some possible way to reach the jug of water they
had put on the table the day before yesterday. But the old
man was in her way. You would think his bony body had
turned to lead. Wedged as it was in the hollow of the bed,
it seemed immovable. The old woman made many efforts to
push it out, but she wasn't strong enough. The corpse was a
complete obstacle to her. Finally, using the very last of her
strength, she pushed her shaky legs up over the lifeless body
of her husband and worked her way over him. After many
efforts full of panting and distress, a thud was heard in the
lonely silence of the tragic room. The unfortunate woman
had succeeded in falling to the floor. Her elbow was skinned
and she had bruised her hip. As she was only skin and bone,

the pain nearly drove her mad. She began to howl loudly, sobbing like a child. Her moaning continued for hours. Without hope of help from anywhere, she had no idea of how long she remained there crying.

The constant agony of thirst which now tormented her unbearably gave her strength to make fresh efforts to pull herself as far as the table in order to reach the jug. Her aged body looked like some strange paleolithic serpent as it dragged itself slowly over the grease-stained floor. Her loose faded clothing bunched up into a knot around her chest leaving her thighs uncovered. Wrinkled and skinny they were an appalling sight. Her piteous efforts to cover the small distance from the bed to the table were full of tragedy. But what followed was even more frightful.

What despair, my God! While she was trying to prop her sluggish body into a position to grasp the jug, the unfortunate woman slipped. In her dizziness she grabbed at the corner of the tablecloth only to find herself sprawling flat on her back, together with all the things that the old man had left unwashed and scattered on the table. Plates with left-over food, greasy knives and forks, half a bottle of oil, a flask of wine, and worst of all, the coveted jug, came tumbling on to the dirty unswept lino with a fearful crash. Cooling water showered onto the old woman's clothes. A dry crust of bread filled her with longing and a wild joy. She sucked the drops of water from her hands and wiped her face with her wet clothing. Like a foolish child she scooped the dry remnants of food from the fallen plates. After pulling herself close to the heap of crumbs, she stretched out bony fingers and with trembling movements took a handful and began to suck. It was all her toothless mouth could do to manage it.

All these efforts took time, and wearied her. Her head sank to the ground. Worn out by the agony of the long day, the poor thing fell into a seemingly endless sleep, a sick slumber, full of delirious groanings. Despite all the unfortunate creature had been through, death still did not take her. She woke up! Woke once again, alive, woebegone, and in misery. How many hours or perhaps days she spent sunk in this lethargy no one will ever know, and she herself was never aware.

It was late afternoon. The first thing she was conscious of
was a heavy unbearable smell. It pervaded the whole room
which had been closed for so many days. "Perhaps Manolio
has begun to smell already . . . " The half-eaten crust had
become like stone, but her mind, affected by the long tiring
period without food, concentrated entirely on this one
morsel. She clutched at it again and tried to eat a tiny piece;
but she only succeeded in hurting her gums and filling her
mouth with blood.

Poor old soul! What a tragic end was in store for her! It
was indeed a black page on which Fate had inscribed her
destiny. But there were moments when she even laughed.
"Hi, hi, hi! Where are you Irene? The baby wants feeding.
Irene, silly Irene, you're supposed to be a mother but you're
letting your child die of hunger, the poor thing. Hi, hi, hi."
Irene was back in the village in Greece. She was her sister-in-
law, but her husband Nickolas was not like his brother
Manolio. "Dry bread and onions will do me, Manolio. I'm
never going to move from here, the place where our mother
bore us. You're welcome to all the wealth and comforts."
Thus Nickolas had written to Manolio.

"Irene!" the poor woman kept shouting. "Irene, feed your
baby. What's the matter? What's the matter, stupid? Don't
say you have no milk with those huge breasts as big as a
cow's. You're lazy like all the rest of your family. You'll
be the death of the little one."

"Ah, mother dearest, I'm going away. Going to escape
from all this devastating poverty. Mother, don't cry! Don't
cry! I can't stand it, don't cry!" The old woman began to cry
herself, foolishly, loudly and tearfully. "See how fat I've
grown!" she murmured, noticing the bare flesh which stuck
out of her ragged clothing. Her skin had swelled strangely
like a toy balloon that children play with on New Year's
Day. It stretched and hung down as if it were filled with
water. The skin on her calves could not stand such stretching
and a browny-yellow fluid, like pus, ran down her legs and
dripped on to the lino . . .

How many days did she drag on like this, a filthy serpent
on the floor? What expectations could she have had, so persistently to hold on to her soul, refusing to surrender it up to

the angel of death? Did she imagine she could ever escape from her frightful affliction; that she could free the archangel from the torment of waiting which he was enduring for her sake?

Her lips became like drums and it was only with difficulty that she could close them at all. Her eyes were hidden in her swollen cheeks. "Manolio, get up! I want water," she whimpered tonelessly, repeating the words over and over. "I'm hungry. I'm hungry, Manolio. Call mother to knead the bread. Tomorrow's Sunday. It will soon ring for evening prayers . . . Manolio, where is Stamatis? See you go and get the English barber to cut your hair. Tomorrow we will go to church . . . Stamatis, is that you walking in the hall? Have you lit the stove? Your father is coming, Stamaty. Run and light the stove for tea . . . Mother, I'm hungry . . . Manolio! . . . Nickolas got a lazy wife. She was frightened of all the work in Australia . . . The silly woman grabbed your brother, and took him back to the village. Ha, ha, ha! They cleared out . . . they gave no notice . . . didn't care that they had nothing. Ha, ha, ha! Irene where are you, woman? You turned out a good-for-nothing wife. Sweep the kitchen a little. Hi, hi, hi! Mother dearest, I'm thirsty, I'm thirsty . . . "

The old woman began to cry once more. She turned face downwards, spread out and sprawling on the floor. Her dress, from all the dragging about, had become a bundle of rags. It left her body half bare and dreadful to look at. "I'm thirsty!" She said it again and again in a complaining monotone, but so weakly she could hardly hear it herself. She tried a few times to rise, but only her head moved, and then fell, showing for a brief moment that she was still alive.

Oh God, what a tragic fate your creatures endure, but who still, despite such vile and piteous conditions, retain the desire and strength to hope for life in you! Oh God, forgive the ill-fated poor wife of old Manolio, who was weary and went to sleep, unable, in the end, even briefly to raise her head, but who still believed and hoped that she would live.

A heavy nauseating stench pervaded the room when the local police broke into it. Outside a brightly shining sun seemed to smile with calm joy on the cobwebbed landing near the door. What a beautiful day! The grass was growing, and with it fresh hopes for the new year with all its crops.

All homelands are sweet in the clear light of day, with pastures bringing hope and joy. It is only in the soul of man that things are otherwise. This strange immaterial substance which can be our slave or can enslave us! It can shine forth in the most clouded black night of our life; or it can darken and confuse the brilliant light of day.

Oh God, forgive the tortured and tormented souls of Manolio and his old wife. They went on living year after year in the clear light of your sun, without ever noticing or loving it. They searched honestly and worked hard to find happiness; but you only gave them misery and pain!

On the country news, between a lot of insignificant items and comments, the announcer reported an odd fact: how a couple of aged pensioners had been found dead in their house some days after the event.

To Discuss the Possibility of . . .

Ugo Rotellini

He moved across the seat and grasped her possessively, lovingly, aware of the tension cocooning her movements.

"Sandra?"

She said, "I won't be seeing you again."

"What do you mean?"

"What I said. This is the last time."

For some moments he was silent, then he said, "But why? I thought . . . "

She struggled in his arms, restless, insistent, her tone taut with despair, the words a defiant apology.

"I can't stand it any more!"

He moved close to her again, caressing her face.

"Let me come. I'll explain to them." She pushed his hands from her, turning, backing away from his concern.

"How?"

"All I want is to be with you."

She shook her head. "You don't understand."

"That's it, isn't it. *I* don't understand."

"Please, just go away," she pleaded.

She moved abruptly, pushing open the door of his car. He saw her pause, a hint of uncertainty, before moving away. He followed her and pulled her to him, his face creased with hurt and frustration.

"Christ, you can't just order me out of your life like that."

She looked at him, sobbing quietly.

"I'll do what ever they ask me to do," he added.

"Will you? They'll want you to marry me."

The look on his face betrayed his surprise, his bewilderment, at a commitment he had never considered.

He never approached her again. Avoiding each other was not difficult.

Soon she left, preferring she said, the intimacy and convenience of the Catholic school near her place.

There were no more commitments, she merely tolerated contacts that were brief and transitory and bearable. Her memories remained vivid and constant, fragments of conversation ever-present. She had been caught unaware, her Italianness no longer a myth or romantic side-effect of her life.

One evening the conversation she had always dreaded took place.

Her father began, "Sandra, there's a young man," he paused, then continued, "a nice Italian boy, you understand. He has seen you. He would like to come here, to meet you, with Enzo, and then perhaps discuss the possibility of . . . "

"No!"

"His name is Tony Cupo. I've met him briefly. I'm told he's a pleasant boy. With good prospects . . . "

"No, I said!"

"At least meet him. If you don't like him . . . " he held his hands out in a gesture of resignation.

"Sandra, you're twenty-one," her mother added, "soon it will be too late."

And so, subdued by her parents' insistence, and drawn by a need that was both ambivalent and compelling, she relented.

"Enzo! Come in! Come in!"

In the hall Enzo stopped, and turning to his companion, held him gently by the arm and propelled him forward. "Livio, Maria, this is Tony. What do you think?" "Well," there was a deliberate pause, a subtle reprimand to be less obvious, less partisan, "Tony, we are happy to have you in our home. We have heard a lot about you."

"Thank you. Enzo has spoken often of you and . . . Sandra."

The other three looked at each other. Enzo put a hand on Tony's shoulder, "He's a good boy," he insisted.

"Come in, please come in," beckoned Livio. "Here, through here. In the lounge."

Enzo was calm, relaxed, with a role to play, which would include highlighting and exaggerating the right qualities, and

directing and prodding the discussion when necessary. Tony
would talk a little, not too much, no arrogance, yet giving the
impression of having confidence, and showing respect and
courtesy.

"Tony, please, here, sit here. That girl of ours. Maria will
you go and see. Get Sandra."

The women returned together, Sandra leading the way.
Her father and Tony, still standing, moved slightly towards
her. Tony paused, uncertain of how to react. "How are you,"
he finally said in English.

There would be little said between them. For now personal
exploration would be through side-long glances and deceptive
disinterest, with any enthusiasm remaining muted and
restrained.

"Tony here, sit here, next to my friend." He paused, then
continued, "Enzo and I have known each other a long time."

"Since fifty-three? God, the 'Roma', remember her?"

"How can I forget. I was sick the whole voyage."

"One month," Enzo murmured, turning to Tony, "can
you imagine. How can anyone be seasick for one month."

"I thought I was going to die."

"Eating . . . five pounds wasn't it? of bananas didn't help."

"You recommended it. You said it would cure me. Like
hell. What agony."

"It was worthwhile Livio. This country. This home. Your
family together."

"It was worthwhile, yes . . . Maria will you get something
to drink? A bicchierino. Then Enzo, I want you to try my
wine before your palate is spoiled with any other rubbish."

"Well, do you like it?"

"Yes, why not, it's almost as good as ours. Tony?"

"Good. Yes. Better than ours."

"So, you're at university?"

"Yes, I hope to finish this year."

"This university, it's far?"

"Not really. But I have a car."

"At your age I had a donkey. I did up to grade three,"
said Enzo, "and you Livio?"

"I'm more intelligent than you, remember? Fourth grade.
You know, we learnt more in those days. School was a

serious business. Teachers don't care now. Not only here."

"Papa, how can you say that."

"Why not? Not you, but I see some of your friends, the way they dress, their behaviour."

"So?"

"Sandra," her mother interrupted, motioning her to refill the glasses.

"Would you like some more?" she asked Tony in a formal, subdued tone.

"No, no, I don't drink very much."

"Well, so you're going to be a chemist," Livio said.

"Hopefully."

"It's going well?"

"Oh yes, I shouldn't have any trouble."

"An Italian-speaking chemist Livio, the possibilities are there. What do you think Tony?"

"Of course, yes. But who can tell of the future."

"Perhaps a nice little shop around here," suggested Enzo.

"You'll have to work and live somewhere," added Maria.

"Do you like this area?" asked Enzo.

"Yes. My parents have bought a block near here."

"Ah, for you?"

"We plan to build a house. When I . . . settle down."

The conversation went well. It was obvious the boy was intelligent, with the right combination of humility and confidence.

Soon the wine and liqueur, the amaretti, the plates of cheese and salami, were taken away to make way for the coffee. A touch of anisetta.

Throughout Sandra was busy, clearing things away and bringing others.

"Well Tony, I think it's about time we went," said Enzo.

"What can I say," began Livio. "Thank you for coming. From all of us. It's been a pleasure meeting you."

"Thank you. For me to have met you and Sandra has been very important. I would like to come again."

Livio looked at his wife. "Of course, you'll be welcome. And please give our best wishes to your family. Perhaps next time if your parents would like to come . . . "

"I'm sure they want to meet you all."

"Good. And we'll have a good talk, all of us."

"Thank you again."

Livio walked out with the two men, the women waiting in the open door, waving a last time, before moving inside.

"Livio listen, I want to say a few words to you. Tony I won't be long. If you want to wait in the car . . . "

"Well?"

"There's a little problem Livio."

"Problem?"

"Nothing serious."

"What problem?"

"Tony."

"What about him?"

"He's er . . . not a Catholic."

"He's Italian isn't he?"

"Of course."

"Well then."

"It's not exactly Tony. He doesn't really care. But his parents . . . "

"Enzo come on, stop this crap. What are you trying to say."

"Well . . . they're Jehovah's Witnesses."

"Come on!"

"They converted."

"Oh shit. It's becoming a bloody epidemic! Italians are so stupid. By God, Enzo."

"Listen, remember it's Tony who has to marry your daughter."

"You're joking."

"What do you mean."

"I mean nothing's settled. That little shit didn't open his mouth in there about this little problem did he eh? Why didn't you tell me before bringing him here?"

"It's for them to decide surely."

"For them to decide what. Don't forget whose daughter she is. Don't forget that."

"Look, what do you care about the parents."

"What do I care? Jehovah's Witnesses! They're crazy. Fanatics. All they want to do is convert people. A couple came around here a few weeks ago. I told them I was a communist. Do you think they listened. They couldn't even speak proper Italian, the bastards. My daughter is not going to be dragged in by that crowd. I should have guessed though, after all they're related to Broccoli."

"What does that mean?"

"You know what that idiot, what she said to her daughter, her six year old daughter, when the little girl was bitten by a dog? Eh? She said, why didn't you bite it back? And she hit her, she said she must have provoked the dog. And you remember the time they had that plague of cats and they tried to kill them by burying them alive, and after a while all those cats crawled out. And when they painted that 'For Sale' sign on their goat?"

"What have those madmen got to do with Tony marrying your daughter."

"Jesus you want my daughter mixed up with that lot!"

"You've got it all wrong. You're exaggerating. He doesn't care. His parents are crazy about him. Even God and Jesus Christ and all his angels praying for the next hundred years and promising them kingdom come wouldn't affect them. If he tells them to wipe his arse, no problems. He doesn't care."

"I care."

"He used to be an altar boy you know."

"So what?"

"So . . . he's flexible. He had his eyes opened as a kid. He's told me he doesn't give a shit about religion. He knows what he wants. But you saw him, the way he was looking at her, at Sandra. If you say they marry in a Catholic church, I tell you there are no problems."

"Why are you so anxious for this?"

"Look, I set this up. How do you think I feel. I tell you his prick is like a rigid rod by now. And Sandra is interested. Very. I can see."

"I was interested."

"Surely you're not going to . . . "

"Do his parents know about this?"

"Yes I told them. I told the father. Tony spoke to his mother."

"What did they say?"

"About what?"

"Come on!"

"Nothing. I told you. Whatever their son wants. And the father I think just goes along with the wife. You can talk to him. She's the crazy one — about religion."

"She's discovered religion. That kind of woman is formidable."

"She trusts me."

"She trusts God more."

"God speaks in strange ways. A hen today is better than an egg tomorrow. You know me, I can talk to *anyone*."

"To a madwoman who thinks she's heading to the promised land and won't be able to take her baby with her?"

"Look Livio we can't just let it go. We've made a commitment. What do you care about the parents. They're irrelevant. You've got the daughter."

"So they're paying you."

"Insulting me isn't going to resolve our problem."

"It helps."

"By God Livio, Sandra's twenty-one. She's a teacher. She's not exactly a chi . . . "

"She's my daughter."

"Listen, you spring this on her now, remember this is Australia."

"My daughter tells me there are one million of us here. One in fifteen. They were the odds my friend, that she'd marry an Italian, any Italian, and when you told me about your little protégé, I thought it was settled, wrapped up. I wouldn't have to worry about the language and the . . . "

"He speaks Italian well doesn't he?"

"Yes. You told him to mention the block too. Impressive. We listened. And where do you think his mother will live when this nice new house is built?"

"He loves his mother. That's a good quality. But I'll have a talk to him. Listen you don't think I want the best for Sandra too? I'm her compare. I baptised her, her spiritual father."

"No more bullshit Enzo please."

"Come and talk to him."

"And say what?"

"Find out what he thinks."

"You told me what *he* thinks. It's the parents. What do they think."

"We're going around in circles."

"A circle that never closes. OK. How can we get together with the parents?"

"No problems. Leave it to me."

"You won't tell me that they have any strange blood next? His grandfather didn't fuck some Abyssinian in honour of our late Duce, and bring her back to Italy?"

"What about next week?"

"See what you can do. I'll have to speak to Sandra first though."

"That's fair enough. You can be a reasonable man sometimes Livio."

"I'll hear from you soon then."

"Tomorrow."

"Say goodbye to the boy for me. Be subtle."

"Always. I'll be in touch."

"Tomorrow then."

"Tomorrow."

Giovanni's Courtship

Vic Caruso

A whole car load of them, each Italian to the core, all looking like something out of Mario Puzo, all in a recent model Valiant.

The eldest, of course, was the father, Don Nunzo, cradling a great pot belly which slumped on the front bench seat like a sitting Buddha's. The coat of the dark indigo suit struggled incessantly to maintain its reach around the incredible girth, and the button holes had long ago resigned to what seemed to be a daily growth. They extended a full inch, open, behind the tense buttons. Don Nunzo's belt was down there somewhere in no man's land, beneath the summit of his barrel-like stomach. Otherwise he looked quite a neat man.

The women, of course, were in the back seat, with Angela a grain of wheat between two enormous millstones — one on either side of her, crushing to her left or right depending on which direction the car turned. She was a dainty little flower, a thirteen year old Madame Pompadour with a quaint little plastic flower planted in each long curl. The little garden of hair was even scented with the perfume of the age, VO5 — by "Alberrtto", as the clever Don Nunzo would say each time the ad flashed through the family's living room.

"I think it's in the next street, *va piano!*" It was the officious voice of Carlo Puiastro, matchmaker for a day. He was short, hiding behind a moustache that struggled to grow on his barren upper lip. He endeavored to create a reputation as an impeccably dressed, stylish man. Thus he was the only member of the party to be wearing a pastel shirt, striped at the collar, and an artificial breast-pocket handkerchief with six peaks sprouting as though the rest of the *Cutty Sark* was there also. His hair gleamed, thick and straight as it was.

Don Nunzo looked out of the car window, observing the houses. Red brick, cream brick. He was quite impressed.

"Good neighborhood," he commented, "I must compliment you. Carlo." Smiled Carlo — a smile of "I told-you-so" and "but of course."

"Yes, you picked the right girl for my Giovanni," Don Nunzo added.

Giovanni, driving, tightened his grip on the steering wheel. His fat mamma in the back seat could sense that Giovanni was doing his bit to express that he didn't like "Giovanni", preferring "John". Giovanni could have made a fuss about this as he usually would, but now his mind was occupied. What would she be like? Not fat, I hope. Not skinny, either, unless she looked like Audrey Hepburn. Not a chance! After sorting through the line-up of various Italian girls in his mind, his heart gained a couple of beats more than usual, and his mouth drooped . . . "Fat!" he said it aloud.

"What?" asked Don Nunzo, his eyes still on the infatuating red and cream bricks.

"*Nienti*," replied Giovanni. "Just thinking aloud."

Don Nunzo finally turned his head towards where the car was travelling, looking at the long street ahead. "You know, Carlo, the more I see of Fawkner the more I must compliment you! This girl must be a princess to live here." Carlo laughed — he could not hold back his delight for such praise.

"*Si, si*," he began, trying to metamorphose the laugh into serious words. "They come from near Naples, you know — but of course, I told you that. And what's more, they've got, er, ah, taste, yes, taste; you know how the *Napolitani* are."

It was Don Nunzo's turn to smile with satisfaction. His son from the depths of Sicily's Catanzaro was marrying into virtual nobility. He tossed his head with more satisfaction, and thought: "Nobility, yes, nobility!"

Once more he turned to view the houses and exclaimed: "Fawkner! My my, Fawkner!"

Little Angela did not have her father's real estate appreciation of domestic abodes, but nevertheless she felt obliged to comment. "When are *we* moving to Fawkner, Papa?" she asked, leaning on the front seat's backrest. "I don't like Brunsuwickki," she said.

All laughed. Fat sister at her side, with just a hint of a sharp tongue, reminded her that life was not always "Brunsuwiccki", for it was much worse in Catanzaro.

Giovanni kept driving, the car bouncing along smoothly under the weight of its occupants. Don Nunzo himself had thoroughly washed it that Sunday morning, and he had felt an air about himself there in the driveway, poised with rag and bucket in hand. As people were returning from church dressed in their Sunday best he had not been perturbed at cleaning away there in his Monday worst. After all, theirs was the most recent model Valiant in the street, its iridescent orange like the bush of Biblical fame, burning there for the adulation of all passers-by.

"Not so fast, Giovanni, we might miss the street" — it was Signor Carlo again, fully in charge of the situation as a proper matchmaker should be. "You might break the springs, too," came advice from Giovanni's mamma, sitting bored and apprehensive in the back. She was half-smothering Angela, pinning her fast to the seat.

"Impossible!" retorted Giovanni. "Valiant springs are like a truck's", he said with pride. He resented women — including his mother — interfering with his driving or making comments about things mechanical. That was a man's field, remote from a woman's domain between the kitchen stove and the kitchen sink.

"Of course they are," added Don Nunzo. "Nothing like the springs of a *Valiante*! Right, Carlo?" Carlo just grunted. He had a Falcon, considerably older than the Calvari's Valiant, and if anyone wanted his opinion, Falcons were the best cars on the road!

"You have to see it on a dirt track — then you really appreciate the springs," said the proud Giovanni.

"Yes, well just as long as you don't drive madly like you always do when *I'm* in the car," boomed the voice of big married sister. Her wrist looked like a tempting proposition for Angela to bite; then maybe she would rest it on her own lap! But you don't bite the wrist of a sister whose husband has deserted her. However, as the Calvaris would say, the less said about that the better.

Wind and road noise began to give way to the sounds of deceleration as the car was thrown into a lower gear to slow it down — a little too suddenly, perhaps. Abuses! Complaints! "What are you, a maniac?!" the mother screamed at Giovanni, brushing her arms as though the Sahara desert had just blown through the window and settled on her sequined, hand-sewn coat.

"Sh! We don't want to let them see us quarrelling," cautioned Carlo. All part of the expertise required to be a matchmaker.

"Is *that* it?" Don Nunzo was awe-struck. Across the other side of the road, sitting low in all its magnificence and embalmed in cream brick, was the house of his son's future wife. Not a pull-down spring blind in sight, but oceans of white venetians, floral in design, enhanced by silky-white curtains. Roll-away awnings, four of them, one on each of the four windows, each window on one of the four fronts of the house. Garden gnomes basking in the gentle sunshine, guarding the conglomerate of lilies, rose bushes and geraniums. Deep terra cotta tiles rising away to their apex in the roof. And a little black fairy born of wrought iron told all interested — and all not interested as well — that this was number 211, named, maybe, after some mystical Aboriginal place: EMOH RUO.

Don Nunzo wiped his brow. "*Ma che casa! Ma che casa per d'avero!*" Yes, it certainly was quite a house, Angela agreed, but before she could ask why they could not have one like it Carlo suggested that Giovanni steer the car right into the large concrete driveway. "Would it be all right?" Don Nunzo wasn't sure, but he trusted Carlo. Any man who had found a family of this quality had his unshakeable confidence.

Last minute adjustments, advice and wrangling. "Now, Giovannuzzo, don't forget what I said. Act intelligent, don't drink lemonade, drink beer or wine and don't, for goodness sake, take a sip until everyone else has a glass, and you must say *salute* before you drink, and . . . "

One after the other, doors slammed shut as the party emerged. The suspension breathed a sigh of relief as the fat mother, fat daughter and fat father clambered out onto the cement of the driveway. Giovanni was the last out, taking ritual-like pride in securing the doors, pulling on the hand brake and carrying out sophisticated procedures known only to one who has sat behind the wheel.

Don Nunzo was taking the opportunity to survey the very neat angle at which the television aerial lead was anchored to the hole in the roof. "Ingenious, simply ingenious!"

All collected around the side of the car nearest the front verandah. The two and a half women made sure that all was in order with their hems and seams and, with handbags cradled before them, proceeded to walk behind the men up the garden path. Leather and concrete played a tune of their own as the sextet shuffled along. No one saw one of the louvres of the venetians lifted ever so slightly in the room behind the verandah.

It was Carlo who gave a sharp flick to the doorbell, setting it ringing inside the house, just as Giovanni was feeling his pulse rate. Thoughts flew. Who would open the door? Will they *all* come out to greet us? What are they wearing? Should we get right to the point? How well does Carlo *really* know these people? Maybe they are a trifle superior to us. Will the marriage work out? I wonder at whose house we'll have the Christmas dinner? . . .

The signs of animation inside the house made themselves evident. Footsteps, muffled by a thick carpet, became audible. A pause. Vibrations on the doorhandle. Suddenly a big parallel space, temporarily all black and void, embellished by the full view of a woman.

To the right of the hall was the lounge; to the left, judging from Don Nunzo's own reflection in a mirror there, could have been a bedroom. But for the time being the party of six stood, some heads turned towards the decorative plaster ceiling, others eyeing each other, and still others staring at the beautiful woman. All were lost. Even the woman, the hostess, had not got far after the hellos were finished with. Carlo rallied himself to the front of the company and did the honors. A few more moments and the silence would have been embarrassing.

"Signora Madafferi," he began, pointing out the hostess, "this is Signor Calvari," and then stepped back, proud of his proper Italian, letting Don Nunzo Calvari shake hands with the hostess Signora. Then came Don Nunzo's wife, Giovanni, and finally the fat sister and little Angela.

"Please, step into the loungeroom, won't you," beckoned the noble Signora Madafferi. "My husband and Natalina will be here right away — they've been in the garden, you know."

"Natalina," thought Giovanni. It sounded different now that her mother had said it, and there was a certain sweetness that was lost on the numerous occasions Carlo had said the name. Natalina — of course, he'd have to shorten that to Natalie, just like the actress, the American actress.

"Yes, yes, of course," replied Don Nunzo to the Signora, and he took in the laminated buffet neatly packed with glasses for all occasions, cutlery sets, tea sets and the occasional sugar almonds packed in the mock-silk nets. His eyes were parched sponges aching to be quenched by the wonders of the room. And everything was a wonder: old photographs in neat rows on top of the buffet, television and mantel, with some larger ones hanging from the soft-hued violet walls.

"It certainly is a nice house," smiled Carlo at Don Nunzo. He saw in his eyes the laughter that one manifests when one is about to praise.

"Yes, yes, a very nice house," agreed Don Nunzo. Carlo smiled in deep satisfaction: he was the matchmaker, the guest of honor. the go-between, the talent scout.

"Oh, but it's such a bother to keep clean," laughed Signora Madafferi. "Every Sunday morning! We start with the hall and end up on the back porch! Whew! But it must be done."

"Of course, of course, I know just what you mean," retorted Signora Calvari, "We always clean ours!" That was just in case the lovely Signora Madafferi had any wrong notions about the Calvari standard of cleanliness.

"And the neighborhood — it's excellent," dictated Don Nunzo. His tone was beatific. "Fawkner is fast becoming the best, most modern suburb in Melbourne."

"*Si, si,*" replied Signora Madafferi. Somewhere she had read about another up and coming Melbourne suburb which the Calvaris had not heard about: Toorak.

At that moment the keenly awaited footsteps were heard outside the doors to the loungeroom. All heads turned in their direction, and in entered Signor Madafferi, trailed by a humble looking girl of about twenty. Madafferi was a robust man, tall with clearly defined features — almost as well defined as Don Nunzo's. He wore a check sports shirt, almost entirely hidden by a mohair pullover and dark sports coat on top of that. He was fifty, he looked it, and he was proud of it.

Madafferi stopped just inside the doorway, and very quickly eyed the company assembled on the divan, with Carlo sitting slightly higher than the rest, on a kitchen chair. Signora Madafferi lounged in one of the two armchairs.

"Ah, Carlo, you've arrived," he said, aiming his outstretched hand towards Carlo. Not exactly the most appropriate greeting for anyone in such circumstances, but he was lost for words. Carlo, sensing this, knew it was time to take full control, the chairman of the board presiding at the board meeting.

He shook hands with Madafferi, and again began the laborious "so and so, meet so and so," until finally he introduced Madafferi's daughter. The latter had stopped short in the centre of the room, inconspicuous behind her father's frame. When she shook hands with Giovanni she raised her head ever so slightly, but turned her eyes as far up as their sockets would allow. Giovanni, being a man, looked at her squarely, his heart fluttering perhaps even more than hers. He had held her hand perhaps a second longer than necessary, and realizing this he dropped it smartly.

Natalina resigned herself to the outskirts of the room, well away in her place. She was only the bride to be.

Giovanni was up there with the best of them on that couch, but it was his presence, and not his conversation, that was mandatory. Little Angela wriggled helplessly.

"It was a little cold, this morning," said Carlo at last, oiling the machinery of marital protocol. "I'm afraid my few *feet* of tomato got the frost!" He eyed the oil heater, placidly stuck to the wall, silent, vigilant. Signora Madafferi saw the object of his gaze, and promptly gave the command to Natalina.

"Why don't you switch the heater on," she snapped. Natalina promptly flew off her chair and bent over the heater, turning knobs. Her parents were proud. They eyed all on the couch, making sure that they appreciated Natalina's obedience and alertness. Giovanni's heart fluttered as he watched her slender figure — unusual for an Italian girl, and more beautiful than his most daring expectations — bending over the heater, the force of gravity doing its neat work on her upper body. She was not just a stranger — this was his future wife — negotiations going well, that is.

Natalina sat down again in her place in no man's land. It was just then that Madafferi felt the social thirst in his throat. "Natalina, the beer!" Up sprang Natalina, and quickly, though with delightful grace, she left the room. Madafferi turned to Don Nunzo, searching his face for some sign, some expression of acceptance.

"Nice girl, nice girl" — it came from Don Nunzo, just as Madafferi hoped it would. Don Nunzo was nodding his head affirming his own words, looking like a wool buyer's agent at a wool sale advising his client on the merits of the wool. A chorus of words and heads agreed with Don Nunzo.

"She's only twenty years old," said Signora Calvari, more in the fashion of a question than an appreciative statement.

"*Si, si,* only twenty," replied the owners of that obedient girl. "But we think it the right age," continued Madafferi. Naturally, there was no need for anyone to question or ponder: the right age for what? Even little Angela, occasionally moaning and groaning there, a sardine amongst the whales, understood. And she took some interest, too, for half a decade only would have to expire before she'd be sitting in the background switching on oil heaters and fetching the beer.

"And she, ah, she does hair, hum?" Signora Calvari was determined to get all her facts — which had been delivered by Carlo in his brief — confirmed.

"Oh yes, well, you know how it is with a young girl, as soon as she reaches" — Signora Madafferi turned to her husband — "what grade is it?"

"*Form,* not grade, form four," he insisted.

"Form four," continued the now enlightened Signora Madafferi, "as soon as a girl reaches form four, it's that time when her parents must help her as much as possible. After all, what else are parents for but to do the best for their children?" This with the voice of a martyr.

"Right, *si,* of course," agreed Don Nunzo. "It's the same with Giovannuzzo," he began, not to be outdone in matters of martyrdom. "Now, he went to third form — he could have gone on, but the studying! Every night locked away in his room! Oh yes, the studying! It's too much for a young boy, you know. So we talked it over and we decided it was the best he was apprenticed, and now he has his own car." Don Nunzo lounged back with satisfaction.

"And he's a builder . . . ?" queried Madafferi.

"Yes, a builder. It's builders who've built this country for the Australians, us Italians with our own hands." Don Nunzo's fists were clenched, shaking, as he made his point. And all agreed with him, taking his facts as well-known ones, facts which the Australiani would never realize or appreciate.

"Do you find much work?" asked Signora Madafferi. Carlo answered her before Giovanni could reply.

"Never a moment to spare! He did my kitchen a while back. That boy has brains in his head!"

"You'd think he was born with a hammer in his hand," laughed Don Nunzo, looking at his son, who was shying back in embarrassment.

"Even our Natalina," began Signora Madafferi in defence

of her own offspring. "She knows all the fashions, cutting, styling — she knows it all."

"It's a blessing when we have to go to a wedding," added Natalina's proud mother. "Don't have to worry about appointments with your own daughter a hairdresser!"

"True, true. It must be quite a convenience. Hairdressers are so hard to get when you have a wedding coming up, no?"

Carlo sensed the situation running away from him, and before Signora Calvari went on about the scarcity of hairdressers, he intervened, sanctioned by his authority as matchmaker.

"It's the right time for building, all right. I remember when Pascoe Vale was the end of the earth in Melbourne. Now it's right in the middle, thanks to God for the building boom." At least his conversation was more important than trite talk about hair. All agreed with him, and he continued. "And it's we Italians who venture beyond the borders building when the Australians haven't even paid off their homes after twenty years!" More sighs in the affirmative. "And Giovanni is still a boy — it's all there for him: as long as there's land, there's houses for him to build. Not like ourselves, eh, Don Nunzo. Where were we at his age, eh, where were we?"

Ah, but this was the land of opportunity. "America," they called it in the old country. America, where the excess meat was thrown out with the bread crumbs and unused milk.

Natalina returned with the tray of nine long, floral-design glasses, in the midst of which were a bottle of beer and a bottle of orange drink. She placed it on a coffee table in the centre of the company and opened the bottles, filling some of the glasses with beer, and the rest with orange. She then disappeared out of the room, nobody questioning why, for they knew. Customs varied little from house to house. And as expected, she was back in no time with a bowl of peanuts and an empty bowl for the shells to be placed in. She then began to go around the room with the tray, whilst her father talked of wine.

"Beer is all right," he said, "but occasionally we need

wine. Wine is *sincere,* not like this beer: there are too many
impurities in beer and spirits. But wine . . . wine is sincere."
  Angela was listening intently. Madafferi said beer was
impure, and she thought of her own family crushing away
at grapes each autumn in their small grape crusher. And
she thought how dust settled on the conglomerate of crushed
grapes and seeds and grape juice, raw and crude.
  "But wine is dirty!" she burst out, aiming her bit of knowledge at no one in particular.
  "Charming little girl," commented Signora Madafferi, as
though she was noticing Angela for the first time.
  "Zitto!" urged fat sister raising a finger to her lips. Just as
big sister told her, she shut up.

All had a glass of drink in their hands now, and Giovanni
was a little more self-conscious than the others. He glanced
around the room making sure that everyone else had a glass
in his or her hand and then he waited for someone to offer a
toast. *"Al Salute,"* Carlo toasted, repeated by a chorus of
voices who then indeed drank to health. Giovanni wondered
how good a cook his bride to be was. He wondered many
things about her — but there was time enough to find out all
about her after they were married.
  Glasses down, there was a disturbing silence all around the
room. The crunch had come.
  "Well!" began Carlo. Indeed, well. This was the time to
talk, when the festivities gave way to the realities of the
situation, where Carlo's mission came to verbal fulfilment.
"Tony," he said, turning to Madafferi, "I've known you for a
long time. Many times I've come to this house and you've
treated me well. Good. And I know that yours is a family of
respect, and you're known and respected." Madafferi listened
intently. All else listened too, some with heads bowed — just
like when a priest, standing before a couple at the altar,
begins "Dearly beloved we are gathered here today . . . "
  "I can tell from my own heart that you are a good
family," Carlo continued, and all were touched. It is not
often that an Italian refers to his heart unless he has high

blood pressure or similar cardiac complaints. Carlo then turned to Don Nunzo. "And you, Don Nunzo, even you are a man of respect, an honest man. I know that your family cannot speak of any disgraces, and you're all hard workers." Angela buried her chin in her chest. These were high words, oratory to stir the soul, and her own little soul was pricked by the majesty of Carlo's soul-stirring. The fat sister had been through the routine and was interested more in manner than matter. This time the Madafferis had their heads bowed and Don Nunzo listened.

"Giovannuzzo is a noble boy. He is young and benevolent as bread. He is a noble boy indeed. I can only speak the highest regards for him as I am sure everyone can."

Since all either had their heads bowed or were looking Carlo in the eye, including Giovanni, Natalina ventured to take a good look at Giovanni. The top of his hair was curled, and one could see in his face the boy reluctantly giving way to the man. His shoulders were broad, and his light grey suit clung to him, doing justice to his strong build. There was the man who would take her away from her parents' domain and furnish her with a house and family, to be cradled in his loving care. What was he really like? She knew he had not been in Australia as long as she had, and having read English and American novels at school she could not help but be influenced by their romance — something very alien to the Italian culture. She dared not admit it to herself, but she secretly yearned for a life like those novels and Hollywood films depicted: to be nestled in her husband's arms as he called her "Honey" and kissed her goodbye as he left for the office in the morning.

Carlo's talk seemed incessant, but no one objected. This was the proper way to enter into courtship, not like those Australians did, leaving everything to their immature, irresponsible sons and callous, loose-moralled, bitchy daughters. Ah, if only the Australians took a page out of the Italian book.

At last Carlo was through, and conversation, once more

flowed freely. The subject matter now no longer involved mutual compliments, for both families were now virtually as one. Natalina still sat quietly in the background, demure and lovely, her suitor across the other end of the room. They were a pair that fate — or Carlo — had seen fit to unite in betrothal.

"No, no, no," said Carlo in the usual Italian way meaning "yes, yes, yes": Giovanni and Natalina would get along very well.

"Of course, the house I will help them out with myself," added Madafferi, "for she's my only daughter, and I want to do that much for her." They all agreed on a date. It was now May, so September would be fine for the engagement. Giovanni agreed, taking pride in having the opportunity to say yea or nay. But with regards to the wedding . . . now that was a problem.

"I'll have to speak to the caterers again," sighed Carlo, "and see if they can squeeze us in for December. It's not their fault but the council's. All these dances on Saturday nights — if they stopped having them so regularly, maybe the more serious business of having a wedding breakfast could be managed more easily."

Madafferi would personally go along with Carlo to Augustini Catering Service during the week to see what could be done. Don Nunzo was confident that something *would* be done, and judging from what he considered to be the fine, contemporary style of Madafferi's house, the latter would spare no expense in seeing that it would be a grand wedding, and all guests on both sides would be impressed. But the actual details would be worked out at a later date, when the board once more resumed, with Giovanni or his father taking over Carlo's role as chairman.

"Giovanni! Giovanni! Look out, there's a car!" Giovanni jumped in his seat, spinning the steering wheel violently to the left, almost running the Valiant into the gutter, braking frantically at the same time. The other car had screeched out of a side street on Giovanni's right, blasting Giovanni with his horn. Giovanni's cheeks were burning.

"But what are you, mad?" Once again his mother yelled.

No, not mad, but in a daze. She was trailing them, behind, aloft in the air, shy, beautiful, wide-eyed, Natalina, a vision, a wife to be. Who can concentrate on the road when his mind is on such a vision?

"Don't get alarmed, Anna," said Don Nunzo. "He's got other things on his mind!"

"*Bella famillia, no?*" stated Carlo, lounging back in the car seat.

"She seemed a good girl," commented the mother.

"*Si, si, bella ragazza,*" agreed Don Nunzo, nodding discreetly. "You're fortunate, Giovanni; what a girl, eh!"

Giovanni drank from the cup of contentment which his family and Carlo offered. He would marry a vision, a blushing, shy vision, a little lamb he would overwhelm with his manhood. Wonderful Carlo, wonderful parents, wonderful Valiant.

"Not so fast, Giovanni, you're going too fast!" came the voice from the back seat.

"Shut up, Ma, I know what I'm doing!" came the voice from behind the steering wheel.

The Strength of Tradition

Judah Waten

Mr Ekdom did not accept the fact that he was living in a new country with different attitudes. He was still at home back on the small island off Rhodes, and not in the inner Melbourne suburb of Richmond. A short, fat man with a dark, soft face, he believed strongly in keeping a stern watch on his three daughters. The eldest, Sophie, who was sixteen years old, had been promised when she was only six to a man on the island before they had migrated to Australia. The amount of the dowry and the final settlement had been put down in black and white.

There were also two sons, one a child of four and the other, the first-born, a young man of twenty-two with stiff black hair and long sideboards. He was also expected to marry a girl from the island, this also having been arranged with her parents. But Mr Ekdom did not attempt to exercise any tight control over his son. Indeed he believed young men should sow their wild oats before marriage, unlike the girls, who were only to start their sowing on their wedding-night, and never, ever, to stray from the family patch.

Mr Ekdom reared his children on that doctrine, giving his wife strict instructions to meet the three girls after school or if she was unable for one compelling reason or another, she was to make sure that they all arrived at home together. The girls were never to dawdle on the way, and above all they were not to talk to the boys from the Tech, only a couple of hundred yards away from the Girls' School. Mr Ekdom had heard some alarming stories about those boys. Most of them had motor cars or motorcycles and they were girl-mad. Mr Ekdom could hardly bear to think of what could happen to his daughters, the eldest in particular, if they were not properly policed.

Mrs Ekdom acquiesced without a murmur. It would not

have entered her head that he could possibly be wrong or unwise in the new land. She was proud of her husband not only because he held fast to the ideas of their fathers, but also because he put the welfare of his family first. He worked at General Motors in Dandenong during the day and in the evening in the kitchen of a restaurant, to make enough money to put down a deposit on a house.

Mrs Ekdom became a familiar sight outside the school building, waiting for the three girls, and then walking with them slowly down the street, past the Tech, nodding to other mothers who were also escorting their daughters. Now and again a group of Australian girls from the school sniggered at the Ekdoms and made provocative remarks to Sophie.

One afternoon the youngest Ekdom girl was the last to come out of the school, which was unexpected, for the Ekdom girls were generally among the first. Mrs Ekdom had become quite agitated and was about to send Sophie to look for the girl when she appeared.

"Where have you been? Were you kept in?" Mrs Ekdom asked.

The girl refused to answer until they were well out of sight of the school.

"I wish you wouldn't wait outside the door, Muma," she finally said. "We're big enough to go home ourselves, aren't we?" she addressed her sisters.

Mrs Ekdom looked at her youngest with some surprise.

"You don't want me to meet you?" she repeated several times.

Then as she looked from one girl to the other her face assumed a tragic expression.

But it was not incidents like this but the buying of the house that changed the familiar pattern of their lives. Mrs Ekdom was compelled to get a job in a nearby clothing factory: the joint efforts of Mr Ekdom and the eldest son Jim who drove a taxi were not enough to pay off the house and to meet the family expenses.

There was the problem of the girls, now more serious than ever as far as Mr Ekdom was concerned. He said to Jim:

"You will have to try and drop in after school."

"I'll try," Jim said. "But you know I could be at Tullamarine or anywhere at that time."

As Mrs Ekdom had found a lady in the street who was prepared to look after the little boy, Mr Ekdom thought that perhaps she might also keep an eye on the girls.

"Not possible," said Mrs Ekdom. "Mrs Patselis looks after twelve small children already."

It was all very depressing for Mr Ekdom who could not stop worrying about his daughters. But now and again Jim stopped outside the house and went inside to see what his sisters were doing. He was harsher with them than were the parents. He would not permit them to look into the street, let alone walk or play there.

"That's not fair," the youngest protested.

"If you won't obey your brother you won't obey your husband," he said aggressively.

Sophie turned on him.

"Sometimes you sound very silly," she said.

He became angry and threatened to hit her if she contradicted him again. He raised his open hand as if about to strike.

"Don't you dare," she said, fearlessly looking him straight in the eyes.

He stepped back, but he continued to make threats until he left the house. Sophie had surprised herself: she was expected to obey him, especially in the absence of their parents. Yet she hadn't: was it because she had acquired new ideas at school? She did not ask herself this question, but she was determined she would never be subservient to him again.

Lately Sophie had softened towards those Tech boys who were always pestering her. Once she would not open her mouth, pretending she wasn't seeing them, but now she exchanged banter with them, even though her sisters were listening and casting sly glances at each other. Innocent though she was, Sophie was nevertheless not unaware of how desirable she was to the boys. She was a large, slow-moving girl, well developed, with big dreamy eyes.

There was one youth more persistent than the rest. He thrust a note in her hand. She read it quickly:

"Meet me here tonight at seven."

Her sisters stared at her burning face.

"Let's read it," one of them said.

"No," Sophie said emphatically, and put the note in her school bag.

At home her sisters prattled about the letter and the Tech boys, especially the letter-writer. Sophie angrily tore up the note in front of her parents.

"I don't even know him," she said.

They were prepared to believe her but they suffered some uneasiness on account of this incident. The girls were really unsupervised for most of the day now that both parents often had to work overtime as well. The responsibility of having a girl like Sophie on their hands would get too much for them. There was only one way to calm and safety, and that was to get her married as quickly as possible. Could they induce her husband-to-be to come to Australia soon?

"I will speak to his uncle," said Mr Ekdom.

Uncle Con had a prosperous catering business patronized by leading members of the community.

"Don't delay," said Mrs Ekdom.

"I'll go tonight," he said.

Mr Ekdom returned from his visit to Uncle Con with an excited expression on his face.

"Remarkable! He was about to get in touch with me to tell me that George would soon be coming to Australia," said Mr Ekdom. "A remarkable coincidence. A good omen I believe. George will be catching a plane that will come straight to Tullamarine."

"That's much better than having to change in Sydney," said Mrs Ekdom. "I've heard of people who got lost on the Sydney airport and missed their planes here."

She had suppressed her pleasure, afraid of tempting fate. Something could always go wrong at the last moment.

Sophie listened to the discussion as though she were an outsider. Until now she had never really believed in the reality of this husband-to-be, despite the photographs of him, a handsome, well set up man in his thirties. It was impossible: the very idea of such a marriage ran counter to all her feelings.

"Aren't you glad?" asked Mr Ekdom.

"But I'm still at school," said Sophie.

"But old enough to be married," said Mrs Ekdom.

"I would like to stay at school and finish typewriting," Sophie said.

The news of George's impending arrival spread through the school. Several Greek girls congratulated Sophie who couldn't help looking proud.

An Australian girl said:

"I'll marry who I want, not somebody I'm told to."

"He isn't an old man is he?" still another girl asked, remembering that a foreign schoolgirl had been given in marriage to a man of sixty.

"No, he isn't," said Sophie. "He's good-looking."

"You're very lucky," came the reply.

Sophie wondered. She was going to marry a man she didn't even know. Yet she did not feel strong enough to resist her parents and repudiate the solemn contract to which they attached so much importance. In a vague kind of way she felt she should oppose her parents, but she was hardly cut out to be a leader of her sex in her community. She was torn by conflicting feelings and demands.

At last George arrived in Melbourne and a few days later he came to the Ekdom house with his uncle. He was even better looking than his photographs, Sophie told herself. And he had good manners, better than those of his uncle who spoke loudly and was accustomed to giving orders.

George looked his intended up and down with an appraising stare. She was certainly a fine-looking girl, he thought. But the house, of which the Ekdoms were so proud, depressed him. The dowry arranged back home so many years ago belonged to goat and donkey days, not the present day of the car. What could you get for it in this country? Next to nothing, he thought with some contempt.

"Work is hard to get at the moment," Mr Ekdom said. "But I think I can get you a job in my factory. I have been promised —"

"I won't need it," George interrupted him. "I will go into business."

"He has a business head," said Uncle Con. "He has worked in Athens in the last five years. And in Munich."

When they left Mr Ekdom looked a trifle puzzled. George was not quite the man he had expected. But as though to allay unexpected misgivings he said loudly:

"I am sure he will make a good husband."

Mrs Ekdom nodded her head. Sophie said nothing. What could she say? She would go through with the marriage if only to make her father happy.

Within a few weeks George was installed in a tourist agency, apparently having had experience of that kind of work. He appeared at the Ekdom house in a new blue denim suit. A traditional table was laid: cold fish with the skin on it, goat cheese, olives and imported Cretan dark red wine, and lamb with okra.

"A taste of our homeland," he said, praising Mrs Ekdom.

Mr Ekdom managed to speak to him on his own before he left.

"About the wedding date," Mr Ekdom began. "Will I speak to your uncle?"

"I will speak to him as soon as I have properly found my feet," said George.

As soon as the door shut behind George, Mr Ekdom gloomily announced there was still no wedding date. For some reason Sophie who had been solemnly staring at the wall, suddenly became gay and laughed at everything.

But Mrs Ekdom began to have many restless nights, frequently waking up to look out of the window at the high brick wall of the factory next door. One night Mr Ekdom woke up to find her in tears.

"What are we going to do?" she asked.

George was invited to lunch the following Saturday. Mrs Ekdom spent the whole of the previous evening preparing honey cakes, garlic pastes, and a special sauce for the dolmers, now rarely made in Australia, since women worked during the week like the men.

But though George had promised to come, thanking Mr Ekdom profusely for the invitation, he failed to arrive. An hour passed before the family began to eat the delicacies.

The meal was no sooner over when Jim jumped up from the chair and shouted:

"I'll find him and fetch him even if I have to maim him.

He will not humiliate you," he shouted into Sophie's face.
"Oh, no please," Sophie whispered. "He may have been
delayed at his business."
"I will kill him," Jim declaimed.
His eyes were blazing and his stiff black hair seemed to be
crackling with electricity.
However he did not move towards the door: it was as if he
was acting out the first part of a ritual drama, a brother
passionately defending his sister's honour.
Mr Ekdom settled the matter.
"I am going to find him and bring him here," he
announced. "It is my responsibility, not yours," he added
looking fiercely at Jim.
Mr Ekdom left hurriedly while the rest of the family
remained at the table, as though still expecting George to
walk in. But Sophie soon got up, unable to bear her brother's
bloodthirsty talk. She went out on to the verandah and
stared around, nodding to acquaintances but not encouraging
them to stop. Her pride had been injured despite her
ambivalent feelings about George. What would she say at
school if he never came again? How would she explain the
whole affair away? But maybe he would turn up at teatime.
He could have made a mistake about the time.
Suddenly she saw her father in the distance, coming
towards her. As soon as he caught sight of her he began to
run clumsily across the street.
"He's left Melbourne, he's cleared out," he almost sobbed,
a dull, uncomprehending look in his eyes.
"Cleared out," she repeated.
She should hate her father, she suddenly thought. He was
to blame for everything. Intolerable recollections broke
through. Yet it was just as well things had now turned out
the way they had. She forgot her old anger with him: only
loving kindness remained.

PART 2

The Second Generation

The Economies of Mourning

Zeny Giles

"Sophia, we could not possibly offer coffee now," said Evthokia. "There must be at least twenty minutes between the brandy and the coffee."

Sophie's mother had warned her about Evthokia and so had her cousin Yanoula, but how could a woman of thirty, who had lived most of her life in Australia, insist on speaking Greek all the time and get herself so worked up about a funeral.

"Sophia, you can take this other tray of brandies. But remember, relatives first — men according to age and women according to age, and only then do you serve the outsiders."

The girl picked up the tray and walked towards the lounge room. Already as she approached she could hear the wailing. A new group of mourners must have just arrived, so it was no good going in. She put the tray down on a small table and prepared to wait.

Sophie had fought to come to this funeral. "I'm fourteen — why shouldn't I go?"

"Funeral no good for you, Sophia," said her father. "You better going to school."

"It doesn't matter if I miss one day of school, Dad. Anyway I'd like to help Yanoula and Thea Eleni. After all, Theo Vassili was my uncle."

But she knew, even as her parents joined in one of their Greek consultations, that her wanting to go had little to do with her uncle or his widow or even her married cousin Yanoula. She had felt the thud of the words "is dead". She had felt herself stunned by that finality. Her mind curled with questions and she itched to see — at least what there was left to see.

"We have decided you may go to the church," said her father. He spoke in Greek to impress her with the seriousness.

"But not to the cemetery, Sophia," added her mother. "After the service you can go back to the house to help cousin Evthokia."

When Sophie had seen her aunt the first time — weeping, pulling at her hair, beating her breast — she had turned away, not able to face such terrible grief, and feeling the comforting surge of her own tears as she joined in weeping with her aunt, her cousin and her mother. But at the church, as she watched the adults crying, she felt a kind of tickling inside her and when old Barrba Yanni had thrown himself to the ground screaming and crying, she had stared with a kind of shocked wonder at his undressed emotions.

She did not feel like that any more. Barrba had not come back to the house and somehow she was learning to read the pattern of her aunt's grief.

There — the weeping had stopped. Sophie's mother would be giving Thea Eleni water to sip and Yanoula would be wiping her brow. Then they would all begin to talk — awkwardly at first, but within five minutes, if no new mourners arrived to begin the whole procedure again, they might even be smiling.

"Oriste," said Sophie as she offered the tray to one of the men she recognized as a relation. He said the appropriate words about the repose of Vassili's soul, picked up the glass and tossed back the brandy with one gulp. Sophie offered the tray to his wife. The woman repeated her husband's words and raised the glass until the brandy barely touched her lips.

Sophie returned to the kitchen with two empty glasses and four others which had been scarcely touched. "What a waste," she said to herself as she poured the remaining brandy down the sink and began to rinse the little crystal glasses.

"No, no, Sophia, we do not throw out the brandy," said Evthokia impatiently. "We just fill up the glasses again for the next people. You take out these coffees and I'll fix the tray. But remember, the coffees are to go to the people who came first, and some of the men have already gone out to sit in the back room."

"Well," said Mikhali, the widow's younger brother, "this table has seen a few card games, eh boys?"

The men around the big table nodded and sipped their coffee. They spoke to each other in Greek.

"He liked his cards, did Vassili," said Andoni, the elder brother. He tapped his cigar ash into a saucer. "Well, his card playing days are over now."

"At least we think they are," said Manoli, husband of the widow's sister, Katina. "Paradise might be one long card game."

"As long as Vassili doesn't have to lose," said Mikhali smiling. "Remember Vassili's long face when he was losing."

"Not as bad as old Barrba though," said Manoli. "Roaring and laughing like a madman if he's winning, and weeping and groaning like a madman if he thinks he's going to lose."

"To tell you the truth," said Andoni, "I don't know how Vassili tolerated Barrba. He used to be here almost every night."

"The old boy put on a good act again today," said Mikhali. "I thought the son would throw him out of the church. You've got to admire the old fellow's spirit, though. Eighty if he's a day, and I can tell you, Andoni and I had trouble getting him into the back of the car."

"Why does he go on like that?" said one of the younger men. "Doesn't he know what a fool he looks?"

"That's the way of the old people," said Andoni, tapping his ash into the saucer again. "That's the way they show their sorrow."

"Sorrow be damned!" said Manoli. "That's the effect of too much brandy and too little brain."

"That's not true," said Andoni. "Barrba loved Vassili, and this is his way of showing it."

"Now you tell me," said Manoli, "what is the point of all this weeping and wailing? Look," he lowered his voice, "I didn't want my daughter to come today. I didn't want Sophia seeing the way the old girls are going on inside." Manoli looked in the direction of the lounge room. "You don't see Australians going on like that. Do you know, the woman a few doors down from us lost her son — he was killed in a car accident. She didn't wear black, she didn't even cry — let alone go on with this other nonsense."

"Not weep for a son," shouted Andoni. "I've always said these Australians don't feel the way we do."

"O come on Andoni," said Manoli. "What do you mean the way *we* do? What makes us so special?"

"I am a Greek," said Andoni, "and so are you, Manoli. You can't deny that."

"It might surprise you to know, Andoni, that I consider myself an Australian."

"Manoli," said Andoni in a mocking tone which did not disguise his anger, "you are using Greek words to tell me you are an Australian. Do you realize what a contradiction that is?"

Manoli shrugged his shoulders and gestured with the palms of his hands. "What difference makes it — Greek words — Australian words? I am Australian."

"Well you're a fool then," said Andoni. "You were born in Greece — till you die you will be a Greek."

"You listen to me Andoni," said Manoli, reverting to Greek so as to make his point. "What did Greece ever do for you? Did it give you enough food to fill your belly? You're just sentimental about all this Greek stuff and so was Vassili — making a song and dance about the Greek church, the Greek Brotherhood . . . "

"Go to the devil," shouted Andoni. "It makes me want to vomit when I hear you abusing your nationality like this."

"Manoli, Andoni," called Katina as she rushed into the room from the kitchen. "Eleni can hear that commotion in the lounge room. Have you forgotten our dead Vassili?"

He could see as soon as he drove into the street that the house would be crowded. They'd even blocked the driveway. His own parents' house and he couldn't park outside. He hated all this rigmarole. He knew his mother was upset but did she have to go on with all this weeping and lamenting?

As for that fool Barrba. He should have been stopped at the church. Just look at his antics at the cemetery —

struggling like a little crazed monkey. And Carole and her parents had to see all that. Didn't these Greeks have any restraint?

He walked up the side path to the back door. The men were sitting around the table — talking, smoking, sipping coffee. It was a wonder that they hadn't started a card game.

"Eh Pavlos," they called when they saw him. "Come and sit with us and have a drink for your father's soul."

"Later, later," he said to them as he pushed past their chairs and into the kitchen.

It irritated him to find his spinster cousin, Evthokia, in charge of his mother's kitchen. Platters of food had been spread on one side, while the area around the sink and the stove was set apart for the trays with brandy, water and coffees.

Evthokia took his hand, "Ah Pavlos," she said to him in Greek, "you poor boy, left now without a father. Where will you find another?"

He took his hand away and ignored the ritual question. He caught his sister by the arm as she walked into the kitchen. "Yanoula, don't tell me we're expected to provide a meal for this lot."

"I wasn't aware that you were providing anything for anyone! It's two hours since we arrived back from the cemetery. Thea Katina and I did all the cooking this morning, and don't you dare upset Evthokia. I don't know how we would have got on without her and Sophie. We had little enough other help."

"If you're suggesting that Carole should have come."

"I'm not suggesting anything. But don't you start telling us what to do. Mum's been asking for you ever since we arrived home. I didn't know what to tell her."

"Will you two stop arguing?" said Thea Katina. "They'll hear you inside. And Pavlos, you ought to go in to your mother."

He could feel his stomach churning as he walked inside. At least there was no sound of weeping.

As he walked into the room, the conversation stopped. His mother stretched out her arms to him, "O my Pavlos, my only son, what will we do without your father?"

He came towards her and she stood and leaned her head against him. She was weeping loudly.

"Mitera," he said to her, "you must try to be calm. You must not weep in this way."

She continued to wail, "O my husband, O my Vassili," and now the women around her were weeping — his aunts, his cousins, his mother's friends. He saw them carried away with hysteria and the whole display sickened him.

"Mitera," he said as he sat his mother down. "You must not make all this noise. You know my father would not have wanted it."

"O my son, my only son. Where will you find another father?" She sobbed and caught her breath.

He said to her sharply, "If you cannot control yourself — stop all this weeping, I will have to go."

She turned to look at him. "But my son, you have just come. Where have you been? This is the day of your father's funeral and you should be here in his house."

"I went to take Carole home. She was upset."

"We are all upset, my son. Why couldn't your wife have come with you to the house?"

"She is pregnant Mitera, don't you understand?"

"I understand what it is to carry a child. Does she understand what it is to lose a husband?"

He did not say anything. He sat a little longer and then walked out to the kitchen.

Evthokia, Yanoula, Thea Katina and Sophie were busy setting out the food.

"I still don't see the need for all this," he said as he watched them. "Why do they have to stay? And people like that busy-body Assimina and that old troublemaker Panayota."

"You speak to him, Thea Katina," said Yanoula. "If I say anything there'll be a fight."

"Paul," his aunt said to him in English, "these people come to the house after the funeral because that is what is expected — what your mother expects. Why are you making such a fuss?"

"Making a fuss! That's just what I'm complaining about. What did these people care about my father? I hate to see my

mother used in this way. It was the same last night. As soon
as they found out, they were ringing up to see if they could
view the body. Well, I said they couldn't. I said it wouldn't
be possible."

"What right did you have to say that?"

"I've got every right. It's a barbaric custom."

"How can you say that, Paul? How can you say that when
you saw how happy it made your mother, this morning?"

He left her and walked over to the kitchen window. Yes,
his mother had been delighted. She talked afterwards like a
silly girl — telling him how beautiful it was and wanting him
to look too. Well he wouldn't. He would not look at this
dead father of his, made up with paint to appear alive.

He was shivering. He mustn't think of it. He poured some
brandy into a glass and drank it quickly. It burned his throat
but he could feel the warmth comforting him. He replaced
the cork and moved the bottle further back on the bench.
Then he noticed the four empty bottles standing in the
corner.

"My God," he said to himself, "there's no doubt about
this lot. They've just about cleaned up the five bottles."

"But cousin Eleni," the elderly woman said to the widow,
"while the others are clearing away the meal and we are
sitting here alone, I must ask you. Why did you hurry in this
way? You've wasted him. Thursday night the poor man dies
— by Friday afternoon you've put him under the earth. There
must be people in our community who do not know even
now that our Vassili has died. Was all this hurry really
necessary, Eleni? Couldn't you have waited until Monday
Then everything would have been done the proper way. He
would have been brought home and all of us would have
come to say our good-byes to him."

The widow wept. She beat her breast and began a slow
wail, "my Vassili, my Vassili."

The widow did not give her cousin an answer because she
was irritated that Assimina should criticize. But as she continued her subdued wailing, she began to think. Why had she

agreed? She knew that it would have been better to have waited. Why had she allowed her children to talk her into this hurried funeral?

"It will be better for you, Mitera," her daughter had explained. "This way the funeral will be over quickly and you will be able to rest."

"Look," said her son, "I'm not going to talk about it any more. You can't wait all weekend. Think of the inconvenience to all of us. The funeral should be tomorrow."

Why did it have to be? Why had she listened to them? And her son who was so definite — where was he? He had barely stayed two hours and then had gone back to his wife. Cousin Assimina was quite right. Her beloved Vassili had been wasted — rushed away to a funeral parlor and here it was, only a day later and he was hidden under the earth. Vassili, who had loved dressing up — who had all his suits specially tailored — who had been so fussy about the way his shirts and handkerchiefs were ironed. And she was the only one to see him laid out — to see him looking immaculate, just as he always looked when he was going somewhere special. She moaned at the waste — the terrible waste.

There were not as many at the funeral as there should have been. She could think of dozens who were missing — all of them people who had loved and respected Vassili. Of course all the official organizations had sent wreaths. He had been on so many committees — interpreting for them, organizing, keeping the books. If it hadn't been for Vassili, the new church would never have been built. And that church was only half-filled for his funeral. Why hadn't she waited? Why hadn't she insisted? Why had she allowed these children of hers to influence her in this way?

She began to sob hard again. The other women had come back to sit a little longer with the widow. They wept with her.

"Eleni mou," said Katrina, "Vassili is at rest. You know he did not suffer."

"Mitera," said Yanoula, "take this little sip of brandy to calm you."

There was an unexpected knocking at the front door. The widow looked up. Who would be coming to visit so late?

Perhaps her son was back — perhaps he had brought that wife of his with him.

"Well, who is it, Katina?" she asked her sister. "Why don't you bring them in?"

"Eleni," Katina hesitated. "It is Barrba Yanni. I told him to go home. I told him how much he had upset you at the funeral. He insists he wants to see you."

The widow frowned. "I shouldn't let him come after what he did today."

A croaky voice wailed from the door, "I want to see Eleni. I must weep for Vassili."

The widow gave a long sigh. "Let him come. He has caused me pain, but my Vassili loved him."

The old man was thin and straggly. His trousers were crushed and his shirt, undone at the neck, showed his grubby woollen vest. His whole face was absorbed in his grief, his eyes were red and streaming. His cheeks, nose, moustache and mouth were wet with his noisy blubbering.

"O my Vassili, my Vassili," cried the widow, giving her uncle the cue.

"Vassili," he gasped between his tears.

"Vassili, Vassili," wailed the widow.

The old man stretched out his arms. "Nephew, I tried to follow you but they would not let me. They dragged me back to life."

"Vassili, Vassili," called the widow, but she could think of nothing to say, and confused and annoyed burst into tears.

Katina reprimanded the old man, "Quiet now, Barrba Yanni, you are upsetting Eleni again. See how she weeps. You must sit quietly over there, or I will have to call Mikhali to take you home again."

The old man sat meekly on the other side of the room. He wiped his eyes with a very dirty handkerchief.

The widow was resentful. Why did he have to come? He had been like this at the church — at every stage outdoing her grief with his noisy wailing and the abundance of his tears. Then, as Vassili's coffin was about to be carried out of the church, he had thrown himself to the floor — weeping and screaming. Pavlos had been so angry he had wanted to throw him out there and then.

But that would have been unseemly, so she, in the midst of her own great sorrow, had to take him by the hand and try to calm him.

He was her uncle but she was ashamed of him. Didn't he know what was expected of him? As an uncle — even an uncle by marriage — he should weep, but to go on with all this crying out — this throwing himself about.

And that had not been the worst of it. At the cemetery, when she felt that she would faint because she could not bear to see Vassili being lowered into the grave, Barrba Yanni had broken away from her two brothers and had tried to throw himself into the grave — on top of the coffin and the flowers.

What a shameful thing! What confusion! All the attention had moved to this half-crazy old man. That had finished it. Her brothers had picked him up as he struggled and wept, and had driven him home.

Now she wondered at her own generosity in letting him stay. She could not deal with the fervour of his grief. So many tears. So many tears when her own son had not shed one tear for his father. How could a son be so cold — so unaffected? How could he refuse to look at his father prepared so beautifully for burial?

And then, when he had finally come home after the funeral, he had reprimanded her for her own weeping. He had told her to be restrained. Why should she be restrained? She had lost a husband — "O Vassili, Vassili," she moaned, "how will I live without you?"

Barrba Yanni roused himself from where he had been sitting and walked towards the window.

She wiped her eyes and looked with disapproval at her uncle.

"You weep, Eleni!" the old man said to her, "but my grief is greater. You have lost a husband but I have lost much more."

The widow was furious. Really he was too much for her — why didn't someone take him away? She turned to her sister.

Katina ran out to where the men sat talking around the table. "Mikhali!" she called to her brother. "You will have to come quickly! Old Barrba is going to cause trouble again. He'll have to be taken home."

Mikhali and the other men followed her back into the lounge room.

Barrba Yanni stood facing the window. The mourners sat forward. The widow waited with tight lips.

"Eleni," Barrba Yanni went on, "you have lost a husband and you weep and that is right. But what have I lost? I have lost my nephew, my companion at cards, my drinking partner. I have lost my interpreter, my accountant, my lawyer, my doctor.

"Should I not weep even louder than the wife? Should I not try to climb into the grave of Vassili, who was more to me than wife or friend — who was more to me than my own life? This Vassili was the son I did not have," and the old man crumpled to the floor, crying like a child.

The widow looked at her uncle and she was sure that she had been wrong. She had been wrong to listen to her children. What did they know — young and born in Australia — what did they know of the need for grief worthy of her Vassili. This old man knew. And Vassili would have been proud. She knew he would have been proud.

The widow walked over to her uncle. "Ella Barrba mou," she said as she took the old man by the hand, "come and sit here next to me and we will weep for Vassili together."

But Your Ways are Strange to Me

Zeny Giles

We watched from a distance as Mikhali helped his mother through customs. They looked an ill-matched pair — this black-clad old lady, no bigger than a child, and the tall, thickset man beside her.

"Why is she all in black?" asked our son, John.

"You've seen the old ladies at church," said our eldest child, Zeny. "And old Thea Assimina has been wearing black since Theo Yanni died last year."

"But your grandmother has been wearing black for a very long time," I explained to them. Her husband died when your father was only eight years old. So Yaya has been in black for the last thirty-seven years."

"That's terrible!" burst out Zeny, her sense of justice outraged. "Why should anyone have to wear black for all those years?"

"It might seem terrible to you, but no widow in a Greek village would think of wearing any other colour but black. This is a sign of respect for her dead husband."

The children said no more, but I could tell from their eyes that they did not understand.

Yaya wept as she embraced us and we were all moved by the meeting. She insisted on giving the children the gifts she had brought them and she tried to open the box which contained the little gold crosses. We noticed how much her hands trembled. Apart from this sign of age, she seemed a very wiry old lady. The skin on her face was like creased brown parchment — she had obviously worked long hours in the vineyard, and her hands also showed signs of hard work. Her head was covered by a black kerchief. Her eyes were grey-brown and her smile showed worn teeth with gaps in the gums. She wore a black woollen dress, black shoes and black stockings. Her legs were slight and her feet so small, she gave the impression of a girl in school uniform.

I had anticipated the difficulties for a seventy year old woman making the transition from her village in Cyprus to a suburb in Sydney. I had tried to point these out to Mikhali when he was still deciding if he should send for his mother to join us. But I had not realized how uncomfortable it would be for the rest of us. We had warned the children to be considerate and not to speak English in their grandmother's presence. The result was not what we expected. The children seemed to avoid Yaya and because they were used to speaking English amongst themselves, spent more time in their bedrooms.

The situation was made worse by Yaya's shyness with me. She would spend whole hours in her room reading a book she had brought from her village, or she would sit self-consciously in the living room while I tried to start some kind of conversation. She seemed more relaxed with her son and the days seemed long as I waited for the children to come from school to break the uneasy quietness of the house and Mikhali to come from work so that he could talk for a while with his mother.

The midday meal caused special difficulty because Yaya would not tell me what she wanted to eat. In fact, she would never admit to being hungry enough to eat at all. One evening after a particularly uncomfortable day, I complained to Mikhali.

"At lunch time, Yaya said she was not hungry. I just happened to put that left-over chicken on the table and she ate the lot. She must have been starving. Why can't she tell me? What if I'd taken her at her word and given her only bread and olives?"

"Don't take any notice of what she says," said Mikhali, growing tired of new problems each day. "She would never admit to a daughter-in-law that she was hungry. In fact she probably wouldn't tell me. You'll just have to assume every time that she is hungry."

I continued to feel irritated, not understanding why communication had to be so difficult. And in spite of Yaya's shyness, her feelings of dislocation became quite clear to us.

On winter afternoons, Yaya would sit on the sunny front verandah which faced a busy road. Fortunately because of her deafness, the noise of the traffic did not bother her, but she seemed intrigued each time she would see a black funeral hearse bearing the caskets and flowers. After a little time, she confided her fears to Mikhali.

"My son, I do not think that Australia is a good country in which to raise your family."

"Mother, Australia has given me all that I possess — secure work, a big house, a car."

"I know that these things are good, Mikhali, but I am sure it cannot be safe to live here. Too many people die."

"Whatever do you mean, Mother?"

"Today as I sat outside," said Yaya with a worried expression, "I counted ten funerals go by. And it is the same almost every day. In our village, ten people would not die in a year. There must be a great deal of sickness in this land."

It took Mikhali a long time to try to explain that the road in front of our house led to one of the big Sydney cemeteries and that there were very many more people in Sydney than there had been in the village. The difference in the size of populations was something Yaya found impossible to understand.

Then there was the problem of the shoes. In summer, the children loved to go barefoot. In fact, Mikhali and I would also take off our shoes in the house on hot days. This must have caused consternation for Yaya, but she said nothing to Mikhali and me. She would begin with our five year old, Christina. She would take the child's shoes and try to put them on her. When Christina protested, she would call to the older children. "But Yaya," each of them would say, "it's too hot for shoes." After a while, Yaya became so exasperated, she spoke to Mikhali.

"My son, why do the children go outside without shoes? This is a shameful thing and you should forbid it. Don't you know that the neighbours will say you are a family of paupers?"

No amount of talking would convince Yaya that the absence of shoes was not an instant admission of poverty.

Slowly as the weeks and months passed, life with Yaya fell into something of a pattern, and although we were not altogether comfortable with one another, we found a working solution.

Yaya would spend most of her days sitting in the living room or in a place in the sun, reading her religious book. She had gained sufficient confidence in us to sound out the words aloud in our hearing. Then she would say her prayers, thanking God and asking for blessings to be heaped upon each of her loved ones in Cyprus and Australia. She began to include in these prayers, requests which concerned the everyday happenings of our family. When Christina was having a birthday party, Yaya asked God to send fine weather. The day proved cold and rainy, but Yaya was resigned. "God must have had too much to do today, so he could not look after the weather for us." We learnt to smile at the simplicity of Yaya's faith and we grew to accept her as the little old lady whose trembling fingers were happiest holding her devotional book. On occasions, however, she would jolt us out of our smugness.

One day, Yaya and I were visiting a cousin who lived nearby. As we walked in the garden, we noticed a tree laden with nectarines. The cousin complained that the best fruit was at the top of the tree — quite out of reach. Before we could stop her, Yaya had clambered up the tree as nimbly as a monkey and was dropping the fruit down to us. How she managed to climb securely when her hands trembled so much, was something that neither my cousin nor I could understand. That night, I had great difficulty convincing the children and Mikhali that Yaya's tree climbing had been an actual fact.

It was some ten months after her arrival that Yaya came into her money. I happened to find out from a neighbour, that because Yaya came from Cyprus and was a British subject, she was entitled to receive an old age pension immediately.

She was puzzled by the whole situation.

"But Mikhali, why are they giving me money? This is not my country and do they give you money for being old?"

"It is a way of helping old people to be independent, Mother. Now you must accept it and use it as you please."

Yaya was preoccupied during the next few weeks. She did

not seem to be able to concentrate on her book and we could hear her talking to herself. In three weeks, she came to a decision. After the evening meal, she spoke to Mikhali.

"You, son, will take half the money for the house and my food."

"No Mother, I don't want to take anything. We have enough money. There is no need for you to give this."

Yaya was firm. With unusual conviction, she said, "If you do not take it, I will have to look for a little room. Assimina at church says that there are little rooms near the church and I will be able to walk by myself."

"All right, all right," said Mikhali, seeing that he'd been defeated.

"Now the other half," continued Yaya.

"The other half of what?"

"The other half of the money, Mikhali," she said sharply, growing irritated with his lack of concentration. "Each week I will give the children two shillings and sixpence each. That will leave another twenty shillings. That money, my son, I wish to save."

"Of course, Mother," said Mikhali who was embarrassed by the whole subject of the pension. "You keep that in your room and then if you need something, you can ask Nina or one of the children to bring it for you from the shops."

"No, my son, I want you to put it away for me."

"All right, Mother, I'll open a bank account for you."

The possession of money changed Yaya. It was barely noticeable at first, but it was certainly there. Of course the children loved to receive their money. It was enough to pay for a trip to the pictures or some other treat. But Yaya seemed to enjoy handing over the money, even more than they looked forward to receiving it. Every Saturday morning she followed the same ritual. She would call the children into her room. Then she would take her purse and with trembly fingers, open the clasp and count the coins into their hands. And with largesse came the strings. No longer would she take the children aside to tell them surreptitiously to put on their shoes. She would nag them from the living room, lifting her head from her reading to tell them that the neighbours would think they were paupers. And when in their enthusiasm, the children burst into English at the dinner table, she would give a look which told us all exactly what she thought of that foreign language. Yaya disapproved of John having to take his turn at wiping up, because she believed that domestic tasks were the exclusive domain of the women of the house. She was also very critical about the clothes the girls wore. She disapproved of shorts or slacks and the thought of Zeny wearing a bathing costume was enough to make her very angry. She did not like to see the girls whistling or crossing their knees and I had to be extra careful to see that I was not guilty of either of these crimes.

As the house became noisier with the open signs of friction, Yaya and I were gaining a better understanding. No longer did Mikhali need to act as the go-between. Now that she was contributing to the family purse she was prepared to tell me that she did not like fish and that large portions of meat were difficult for her to digest. She even began preparing her own vegetable dishes on a Friday because she did not eat meat on that day. She would fold the linen for me after the weekly wash and because she had never been used to an iron, she had learnt the skill of straightening clothes with her hands so that they looked smooth and neat. The final seal on our new relationship came when she asked if she could wash up after breakfast. At first I would listen anxiously as she clashed the dishes with her trembling fingers but I learnt to get on with the other household jobs and Yaya's morning wash-up became part of the daily routine.

Yaya's relationship with her son also changed. Mikhali did not agree with the strict fasts of the Orthodox Church and during the long fast periods would try to talk Yaya into taking a little milk or an occasional egg. Before, she had weakened. Now she was resolute — insisting that she keep the fasts to the letter. And when he would try to talk her out of attending one of the many long services of Holy Week, or promise that he would drive her to a particular service and then come late, she would inform him quietly that she was thinking of getting a little room near the Greek Church so that she could arrive at all the services on time.

Mikhali and I would joke about Yaya's growing independence and would make guesses at what she was planning to do with her savings.

"Perhaps she wants to buy herself one of those little rooms she is always talking about," Mikhali said with a smile.

"Your mother is more realistic about her money than you give her credit for," I said to him. "She is probably thinking of having something to leave to her grandchildren."

But the explanation came much sooner than we expected. Yaya and I were sitting in the living room. I was knitting and Yaya was working laboriously over a piece of crochet she had learnt to do only in the last few weeks.

"Daughter," said Yaya as she tried to keep her hands steady so she could catch the new stitch with her crochet hook, "what would it cost for me to have a dress made?"

"The flannel is expensive because it is pure wool, then there is the cost of the dressmaking. I think twelve pounds would cover the whole cost. But now that I think of it, Yaya, there is no need to buy more material. I have another piece of the black flannel left over from the dress we had made for you at Easter time. Will I ask Dhespina if she has time to sew it for you?"

"I do not want black flannel this time."

"But Yaya, you said you liked the flannel for all parts of the year because it stopped you getting back-ache. If you are finding it too hot; why don't you try black cotton this time?"

"No, no, the flannel is good, but I do not want black for this dress."

I stopped my knitting. Only last week I had trouble persuading Yaya that it would be respectable for her to wear cream flannel to bed. "Are you sure you want a colour, Yaya? Remember the nightdresses."

"I am quite sure; it must be a colour."

"Well, what about brown or dark grey?"

"No, I thought I would like something of the colour you were knitting for Christina."

"Oh, you mean the navy blue school jumper?"

"No daughter, I mean the one you made for her to wear to the midnight Easter service."

"But Yaya, that was pink."

"That is the colour I would like."

At that I burst out, "Yaya, you have been wearing black since your husband died nearly forty years ago. How can you go out now, dressed in a colour that only a young girl would wear?"

"But I will not be going out in it."

"Do you mean that you will wear it only in the house?"

"No, my daughter, I will be wearing it in my coffin. Haven't you heard that it is bad luck for anyone, even an old lady to be buried in black clothes? Now that I have money, I want to get everything in order, for when I die."

I sat stunned as if Yaya had mouthed some obscenity.

Yaya sat calmly crocheting.

"Yaya," I said shakily, "I am going to make a cup of tea. Would you like me to bring you one?"

"No daughter, I do not need tea. It always spoils my appetite for the evening meal. But come back and drink yours near me. I want to talk with you about the stockings, the shoes and the scarf for my head."

Bobbeh

Morris Lurie

A hard woman. On her last day in Poland she buried the silver samovar, to spite the *shkotzim,* the *goyim,* but took the other, the everyday one, the ordinary one, the plated nickel, which she gave, when she came here, on the other side of the world, to my mother, who set aside a morning every month, with polish, with powder, with brushes and rags, and made it shine, made it gleam. Once a month, twelve times a year, a dutiful daughter. But not once did the *bobbeh* ask to see it. Sentiment was not part of her life.

Nor was the samovar, really, of ours. It stood in the garage, on a dusty table, shining in the gloom. Why? I asked my mother.

My mother frowned, annoyed, my question unworthy of a reply, the fire in her eyes answer enough. The *bobbeh's* samovar! Didn't I understand anything?

A hard woman. She kept chickens. Two in a wire coop in a corner of her hard, concrete yard, and every Friday, Friday morning, the chicken man brought her a third. Handed it to her by the legs at the back gate, the chicken squawking madly, wings beating, hanging uselessly upside down. This chicken went into the coop for next week, or the week after. Its turn would come. Pushing it in, the *bobbeh* would grab for one of the two in there. For *Shabbos.* The *Shabbos* meal.

Except what happened, happened every time, was that the moment she opened the coop, the two chickens in there would run out, run into the yard, and then the *bobbeh* would drop the new chicken, so now all three were rushing about, crazed with fear, and the *bobbeh* would swoop and shout and get nowhere and then seize from its hook in the shed either Uncle Hirshel's tennis racket or the carpet beater, that plaited pattern of wicker arabesques on the end of a long handle that she had brought with her from Poland, from Bialystock, where she was born, seize whichever came to hand first, and then, darting, swinging, shouting curses in Yiddish and Polish and Russian, the vilest things, she would whack and thrash all three chickens into either senseless submission or the coop — an old woman, mind you: oh, how slowly she walked — and then, her blood up, muttering, still cursing, shaking her head, no time for a rest now, stuff today's chicken into a string bag and hurry with it to the *shochet*, the ritual slaughterer, who was two blocks away. The *shochet* slit the throat, nothing else.

Then the *bobbeh* would hurry back and sit down on the wooden bench in the yard and pluck out the feathers, the just-dead chicken laid out on the hammock she made of her apron between her spread-apart knees, and then she would come into the house, into the kitchen, and fill it with the foulest smell as she singed off the feather ends over the gas stove, turning the white body, over and over, round and round, slapping it with her hand whenever a flame appeared, her bare hand, immune to pain.

Or gave it to my mother, let her slap and burn.

I didn't want to go there. I never wanted to go. What for? There was nothing there to do. Couldn't I just stay home? I'll be all right by myself. Really. Please. I whined, I nagged, I sulked: a dreadful child.

My mother was outraged. "The *bobbeh*?" she said. "You don't want to see the *bobbeh*?" She was insulted. She couldn't understand me. What was the matter with me? But enough, enough! She dressed me in my best clothes, my best coat. Shined my shoes. Pulled up my socks. Combed my hair. Wetted a corner of her handkerchief in her mouth to wipe away at my mouth, my eyes, my ears, a mark on my knee. Buffed me. Polished me. Tugged and straightened. Made me look nice. And then, there, the minute we were there, ignored me. Forgot all about me. She had no time for me now. She was with the *bobbeh*. Her mother.

And the *bobbeh* would snap, "Go outside. What are you standing here for? Go and play."

Play with what?

The *bobbeh*'s yard was concrete, concrete and iron and brick. Nothing growing, nothing green. Glary in summer, in winter you froze to death. The high brick side of the house next door loomed over it. The other side was a corrugated iron fence. A washing line stretched across, held up with a long split-ended pole. An open shed. An outside tap. The chickens. (I was frightened of the chickens.) The back gate was corrugated iron, too. It scraped on the concrete when you opened it. When you closed it, the whole length of the fence shook, and clanged like a coupling train.

"Take the ball," my mother would suggest. "Play with the ball."

The ball. A bald tennis ball. There was always one there. I don't know where the *bobbeh* found them. Uncle Hirshel didn't play tennis any more. He didn't have time. He worked hard, long hours, selling underwear and socks. He had not yet married, and lived with the *bobbeh*. (As did my unmarried Auntie Dora, too.)

Uncle Hirshel was a thin, nervous man with a long nose and sticking-out ears and a stutter, and he was obsessed with fitness. He exercised daily, first thing in the morning, swinging and springing and touching his toes. He rode a bicycle to work. His body didn't have an ounce of fat. "F-f-f-feel!" he would command me, flexing his arm. And I would touch him there, feel his muscle like frightening iron under his shirt, impossible-to-squeeze steel. "Ah!" Uncle Hirshel would cry. "You see? S-s-s-strong!"

But a gentle man, like all the men in the family. Obedient. Quiet. I don't think I ever once heard him raise his voice. And frightened. Once, in Bialystock, he had thrown a stone which had accidentally gone through the window of the house next door. Non-Jewish people. *Shkotzim.* Uncle Hirshel had run crying to the *bobbeh* and then hidden under her bed, and the *bobbeh* had had to order his brother, my Uncle Sam, to go outside in his place and take the beating.

While her husband, the *bobbeh's zaydeh*, sat, said nothing, did nothing.

We called him the *bobbeh's zaydeh*, always that, never anything else, to differentiate him from the other *zaydeh*, my father's father, who was simply *zaydeh*, and who lived with us (his wife was in Israel or Palestine as it was then),

but there was more to the title than that. Look at the owner-
ship it proclaimed! Look at the subservience!

He was a small man, made even smaller by the hat he
always wore, inside the house and out, the hat casting a
shadow on his hollow-cheeked face, the brindley moustache,
the vague, faded eyes that looked always wet. He sat and
smoked and drank tea — or sometimes a glass of *bromfen*,
brandy — and never said a word. Even on *Pesach*, enthroned
on feather pillows at the head of the table, running the *seder*,
you felt he was a puppet king, the *bobbeh* in real control.

Three days after he died, she took me into his bedroom.
On the bed was an old suitcase. She opened it. Inside it was
filled with socks and ties. "From America!" the *bobbeh* said.
"Take!" He had gone there for a year, to make his fortune,
believing all the stories, overnight millionaires, streets paved
with gold, and a year later had limped back with this, just
this, and then sat silent for ever after, smoking, drinking, wet-
eyed under his hat.

"Take!" the *bobbeh* cried. "He never wore them. It's like
new." Grey socks. Grey ties. The *bobbeh's* fingers plucked
them from the ancient suitcase, threw them before me on to
the bed. I fled.

The *bobbeh* knew everyone and everyone knew her. The
back gate clanged with endless visitors. Gossip. News. The
kitchen bustled with tea and talk. An engagement. A
marriage. Business deals. A death. What did it all mean? I
couldn't understand a word. I sat in a corner, flipping
through Auntie Dora's movie magazines and, when I couldn't
do that any more, I walked through the house.

Auntie Dora's room smelled of powder, make-up, cigarettes.
There were photographs of movie stars stuck up on her walls,
pink pictures of Clark Gable, Van Heflin, Alan Ladd. I stood
in the doorway. I didn't dare go in. Uncle Hirshel's room was
neat and bare. A bed, a chair, a chest of drawers, a dark wardrobe. No clothes, no pictures, nothing lying about. I didn't
go in there either.

I tiptoed around the house, shoes creaking on the cold
linoleum. Everywhere was dark and cold and smelled of
polish. Hand furniture. Locked cabinets. The dining room
table was topped with glass — don't touch. Heavy door

handles. Stiff doors. In the hall a strange blue light fell on the floor through the glass on either side of the front door, the front door that was never opened, no one ever came in that way. I was restless. I was bored. I wanted to go home. When would we go home? I felt the house filled with something more than cold and dark and that smell of polish.

In the kitchen, everyone sat. Talking. Shouting. Drinking tea. Smoking. Eating cake. Except for my mother. She never sat down. She didn't have time to sit down. Whatever the *bobbeh* said, she did. Look in the oven, it must be ready in there! Get more plates! Where's the tea? A knife, a knife, we need a knife for the cake! The back gate clanged. Someone else came in. A chair, a chair! the *bobbeh* ordered. Get a chair! Aunty Dora sat, Uncle Hirshel sat, the *bobbeh's zaydeh* sat, everyone sat and shouted and ate and drank, but not my mother. In the *bobbeh's* house my mother ran like a servant.

My mother was the favourite. Everyone said that. The oldest of three daughters, two sons, she felt the responsibility. It was she who came here first. This was in '33, '34, Hitler already looming. Her visa was for America, passage booked, bags packed, the *bobbeh's zaydeh* already there, walking those gold-paved streets. And then it was discovered that the *bobbeh's* lungs were scarred. Old scars, dead tissue, but scars nevertheless. America, for her, was closed. And my mother? Save yourself! everyone cried. Run! Go!

No, my mother said, and came here instead, knowing no one, alone and frightened, sailed to Australia, where there was no law about scars. Found a place to live, found work, saved, saved every penny, saved to bring out her brothers and sisters, but before them, the *bobbeh*. She brought the *bobbeh* out first.

We were *kosher* because of the *bobbeh*. Bought separate plates for *Pesach,* finer by far than those we normally used, white plates with a rim of gold that lay hidden under brown paper on the top of the cupboard for the fifty-one ordinary weeks of the year.

For the *bobbeh* we went to *shul,* dressed in clothes we couldn't afford. Then walked with her from *shul,* where she was always the slowest, the last, she couldn't leave until she had spoken to everyone, wished them a *Gut Shabbos,* a *Gut Yomtov,* and then the gossip, the news, the slow walk home, at least an hour it took her to cover that kilometre, a step at a time, until, at last, exhausted, famished, we arrived, and sat. Except for my mother, who became, in the *bobbeh's* kitchen, that rushing servant.

Everyone married, everyone left. She found a wife for Uncle Hirshel, a husband for Auntie Dora, that dreamer of movie stars. A miracle, everyone said. The *bobbeh* moved to another house, a smaller house, she had no need now of all those rooms. The yard here was lawn, and for the first year Uncle Hirshel came weekly and mowed it, and then the idea came to him of concrete, green concrete. "It looks the s-s-s-same," he said. In summer the *bobbeh* stood and watered it, the lawnmower slowly rusting in a shed.

Then the *bobbeh's zaydeh* died, and this house that had been so small was suddenly too big, empty and echoing wherever you looked, but the *bobbeh* refused to move again. There was a place for her with any of her three daughters, either of her two sons. No. She wouldn't hear of it. No! she shouted, shaking her head. And when the *bobbeh* said no, there was no argument.

So we visited, once a week. On the weekend. *Shabbos.* Sunday. And in between the visits my mother would drop in, as she put it, and clean the *bobbeh's* windows and sweep her yard and polish her floors, arriving home late, tired, exhausted, dark under the eyes. And then, the next day, go again. "She's alone," my mother would say. "How can I not go?"

My mother died before her. Died of exhaustion, worn thin, worn out. Twenty years ago, but I am there now. I stand in my suit, in the *Chevra Kadisha.* I can see the *bobbeh* being led in, supported by my two uncles, Uncle Hirshel and Uncle Sam. Her head is bent, her face is hidden, there is no face there at all.

The service begins. And then suddenly she breaks away, she tears herself from her sons, she falls upon the coffin, she screams out my mother's name. She has to be constrained, she has to be pulled up, she has to be pulled away. And now she begins to wail. She wails with a sound I have never heard before.

My hair stands on end. I am frightened to look at her, to look at anyone, but especially at her. I stand, head down, my eyes squeezed tight. I am frightened, and then I am outraged. This is *my* mother, my mother is *dead*, and here is the hard woman who caused it, who worked her like a slave, pretending this grief. My face burns with outrage, but no, it is not outrage. How can I have been so innocent, so foolish, so unfeeling, so dumb? I bow my head, made humble by the *bobbeh's* towering love.

A Beacon in the Night

Morris Lurie

Allow me to present for your edification and respectful awe that sterling figure, that man, that — well, here comes Yossel Shepps. Not much to look at, I admit — five five when he stands up straight, big clumsy hands and feet, cheeks like emery boards, a droopy left eyelid, a funny way of not quite looking at you when he looks at you. But make no mistake. Yossel is a beacon. Yossel is a signpost in this murky world. Yossel is a light so straight and true your heart takes one look and wants to fly up and sing. He's only twenty-two, and look, the kid's practically a doctor.

So?

I know, I know, Jewish medical students are a dime a dozen, but tell me this. How many of them speed straight from lectures to help out their poor struggling parents? How many of them cram till four in the morning and then leap up, fresh and eager, to serve up Sunday lunch?

Yossel does. Yossel is a miracle. According to my father, Yossel is a golden wonder, a blessing, a saint. He is a shining example such as rarely comes along, and each Sunday, when we troop into the Café Zion for lunch, he allows us to bask in Yossel's light. Hoping madly something will rub off on us, his two moronic sons.

For the record, let me state that I, aged fifteen, have not completely ruled out medicine as a career. It's a faint possibility. A lot of things are possibilities. At the moment though, I'm mainly interested in being a film director. Or a sports journalist. My brother, aged twelve, doesn't know what he wants to be. But he's young.

Back to Yossel Shepps. But before I tell you about him, I'd better tell you about the Café Zion. Maybe though, to get some sense into this, I'd better tell you about my father first.

He's a fruiterer. It's a nice little business, except he has to
get up at five in the morning four days a week and drive off
in the truck to the market (sometimes with his pyjamas on
under his clothes), and he doesn't come home till eight or
nine at night. Mum serves in the shop, and they usually come
home together, so you can imagine the quality of the meals
we eat. Except for Sunday. Sunday we all relax. We have
lunch in a restaurant. But if you think that means candlelight
and sweeping violins, you don't know my dad.

My father's idea of a good time is big portions. So what if
the lighting is stark and bright, there's no carpet on the floor,
the chairs wobble, the cutlery doesn't match? So what if the
tablecloth is a little bit stained? What's that? You found a
hair on your plate? Don't eat it.

For about a year we went to a restaurant that was just like
that, with a waiter who was at least seventy and who used to
groan over to the table, wearing what looked like his
deceased great-grandfather's clothes from the Old Country,
and as he spilled soup all over the place he'd tell us about his
aching feet, his rotting teeth, his unmarried forty-year-old
daughter, and a strange pain in the back he'd had for eleven
years. There was a menu, but it didn't make any difference,
everything tasted the same. Monumental portions. You'd
stand up at the end and want to die. "Come again," the
owner used to say to us as we dragged ourselves out, and for
a whole year we did, and then suddenly we switched to the
Café Zion. Which is exactly the same as the first restaurant,
except for one thing.

Yossel Shepps.

"Hello, Doctor!" cries my father, as we troop in for our
weekly feast. "How's it going, Doctor?" he booms across the
room. "Everything all right, Doctor?"

Doctor. Doctor. My father is enamoured of the word. He
can't say it often enough. It is honey on his tongue.

We sit down. The tablecloth boasts a few new stains and is
rolling with old crumbs, some of which I manage to sweep to
the floor. My fork is so twisted it looks like a piece of
modern sculpture. I reach for the menu, purely for something
to do. I know everything on it without even looking. The
menu at the Café Zion is always the same.

"Ah!" says my father, swivelling around in his chair. The Doctor has arrived.

He stands, pad in hand, smiling his curious smile, giving our table one of his not-quite-looking-at-you looks. He clears his throat. I hear my father getting ready to speak. I make close inspection of Yossel's truly monumental feet.

"Good afternoon, Doctor," says my father.

"Good afternoon," whispers Yossel Shepps.

"Well," says my father, "how are the studies?"

"Very well," says Yossel Shepps, very quietly.

"You don't find helping in the restaurant takes too much of your time, Doctor?"

"No, I manage."

"Very nice," my father beams. "Tell me, Doctor, when do you finish?"

"In three months," says Yossel Shepps.

"Ah! And then you'll open a little private practice, ah, Doctor?"

"Not at first," says Yossel Shepps. "I have to do a year in a hospital."

"Pardon me, Doctor," says my father. "I forgot. A year in a hospital. Good experience. And then you'll open up on your own?"

"I think so," says Yossel Shepps.

"Very nice," says my father. "A beautiful future."

He turns then to my brother and me, and the look he bestows upon us I'd rather not describe. We make, of course, no reply. How can we? It'd be like putting our heads in a lion's mouth.

"Well, Doctor," says my father, picking up the menu. "I think I feel like a little soup. What would you recommend?"

We order. Dr Shepps shuffles away. He certainly is a strange looking chap, but it takes all sorts to make a world. Looks aren't everything. Dr Shepps. Personally, I wouldn't feel too happy having him peering at me if I was severely ill. Lying there, close to death, maybe with one of those tubes going up my nose, and him giving me one of his not-quite-looking-at-you looks.

My father, still radiant from his encounter with Yossel, looks around the room. There are about ten people here, not counting us, all looking miserable as they ingest their massive portions. Then from out of the kitchen pops Mr Shepps, just for a second, and my father gives him a big wave.

"Hello, Mr Shepps!" he calls. "How's everything?"

"Good, good," says Mr Shepps, with a weak smile, quickly popping back in again.

Poor Mr Shepps. He looks terrible. His face is grey, his cheeks are sunken, his brow is creased with lines. He looks about a hundred and ten. I catch a glimpse of him through the servery window, as he stirs a big pot. He is almost a ghost.

Mrs Shepps is in there too, but you rarely see her. A grey little woman, haggard with work.

"They work very hard, don't they?" I say to my father.

"It's a privilege!" says my father. "They're putting a son through medical school!"

"But Yossel's always wearing new clothes," I say.

"So?" says my father. "What do you want? You want him to look like a beggar? He mixes with top people, he can't afford to look bad."

"And the car?"

Mr Shepps has bought for his son a brand-new car, a shining two-tone blue sedan, which is parked right now just outside the front door.

"Idiot!" says my father, raising crumbs as he bangs the table. "What do you think the car is for? So Yossel can hurry back here from lectures. Not waste time on a slow bus. Don't you understand anything?"

"Sorry, dad," I mumble, and keep my head down for the rest of the meal.

The months come and go, and one day when we troop into the Café Zion, what should we note but the absence of Yossel Shepps.

"Ah!" says Mr Shepps, who has graduated to waiter. "He's in the country."

"He passed all his exams?" my father asks.

"With honours," says Mr Shepps. "He's in a very fine hospital. We hardly see him, he's working so hard. He comes home only two or three days a week. Exhausted! You should see him."

"It's a hard year, the first one," my father says. "And how are you? How is Mrs Shepps?"

"Good, good," says Mr Shepps, who looks more terrible than ever. He seems to be working twice as hard, running backwards and forwards, sweat glistening on his brow. I mention this to my father.

"Fool!" he cries. "Don't you understand anything? They're proud to be working so hard. They live for their son."

The situation doesn't make sense to me. Exhausted parents, exhausted son.

"You'll see," says my father. "In two, three years. Dr Shepps. A beautiful future."

Social engagements keep us from the Café Zion for the next three weeks — a wedding and two barmitzvahs — but on the fourth week we're back, starved for real food. In we go, but what's this? It's all different. The sign's on outside, but there's no one here. Where is Mr Shepps? Mrs Shepps? A strange air of gloom permeates the place.

Nevertheless, we sit down, at our usual table. The table-cloth, anyhow, hasn't changed. We toy with the same twisted forks. My father swivels in his chair, looking round the room.

Then from out of the kitchen comes a man we have never seen before. He looks about sixty, with sad eyes, like a dog, and a shining bald head.

"Oh?" says my father. "Mr Shepps not well?"

"You didn't hear?" says the man.

"What?" says my father.

"Oi oi," says the man, shaking his head. "He hung himself. Excuse me, I'll bring a chair. I'm having terrible trouble with my feet."

We sit in stunned silence, no one saying a word, as the man brings over a chair from the next table, and sits down with a weary sigh. Who has hung himself? When? Why?

"A terrible business," says the man, shaking his head.

"You haven't heard a word?"

"Nothing," says my father.

"Oi oi," says the man, with more head shaking, and then he tells us, slowly, the whole story. It's all about Yossel Shepps.

"He was never a doctor," the man tells us. "They threw him out in the very first year. He didn't have the brains. So what's he been doing all these years? He's got himself a *shikse,* and every day he pays her a little visit. In the nice car his father bought for him."

My father, I note, is fiddling with his napkin.

"So what happens?" says the man. "Last week Mr Shepps phoned up the hospital in the country — he wanted to remind his son about something — and what does he hear? They haven't got a Dr Shepps in that hospital. Never."

The man pauses here to blow his nose in an enormous handkerchief, a good half minute required to pull the voluminous folds from his trouser pocket, another half minute to stuff it back again. No one speaks. He blows. He continues.

"So Mr Shepps waits for his son to come home. Here he comes, in his shining new car. 'Listen,' says Mr Shepps. 'I talked to the hospital this morning. They told me they never heard of you.' His son tells him the truth. How can he hide it now? 'I never wanted to be a doctor,' he says. 'You forced me. You pushed me. I couldn't tell you I was thrown out. I didn't want to break your heart.' Mr Shepps hears this story, runs upstairs and throws a rope over a beam. Have you ever heard such a thing?" he asks my father. "In this country?"

He goes into another routine of head shaking, this time with some low moans and a pursing of his lips. Still no one at our table says a word.

"He was practically hanging," the man goes on, "if not for Mrs Shepps. Oi oi. A terrible business."

"Where is Yossel now?" I ask.

My father shoots me a mean look, but the man answers, and my father turns back to him.

"Who knows?" he says. "He ran away. I hear he took a job somewhere. In a factory."

"And Mr Shepps? Mrs?"

"I don't know," the man says to my father. "I think they're at the moment with friends. You know a Mr Polonski? He is buying this restaurant. A very nice man. Well," he says, standing up, "would you like to order now?"

We eat. The food, despite everything that's happened, is exactly the same. Large silent portions. Finally my brother speaks.

"MD," he says, "Master of Deception."

"Quiet!" my father roars. "Jokes I don't need."

He is in a terrible mood. He doesn't say a word until we get to the apple compote. Then he speaks.

"Today's children," he says, "are not worth a *fortz*."

"But he never wanted to be a doctor, dad," I say. "It was all because his father pushed him."

"So what's wrong," says my father, "if a parent wants something a little better for his son? Something a little better than his own miserable life?"

"Yes, dad," I say.

By the time we've finished lunch, my father has managed to swing the whole story around. Now it has become a moral tale about children's ingratitude to their parents. I sit there, not saying a word.

Actually, I'm thinking. Yossel Shepps not being a doctor doesn't surprise me all that much. He didn't really have the manner. Do real doctors ever have such enormous feet?

The thing that is remarkable is how anyone with Yossel's looks could win himself a girl. A *shikse*. Coming home exhausted, day after day. Yossel Shepps. It's unbelievable. Who would have thought, under that exterior, lay a Casanova, a sleek lover, a boudoir snake? Yossel Shepps is a beacon in the night, a shining example to us all.

Jim Christos — the Cuckold

Nicholas Athanasou

In the conviction that nothing would ever change Jim
Christos always spoke of his business as "doing well", and of
his wife and children as "beautiful" and "cute"; for him
Souths would always lack a good centre, taxes would always
be too heavy and the Labor Party nothing but a bunch of
socialist mugs. The celestial relationship was for him incon-
trovertibly fixed: the earth rotated but did not revolve and
he enjoyed twenty-four hours of consistent existence.

His conversation, tasteless, colourless and indiscriminate,
like the water from a dirty garden tap, remained indistinguishable from one day to the next. His pocket philosophy
was expressed conveniently in a number of stock phrases
which he often declared with an astonished mistaken sense
of his own originality. He waved his hands majestically as he
talked and threw his corpulence into every frequent oath and
dirty phrase he swore. Once started on a subject he was
difficult to stop; for he loved what he created and found it
irresistible.

The figures from yesterday fled the thick round lips of Jim
Christos: they were the lips of a fat trumpet player who rises
from the midst of a band to play the most deafening high-
pitched solo. They caressed the mouthpiece and blew into
the phone as into some fat woman's arse. He loved the
cavernous indefinite echo of his own voice and, as he listened,
doodled with his pen on a small pad. He asked Larry to
repeat the figures and smiled in amusement at the hesitation
and deliberate pause which preceded each number. He was
surprised to discover that he had not made any mistakes and
now felt more inclined to get rid of the bastard.

"Goodbye Larry. See you Monday."

"Ta ta Jim. See you."

He smiled to himself. "Ta ta." What sort of way was that

for a man to say goodbye? The bloody infant. The bastard. Everyone but me.

Christos opened his drawer and placed the sheet that contained the figures back in his folder. They would probably want to hear those figures again this afternoon at the weekly meeting that was held in Thompson's office. Anyway it would be a good idea to keep them handy just in case Thompson asked for them. Not that he feared Thompson or any of the others on the board. He could more than hold his own with most of them and felt that, given the chance, would be able to complete their work in just a fraction of the time it took them. It was just that Thompson's old man was chairman of the board and you couldn't shift old Thompson with a ten-foot pole.

It was old Thompson who had given him his first job with the company. He had been just a boy then, seventeen years old, but a real go-getter all the same. His eagerness had caught old Thompson's eye and he had been able to get on the right side of him,; so, by a combination of arse-licking and hard work, he had managed to reach his present position, assistant manager of the Sydney branch. And as he often told his friends, he would be running the business in a few years. Why, he was almost managing the place single-handed as it was.

And Christos felt that he probably would have gained that top position already were it not for the fact that he possessed a Greek name. At least that was the reason he gave his friends. Christos often had cause to resent his Greek name, not only because it interfered with his business ambitions, but also because it automatically tended to lump him with those Greeks whom he regarded as his inferiors — Greeks who could not speak English, Greeks who worked in factories and went to soccer games, who drove their Valiants like typical dagoes, who were a bloody nuisance and got their names in the paper. He had never grown accustomed to the difficulty that people faced in spelling and pronouncing his name correctly nor to the manner in which they seemed to look askance at his dark skin and black wiry hair. As a matter of fact he spoke very little and very poor Greek; he had played rugby league and not soccer at school; he had always sought

the company of Australians and felt foreign to those Greeks
in Newtown or Enmore who could be seen playing with their
komboloia on the street or sitting in *kafeneia* gesturing and
shouting about soccer or Greek politics. He preferred the
close warm atmosphere of a pub and the cool beer that
relieved the fever of his thoughts. Yet often when he was
talking to Australians, even with his wife Karen, it seemed to
him as if there was a persistent inner voice reminding him:
"You are Greek; they are not. There is a difference!" Then
Christos would begin to swear more loudly and freely; for he
was afraid of the difference and wished to escape it.

At that moment, Christos pictured his wife Karen and felt
the quiet lazy manner with which she attracted him. She was
like a blank tablet on which he was able to heavily impress
his thoughts. She submitted so quietly to his will that he
liked to think he owned that tall blonde figure, her soft waist
and hard breasts. She had borne him two children but he felt
less as if he owned them. The two boys were fair, soft-
skinned, blond-haired like his wife and did not resemble him
at all. Although he took them to visit their grandmother at
Easter and Christmas, they would complain before going,
hide behind their father's chair in her company and appear
anxious to escape her embraces.

The phone rang and his secretary announced that the
weekly meeting was about to commence. Christos brushed
the sweat from his mouth and combed back the horseshoe of
hair that remained on his head. He put on his coat, gathered
his papers and walked toward Thompson's office. He met
Taffy Nicholls the sales rep on the way and agreed to meet
him in the pub for a few drinks after work.

The Kings Head was full when he entered. Office workers
who had thirsted for their freedom all the week now celebrated their Friday release. They crowded the bar, raised
their voices and dimmed the atmosphere with their smoke.
Taffy signalled to him from a table in the far corner and
Christos pushed his way through the crowd, disregarding an
angry shout from a drunken white collar who had spilled his
drink.

"G'day Jim. What took you so long?"

"Aw, bloody interstate call. I don't know why they always

manage to call up on Friday arvo at this flaming hour. And when you need your bloody secretary, she's gone ten minutes early, as usual. So I've got to do her work as well. It's a bloody disgrace."

"Ah well Jim, it's Friday." Taffy said cheerfully. "Try and forget about it. What are you drinking mate?"

"Make it my shout, Taff'. Beer?"

"No mate, it's mine. You just sit tight and I'll be back in a jiffy. Beer isn't it?"

For the first time Christos noted Taffy's merry red expression. He wondered exactly how many drinks Taffy had finished before his arrival. Christos was not inclined to push his way through the same crowd and he gratefully accepted his offer.

"I'll be back in a jiffy," he repeated.

Taffy said this with a laugh, acknowledging his own cliché. Christos remained seated, sliding an empty beer glass carelessly along the table from one hand to the other. The moisture formed from many drinks lay in a shallow pool upon the table. The empty glass rested in this pool, and as it was slid across the table, cast a pattern of moistureless areas on the surface. After a short while he began trying to form a lake, moving his glass in different patterns in an attempt to coalesce the separate pools. But his slightest movements left small billabongs or pools which, the more he tried to unite, the more tiny, disorganized and isolated they became. Then his friend returned with the drinks.

"Cheers Jim."

Christos raised his glass in reply.

"You were bloody good in there today, Jim. You really tore strips off young Thompson."

Christos smiled as he lowered his glass. He wiped the froth from his mouth but the smile remained. He welcomed the praise and felt it was his due.

"Well, he's had it coming to him, Taff'. He's the only log we've got in the business. If it wasn't for his old man he'd be out of there like a shot. I hope I didn't go too far this time, though. He might go crying to his papa."

"Don't worry about that mate," said Taffy. "This time

even old Thompson was impressed with what you said. You could see that."

"These young blokes like Thompson with their University education don't know what it is to do a good day's work." Christos announced this proudly as if it was a new discovery. "All they know is how to think about what they're going to do. They never get the bloody job done. I passed the Leaving; didn't matriculate though. It didn't matter anyway; I had no plans to go to Uni: and I did all right for myself. I'm earning more than most of those longhairs put together; hard work mate," he pressed his finger into the table, "that's what got me where I am today. Hard work and nothing less. Not sitting on my arse all day thinking about the bloody work before I go out and do it, like the longhairs you find nowadays!"

"Ah, you're right there, Jim. Of that there's no doubt. Hard work never hurt anyone and most of the young fellas nowadays don't even know the meaning of the word."

"So you think old Thompson liked what I said?" Christos asked. He wanted, needed reassurance.

"I'll say he did. It won't be long Jim, I'm telling you. You'll be running the Sydney branch, sure enough . . ."

"Another beer?" Christos asked.

"I won't say no."

For two hours Taffy agreed parrot-like to every stock conviction that Christos proposed, and Christos, like a balloon, swelled with each assent. They shouted each other drinks until each was satisfied that the other had not been cheated. Then Christos helped an unsteady Taffy out of the pub and into a nearby taxi.

He walked back the way he had come. He was slightly drunk and the cool night air refreshed him. Cars roared down William Street; the richly coloured neon lights winked on and off casting the people who passed him in high relief, and just for a moment, causing him to believe that all this had significance for him alone, that only he could understand the true nature of the night and its people. He quickly dismissed the thought but for a moment was almost convinced.

He collected his car from the parking station and pulled quickly out of the driveway to gain advantage of the green light. The tyres of his Falcon squealed as the car rolled awkwardly across the lane. He swung the wheel round, narrowly avoided another car and raced toward the lights managing to cross just before they could change. Christos often drove in this manner, accelerating aggressively before green or amber signals and swearing aloud at each red light that forced him to stop. He would feel genuinely happy after managing to successfully negotiate a set of traffic lights without stopping. It was as if he had defeated the devil who was trying to interrupt his destiny. He would exult in his victory but never pause to examine the nature of his happiness, composed as it was of trivialities.

He sped past a number of cars then took a short cut that he had discovered himself through a number of back lanes in Surry Hills finally emerging at Redfern near the glass works. He silently congratulated himself on the speed of his journey.

He paused at a set of traffic lights and turned to examine the cars around him. A young couple were seated in the car next to him. The girl looked straight ahead and nodded as the young man whose fingers danced on the steering wheel was speaking to her. Behind him three or four dark oafish looking bodies were crammed into the front seat of an old Zephyr. Before him in the back seat of a Mercedes, the silver hair of a Vaucluse matron was seen by the light on the expressway. The lights changed and the cars set off, one following the other.

Along the road to the airport his thoughts were lulled by the monotonous sound of the engine, the straight road and the succession of bright lights that flashed across his windshield and caused him to squint. Cars pursued him, passed him and allowed him to pass them. He obeyed the signals without thought and changed the gears mechanically. His lips moved silently once or twice and his fingers held the wheel so tightly that the colour was pressed from their tips.

Dimitri Christoforos — that was his full Greek name before he had contracted it to Christos about ten years ago. Dimitri Christoforos. His lips curled around each syllable. He had changed his name to Christos so that it would be more acceptable to Australian ears. His mother had been against the idea saying that she would prefer to carry the name of her husband to her grave. But with the help of his brothers Christos had finally managed to bring her round. As it turned out it made no difference; the bloody Australians had just as much difficulty with Christos as Christoforos.

An image of his mother, a small bent figure wrapped in black, rose before him. He had promised to visit her tonight but had let the time slip by while drinking with Taffy. It was too late to turn back now. He would just have to telephone her when he got home and apologize saying that he had been forced to work back at the office. It would at least avoid facing her directly and trying to lie in his broken half-Greek half-English. Her sour lizard face and rasping voice still had the power to freeze him and to force him to listen to her advice. She was particularly suspicious of Australians — it was a legacy of her early days in Australia — and she was always counselling him not to trust them in his business. She disapproved of his marriage and never failed to remind him that he alone of all her sons had taken an Australian wife. Although he had no wish to break with her altogether, Christos had begun to visit his mother less frequently of late. He no longer bothered to argue with her anymore. He was convinced that it was useless: "just like talking to a brick wall," he would tell his wife. Besides, his Greek was too meagre to argue effectively with her.

At the sound of an angry horn from the car behind him Jim Christos awoke with a start. The driver was urging him to go faster or at least move over to the inside lane so that he could pass him. Christos changed lanes. He was too startled to do otherwise. He could not understand how he had become so completely lost in his thoughts. It frightened him and instinctively he turned round to see if anyone else had noticed.

When he arrived home he turned into the driveway, stopped the car, got out, raised the garage door and parked his car in the garage: then he collected his papers, got out of the car and pulled down the door. He silently cursed the uncomfortable ritual that he had to follow every morning and evening just so that he could get his car in and out of the garage. He walked toward the front door and withdrew the key from his pocket. The house was in darkness. His wife's car was missing but that was not too unusual. She had probably gone down to the club and left the children with one of her friends. He was almost looking forward to a quiet night to himself.

He stepped inside and was instantly surprised by the darkness and silence which greeted him. Normally the first thing he heard on opening the door was the sound of the television in the back room. He flicked on the light switch and made his way into the bedroom. He took off his coat, twisted off his tie and undid the top button of his shirt. He sat on the bed and pulled off his shoes replacing them with a pair of time-worn slippers. He entered the bathroom and washed his face with cold water, drying it with a towel that he replaced carefully, the way Karen liked it. His mouth felt dry and he took three or four gulps of water directly from the tap. He spat out the last mouthful and allowed the water to drip from his lips onto his shirt.

He moved into the kitchen and checked the oven. Karen would have left him something to eat. It was empty. He looked around him. Everything was clean and in order; nothing was out of place. He opened the fridge. At least there was still plenty of cold meat and some beer. He pulled the ring off a can and took a preliminary sip before downing half of it in one huge gulp. He wiped his mouth deliberately and smiled. It was as if the smile had been made for effect even though he was alone in the room. But the smile mirrored the satisfaction that he felt within. He felt secure and happy in his own home, surrounded by familiar objects, things that he owned. He appreciated the silence all the more now for it gave him the opportunity to bask in these thoughts.

He finished the can in two more gulps then rose to switch on the television. Canned laughter. A British comedy was playing. He changed to the movie — a western — then to a crime series. He eyed with interest the two cars that chased each other across the screen but felt cheated when a commercial appeared at the climax of the chase. He was about to turn away when he noticed a piece of paper lying on top of the television. It was a letter addressed to him; the writing was Karen's.

The note was only a short one and he read it quickly

skipping words and scanning the sentences freely. When he
had finished his head jerked back abruptly as if he had been
struck on the chin, and like a full blown balloon suddenly
released, his brain seemed to jet madly about the room,
finally coming to rest in a noisy sorry expulsion. He read the
letter a second then a third time. He read it slowly now concentrating on the individual words and trying to guess the
exact thought that lay behind each expression. He crumpled
the note and threw it to one side.

"Bitch," he said aloud. "Bloody bitch."

He clenched his fist and pressed his knuckles into the table
until it hurt him. He swore aloud to himself for about a
minute not moving from the spot where he had first read the
note. He could not believe it. This could not be happening to
him. He picked up the note again and spread it out on the
table. He stared at the paper but did not read it. There were
several grammatical errors, and he noted that the letters were
wide and ill-formed as if they had been written by a child. He
picked out one or two words and then a name, Joe Ryder —
one of those Australian goons who was on the committee at
the club. Christos had never thought to notice him before.
He had always regarded him as a fool and now that fool had
run off with his wife and both his children. Wasn't he already
divorced with children of his own? The bastard. He would fix
him. He must.

He paused in the middle of the room, his head to one side,
then swung round suddenly. The sound of a car turning into
his driveway. He raced toward the front room. It was
nothing. She had not deceived him. He would forgive her. It
was all a joke. He peered through the window into the darkness. No joke. The neighbours were returning from a night
out on the town. Noisily they scraped the gate against the
ground as they opened it. The husband was drunk: he was
shouting loudly at his wife. She had lost too much money on
the pokies, it seemed. Christos turned away from the window
in disgust.

He walked slowly back to the television room. He lit a
cigarette then sat down before his own image on the empty
television screen. His image was stretched, drawn and
anguished. He rubbed his hands slowly over his face and

pulled up the corners of his eyes. He felt tired and weak. His head was full as if he had drunk too much and he had trouble sorting out the contrary ideas that surged through his mind. What was he to do? He had never expected Karen to do anything like this. His several visions of her blurred and confused themselves with those of Taffy laughing in his beer, the petty victory he had gained over young Thompson and the couple he had seen in the car tonight. Perhaps Karen too was in a car somewhere with him. His heart beat faster and he was seized with a tremor of apprehension.

He was overcome by a strong desire to have it out with the two of them. But where was he to begin? He telephoned one of his Australian friends. He was not at home. His wife asked Christos whether he would like to leave a message. Christos was on the point of telling her everything but stopped himself just in time. He could not be sure that she had not been in on this whole affair right from the start. She must have known what was going on for some time. She was one of Karen's best friends. What's more, she was probably laughing at him right now. They would all be laughing at him now. No. He would trust no one, least of all an Australian. Christos told her that it did not matter. He would call again. It was not important. Karen? Yes, she was fine. No, she was not at home. She had gone out tonight with a friend. (Oh, what was he saying?) She would be home late. Yes. That was all he knew.

He put down the phone but kept his hand on the receiver. He felt faint as if his knees were about to give way under him. He was keenly aware of his own vulnerability. He was possessed by a vague mysterious fear that this catastrophe had been developing for some time and that he alone had failed to notice it. But what had he done? He could not understand it. He wished he could see his own face and judge how all this was affecting him.

He telephoned one of his brothers. He felt that he must share his secret with someone. There was no answer. The whole family was probably over at his mother's house. He rang these.

"Allo." It was his mother's voice. Christos choked on his reply.

"Allo, allo . . . " she repeated several times.

Christos kept silent. He recognized the voices of his brothers in the background and tried to picture the scene at the other end of the line.

"Allo." The voice was angry now.

A reply formed on his lips but he did not sound it. There was so much that he wished to tell his mother now. He felt lost and sorry for himself and wished that at this moment his mother could take him in her arms and let him cry in her lap as when he was a boy.

"Allo."

But things had changed. Christos was no longer a boy and his mother had grown hard, bony and adamant. They no longer shared the same life. It was simply too much of a defeat for him to tell her what she had prophesied from the beginning. She would find it out in time, he thought. No, he must not speak even though it left him with nothing.

The phone went dead. Christos kept the receiver to his ear until the last possible moment then returned slowly to his chair. He sat down and looked sadly about him. The objects in the room seemed to shrink from his gaze, and the light, so sharp and brilliant, appeared to illuminate the emptiness that surrounded him too clearly.

He sighed deeply and let his head fall back on the chair. He stared into the light above and was struck by the reflection of his own emptiness. He was weak, humiliated, pitiful and slightly drunk. His heart cringed faintly. He felt cold and knew that he was alone.

Kapetan Nikola

Nicholas Athanasou

Sydney, 1948.

It was still dark when Kapetan Nikola opened the shop. He stepped inside and groped his way toward the light switch at the far end of the room. He traced a path around the sack of potatoes near the door, between the rows of sloping shelves filled with fruits of all kind and the counter on which lay the cash register, the sweets cupboard and the open sheets of newspaper, then edged his way carefully toward the wall. He trod on the leaves of yesterday's vegetables and heard them crackle drily underneath. The naked brightness of a hundred-watt bulb showed him the work he would have to do that morning.

He followed methodically the routine he had established over the last two months. First he swept the floor, then he went over it again with a wet mop; he wiped the shelves and the counter vigorously with a damp cloth. He restored the display of apples, pears and oranges, replacing any fruit that had fallen to the floor during the night. Then he emptied the rubbish into the garbage tin at the back of the shop, stored the empty bottles of soft drink into a box, carried in the milk and cut the double sheets of newspaper used for wrapping, into single sheets. His last job was to sharpen the knives which were used for slicing the vegetables.

Kapetan Nikola pulled out a packet of cork-tipped cigarettes from his pocket and sat down behind the counter to enjoy a smoke. He gazed at a mirror above the rows of fruit and brushed back an untidy shock of white hair that had fallen over his brow. He was wearing a collarless white shirt, buttoned to the top, and a pair of blue-striped trousers held by suspenders. He was not tall but broad shouldered, and his hands were thick and hairy. His immobile expressionless face was thrown into areas that reflected the light differently. His cheeks were shiny and smooth, his lips, beneath a thick grey moustache, thin and colourless, and his eyes, dark and thoughtful. He stared fixedly at the objects before him and blinked deliberately.

His work took no longer than forty-five minutes but often, like today, he could stretch it to the hour. Now he had only to wait for Tony his son-in-law to return from the markets with a fresh load of vegetables and fruit. He had nothing to do till then. His daughter, Evangelia, and the other women employed in the shop would arrive in a few minutes to officially open the business. For Kapetan Nikola could neither speak nor understand English, so even if a customer had chanced to enter the shop, he would not have been able to help him.

Six months ago, he had left his island in the Aegean and emigrated to Australia. The war had devastated the small island, and most of the inhabitants had been forced to migrate either to Australia or America. During the war, he had transported refugees from Cyprus to Port Said in his own caique, and had managed slowly to scrape together the passage money to Australia for each of his six children. Why Australia? Simply because others from his own island, Kastellorizo, some even before the war, had already settled there and had sent back favourable reports of the country. So first, he had sent his eldest son to scout the land, weigh its people and plan his family's settlement. But in his first letter his son had written that this was no place for foreigners, " . . . Here, they work you in the markets for fifteen hours a day and pay you barely enough to live on. The people swear at you and laugh at your appearance . . . they hate your dark skin and the way you talk . . . I hate these people and their damned country . . . " Kapetan Nikola had pitied his son but knew that there was little else he could do. His son was young and would adapt quickly, and he had expected the letters which followed to be more hopeful. Once his son had become reasonably established in the new country, Kapetan Nikola sent out his four daughters, singly or in pairs, and with this injunction to his son: "Find them husbands, men from our own island." So each girl had been matched either while en route or soon after her arrival in Australia.

He had been the last to come himself. For now that the war was over, there was trade in neither people nor goods among the islands. Everyone had spoken of bad times and even worse ahead. Before the war, Kapetan Nikola had seen good times, sailing regular trade routes between the islands and even venturing as far as the mainland, Cyprus and Egypt. But the islands were now for the most part deserted, and what little trade existed was taken over by the big companies with their larger and more efficient vessels. On Kastellorizo, just a handful of people had remained, and Kapetan Nikola had sat in *kafeneia* filled with only the oldest men. Almost every week, he had found himself farewelling relatives or friends setting out for other countries. They would embark saying, "We shall see you in Australia. Don't you worry Kapetan Nikola. This will not be the last time." His family had sent numerous letters clamouring for his presence, but he had continued to postpone departure. He had been reluctant to leave the things he knew so well. Finally a generous offer was made for the caique, and Kapetan Nikola found that he could delay his departure no longer. He had gone the rounds of all his friends and relatives to bid them farewell. He had felt them slap his back and toast him one more time; he had listened to their well known stories and had wondered whether he would ever hear them again. His cousins had cried and embraced him. His own voice had choked and the tears had flowed slowly down his cheeks. And before leaving, he had walked down to the pier and had gazed at his caique for the last time. The brass of her wheel had shone in the moonlight and her masts had stood bare and tall. The rope had been pulled taut, the caique had groaned to be set free, and a gnawing sense of emptiness had overwhelmed him as he had felt in his heart that this life was over and he would never know it again.

Kapetan Nikola took out his pocket watch to check the time. It was almost 7:30, time for his daughter to come down from the rooms above, where they all lived together. He extinguished his cigarette and began to whistle a Greek melody, but he seemed to run out of puff half-way and could not end it satisfactorily. He moved to the window and looked out through its misty pane at the early Sydney morning. On the other side of the road, two women stood at a tram stop, talking to each other. They signalled a tram but it raced past them, ignoring their angry shouts and gestures.

He was about to turn away when he noticed that one of the apples in the window display was missing. He picked another from the box behind him and gently tried to wedge it between the others. But he succeeded only in upsetting the balance completely so that the apples went tumbling down. Kapetan Nikola swore aloud. He began to gather the apples but when he had collected an armful, did not know what to do with them. He placed them on the counter nearby; then, just as he turned round to collect another armful, he spotted some of these apples rolling toward the edge. He dropped what he had and turned to stop them — but not quite in time. Five of them had already fallen to the floor. Kapetan Nikola swore aloud again.

"What are you doing there?" a shrill voice cried in Greek from the back of the shop.

Evangelia, Kapetan Nikola's daughter, strode into the room, paused, and surveyed the disaster with outraged authority. She was a slim young girl with a smooth olive complexion and thick, wiry, chestnut hair. Her lips were compressed tightly into a thin angry line as they regarded the hapless Kapetan Nikola. He looked so awkward there, beside the counter, his arms outstretched in both directions to prevent more apples running off the edge.

"Father, what are you doing there? You've wrecked the display. Why are all these apples on the floor? Look, they're all over the place. Now they're soft and have been opened. We won't be able to sell them if they've been opened. You know that."

From the moment his daughter had entered the room, Kapetan Nikola had been expecting this tirade, and to some extent, he felt he deserved it. But his attention was strangely less taken by his present embarrassment as by the Greek word that his daughter had used for "floor", *flori*, a borrowing from English, rather than the correct word *patoma*. He let her continue until she had worked off most of her indignation.

"Well, haven't you got anything to say, father? At least do something!"

"Come here and give me a hand, daughter, and stop gabbing away! Come on!"

She appeared satisfied that her point had been made and went over to help him.

"But what are you trying to do?"

"I was trying to rearrange those apples. That's all."

"Oh silly, it's always like that. You can never get that row filled tight."

"How was I to know that?"

They checked if any apples had escaped their notice.

"No more?" she asked.

"None."

Kapetan Nikola watched in silent resentment as his daughter began to check and rearrange what he had already done that morning. She chatted about her sister's baby and Kapetan Nikola agreed that he did look a little like him. They stood facing one another. Evangelia seemed to pause deliberately before saying, "Listen father, Tony and I have been thinking. We don't really need your help that much in the mornings. We're very grateful that you do it, of course, but if you'd rather stay upstairs and rest in the morning, we can always get someone else to do this. It wouldn't cost much, really."

Kapetan Nikola looked kindly at his daughter. Yes, she meant well by it. She was a good girl. But how long had she been wanting to say all this? He tried to answer in as unconcerned a voice as possible:

"No use throwing good money away, girl. It's really no trouble. And I've little enough to do now anyway."

She shrugged her shoulders; she said "All right . . . ," but asked him to think about it anyway.

With order restored, Evangelia cheerfully kissed her father and ran up the stairs, promising to bring him down a cup of Turkish coffee? He was about to light up another cigarette when the door opened and the Australian shopgirls, Moya and Sandra, entered.

"G'day pop, 'ow are ya?" said Moya, the livelier and more friendly of the two.

" 'Allo Moya, 'allo Sahndra."

Sandra did not acknowledge his greeting but walked

straight past him. She looked into the back room then turned round and asked abruptly, "Where's Angie?"

Kapetan Nikola did not understand at first but when Sandra repeated "Angie" more loudly and clearly, he pointed upstairs. Kapetan Nikola did not like Sandra. Her large figure reminded him of a sow. She spoke roughly to him even when his daughter was present and called him such names as "dago", "wog", "Balt". She often laughed unfairly at his strange-sounding language and his inability to express or comprehend the simplest ideas in English. He hated the advantage this gave her. Normally he would have had nothing to do with her, have never given her a thought; but he had no choice here. He was forced to notice her.

The women retired into the back room to store their bags and prepare themselves for the morning's work. Evangelia returned with the coffee and a glass of water. She asked him how he felt and when Kapetan Nikola repiled that he was fine, pecked him quickly with a kiss and ran off. He drank his coffee slowly, savouring its strong rich taste, then gulped down the water quickly to clear his mouth. Evangelia came down again, this time dressed for work. She opened the cash register and counted the money into the till. The women returned and awaited the first customers. Kapetan Nikola saw that there was nothing else for him to do downstairs, so he went up to his room with the empty cup and glass. He washed these in the sink, dried them carefully and put them away. Then he sat in his cane chair and rested his head on a cushion.

Eleven o'clock came and found Kapetan Nikola asleep in the same chair. His sleep had been dreamless and satisfying but finally disturbed by a series of loud thudding noises. He stirred half consciously and gradually began to recognize the passage of time and where he was. He yawned, passed his hand through his hair and stretched out his arms. He heard the noise again and identified the familiar sound. Yes, it was Tony unloading the truck. Had he really slept that long? He rose quickly and went downstairs. He passed through the crowded shop and out the door where he found Tony struggling with a sack of potatoes.

"Antoni," he shouted, "let me give you a hand with that one."

"Oh, there you are Pop. Okay, let's go."

They carried the sack into the shop, one of them grabbing each end. After a few seconds, Kapetan Nikola began to feel the weight and wanted to let the sack go, but he managed to keep hold of it. After they had deposited the sack in a corner, Kapetan Nikola noticed that his forearm muscles were rhythmically contracting and that his hands were shaking slightly. They went outside to carry in the rest of the goods. As it turned out, Tony had already done most of the work.

"You were a bit slow today, Pop."

"I overslept."

"Ah, you're getting old Pop. Anyway, there was no problem. I could handle it alone."

Although his son-in-law had been born and raised in Australia, Kapetan Nikola liked Tony. He was certainly Greek. In fact, he had known both his parents back on Kastellorizo. They had migrated early, after the first war, and had brought up their family in Australia. He could not help feeling, however, that they were a different breed, these Greek-Australians. They spoke English with a broad accent that differed even from the type he had heard in Cyprus. Their Greek was imperfect and poorly pronounced. Often they used a mixture of the two tongues, preserving in Greek the more basic words and resorting to English or anglicizing a Greek word when a difficult or abstract expression was required. But in the eyes of Australians, there was no difference between a fresh immigrant and a Greek who had lived all his life in Australia. This, above all, united them.

So it was with Tony. He maintained the Greek customs, respected both the church and the family and tried to preserve the language. Kapetan Nikola could also see that Tony knew the way to survive in Australia. He was a hard worker. His shop was open seven days a week, eight in the morning till eleven at night. His other daughters had taken similar husbands and his sons had adopted the same policy of survival. He was not worried about the fate of his children in Australia. Under their care, they would easily adapt.

"The shop looks busy."

Kapetan Nikola meant this remark as an invitation to talk.

"Good. I suppose I'd better get in there. They like to see the owner of the shop, you know."

"Won't you be needing me this afternoon then, Antoni?" Kapetan Nikola asked before Tony could turn to disappear.

"No. Don't think so. Why don't you go down to the Leski in town, Pop? Anyway . . . " Tony added in English, but he did not finish the sentence as he noticed two more customers were entering the shop. He followed them inside. Kapetan Nikola watched the short steps of the retreating figure and thought to himself, "Yes, I cannot help but like this man. Even though he leaves me here with my mouth open, gaping like a fool. For he will ensure that my daughter's future in this country is secure. Besides, it is the way of people here — to act like that."

The tram lurched down Anzac Parade, rocking its passengers back and forth monotonously. Kapetan Nikola sat at the back of the tram staring absently out of the window. He was now dressed for the Leski, having added a grey vest, a striped coat and a wide black hat. Whatever Kapetan Nikola knew of Sydney had been learnt from this tram route. He had come to recognize each of the streets, the shops and the pubs along the way. He had tried to guess the message of posters on bill-boards and the sides of buildings. He enjoyed the colourful illustrations of oversize jars of food, packets of biscuits, tea and cigarettes. He particularly liked the paintings of sporting events and beer glasses that decorated the walls of pubs.

As the conductor drew near, Kapetan Nikola prepared the exact change for the fare. He turned to face him and got an impression of a dark blue uniform, a badge, smooth white skin and a wide ill-formed mouth.

"Ox-for Stree'," he pronounced very slowly.

"You'll need more than that, mate. Fares 'ave gone up. 'Aven't you heard? Costs thruppence now."

Kapetan Nikola did not know why the conductor refused to accept his two pence as all the others had for the last two months. He could not understand what the conductor was saying. He repeated, "Ox-for Stree'."

"Look mate. Fares gone up. No good this," and he pointed to the coins in Kapetan Nikola's outstretched hand and shook his head, "Need more — thruppence," and he indicated this by raising his middle three fingers, "three — sabee."

"But Kapetan Nikola could not see why things should change today or any other day. He still believed that the conductor could not understand his poor English and he repeated even more slowly, "Ox-for-t Stree'."

The conductor tore off a threepenny ticket and pushed it under Kapetan Nikola's nose.

"Thruppence, see you bloody wog. You ignorant old dago. Why don't you bloody well learn English!"

Kapetan Nikola recognized the words of abuse. He pushed away the conductor's hand and pulled out an extra penny. The conductor took the money and purposely dropped the ticket onto the floor. He walked away grumbling to himself.

Kapetan Nikola bent down to pick up the ticket. He fingered it nervously with his thumb. He looked out the window but now found it difficult to recognize the landmarks. The colourful advertisements whose meaning he could only guess now seemed to mock him. His mouth felt dry and he was strangely conscious of his own breathing. It was somehow too deep and too loud. He could feel nothing but shame for his ignorance and hate for all Australians and this conductor in particular. He looked down wishing to avoid the accusing stares of his fellow passengers. But it was not his fault. He had never wanted to come to this godamn awful country. He could not speak English. So what? Could they speak Greek?

With relief, he escaped from the tram at Oxford Street. He crossed the road and walked up a narrow set of stairs into the Kastellorizian Leski. This clubhouse was little more than a large upstairs room into which were crowded five or six round tables with chairs and a tiny bar that served coffee, spirits and beer. Smoke rose heavily from several tables where the men were playing cards, backgammon or just talking and drinking together. Kapetan Nikola nodded to one or two of his friends, refused an offer to join in a game of cards saying that he did not feel like it, and then went up to the counter where he ordered a coffee without sugar.

"Yassu, Kapetan Nikola."

Kapetan Nikola turned to meet a short old crony with a bald head, a prominent fleshy nose and a wrinkled blemished face. He saw that he was drunk again.

"Where have you been since Sunday, Niko?"

"Yassu, Manoli. What do you mean, where have I been? It's only Tuesday today. I can't spend all my time here, you know. I've got to help Antoni at the shop."

Kapetan Nikola did not often use gestures when he spoke, but this time, he waved his right hand impatiently and spoke in a loud voice to his friend. He was immediately ashamed of his loss of temper; he apologized and asked him more gently, "Did you see the doctor yesterday?"

Manoli nodded.

"Well what did he tell you?"

Manoli's face brightened.

"He told me to stop drinking. Can you imagine that, Niko — me without a drink? Otherwise, he said, my belly would get bigger. My son told him he'd do his best to persuade me to stop but, as you can see, he hasn't been too successful."

And here, he took another sip from a cloudy glass that was filled with ouzo and water.

"You ought to listen to him. You remember Kapetas back on Kastellorizo. He went that way. His belly grew to be as big as a house before he died. Remember, the doctor kept taking out fluid but it just kept coming back. It was awful to see."

"Yes, I remember. But he was much older than me."

"But he suffered for years, Manoli."

Manoli grew thoughtful and paused to take another sip from his glass. He seemed to gain fresh heart.

"Suffering eh! And aren't we suffering here now, Niko, with nothing to do all day except play cards, drink and wait for death?"

"Shut up, Manoli. You're talking donkey shit."

"No listen," and here he touched Kapetan Nikola on the chest with one of his fingers that was wrapped around the glass, and brought his face closer to that of Kapetan Nikola to whisper confidentially:

"Today my son said to me, 'You're a pisspot, dad, a bloody pisspot.' You know what that Australian word 'pisspot' means, Kapetan Nikola? A 'metho', a drunkard. He called me, his own father, a 'metho'. I went after him with the first thing I could lay my hands on, a hammer I think it was. And do you think he begged my forgiveness like a true son? No, he twisted my arm and wrenched the hammer away. He pushed me off and told me to go to my room and sober up. And I wasn't even drunk, Niko, I swear it. I couldn't believe it. What are our children coming to in this country when they begin to swear at their parents and even raise their hand against them!"

When Kapetan Nikola did not reply, Manoli stared at him for a while before asking softly, "You're not drinking, Niko?"

"No."

Manoli moved off to annoy the backgammon players with the same story. One of these players, the former policeman on Kastellorizo, a dark fat man with a bald head was angered by his intrusion and shouted at Manoli to go to hell. Kapetan Nikola took pleasure in watching this man play backgammon. He took every loss as a personal affront; he revelled in each victory, pointing out the superiority of his play and his opponent's mistakes, but cursed the dice when he lost.

He concentrated wildly on the game, never raising his eyes from the board but staring at the position of all the men and holding his breath at each roll of the dice.

The kafetzi returned with his coffee and a glass of water.

"How's it been, Kapetan Nikola?"

"Not too bad. Yourself?"

"All right."

He carried his cup to the only vacant table in the room and sat down to enjoy a smoke with his coffee. For a brief moment, the odour and taste of the coffee, the sight of the men playing cards and backgammon reminded him of the quiet sleepy *kafeneion* he had left on Kastellorizo. Yes, if he were to close his eyes the sounds would be the same. He heard the roll of the dice over the board, someone curse his luck, a murmured bid, cards being shuffled and the loud sipping of coffee. Outside, a truck roared past and blew its horn; Kapetan Nikola opened his eyes.

Laughter rose from the next table. It was Manoli again, this time telling his story to a group of younger Kastellorizians and Greek-Australians.

"But you are a pisspot, mate," one of them said in English.

"And a bloody fool too, just like Kapetas," another added in Greek.

Manoli glared angrily at each of the mocking group. Kapetan Nikola feared that Manoli might go too far and start a fight with them. He was about to get up and restrain Manoli when Manoli suddenly turned and faced Kapetan Nikola. Manoli seemed to look past him as if he did not recognize him. He groaned softly and covered his face with both hands. Kapetan Nikola went over and placed his hand on Manoli's shoulder, and tried to make him sit down. He looked at Kapetan Nikola and whispered, "See! I told you." Then he tore himself away and ran out of the room.

Snap! The group at the table burst into laughter. Several other tables joined in.

"Just like Kapetas, didn't I tell you? He'll go the same way."

Hooligan, liar, thought Kapetan Nikola. How could he treat a dog, let alone a man, that way? And how could he have known Kapetas, the drunkard? He grew sick and died well after this fellow had migrated.

He resented these new "Cassies", as they called themselves, who boasted of the good old days back on Kastellorizo, days which they had never known. Most of them had migrated when they were very young, and from the gossip they had heard at the club over the years, could identify most of the characters who had lived on the island. But now it seemed to him as if they had become their own characters, and as if the island had belonged to them alone. He was secretly ashamed that one of these "Cassies" had shared his own thought.

He did not bother to finish his coffee but decided to follow Manoli. Perhaps he would need to be taken home. He crossed the room as quickly as he could, the laughter of the "Cassies" still echoing in his ears. Outside, in the busy street, he walked up and down and looked for him in every direction; he checked the lanes and the shop fronts but could find no trace of Manoli.

He checked his pocket watch. It was still too early to go home. He pulled down his hat and struck a path in the direction of the city. He walked briskly and absently, with bent head. He did not regard the people who passed him nor did he care to look about him on the street. However, occasionally he would pause and become conscious of things, as one aroused from a deep sleep who wakes and says, "Ah yes, I know you," then instantly falls to sleep again. He strode down a steep hill following the easiest most available path. By moving to the side of the road, he automatically avoided a group of children who were playing hopscotch on the pavement. He stopped to watch a young girl spin a hoop around her waist and heard her mother call her inside. He passed a pub with its door half open. Inside, he saw a crowd of big-bellied men, some of their shirt sleeves rolled up to the elbow shouting to their mates, others, red-faced, leaning against the bar, sipping their beers.

He crossed a wide main street among a crowd of people then held straight on. The road seemed to close before him so he turned down a more comfortable side lane. He passed rows and rows of houses, all old, all the same.

Toward evening, he found himself at the edge of a wide curving road. Opposite, there were a number of tall green warehouses. There were large numerals painted in yellow on the doors. He began walking along the road, then stopped abruptly when he saw in the gap between two of the buildings, the black hull of a ship. He looked up. There was her funnel and her masts. He was at the docks. But how had he failed to smell the sea? He crossed the road but found his path blocked by a wire fence. He gazed through the holes in the wire at the long black hull. She was a Norwegian cargo vessel, about ten thousand tons. The Plimsoll was high; she was unloading.

How many times had his caique passed one of these giants in the Aegean? And how often had he asked himself where was she going? what was her cargo? who was her captain? and what manner of men had chosen to sail in her? His caique would blow her shrill little horn in greeting, and the ship like a dying god would sound a deep mournful reply.

He followed the line of warehouses until he reached the end of the fence. At this end, there was a wharf to which were tied a number of lighter craft, then further on, a jetty where a few misshapen fish hooks and some leftover bait wrapped in newspaper were scattered.

He sat down on one of the pylons at the water's edge. He took off his hat and was grateful for the cool breeze that refreshed his brow. He watched the traffic cross the bridge, a tug butt its way madly across the harbour. He listened to the screeching of the gulls, and in the distance followed the bright lights of a ferry as she approached the quay. In Kastellorizo, he had often sat for hours by the water, enchanted by the perfect stillness of the evening. He had felt so tiny before that huge dark expanse of sea and sky; but it seemed to give his life a sense of design to think that he, too, was part of such a moment; he had felt at peace with the world — content.

He looked across the bay toward the North Side where the square yellow lights of the houses and flats betokened warmth and comfortable living. He smiled at the irony which left him alone, out in the cold. But this was as it should be, he thought, for he was the outsider here, the man with the funny looking hat who could not speak the language and whom they laughed and swore at in the street. The cold sobered him more than he wished. His smile no longer seemed natural but rather weak and foolish. Not for the first time, he found himself regarding his life critically and demanding to know in what direction it was leading him. But his answers were always the same. The life was different; the people were different. Here he searched vainly for things to occupy his time. In Kastellorizo, at least his days had been full; and moreover, he had been somebody. Kapetan Nikola. It had been enough just to say his name. Everyone had known him.

He had never expected one side of the world to resemble the other. There, he had made his living with sail and motor, pursuing a retreating horizon he had never expected to capture. Here, he stood face to face with dirt and grey, the work of fruit shops and markets, and the insults of strangers he had no wish to understand. It was as if what he had been pursuing all these years in the Aegean had suddenly turned about and devoured him.

He paused to watch a launch pass in front of him. In its wake it blew a cool spray that thrilled his cheeks. His neck felt stiff and he threw back his head and looked up at the night sky. But he could not identify any of the bright stars; the constellations were different in the south. He sighed aloud and felt the heaviness of his body; his heart was empty. Not since he had seen his caique for the last time had he felt this way. For now, as then, he understood the void and knew nothing would ever fill it.

He turned his eyes to the dark waters below him and watched the moonlight play on the surface. It had always seemed to him that the dark waters of the night concealed a secret, and that if he were to gaze long enough at the rippling surface, the waters would open and he would be granted a glimpse of the mystery. Now he considered discovering the whole truth. He shaded his eyes from the glistening water; his thoughts were strangely empty and he could hear nothing but the sound of the water gently lapping the pylons.

He groaned aloud. No, no, no, no. It was useless. It could never be. This was no solution for a Greek. His hands shook; he was sweating all over. He took off his hat and wiped his brow. He was surprised to feel the trail of two hot tears that had involuntarily run down his cheeks.

Kapetan Nikola sat there a while longer, rose, then walked slowly back the way he had come. He stopped once to listen to the night. The stillness was now complete.

Barbecue

Angelo Loukakis

He was glad to get away from the others and go for a walk
alone. He walked close to the bank, having left them at the
picnic area preparing the barbecue. He was supposed to be
looking for wood but, after a few minutes, he had found a
peaceful corner where the river seemed to bend around him
to the left and right. He stopped and sat down. It had
become a real question of just how much longer he could go
on playing these parts.

In some ways it made sense to do what he was doing.
Strategies were useful. But as a way of life? There were times
when it was all of no consequence, when he felt it was just
elaborate theatre, and there was nothing at the centre.

Others had done their bit too in giving him so many parts
to play. It wasn't solely his doing. Not only were they roles
that were desired of him, they were characters he was
expected to play. Rounded and believable.

To his mother he was a perfect son. Classic case. The more
he did to her the more perfect he became in her eyes, the
more she loved him. To his father he was a scholar. To his
wife he was friend and lover — she despised the use of the
term "husband". To his colleagues he was an aspiring and
quite talented but junior lecturer in sociology, particularly
the sociology of migration. To the kids in the neighbourhood
he lived in he was, because of his dark and swarthy looks, a
wog. To his in-laws, an enigmatic but likeable sort of a chap.

Why did he accept all this quietly? Well, to some extent it
was out of his hands. People were lost without a definite
view; they imposed it on others. And it would get him
nowhere to go around challenging people's prejudices or
expectations all the time. At the age of thirty he was tired
enough. Anyway, some things he could live with. Like his
old man's idea that he was a scholar. But it would help if one

day he sat him — and a few other people — down, and told them some truths about George Montidis.

Looking for an image of himself as more assertive and aggressive than he was today, he finished up in childhood. He used to fight a bit as a kid, but what can a child, even if he is assertive, teach a man? There was a tendency also to glorify his childhood. People thought of him as the son of migrants who had exchanged rural squalor for an Australian inner city slum, who had brought him up repressively. He was someone who had been damaged by circumstances but had pulled through splendidly. It was all only a rewrite of history.

The worst that had ever happened was being called names. His parents were shopkeepers, petty bourgeois; there had always been food and money and clothes, even intellectual encouragement. Intellectual encouragement. Ha! Dictionaries and encyclopedias bought at Woolworths. He felt guilty that he sometimes let acquaintances go on about what it must have been like for him as a child. But finally he had capitalized on such patronage. Why not?

There was no message in childhood. He tried. But all there was just added up to a funk, the moody, cranky funk that everyone lives in as a kid. One thing. At least in those days he wasn't trying to please everybody.

If he had been true to himself he wouldn't be where he was today, sharing an office with a crazy woman in a crummy College of Advanced Education. Her and her doctoral thesis, her Marxist interpretation of D. H. Lawrence, and her troop of lovers who were always on the phone, and her empty sultana packets and yoghurt cups spread all over the place.

Was this what his father had wanted for him? They had such faith in education those old bastards. Get an education means use your brains not your hands like your father. Means cushy job. Easy money. Respect. It was possible that he himself had believed some of this stuff once, again, a case of reacting to others. What would his father think of Monica, if he were ever to come to the College? He could hear him now. She looks like a tart. But she's got the brains probably. Brains is everything in this world.

No. If he had been true to himself he would be doing something else. What? . . . A fisherman . . . The thought made him squirm. An undergraduate crying on Linda's arm. Linda who wouldn't love him. He told her that it was too much, the falseness of the social world which demanded that he be this or that, do this or that. She'd asked him — How would you live your life then? A fisherman, a man in a boat, he replied. All so dramatic. But there was a drive for a simple life.

What was so complicated about what he was doing now? He was a sociologist. Really only like a stamp collector or a census taker. You have the form, the page, you stick in the stamp, the information, you add it up. Conclusions. That there are thirteen stamps from Antigua in my album. That there are approximately 532,000 Italians or 460,000 Greeks in Australia. This is what they think, according to my surveys, my study. This is what they do. Nothing very complicated about life as a sociologist. Easy in fact. Except that he felt guilty about the people who made up the numbers. The two who were his parents had worked hard — not that they'd made any money — and yet the amount of physical effort they'd expended in their lives worried him less than the loneliness he saw in them. They had no friends and their only acquaintances were customers. On the other hand, whenever he had confronted them they always said they were happy enough.

It could be that he was just being obsessive about their being unhappy. An idea about personal misery. That was the real obsession. In the West everyone was obsessed with their own psychic state, and the whole thing had reached the proportions of a social neurosis. In so many instances what counted for personal misery was just so much bullshit. What about real suffering? He worked with people whose greatest concern in life was whether their latest dinner party had been enough of a success, whether they should have served an Australian red instead of the Beaujolais (in deference to that latest resurgence of pride in things Australian), or whether their dumb thesis was going to get a first or not.

If they weren't lonely why did they want so much for him and Julia to come and live with them? They were being unnecessarily demanding. He tried to translate that into language they would understand. He couldn't.

Across the river from where he sat was another little barbecue area, the park was full of them. On either side of it the bush was quite thick. It was like an island. He watched the natives wandering around, gathering wood, lighting fires, preparing food, eating, sleeping. Some of the older ones were laughing, some of the younger ones were crying.

He remembered that he too was meant to be participating in a barbecue. The wood. He looked around quickly and saw that there wasn't much around. He stood up and walked to the base of a nearby tree where there were a few small, broken branches. But instead of picking them up he lowered himself against the tree trunk and pulled two or three bits close to his side. He wasn't ready to go back just yet. The company wasn't all that appealing.

He was tired of the Crofts, Peter and Alice. He had been a student with Peter, what they once had in common was no longer that obvious. They weren't often in Sydney. Peter was Canberra-based, doing research for Foreign Affairs, and it had been his idea to have this get together. They were Catholics, according to their variant definition of that religion, a deviant definition no doubt according to the Church. Alice looked like a folk singer, long blonde hair and still wearing kaftans and sandals.

His father would never believe that Peter worked in Foreign Affairs. Peter with that owlish face and those glasses, wearing Bermuda shorts and long socks. To his old man Foreign Affairs was big time. Heroic figures. A conversation on that subject nearly always led to talk of Herb Evatt, his father's only Australian hero, to talk of his work for the UN, and how Robert Menzies had finally destroyed him. He had not been a typical Aussie, that one. He had welcomed the migrants.

All those lectures he had heard as a kid about the bad deals Greece had collected at the end of every war. At Versailles.

At Yalta. How the old country had never been given what it had been promised by England or the Allies. Foreign affairs? It's all crooked business, dirty business. Peter? Doesn't look like anything much, looks like a school boy to me.

But then even the old man's idea of school kids was so wrong. He looked across the river again. They all had short shorts and thongs and T-shirts, like the kids in Glebe where he and Julia lived. Wonderful kids they were. Last week going to the post office, one of them had said something to him that hadn't been said to his face in years. He had brushed past a little girl of about ten standing outside near the boxes. As he pushed the door to go in he heard her say "Wog!" And when he turned they took off. He was a fool to think all that was finished.

It occurred to him that this was one reason he needed all the academic friends he had acquired, and the enlightened middle class in general. They were a kind of protection. He despised their empty indignation and their politically correct views, but their willingness to accept him was useful in a way. They took him seriously enough, and in return he added colour to their lives. A bit of the exotic. He had an interesting background they all liked to question him on.

What *was* that background? What did his origins and his ancestral culture mean here under these trees on a river bank in the Royal National Park? What did it matter if you were Greek or Turk or Yugoslav or Italian, or Anglo-Irish or whatever, in this place? If you took it as other than rhetorical he supposed the answer depended on who was around. It didn't matter to him, but it might matter to a racist if you were a Lebanese or whatever. Because if you were the latter you were likely to be disturbing the peace with that noisy music and chanting and dancing. Nature here was not that much of a leveller.

But whatever nature was doing now had no philosophical significance, the sun filtering through the tree overhead and sounds of the bush were simply making him drowsy. He looked at his watch. He had been gone about twenty minutes, though he could find no energy to raise himself. There was still time.

There wasn't really. A minute or two later he decided he'd better get a move on and so, picking up the few sticks next to him, made ready to go back. He had walked a little way along the grass by the bank when he saw Peter coming towards him. He was pleased that he had been come upon while looking as if he was doing what he was meant to be doing, rather than lazing under the tree. He could say he was late because wood had been hard to find.

"Where've you been? We thought you'd been kidnapped," Peter grinned at him.

"By Aborigines from a lost tribe living hidden in the bush?"

"Yes. Something like that."

"Of whose tribe I'd become a member and renounced my white ways?"

"Yes! Yes!"

"No! That's not what happened at all. Wasn't much wood."

"Oh. Right. We've started the fire with what we found around near the pits. What you've got there will help though."

Thanks Peter, he felt like saying. He could do without the positive reinforcement.

He walked alongside Peter for the rest of the way back without speaking. They entered the clearing with the barbecue pits and the two women, seeing them coming, began to clap and cheer. Peter took a bow.

He felt foolish having brought such a small amount of wood. More so because some of the other picnickers had heard Julia and Alice's carry-on and were looking his way. He noticed one fat specimen in particular who kept on looking. He was wearing a T-shirt with an indecipherable message on the front, his mouth hanging open as he absently turned the chops on the grill plate in between stares.

Going to their own pit, he inspected the fire Peter had started earlier with help from Alice and Julia. It had burned down to embers all right, but there were not enough of them for the amount of meat to be cooked. He was a little angry for some reason and felt like blaming someone. The people he had fallen among (or was it chosen?) were so incompetent at ordinary survival. For all their faults his parents knew how to perform simple, useful tasks like getting a fire going properly.

"Needs more wood, I think," he said.

"Are you sure?" Alice asked him doubtingly.

He let a few seconds pass, doing his best not to show any emotion. When he finally replied "Oh, yes," he spoke with as jolly a tone as possible. In this mood, he needed to keep himself under control. Peter came to him with the skewered meat on a plate.

"Ready to go?"

"Not really. But we can put some more wood in if it dies down." He took the meat from him and arranged it on the grill. The others stood near and watched him do it. There was a chorus of hoorays.

"Oh God!" Julia exclaimed. "I'm so glad I married a peasant!"

"Yes. It must be very nice to have someone who can do practical things," Alice added.

"I think that was meant partly for me George . . . if it wasn't then these women are very nasty. Sarcastic almost, wouldn't you say?"

"I wouldn't know. I'm too innocent a lamb."

Alice looked at him quickly, this was an opportunity not to be missed.

"Greek lamb!" she shouted.

"Enough!" He raised his arm in a grandiose manner, pretending to be a general quelling noise from the ranks. But the word was more than half-meant. He wished they would shut up.

He turned the meat and looked up at the ridge across the river from where they were standing. Six years ago, while on a university geography excursion inspecting that ridge's formations, he first spoke to the person who was now his wife. Not having seen her in lectures or tutorials, he had been unaware of her existence until that day. And this afternoon he didn't know whether to curse or bless geography. Curse or bless Julia.

"Say hello to her, Father," he remembered muttering in Greek to his old man when he first took her home. He thought he would have to do the same with his mother until she spoke without prompting. "Hello love," she'd said, not wishing to be thought impolite. They didn't know what she was, what she meant. Correction. His mother knew. This Australian girl brings trouble to our house. She comes to take my boy away. How right she was.

To please them, or to escape them, or to take the best course, or whatever, he would get married. Julia wanted to get married. While she had sets against many things, she had no set against marriage. "Just think! All the Greek food I'll be able to eat!"

Julia was a Hellenophile. In the early days that was the basis of their seeing each other. Going to restaurants, Greek plays. Reading Plato for the courses in government they were taking. Come to think of it, she was the first person he had known who wasn't Greek who knew something about the culture he came from and wasn't indifferent or hostile.

For her he had pretended to be more Greek than he actually was, or felt like being. It was pretty hard for a boy who was born in Balmain. So many things he did for her. Like going to the library to find out about Greek Orthodoxy, the religion he had been baptized into, knew nothing about and was constantly questioned on by Julia. The rituals interested her, the Easter services. The memory of educating himself in things Greek to please her made him wince. Play-acting was all it had been, all it was.

From the time he had slipped into playing parts things had begun to go wrong. That was the beginning of the end he had reached now. Weighed down by things he would have to throw off. If that meant people too, OK he would do it. He would begin by dropping the makeup and the characterization.

"Hey, what about the food?" Julia asked in the background.

He tilted his head in her direction, looked back at the meat, then faced her.

"Two minutes."

"Great, we're starving."

You're starving, he thought, I'm doing worse than that. However, whatever I choose to do, and whatever new way I manage to find, I won't punish anyone. There is a personal, existential question to be settled here. Any chaos caused will be caused by others. I will wander away from the noise and emotion like Mr Magoo. Smiling. Unaffected.

As they came to him to have the meat shovelled onto their plates he remembered that Mr Magoo was short-sighted. Something to avoid. In reality, there were so many things to be sorted out. He hoped to have some time alone after lunch. Then he would sort them out. The time had come.

Everyone had eaten with relish, they all approved of his efforts. He too had eaten well. His appetite was larger than he had suspected and the wine they had brought had helped him into a better state.

With the last of the food gone, Peter and Alice arranged themselves on a blanket to take a nap. Julia took it upon herself to clean up. Gathering the scraps into a bag, she headed for the bins which were some way off near the entrance to this area.

He took the opportunity to find his own spot a little closer to the water. He settled himself and pretended to be asleep. When Julia returned she came to where he lay. He was aware of her looking at him for a few moments, then going away. He was relieved that she hadn't stayed.

Opening his eyes again, he noticed the ring of small, decorative trees artificially planted around the edge of the barbecue area. The natural growth, the original trees of this clearing stood behind them, towering in the background. The old and the new . . . The old and the new. Everything fell somewhere between being old and being new. Introduce human will and you have the origins of conservatism and radicalism; we want to keep things as they are, we want to change, to begin again.

Julia was part of the new. There was no point in worrying her with things finished, as he'd done so much of late. Represented by an ageing mother and father, much of an older period was finished, what they stood for being gone or of no use any more. But what do you do about them? Old people's home? Not possible. They wouldn't go. He wouldn't put them there anyway.

"In Greece parents and children live together. When a son marries he brings his wife to his parents' home and they live together. When the parents die the son will have the house for his own, to raise his own children. That's the way to do things."

Is it? How foolish and dogmatic it all sounded. How many arguments he'd had with them. That way of life makes no sense here. People don't live with their in-laws if they can help it. Julia wouldn't want to do that, and he didn't blame her either. Not that she wasn't without her own definitions of right behaviour.

He couldn't hold Julia to account for anything though. Her definitions were attempts, tentative, she always had their best interests at heart. She was a good woman. She had her flaws, as did the best of them. She got too fired up over politics, women's questions, international problems, her area of responsibility was too large for her to do much effectively on any one matter. She used up a lot of emotion. But she was kind. A bit of a culture vulture. But generous, very generous. If she were in need of anything, it was a pruning job. This was something he felt himself to be in need of more than anyone he knew.

Really, that's it, isn't it? To cast aside all those definitions that finally trap one. All right, begin. No particular order.

This food business for one. Why was he always cooking lamb on skewers for everyone? It wasn't such a terrific meal, Greek maybe, but not so fantastic. He was bored with the culinary emphasis in life. And bugger the baclava too. From now on, it's Chinese, or whatever. It wouldn't do harm to profess occasionally that he didn't like Greek food.

And what about being typecast at work, where it was naturally assumed that he was desperately interested in studying the lifestyles of fellow migrants? Simple. He would apply for something else. Anything. Go back to teaching high school, that would be of social significance.

They would have to live with less money sure enough. Perhaps Julia could go back to full-time work. It could be organized. Parents? A new job would probably mean moving away, and if it means interstate so what? There's the parent problem answered. Fending for themselves emotionally could be the best thing to happen for them. They're survivors, they'll keep. Get right away from them and their expectations and demands. Other people had done that sort of thing, there was no reason why he couldn't.

Friends. What friends? If he no longer played the migrant who had struggled and made good, the people who were impressed with that sort of thing would disappear from around him anyway. The Crofts and such-like were, let's face it, just tiresome. They didn't really care what happened to you. If something were to happen to him, what would they offer? Sympathy. At least the Greeks would lend a helping hand. Even money.

He stopped for a moment. Those kinds of comparisons can't do anymore either. That was part of the plan, that the cultural idea was bullshit.

The plan is OK, the will had been engaged. What about acts, getting started? When? How?

He wondered how Julia would react to such changes, especially those she might interpret as personality changes. He would explain that they weren't, these were answers to the question of how to live. Carrying on about things Greek would have to end. They would have to find other interests. And these interests were non-essential. When she was alone with him she was warm and gentle, she had humour. He hoped he related to her in similar ways. It was only other people that brought our what little there was which was annoying. They were at their worst when people like the Crofts were around putting pressure on them. Julia thought she had to compete or she would be put down. From now on they would keep right away from the superficial. And excise the unimportant.

Among the trivia they would have to abandon was the terrace house in Glebe they were living in. Living there was nothing more than a concession to the lifestyle of the people he and Julia had worked with over the last few years. The trendy, young, middle class. There was absolutely nothing he could see to recommend bare, sandstock, brick walls and shaggy pile carpets. One shed sand and dust, and the other collected it. Very fashionable. He would be more content in a fibro shack with lino on the floors, and a radiator instead of a smelly, open fire. That sort of place would be more likely to feel like a home. A real home is what was needed.

Going to restaurants three nights a week would be completely out, and he would take up a sport to get fit. Enough of the sedentary life.

Right. What matters — A decent marriage, free of interference from acquaintances and relatives. A decent home. Decent friends. Work that is satisfying and useful. Health. Heart.

What doesn't matter — Play-acting. Pretence. The upwardly-mobile. Sociology. Trying to please everybody. High culture. The culinary arts. Ethnic culture (including Australian). The past. The past. Things from days gone that weigh one down.

He looked up from where he lay. The river was cool and flat, a few slow ripples, the afternoon light reflecting from the surface. The other bank fifty metres away. The ridge beyond covered in green.

He looked behind him. The Crofts seemed to be sleeping. Julia was sitting up, cross-legged, contemplating something. Her hands were in her lap. She was playing with her fingers.

He stood straight up. The moment had come. He took his shirt off quickly. He kicked his shoes off. Behind him he heard Julia shout "George! What's the matter?" She sounded frightened.

He went to the edge and dived in without hesitation. He would swim to the other side. A few metres out he turned to see them standing at the bank he had left. Julia shouted again. "George! George!"

He stopped for a moment.

"I'll see you on the other side! Talk to you then! I love you!" he called out in reply.

Turning again, he stroked slowly towards the other side.

The Boxer and the Grocer

Angelo Loukakis

Peter Venizelos believed in privacy. Even a shopkeeper should have privacy, or so he would occasionally tell his customers. It was a good philosophy, it helped protect your soul from the likes of Eleni. Originally a *patriotissa* from the same part of Evia as himself, she was now another one of the prying fools who lived near his grocery shop. Like so many of the tired Greeks in Marrickville, Eleni had two or three points to make about *ta pragmata*, and she insisted on making them over and over to the other inmates.

"I have already heard the news," Peter would tell her. He didn't need Eleni asking questions or explaining problems to him. He had done this for himself.

"They know it's better here. How can they go back? . . . Why don't they close their mouths?" So the tirades would run.

On the last day before Australian Easter Eleni entered the shop, bearing a fresh piece of nonsense.

"Peter, listen, my cousin the featherweight champion of Greece . . . is coming. We don't have any more beds, *the 'mou*, and they ask us to let him stay in our 'roomy semi'. They don't understand."

"In the old country they don't understand." He agreed with that part. He shook his head at his own conclusion, his thoughts beginning to go their own garrulous way.

"Are you listening *Englezo*?"

"I am not an *Englezos* and I never was, and *you* blaspheme too much!" He packed her groceries in her bag. He was glad she had finished. But what about her boxing cousin? He liked boxing . . . He could put him up in this place if he wanted to . . . Not for free of course.

"Eleni, I have an idea . . . He can stay here."

"True? True? I will send him to you when he comes, if you mean it, you old Turk!"

Peter was surprised at himself — he had told Eleni he would let a stranger stay at his home. Someone related to *her*. But who could question Peter's generosity? He was not as bad as some people thought.

He was standing on his toes now —

"I will give him a bed. What! Do you think I am a Jew?"

At this, Soula's eyes zoomed to his feet from the other end of the counter. His wife never missed anything that could be interpreted as "madness" — she was hoping that some day he would be struck down from above. But Peter was once a fight fan and he remembered how they would stand on their toes — the boxers, that is. He remembered the pictures of himself in the gym, and that somewhere he still had the half-stubs to "Patrick vs Burns".

As Eleni left the shop, he pulled himself up and said "Freddie Dawson, the Black Panther" out aloud at his wife.

"You wouldn't remember, or Jim Londos either."

Soula shook her head as she added this to the indictment. Why wasn't her son ever around to see these displays?

Stelios Lendounis landed in Marrickville on the first Wednesday after Easter. He headed for the shop to meet his new "uncle" without Eleni, as she had to work her morning shift. Peter was sweeping outside the grocery when he saw the athletic and obvious Greek in a track suit walking down through the local Odeons, delicatessens and bridal shops towards him. He followed Stelios' strides. Why was he alone? Peter rolled up his sleeves — you still have a young man's arms, he told himself. But feel very weak today. He went back inside, thinking of the ugly bodies in Marrickville. He would often watch them — little bow-legged mountain men from Yugoslavia and Greece and Turkey wearing lumpy suits — with their fat, shuffling women nearby. He stood up straight and took a few lordly, deep breaths.

"You're testing the air? What's the matter, not good enough for you" Soula pounced.

"*Sopa* . . . here he is."

When he entered Stelios Lendounis was everything —

smiles, poses, a few mock punches at the refrigerator — he knew he had the crowd. He then introduced himself to Peter.

"*Ghia sou! Ghia sou!* Anything you want boy, anything. I will look after you . . . come to your room. You are another son of mine!"

"Mr Venizelos, I will stay only until I fight for the Championship." He apologized in his best Athenian Greek, and walked in front of the grocer to his new room. He then opened a small carry bag, emptying hundreds of photographs "for the people" onto the bed. Photo of Stelios standing behind a table laden with trophies, his arms outstretched. Photo of Stelios in his Olympic Games suit. Photo of Stelios on the beach etc. etc.

"I will then go home."

Peter had heard this before.

"How old are you?"

"Twenty-seven."

"Have you heard of Hurricane Henry Armstrong? He won a World Championship when he was nearly *thirty-five*, Stelio!" Peter began to lead him back into the shop as he spoke. Stelios, having a closer look as they went, was amazed and lost the grocer's last words. So dirty . . . all tins . . . and he speaks with a mountain accent. Stelios had never heard anyone talk like that anymore, even in the North. Maybe he is mad.

Michael shambled home from school not long after. "Peter's son", as he was known to the denizens of the grocery, was a strange little fifteen-year-old with a big nose. His father introduced him to Stelios.

"He is a smart boy, *o ghios,* going to be an architect."

Stelios sensed the unhealthiness of this boy wearing the too-large school blazer. He reminded him of his own cousin, the Athenian, who was sixteen and wanted to be a philologist, a silly teacher. This one could do with some exercise.

"We could run together?"

"I've got a bicycle . . . I'll ride next to you." Michael prided himself on his quick thinking, a useful survival tactic in the racial wars at school. Peter's son often came home with a bloody nose. He was just an average survivor.

After the grocer had sent Michael on his way, Stelios

moved closer. He turned his back to Soula, who was busy with a customer, blocking her view of them. He had something he wanted to say privately.

"Would you write in English for me to a girl I met on the boat?"

"Yes . . . one night after I have shut the shop, when you are ready."

Michael, who had not retired altogether as he had been told, stood at the door which led to the house and watched them at this moment. How well his family's acquisition — one champion fighter — would go over with the grubs at school!

In the living room that night they were all transported to other worlds.

Thirty-seven years since Peter had left Greece, and in this room there were pictures of villagers in folk costumes, portraits of turn-of-the-century heroes, and some old 78s in a corner.

"They are *still* worth playing, Stelio, still worth playing . . . "

"I am proud of you. So many years and you are *still a Greek.*"

Soula came in from the kitchen, taking orders for coffee. She grinned as Stelios asked for an *Elliniko.*

"Thank you Mrs Venizelos." Stelios thought how true it was what he had heard — that these foreign Greeks measure their patriotism by the number of coffees they make their visitors swallow. He decided he may as well keep smiling, despite the down-at-heel air of the place.

It was now the oracle's turn. He sat up, face shining, and stared strongly at the boxer. There were important things to be said.

"I was a soldier in the Australian Army, you know, and I know this country well. At your age, of course, I was very fit. I will show you a photograph one day 'Auburn Gym 1945'."

Stelios was bored. Why did the grocer think he was interested?

"Peter, listen, tomorrow I must see Mr Rowley about my first fight."

"What? Yes, I will come with you . . . Soula can mind the shop."

"About my training, Mr Venizelos. Can Michael run with me? I don't know the streets. It will be good exercise for him."

Michael appeared at the door of his room on hearing his name. He looked across at his mother. This was her territory.

"He mustn't run Stelio, he sweats."

"*Sopa Soula!* As I was saying — if it was not for the war I could have done something . . ."

Peter continued with the public version of his private history the following night.

"I knew Rowley just after the war when he had a used furniture place down the road. Always talking about the World Championship. Everyone knew he had no brains. Always talking too much."

"But, Mr Venizelos, he has found someone for me to fight in three weeks. And then the Championship."

"No matter, I don't like him."

"Is this champion, Benelli, any good?"

"He is a champion *vlakas*, Stelio. You can beat him too . . . no brains. You are a Greek remember. The day we can't beat a Macaroni!"

Stelios watched the grocer getting excited. He thought of his own father and how he would talk about the Turks. What fools these old men were. They caused all those wars with their arguments.

"What about this letter Stelio, now that Soula is not listening."

"I met two New Zealand girls on the boat, one of them was very good to me."

"Oo Hoo!"

"She used to laugh at me and take me to her cabin. Will you ask her if she is coming to Australia to see me fight? . . . and you must tell her that Stelios misses her."

"Let's go to your room away from my wife, and I will write the letter."

As they sat down together, Peter noticed how the soft skin under the boxer's eyes yielded so easily — it was almost opaque scar tissue, and Stelios was conscious of his host's attention. He began to gently rub around them.

"I don't have much trouble with my eyes, you know, except they become tired after fights . . . Is that letter long enough you think?"

"Plenty. How long have you been doing this fighting job, *patrioti?*"

"Since I left school. I was amateur champion in the army and then I went to Munich . . . not many professional fights, about twenty . . . but I won the Greek Championship last year."

Stelios had no need to think about the words, he had said them before to others. But he could see no reason why the grocer should be interested. He would give him the rest anyway.

"I had to leave the village when I finished school. My mother was hysterical. My brother told her what I had done, but there was no money at first and she could not understand. She said I had disgraced everyone and look at my brother, a rich man in California . . . Today she says to everyone 'my son the Champion', especially when she saw how the village treated me when I went back after winning fights."

"Hmm. Stelio, have you heard of Jim Londos the Golden Greek? He was the world's greatest wrestler of all time."

Stelios was certain that the grocer had heard nothing of what he'd said.

"Mr Venizelos, those people are gone. It's a different business now. Tell me, why haven't you made a trip back?"

The grocer tightened up visibly at this question. He began to answer quietly.

"They are all dead . . . who would recognize me? We never had the money, just as important. Money was always the Big Problem."

He began to liven up.

"When I first came to Australia — Queensland — I worked

for a few shillings a week . . . you probably don't know a shilling."

Stelios looked away from him, as Peter began to redden, becoming both demon and martyr. He was sorry he asked that question for it made the old man strain. He remembered the tragic-cunning expression so often on his own father's face.

"Working for some distant relative cleaning dishes in his cafe . . . in Cairns with the snakes . . . I was sick with the change of climate for months . . . lost my hearing for a time. I went to Brisbane to look for other work. Unions said no jobs for dagoes."

"I am very tired, Mr Venizelos. I should go to bed early for training." The grocer was depressing him.

"*Kala! Kala!* I'm going. Good night to you."

In the bedroom the grocer found his wife muttering to herself. He tried to ignore her as he undressed.

"The boy shouldn't be with rough types, he is too young." Mrs Venizelos was annoyed at the content of her arena these days — there were too many males around.

"Don't worry, Michael is smart enough. It's a good experience for him. There are other things besides grocery shops you know." He listened to himself, wondering how such a diplomatic and philosophical beginning would go down with his wife.

"There might be, but that's all *you* know."

"No arguments . . . please."

"I think you should tell him not to give Michael ideas."

He went back to the boxer's room soon after eleven. Stelios was lying on the bed next to his letter.

"Sorry to disturb you."

"I wasn't sleeping."

"My wife doesn't like fighting . . . she told me to tell you about Michael."

"I know . . . don't worry."

As the grocer left, Stelios lay back and thought about women. How ridiculous they were after a certain age!

The first fight, three weeks later, went to Stelios easily enough on points. Next day Peter began to assault his customers —

"Mrs Rawson, Stelios won the fight!"

Mrs Rawson, like most of his other customers, was ecstatic —

"Aaa ya bloody idiot — Greeks . . . Give us a half-loaf of Abbco."

Stelios spent the day walking stiffly around the shop sporting a black eye. Peter would point him out to his customers at which cue everyone would nod. It was a little hard for Stelios to enjoy this glory. Peter and son would have gone to see that fight had not Mrs Venizelos complained about keeping the shop open. Besides this, she had feared for Michael's tender psyche.

Stelios stepped up sparring for the fight with Benelli, while Rowley soon found some desperate lumps for him to work with. In the next couple of weeks a different face would turn up every second day at the shop looking for Stelios. They almost all had antiquated hairstyles and bulging veins. To Soula they were gangsters.

Stelios had some trouble communicating with these training mates.

"Mr Venizelos, they just grunt all the time, grunt . . . I don't think they have any homes. Where do they live?"

"Behind your gym, in those rooms that Rowley lets. He is a good businessman."

"And they walk like mountain goats . . . I'm glad my mother isn't here."

The Championship fight was on the first Saturday night in June. This time grocer and son were allowed to go along. As they stood outside the shop self-consciously waiting for a cab, two of Peter's customers walked by them grinning. Peter was not used to being dressed up, and his rigid unease was on show as he would never allow it to be in other circumstances.

Michael was embarrassed again when, in the cab, his father decided to spring the boxing mythology on the driver.

"You know, cabbie, the Greek Champion is fighting

tonight. He is a friend. Better than any Australian fighter. Good as Patrick, even in the forties." Silence. He looked at the driver, a swarthy man, Italian for sure.

They arrived at the Pavilion. And entering the main hall they were almost driven back by the smell. Even old Peter.

They finally saw Stelios and he was almost unrecognizable. He had become a nervous animal steadying himself in the corner, waiting for the howls like an ancient pancratist. Peter winced as his eyes moved away. He watched the aisles, guessed the size of the crowd, and wished his son could somehow help him. They sat close to the ring.

When the bell sounded Peter Venizelos shuddered and gripped the bottom of his seat with both hands between his legs as the young Greek bounded out into the centre of the ring.

"I wish he never came!" The grocer shouted knowing that hardly anyone could hear, not even his son next to him.

The facts of his own life were with him again tonight, had forced themselves into his mind again. He, Peter Venizelos, had once had a body like this young man's. He had once felt the warmth of days in his family's olive groves. He had once run up the hills that drift away from the sea at Portonisi. And to think he had left those things behind to become a soldier and sleep on hessian sacks in bush camps, to push a fruit barrow around the streets for a living. He had tried always, for years, not to think too much about what had happened. Promises were finished, but the opportunity this boy had, the chance, just the chance, should have been allowed him once. Everything worked out differently. Things had worked out against him, against him all the way.

But in this place, sweat began to roll down Peter's face and through the hairs of his chest. He wanted it to be all over, to go back to Marrickville where it could all be put out of mind.

No way to turn now, just to sit and watch and hide his face from his son next to him.

Three rounds had ended and Stelios Lendounis had assumed command. Michael listened to his transistor through an earplug — the man said that the Greek was succeeding in confusing the local champ, he kept switching from southpaw to orthodox to southpaw all in the same round. He changed direction all the time and he was fast.

The old man began to weep, the fourth round underway and a cut open above Benelli's eye.

What madness had replaced the dream? He felt the weight of the frustration he usually held back, more strongly this night than he had for a long time past . . .

"Leave him alone." He heard a woman scream as he began to hit someone who had called him names outside his shop, fifteen years ago.

"I can't . . . I can't stop. I have a right too, this country is not theirs only . . . "

. . . A friend looked at him oddly as Peter placed his overcoat over his arm and walked out of the village. He might have been a doctor, but how could he have known that Peter Venizelos would never do anything!

He told them all he would leave, he told them he would try. That's all he was guilty of — leaving. But what else could he do? And why did they never write . . . especially him, especially Kappas . . .

Peter wanted to turn to his son and explain. But he could do no more than look away. The shouting stopped . . . The fifth round had just begun and the fight was ended. The damning, stupid fight was over.

PART 3

The Hosts

The Street

Gwen Kelly

My father was fantasy and love — who else could have created King Beetle stitch and Queen Beetle stitch? But my mother was reality — the chops, excessively fat, that had to be returned to the butcher; the sixpence that had to be explained when the depleted change was placed on the kitchen table.

It did not matter that I never, in fact, saw my father work King Beetle stitch. It was a wonder of gold and green blended with the sheen snatched from the backs of the Christmas beetles in the garden. It zig-zagged across the imaginary doyleys and supper cloths of my mental universe. My father said he could do it, and that was enough.

When I wanted to dream I turned to my father, but I should never have thought of consulting him about our neighbours. That was my mother's territory. The people of our street acquired substance and spirit through her eyes, were limned by her prejudices, suspended in the amber of time with her judgments tacked to them like labels.

I have wondered since if that world were also fantasy. Through a multiplicity of streets in other places, other time, they remain, a mosaic of life and an intimation of death. My mother created a social see-saw in which death joggled with life, where friendship dissolved into resentment. Whatever the reason, living was a pattern of talking and not talking. There was always someone with whom we had broken off relations. My mother's ancestry perhaps? All those Scots feuds were probably burnt into her subconscious.

Our own home was a world in itself where my family's loving and hating were carried on amidst the constant noise of battle. The house was a rambling weatherboard Australian bungalow sheltered from heat by trees and flowers and verandahs. It overlooked a tennis court created after many years' hard labour by my impractical father. Maybe the tennis court gave us status. I do not know, but my mother undoubtedly drew very fine lines of social desirability between herself and her family and most of her equally poor neighbours. We used pots, not saucepans; we washed in the wash house, not the laundry; and we never never never said "bikky" for "biscuit". This divided us both from the aspiring genteel who scorned good down-to-earth proletarian language (could it have been merely Scots?), and also from the rag-tag beneath our notice who dunked bikkies in tea and never washed their hands after using the lavatory.

At the top of the street lived the Moots, usually referred to as the Mootses. They were noisy, brawling, gay and vulgar. They had sisters and brothers and cousins and aunts who spilled every weekend out of the front door and on to the verandah with much shouting and laughter. Some of them arrived, with squealing brakes and hooting horns, in cars that were almost veteran even in the early 'thirties.

The Mootses had an earthiness that marked them as lower class. At least that was the impression I gained from my mother. I never did find out why they were almost, but not quite, socially undesirable. Perhaps it was the brimming glasses of beer that accompanied the Sunday shouts. My own family were, in theory at least, teetotallers, though there were whispered doubts about the fantasy man who headed it. Whenever she passed their house, my mother chattered happily to the Mootses, but at home she watched their comings and goings through our kitchen curtain with tiny grunts and muttered imprecations.

"That Edie'll come to no good if she gets around with that fellow," she muttered as Edie floated out on the arm of what looked to me an eminently desirable young man. I was partial to bow ties and pointed shoes (not to mention rolled socks for my contemporaries) but in view of my mother's scorn I was wise enough to keep these depraved tastes to myself. On these occasions of social enlightenment I never asked questions. If my mother wished to enlighten me she would.

This time she did. "He's a Cosborne," she said. "Mark my words, he might call himself a Gray but he's a Cosborne just like his mother. And no good ever came to any girl by consorting with Cosbornes." I looked at the young man as though mesmerized by a snake. I hoped that I too, in the fullness of time, would meet a Cosborne.

Ivy Moots had a baby. I knew very little about babies. My sisters and brothers stretched away ahead of me and only one small sister came behind. On Thursday evening Ivy Moots brought the baby down to see my mother. It had tiny, waxen features, a fuzz of brown hair, and it smiled when it took my finger. I had never loved a baby before. It was usually dogs and cats at home, and actually I preferred pups and kittens to their whining human counterparts. But I liked this baby. It held my finger. It laughed and gurgled; and on Saturday it was dead.

"You can't tell with convulsions," said my mother. "Convulsions can kill a baby just like that," and she clicked her fingers realistically in the air.

She picked the white may from the garden and she wound it with wire into a wreath. "For the baby," she said. "We liked him." When it was finished she gave it to me. "Take it to the house, but don't go in. Not even if they ask you to see the baby. Death is not for children."

They did not ask me and so I did not go in. I was glad. I was sorry. I wanted to see death. I wanted reassurance; to know that the baby laughed.

My mother did not attend the funeral. We looked through our kitchen curtains and the red coral trees, and the coffin was tiny and blue but much bigger than the baby. I felt my finger for the last lingering touch of life that the baby had imprinted on it. Simply to believe.

We ceased in time to mix with the Mootses. They dared to suggest our stray dog be destroyed. They even offered to do the shooting. He had been run over after six weeks of non-admitted residence with us. My mother lifted his skinny frame from the road and held him in her arms. "We don't need your rifles, Eddie Moots," she said, "and we never shall."

*   *   *

Next door to the Moots lived the Raynards. While my mother lived we never talked to Raynards. I do not know why. Not really. "Exclusive," my mother said dusting her nose with powder from an orange box imprinted with tiny parachutes. Or perhaps they were dandelion heads. I thought it gave her a flyaway air. "Too good for the average worker," said my mother, whisking her duster with Friday cleaning vigour over the chairs. "Well, I won't waste her time with my gossip."

Sometimes I smiled at the woman. I knew she was timid; a pretty woman with bouffant brown hair. I admired her graciousness, her little flutter of shyness as she slipped out of sight down her driveway. She had a huge husband in hanging black clothes who disappeared into the white stuccoed house every evening never to reappear until seven o'clock the following morning, still in the same black clothes.

There was a child, Heather, a good five years older than myself when to be thirteen seemed to me "very heaven". Sometimes I crept by the hedge and peered through. I hoped Heather would notice me. Does thirteen ever notice eight? She too was pretty. My mother disapproved.

"You keep away from there," said my mother, catching me on my rear with a stinging twig as she strode past the hedge, "Mrs Raynard will have you locked up if she finds you with your head in her hedge. She's garden proud, she is."

And so I never spoke to Heather until my mother was dying and the pain of her absence had become for me a monotony to be dispersed as best I could. I looked in the hedge more often as my need for fantasy increased. My father, now unemployed, seemed to have forgotten all his fancy embroidery.

"How's your mother?" said the soft voice. She was standing in the gateway and I tried to sidle away like a frightened cat, but she put her hand on my arm and talked to me as if I were a real teenager. For me she was in every way wonderful. She talked about clothes and books and the things big girls do. One day I discovered she was also a fantasy maker and my love became adoration. Every evening in the late summer dusk I crept out of our gate and stood on one leg outside Heather's gate while she spun fairy tales out of her own dreams.

She never asked me in but she did lend me a book bound in olive green, and every night I pressed it to my heart before I began to read. It opened with a funeral and a boy of nine whose mother had died. Before I returned it, I read the opening chapter again and again, and I wept with a new, painful pleasure that I could not comprehend. I can remember no more. I think that the boy, after much sorrow, found a new home where he was happy. It was unimportant compared with the funeral. For me the mysterious presence of death was no longer a blue coffin. It was an olive green book which my dearest friend had revealed to me.

Next to the Raynards was Wines, an old, bearded, grey man in a grey house. "That old devil Wines," my mother called him, and she always believed he was in league with Hawkins, a man who lived next to us in a big house with big grounds.

Mr Hawkins never went anywhere. Hour after hour he sat in a cane garden chair with an old hat on his head and his newspaper in his hand. Mrs Hawkins was bulk and black silk. She had a car and a chauffeur. Every day she walked on the arm of a servant from her front door to the car parked alongside our unkerbed gutter. Through the curtain I could see the car sag with her weight as she stepped onto the running board. "She eats too much," said my mother stitching frock after frock on her sewing machine, "but you can hardly blame her. She has to put up with him, poor woman."

She did not explain, but when I wanted to collect bottles to exchange for pennies to be exchanged for fireworks my mother said, "Try the bush outside Hawkins' back fence. You'll find plenty there, I'm sure." She bit off a thread with her teeth.

My mother never went to the bush outside Hawkins' back fence, but she was right for all that. Bottles of a quality I had never seen before: long, brown, with a tantalizing odour and grape-edged labels. It was very satisfactory. The bottle-o liked them, too. He paid threepence instead of the usual penny. I was kindly disposed to Mr Hawkins, but my mother thought otherwise.

Our cattle dog was poisoned and my mother blamed Hawkins. "He paid old Wines to do it," she said. "You mark my words. He wouldn't have the guts himself. He didn't like Paddy going through his paddock. Never did him any harm, but property is precious to capitalists like the Hawkins." The tears ran down her face. She had loved Paddy, the red-spotted epitome of canine intelligence. "He paid that old devil to do it," she said looking at Wines' house. "That old skinflint would do anything for money."

I looked at Mr Wines with caution. I skirted Mr Hawkins. I, too, had taken short cuts across the paddock. Perhaps, who knew, I was lined up as Mr Wines' next victim. He was an old man with a pepper-and-salt beard. He reminded me of my own great-grandfather, whom I had loved. God knows why. No one else did. He had appeared to like me too. An old, old man shut up in a narrow dark house in Newtown, who stroked my long black hair and said to my mother, "Don't let them cut the child's hair, Ann, don't let them cut it, whatever you do."

I knew from my mother that he, too, was an old villain who hated my mother's mother and despised his own son, my mother's father, long since dead. As my mother seemed to share his dislike of her own mother, I never did understand why this fact was held in perpetuity against him; but when he finally died, aged ninety-six, my mother looked at my father and said, "I told you so. Mean as dirt. 'Vengeance is mine,' saith the Lord; but trust old John Booth to usurp the Almighty's role."

I did not discover for many years that this piece of rhetoric referred to his will. He had taken the two hundred pieces of property that he possessed and divided them equally by number between his daughter and his daughter-in-law. To his daughter he had left a hundred in the best parts of the country, rich, well-watered land, and to his daughter-in-law he had left a hundred derelict tenements requiring as much in upkeep as they returned in rent.

And so Mr Wines was doomed on two counts. He was a reminder of that blackhearted villain, John Booth; and he was the murderer of Paddy. He spoke to me once, nicely, kindly, like an old man. For a second I stood transfixed, too terrified to move, and then I took to my heels and fled, burying my head in my mother's apron. "He's a dirty old man," she said, "a purveyor of death."

No one called the Badhams dirty old men, although my mother hinted mysteriously there was a touch of bastardy there. My mother's prejudices were deep and very Australian. There were grown-up Badhams and a little Badham my own age called Jean; sweet, well kept, but inclined to be spoilt. "Bitchy," I called it. It was my mother's word, not meant for my use.

Jean insulted my teddy bear as we rocked on a sheet of galvanized iron in the middle of the rain-flooded, still incomplete tennis court. "Your bear hasn't got real eyes," she said, "only buttons." I knew, but I did not want to know. Our dog had eaten the original eyes. My mother had done her best. I loved my bear.

I rocked the tin, and the green slimed water splashed on her white frock. "I'll tell on you," she wept, "I'll tell." She knocked my bear into the water and I bit her hard on the arm. Effectively. She ran for home screaming. I lay behind the front gate watching in terror. My mother was out. Mrs Badham came to the edge of her verandah opposite our gate. She shook a fist in my direction. "You wait until your mother gets home, you little vixen." I poked out my tongue.

I admit I quaked. My mother, when aroused, was a formidable opponent. But Mrs Badham must have queered her pitch somewhere along the line. I could see even at first glance that my mother was inclined to favour me.

"Do you like Jeannie Badham?" she said to me. I hesitated. A lie could be too easily discovered. Jean Badham undoubtedly bore the marks of her encounter.

"She threw my bear in the water," I said. I produced the green-slimed bear to prove it.

"I thought something like that had happened," said my mother. "That's the last time their child sets foot in our grounds. Destroying the children's toys. What happened then?" she asked.

"Jean told tales," I said, calculating rapidly. My mother professed to dislike tales. "She ran bellowing home, and Mrs Badham came out and yelled at me and said she would tell you to make sure I was punished." In conscious virtue I cast down my eyes. "Mrs Badham" — my mother paused and looked hard at me to see the effect of the name on my conscience — "Mrs Badham said that you poked out your tongue at her. If I thought you had been rude to Mrs Badham I'd smack your bottom hard."

"I didn't leave this yard," I said truthfully.

My mother recounted the story to my sisters and brothers and my father, and we no longer spoke to Badhams. Or perhaps they no longer spoke to us. Every night I snuggled up in bed with my younger sister. "Good night Mum. Good night Dad." "Good night darling," "Good night dear." Then under our breath we muttered in unison, "Good night everybody in the world except Badhams."

We did not speak again for two years. It was the morning after my mother died. Mrs Badham brought a cake over to my sister. Jean offered me her bag of sweets. I hesitated. "Have the sherbet," she said. I loved sherbet. We all did. I liked Jean. I always had!

Sometimes, matters that divided us were ideological. Mrs Parkin was lovely, good looking and gracious. *But* — "She is a really nice woman," said my mother to her sister, Bella, sipping tea on our side verandah with her grey-green eye turned to catch our sinful activities, "really nice, *But* —"

That mysterious "but" divided us effectively. You could not be neighbourly to Catholics. They were a race apart. Instead of going to a proper Church, like the rest of us, they went to the little one around the corner. It had a white cross on top of a triangular facia board that reached triumphantly for heaven. "Popery," said my mother. "Don't let me catch you in there, or the devil will get you for sure."

I stood outside the fence. I eyed the white cross with fascination, but I never went in. I feared for my friend, Jimmy Warner, who also lived in our street, because he entered the little building every morning, on our way to school. "The Warners are poor Catholics," said my mother in scorn. Apparently you could not win either way. "The Parkins are sincere. They know their place in the community. John is with his own kind at Joey's. Believe me, the Warners ought to be in their own school too."

Even so, we played with the Warners but never with the Parkins. With Jimmy, my sister and I laughed and feuded through two long summers, glimpsing through him some of the street that was truly out of bounds.

The Dares were out of bounds. I never knew why, but I knew when my mother was serious. They lived at the end of the road in jerry-built houses. They used new words, wonderful expressive words, that I knew by instinct never to repeat at home. I puzzled over my mother's attitude. Did they dip their fingers in their lavatories, or harbour nits in their scrawny straw hair? I never found out. My mother's lips would close firmly. I did not disobey her.

It was not simply a matter of poverty, for the Southeys next door were equally poor but my mother loved the gentle, helpless Botticelli woman. She organized Mrs Southey's life completely. She called herself SouDey, but my mother soon corrected that. The baby was hungry, but my mother prescribed a bottle of arrowroot biscuit-and-milk and he throve. The children were dull, but my mother manoeuvred my big sisters into finding new schools for them. I slid down Mrs Southey's bamboos, plucked the waxen berries from her flowering trees, fluffed open the balls of the cotton bush and drained off the white milk. My mother came and went with advice, and I came and went with her. And so, when she was dying, the pattern remained. We came and went to Mrs Southey as a matter of habit, a pledge to the continuity of living.

My mother died. They gathered around us: the Moots, the Raynards, the Hawkins, Mr Wines, the Badhams, the Parkins, the Warners, the Dares and the Southeys. They brought food and comfort and help.

Finally, we went away, never to return. But I had reached out for life in that street and to some extent I had found it — life, and its reverse image, death.

Wong Chu and the Queen's Letterbox

Tom Hungerford

You mightn't think there'd be a very strong connection between an old Chinese market gardener and a pillarbox owned by the Queen of England — but there was: a long and intimate, and in many ways a romantic one, too.

Both the pillarbox and the Chinaman first knew South Perth as a rushy riverside retreat of cow paddocks and market gardens and bush, where the settlers along the river's bank had their own jetties and flat-bottomed boats for travelling to and from Perth, and horses leaned thoughtfully over every second fence along the one main road through the suburb.

Both were associated, for nearly an entire biblical lifetime, in the same quiet little coign of it; saw it grow, saw gravel give way to bitumen and roadside trees to electric light poles, saw the bun give way to the bingle and the bingle to the wig, the cart to the car and the backyard grapevine to the telephone. Both became so much a part of it as not to be missed until they departed, which they did within a few months of each other.

The pillarbox used to stand on the corner of Suburban Road and River Street — now Mill Point Road and Douglas Avenue — where youngsters who are now grandparents used to turn down, still munching on the morning toast, to take the ferry to town and their first jobs.

I don't know when it was put there, but it bore a florid "VR" and the date 1857, so it might well have begun its long office only about thirty years after the first settlers ventured up the swan-haunted river.

A solid single-towered little castle of reaction, it was in some ways not unlike the dumpy queen-empress who owned it, and under the shield of whose power it took delivery of letters to be sent all over a world which then existed almost solely as an appendage to her Empire.

It was six-sided, about five feet high, and it was painted that wonderful imperial shade of red common to pillarboxes, fire brigades and the jackets of Guardsmen. On top it had a Germanic sort of spike like the one which used to surmount the Kaiser's helmet — perhaps not as sharp, but sufficiently so to make the box completely unsatisfactory for sitting on top of . . . I know, because I used to try, and so did several generations of South Perth children before and after me. Thinking about it inevitably brings back the childhood it presided over, a period now as remote and strange and in a way as unbelievable as life on a quasar.

Mill Point Road was then a ribbon of red gravel flanked by twin ribbons of deep, red dust between a double line of the loveliest trees . . . planes and kurrajongs, gums and cape lilacs, lillipillis from which, on the way home from school, we stoned the tiny, tart "Chinese apples", Moreton Bay figs trimmed meticulously to the shape of opened umbrellas that, nevertheless, kept out far less rain than the straggly old gums.

It was the spine of a suburb which then didn't stretch as far as Fremantle Road — there was still a lot of almost virgin bush even beyond Angelo Street. Our home was on it, and most of my childhood centred between that home and "the shops" where the pillarbox was — Mr Rogers the butcher and Mr Faddy the grocer and post office; there was hardly a day when I did not pass the box on my way to get a reel of white cotton forty for my mother or a twist of hundreds-and-thousands for myself, climb on it or wait at the base while my Lion or Towser or Barney ceremoniously completed the lustrations which, stoically, it bore from a thousand generations of South Perth dogs.

Why, when I look back on my childhood in South Perth is it always summer? I see the urchin who was myself, with other urchins, chuffing happily through the roadside dust past the pillarbox being either trains or flocks of sheep, as the mood takes us, but either way enveloped in a red cloud that eddies up to the dense summer foliage above us. Or I stand transported, every time, as Colonel Le Souef in his open carriage flashes past, at fifteen miles an hour, behind four of the zoo's dinky little shetland ponies: the council watering cart sloshes through the burning afternoon, and we spin like drought-maddened frogs in its spray: scarecrow "blackies" and their stick-insect children, whose tangled black hair and blazing black eyes I can still see, all these long years after they have gone to their dreaming, trudge past our front gate hawking their clothes-props through the streets of the quiet riverside suburb which they used to own. From far off the tinkling bell of the tiny ice-cream cart calls, no louder than the sobbing of doves in the trees by our side fence, but more imperative than the voice of God . . . and throughout the long summer evenings in the shadows of the shop verandah, the laughing and chiaking and softly winking cigarettes of the dread "corner-boys" affronts the righteous. "D'you want to grow up to be a *corner boy*?" my mother threatens me again, over some old misdemeanour: and although nothing could enchant me more than an invitation into that raffish circle — there is a jockey and a fisherman among them — I can hardly tell her so.

The old pillarbox saw it all and heard it all, through childhoods long before mine and long after, meanwhile taking into its stolid care letters written by South Perth parents and lovers and children and wives to men fighting in the Boer War, the Great War and the World War, in Korea and Malaya and Vietnam . . . and, no doubt, because he worked in a garden just down the road, it received whatever letters Wong Chu sent back to his family and friends in China during the sixty-odd years he lived in South Perth.

Looking back, it seems there never was a time in my childhood when no Chinamen padded along the shady, oyster-shell footpaths of our neighbourhood, waved grinning from their big, hooded carts, appeared at the back door with fruit and vegetables — Rome beauties were our favourite apples — sat quietly in the ferry or stood quietly in the shops, a part yet apart in the friendly everyone-knows-everyone affairs of the suburb.

They lived and worked, maybe as many as fifty or sixty of them all told — on the broad strip of superb black soil which fringed the river, behind a dark belt of trees and rushes, almost without a break from close to Mends Street to the edge of Victoria Park.

The gardens, those of "our" Chinamen, anyway, were as

much our playground as the river or our own backyards. Then, of course, we didn't know how beautiful they were, with their patchwork of green carrot tops and pale green lettuce and milky green cauliflower in season, the blood-red of beetroot and the purple of egg plant, and the gold-flecked lakes of melons and pumpkin at the damper, lower end of the garden. Armoured gilgies dozed beside their holes in the square wells scattered among the beds for watering and dipping the vegetables, and in the slow moving waterways by which the run-off of a score of bubbling springs converged on a mysterious underground tunnel leading to the river, bright constellations of red goldfish exploded in all directions as we took after them with — had we but known it — utterly harmless "spears" from the thicket of bamboos down by the river.

Wong Chu — "Charlie" like all the others — worked in the garden below my home. A small, bird-boned man with flesh as brown and hard as sheoak wood, he wore the clothes common to all the "Charlies" — a rough working shirt and dark blue cotton trousers which folded over at the waist like a sarong; never boots or shoes in the garden, and only, in the worst of weather, the big "umbrella" hats of their homeland . . . they seemed to prefer instead the Australian-style tucked-in cornsack in which bobbing about their gardens with another sack tied apronwise around the waist, they looked like an industrious company of monks, or perhaps dwarfs.

Generally they slept in galvanized iron huts at the drier, top end of the garden, having in the middle of the cultivation an open-fronted shed in which the cart was housed and gardening implements stored along with great bunches of seedheads of most of the vegetables they grew; often they cooked and ate in these sheds too. We were fairly free of the garden shacks, but rarely ventured into the sleeping quarters. There were about those, curious shifting shadows, pungent scents and unexpected shapes which evoked all the strangeness and menace of that vast, distant and ancient China where they ate puppydogs and drowned baby girls in the yellow rivers. In their recesses, our friends' everyday eyes were darker and more oblique, their dark hair more uncompromisingly dark and lank. They smoked long hubble-bubble pipes of bamboo, in the little spouts of which they ignited — with a long taper — tiny pellets which we all were then certain was opium, but which, before I grew up, I had realized was only Champion Flake Cut from Mr Faddy's irreproachable coffee-smelling shop. In those sheds, moreover, they conducted orgies . . . everyone knew *that*. Most Saturday evenings they dressed in stiff blue serge suits and unaccustomed black shoes and went into town . . . to play fantan down in James Street: everyone knew *that,* too. They rarely came home until Sunday morning, and when they did they were often followed at an interval by white ladies; up from the ferry, past the fluttering disapproval of Jubilee Street front-room lace curtains and so to those mysterious galvanized-iron living quarters. And orgies.

But if those ladies were somewhat less than kin and more than kind, who is now to blame Wong Chu and Sun Kwong Wah and Ah Kim and all those hard-working, lonely Charlies separated by long years and half the wide world from the much more satisfying loves they had known in their villages in distant Yunnan, or Kwangsi, or Shantung? They were up and working long before the first ferry — then the criterion for early rising around our way — and the fire flies went to bed before them. The gardens were turned over spadeful by spadeful for every new crop, and were fertilized by great heaps of straw and manure brought from the stable up on the dry ground. Planting, weeding and harvesting was all done by hand, and in the musky summer evenings of frog-croak and bittern-cry from the swamp by the river you could trace the passage of the softly effulgent cascades from their huge watering cans — one on each end of a yoke across the shoulder — as they wove backward and forward over the parched beds. Nobody worked harder in South Perth, few were more law-abiding, and none was kinder to the flocks of grasshopper kids — who in the fond belief that they were unobserved as they crept through the rushes at the bottom of the garden — stole their melons and harassed the goldfish in their ponds.

I have two very clear recollections of old Wong Chu. One was of the day when, having caught several dozen crabs from the now unimaginable bounty of the river, we gave most of them to him. He appeared utterly staggered by the gift; he stared around the shed, obviously looking for something to give in return, and finally thrust on us two enormous cauliflowers fresh from the garden. The other time was when he returned from his trip to China, I think in about 1924 — I was about ten years old. Before going he had promised he would bring back a present for me. He did — six magical Chinese kites of featherlight bamboo and flimsy red and green rice-paper, in the shape of some legendary Chinese bird. As you set them on the air they floated off: if I close my eyes, I can feel them in my hands now, and feel too beneath my bare feet the cool damp path of black soil on which, when he gave them to me, we stood in the middle of his now vanished garden.

Suddenly both Wong Chu and the pillarbox are gone. One day late last year some men came with shovels and a truck and a bulldozer and before you could say knife a century and more of South Perth history had been obliterated . . . to be replaced by a hideous functional one-legged red box like a disgruntled oomfah bird with whatever head it might possess tucked under a wing inscribed, not with the lovely florid monogram of a great Queen, but with a legend in white, mean paint suggesting when the citizens of this diminished day might deposit their mail in the expectation that it will be delivered between strikes.

Not long after the pillarbox disappeared, I was not a bit surprised when a friend, whose family had been looking after old Wong's affairs for twenty years, told me, without preamble, "Old Wong's going back to China."

I had been seeing the old chap, a few times a week, ambling down Jubilee Street to the shop — to the shop which long ago had replaced Mr Faddy's burnt-out emporium, along the street on which, those far-off Sunday mornings, the ladies had walked behind him up from the ferry. I don't think he ever connected me with the larrikins who snatched his melons, but he would always pause and say, "Welly ni' day!": or, squinting up at the sky, knowingly, "Maybe lain, eh?"

All the years while we played by the river, outgrew our

childhood, left school and found jobs, went to war and came back, got married or went roaming, grew to middle age and beyond . . . all those years the pillarbox stood on the corner and Wong Chu worked among his vegetables . . . in the finish, with all the other Charlies gone and the gardens destroyed, on a little plot at the end of my street, in his old shack, with his old horse for company until that died, too.

And now both he and the pillarbox are gone. I don't know where the pillarbox is, but the old man is in Hong Kong among the family he had not seen for half a century. I hope he is happy. I hope that Kwan-yin will send a great big celestial dragon with flaming eyes and scales of jade to watch over him, as long as he lives.

Indira

Joe Wright

It was a day in late September when I first saw Indira. A warm, vernal wind, heavy with the scent of flowers, whispered up the valley and sported with the pink and white apple blossoms. I stood by the waggon of Curran Deen the hawker and watched the herd of tired cattle passing by. Bearded drovers, sitting loosely on sweat-caked horses, flicked the lowing Herefords with long black whips, and blue cattle dogs trotted behind, panting, with their pink tongues almost on the ground.

Indira was so beautiful she could have been snipped from the cover of a story book, and as she ambled by with silver mane and silver tail shining in contrast with her chestnut coat, a strange thing happened. She stopped and with velvet ears pointed forward she whinnied, her big, soft eyes fixed on Curran Deen as if she knew him.

The driver riding her swore, as he jerked the bridle and raked her sides with his spurs; then they were gone, lost in the swirl of dust and moving cattle. There was a sad, haunted look on the hawker's face. He seemed oblivious of my presence and I heard him half whisper the name, "Indira."

"Have you seen that pony before?" I asked Curran Deen. He didn't answer. I don't believe he heard. There was a faraway look in his eyes as he stared after the receding cattle. I had a feeling I shouldn't intrude on his thoughts, so I quietly moved away.

San Singh's waggon stood close to Deen's. He was just returning from the creek, his arms filled with dry oak, with which he and Dean always used to build their fires. Being a slow-combustible fuel it was ideal for cooking their jonny-cakes and while burning exuded a pleasant odour. Even now, after all the years that have drifted by, that pungent smell evokes a clear picture of dark-skinned, pink-turbanned men and the covered waggons which were Aladdin's caves for us outback children.

Singh was six-foot-six and enormously strong. He had a glib, witty tongue and was expert in flattery and sales talk. He had visited our valley once a year for as long as I could remember; like most hawkers he seemed able to keep stored in his memory from previous visits the fitting of each customer, whether it was for Ben Wall's riding breeches or Mrs Riley's corsets.

Mostly the hawkers arrived in pairs. I suppose they kept each other company. This year Singh had brought a strange companion who intrigued me — Curran Deen.

Deen seemed neither old nor young, big nor small, yet as he moved about unhitching his team, he gave the impression of quiet strength. His face was beardless and handsome, though somewhat lined; the thing which fascinated me most was the changing expression in his large brown eyes, and his low, musical voice thrilled me.

Being a stranger, he was watched with suspicion; ours was a small, isolated community, somewhat clannish and racist in its views. Even my red hair was a bit too outlandish for local taste, and my schoolmates never allowed me to forget that I was some kind of freak.

I often hung around Curran Dean's waggon, spending the few pennies I managed to earn and wondering about the big books he always seemed to be reading. Sometimes he would read a passage aloud, before closing the volume loudly to scare me, and though I scarcely understood the words, they did cause me to ponder deeply on the riddles of life. I began to watch the changing glory of sunsets; I became aware of the tender beauty of opening flowers, and terribly worried by the truth that everything must fade and die.

I longed for the strange Indian to tell me more, but he seemed rapt in a world of his own.

As I walked slowly home after seeing Indira, my thoughts were of the drovers, the thoroughbred mare, and the haunted expression on the hawker's face.

My one great wish was to own a pony of my own; it was the dream of most country boys, just as now it is the dream of modern youth to own a car. But a beautiful palomino such as I'd just seen would be as unattainable to me as would a Rolls Royce to the boy of today.

Digger's Creek, where we lived, was a pretty spot, especially in spring, when all the cherry and apple trees were in blossom and the ground was a mass of golden buttercups and bluebells, and great frothy clusters of white clematis hid the ugliness of the abandoned mineshafts. Some of the families who lived there had come with the first miners at the turn of the century; others, like ours, drifted in after the Great War and, tired of chasing the golden myth, had struck their roots in that remote corner of New South Wales.

The morning after the drovers had passed I was helping Mum weed her garden before sunrise when old Ben Wall came riding by. He rested awhile and yarned to Mum. All the folks liked Ben and claimed that the white-haired bushman was the best horsebreaker and doctor in the State.

"Did you see the mob of cattle go by yesterday, Uncle Ben?" I asked. Most people called him Uncle, and I was bursting to tell him about the palomino.

"Yes, Ginge," he replied with a twinkle. "And wasn't she a beauty?" Then his face sobered as he continued, "I've had some good horses in my day but I've never seen one I'd love to own more'n that little filly. I went down to the drover's camp last night with some sneakin' hope of makin' a trade, an' who'd ya think was there tryin' t' buy her?"

"Curran Deen," I said.

Ben looked surprised. "Yes, Curran Deen. He almost got down on his knees and begged that drover to sell her to him, but I could see he didn't stand a chance. That character knows horseflesh too well. The hawker'd have more chance of buyin' his wife."

"Why'd Curran Deen want the pony so much, Uncle Ben?"

"Dunno, Ginge, but he sure wanted her awful bad. Strange cove, that Indian. Oh! An' I nearly forgot to tell ya, ya cow's down there aways, mixed up with the drover's herd. Ya better go fetch her. Some of these blokes ain't fussy what they pick up."

I left my older sister, Neta, to help Mum with the weeding and hurried off down the road to find Nancy, our cow, before they'd have time to collect their herd and move on. I passed the waggons and could hear San Singh humming a song and rummaging in his van. Curran Deen sat by his heap of cold, white ash. Neither his eyes nor lips moved when I called "Good morning." I hurried on.

Perhaps it was fate which guided me to where the accident had happened. The palomino lay there, trembling with pain, her broken foreleg twisted beneath her. The drover was lying with dust and blood on his face. I thought he must be dead, but as I crept up with thumping heart he sat up and spat blood, then rose unsteadily to his feet. When he realized what had happened, he cursed the snarl of rusted wire and the careless farmer who had thrown it into the bracken.

"Are you all right, mister?" I quavered.

"Me? Yeah, I'm all right, but look at me mare — busted, finished! The best bit of horseflesh I ever had, an' ta think I coulda sold her to that hawker. Me ol' dad allus tole me 'twas unlucky to refuse a good offer for a horse an' he was bloody well right." Then his face softened. " 'Twasn't your fault ol' girl," he said sadly. "I hate ta have ta do it, but I better go an' get me rifle an' put ya outa ya misery."

I understood the law of the bush, that it is kinder to kill an animal rather than let it linger in hopeless pain, yet I couldn't bear the thought of that beautiful creature being destroyed. But what could I do? Then I thought of Curran Deen, and somehow I felt sure that that strange, silent man had the power to save her.

Faster than the drover's legs could carry him to his rifle, my bare feet flew up the dusty road to the hawker's van. He was still sitting there, motionless as a man of stone.

When I sobbed out my story I saw a new Curran Deen. He barked orders to old Singh in their own tongue as he snatched up bandages and water, and in minutes we were on our way.

The veterinary skill of the hawker soon became apparent. As he worked on the palomino with deft, sure hands, the ghost of a smile hovered on his lips. The drover shrugged, saying, "Well, hawker, she's yours if ya can mend her leg, but I ain't ever seed a horse's leg mended yet."

Some of the spectators looked a question at Ben Wall. "Waal," he drawled, "it's damn hard to get a horse's leg to knit, 'specially if the flesh's torn. I on'y ever saw one horse mend, an' he always limped after, but I'll bet ya one thing, if this hawker cove can't mend her, no one can."

I stayed to help Curran Deen and when we were alone, he said, "We won't worry, will we, Ginge, if our little Indira limps a little?"

I wanted to ask him why he called her Indira, but somehow I thought I shouldn't. Anyhow, it was a nice name and suited the palomino.

Stout posts were erected, and with the help of San Singh the pony was suspended in a sling made from ropes and chaff bags. Curran Deen said she'd have to stay there until the leg was completely healed.

Day and night the hawker fed and nursed his pet and in the afternoons after school I was allowed to help. Our shared love for the crippled mare had erased the invisible barriers of race and time, and given birth to a friendship I would forever cherish.

Sometimes he would brush and groom Indira for hours, until her silver mane and tail shimmered like a lacy waterfall in sunlight, and her chestnut coat shone.

Never since have I met a man of such profound depth of thought who yet clung to so many quaint and simple beliefs as Curran Deen. He would spend hours explaining to me his philosophies of life, death and the transmigration of souls. He saw in birds and animals the likenesses of those who had passed on, and I knew that to him Indira was the re-embodiment of someone he had loved very dearly.

Sometimes I would sit by his campfire, cross-legged in imitation, and listen enthralled while he quoted poetry or narrated stories of his native India. Speaking softly and slowly, he seemed able to gather me into his thoughts, taking me back to childhood when he had played happily with his sister, whose name was — well I guessed, though he referred to her only as "my little sister".

Then with drawn, sad face, he would tell me of the great famine. He would become so intense at the terrible memory that I could plainly see the hovering vultures and the bodies which lay on the blistered earth staring up at the pitiless sky. I could also see a little boy who was Curran Deen, clinging to his mother. Both were crying pitifully and their tears were falling on the still form of a little girl whose eyes were enormously big and brown, like Indira's.

Seeing the distress on my face and the gathering storm of tears, his mood would change. He would pat me on the back and say, "Never mind, Ginge. Bruised petals must ever fall — but seeds fall with them so that the flowers will bloom again."

I think Curran Deen was as happy that spring and summer as his lonely heart could ever be and I was happy, too. I will never forget the first glad day I was allowed to ride Indira. How warm and soft her coat felt to my bare legs! Though she limped a little, her step was light; she moved with the grace of a ballerina and the bearing of a queen.

About a month later, the Indian asked me to ride the mare to school. He said that if she had constant work, carrying a light weight, her limp would gradually disappear.

How important I felt the first day I rode the golden palomino into the schoolyard! There were no more smart cracks from the kids about my ginger hair or patched trousers — just envious, admiring glances as they gathered around reverently to stroke her silken coat. All at once I had become a *somebody*.

Spring slipped away; the valley felt the hot breath of summer, turning the pasture brown and bringing red to the cheeks of the apples which burdened the branches with their abundance and gave off a marvellous, sweet-tangy odour.

Indira's limp had completely gone, but secretly I was worried. The hawkers had stayed overlong, and San Singh was growing restless. When they left, could I expect Curran Deen to leave Indira with me? I tried several times to ask him, but the words always seemed to stick because I was so terribly afraid of what his answer might be.

Then San Singh read in the Sydney papers that it was expected that rabbit skins would bring a record price in a few month's time. The shrewd old fox decided to stay till spring and buy pelts from the locals, so I was able to push my worries into the future. I spent all of my spare time with the hawkers.

Often a half smile quivered on Curran Deen's lips, like a ray of sunshine trying to penetrate clouds on a winter's day, but only once did I see it break right through, lighting his face with warm humour.

"Look, Curran Deen," I cried, "Indira's belly's wriggling." Then I had dropped my eyes, embarrassed, for all at once I knew. I should have known before. When I looked up he was really smiling.

"Yes, Ginge," he said softly. "We'll have to take good care of her now, won't we?"

We wondered whether her foal would be a colt or a filly, and whether it had been sired by a thoroughbred. Ben Wall hinted darkly that the mare had probably been stolen from some famous horse stud in the north of Queensland. After that I was always uneasy when the policeman rode by on patrol, and I knew the Indian was worried, too.

It was a bounteous season that year. Each time the small farms and gardens began to thirst, big, black, woolpack clouds would come rolling over the mountains, driven along by the rumbling wheels of thunder and the flicking whips of lighting; then down would patter the big, cool raindrops until the tanks were spurting from their downpipes and all the creeks and gullies hissed and foamed with the brown, rushing water.

The earth always smelt fresh and good after the storms. By the beginning of March, tall San Singh could scarcely reach the tops of the waving corn, and the apples and pears were bigger and smoother than I could ever remember.

Indira had grown heavy with foal and could no longer be ridden, but peacefully awaited her time dozing with the fat waggon horses.

Day after day the valley basked in autumn sunshine, unmarred by wind or cloud. But the flowers and trees seemed to know their time was short. The corn turned brown and set up a husky whispering, the willow leaves faded from green to gold and began to fall. Russet leaves floated from the apple boughs and farmers started to gather the ripened fruit and golden grain.

By the beginning of June the mornings were white with frost, the fur grew long and thick on the wild animals and prices for rabbit skins had risen sharply, beginning the great fur boom of the 'twenties. One day after school I took six of my dad's old rabbit-traps from the shed; when darkness had fallen my first trapline was strung, far up the valley, among the mounds of abandoned mineshafts.

Dawn broke clear and crisp, the valley floor glistening with frost; by the time I reached my trapline, a red-gold band of sunlight touched the jagged top of the western mountain. My bare toes stung as they crunched the needle ice on the journey to the traps among the mineshafts. I had only caught two rabbits, and foxes had robbed me of both. A pungent, foxy scent and a muddy circle spattered with blood and fur was all that was left. I could see they had been fully grown rabbits and I was furious, because San Singh would have given me sixpence each for their pelts. Glumly I turned for home, and it was then I heard strange sounds coming from an old mineshaft.

Creeping forward with thumping heart, I could see fresh, broken ground where something had fallen. Cautiously, I leant over and peered down. It took a little while to adjust my eyes to the shadowed depths; then I could see and hear something struggling, almost submerged in water some twenty feet below. My heart almost stopped beating, for light from the sky had reflected on two big eyes which looked up beseeching help. Then there was a whinny, and I knew it was Indira. In a second I was on my way, running as I'd never run in my life before.

I reached the waggons in a state of collapse. Curran Deen ran to meet me; as he held me up I tried to speak, but my lungs were fighting for oxygen. The hawker's eyes burnt into mine and read their message.

"Indira! Where?" I managed to gasp directions. Then the faces and vans began to spin, round and round, and I was lost in darkness. When I came to, my head was in Mum's lap and my sister Neta was sponging my face with a damp cloth.

Neighbours had gathered and Curran Deen was throwing coils of rope about his shoulders. The memory of Indira's plight flooded back. I jumped to my feet and started up the valley, ignoring Mum's protests and Singh's offer to carry me.

Pale June sunlight began to wash the flats and ridges, and the ground turned brown as the frost retreated, to climb the mountain in wispy wraiths and vanish in the blue sky.

We stood silent while San Singh, huge legs braced on two stout logs above the shaft, lowered Curran Deen as effortlessly as another man might lower an empty bucket.

We faintly heard the hawker's voice reassuring Indira as the rescue ropes were attached; then Singh was hauling him back. Over the lip of the bank Deen clawed his way, wet and muddied. I searched his face, dreading the confirmation of my fears. I might just as well have tried to read the countenance of a bronze Buddha.

We all moved closer, murmuring advice and trying to lend a hand on the rope. I watched Singh, fascinated at the display of steel-like muscles which flexed and rippled as he hauled the rope hand over hand, while the veins in his neck stiffened out like copper rods, and beads of perspiration trickled down his dark face.

Folk kept arriving, hoping to help in some way, for the story of the drover's horse had already become a legend and the sad-faced Curran Deen had found a spot in most of those hearts. Bare-footed children stood quietly behind the grown-ups, with no thought of mischief.

A cheer went up as the bedraggled animal cleared the shaft and was dragged to a grassy, level spot. Indira made one feeble attempt to rise, then groaned and lay still.

Deen worked rapidly, drying and massaging her stiffened limbs, while Singh kindled a blazing fire. No advice was offered; there was just a fatalistic shaking of heads.

I prayed for a miracle as Ben Wall placed a hand on the

muddied, swollen belly, lifted the wet, frozen legs and watched them fall like dead sticks. He felt her nose and lifted her eyelids, then slowly straightened and like the others shook his head.

It all seemed so hopeless. I began to cry; the tender arm of my sister, Neta, went about my shoulders, drawing me away. There were tears in Neta's eyes, too, as she said, "Come on, Ginge. You'll be l-l-late for school."

As we moved away, I heard old Ben say to Deen that they might attempt a Caesarean if the time was right; but of course that was beyond my understanding.

Vaguely I remember that long day, the silence of the schoolroom broken only by hushed whispers, creaking forms and the hurried scratch of the teacher's pen, and then the bursting flood of pent-up noise as boys and girls rushed through the lunch break. I sat apart, my thoughts on Indira and the Indian.

On my way home, a tide of shadow, spiced with impending frost, seeped up the valley. A cowbell tinkled somewhere beyond the willows. On the ridge a ploughman trudged behind his tired horse, and the evening sun flashed from the polished share as it rattled over loose stones. Weary after the long walk from school, I stood by our front gate. From inside came the subdued clatter of pots and the smell of fresh-baked bread.

Unseeing, my eyes rested on the neat, brown earthen beds where the flowers slept. For a long time I stood there and felt a coldness inside me that was not all due to the gathering frost; then I turned to stare up the valley. What was happening up there where that wisp of smoke curled skyward? And what was that bobbing down the path, indistinct and grotesque in the evening shadows?

It was closer, now. Someone slowly walking, and something which was not a dog trotting by his legs. Surely I must be dreaming?

But no. Curran Deen was speaking, and before my eyes a miracle seemed to have happened, for a miniature of Indira — a tiny palomino colt — was rubbing his soft, damp coat against my bare legs and hungrily nibbling my fingers with silken lips.

"He's yours, Ginge," the hawker was saying in a tired voice. "Lucky you have a cow in milk. He'll soon grow big and strong. Be kind to him, boy." He rested his hand on my shoulder.

Mute with emotion, I stood nodding and rubbing one bare foot against the other. Then Neta was there all starry-eyed and smelling of lavender. "Oh, you sweet, helpless little thing!" She gathered the golden waif in her arms and told Curran Deen all the things I should have said. But I knew he understood my silence, for he reached out and touched my cheek before he turned and vanished into the twilight shadows.

With morning came the prick of conscience. I was calmer now and knew I must go and thank my friend for the greatest gift I'd ever received. But I was too late. The white ash heaps were almost cold; where the waggons had stood the frosted ground was scuffed with hoofprints and two sets of tyre tracks pointed west. The hawkers were gone, and though I didn't know it then, they, like the old prospectors, were never to return.

The dreamy years have drifted away, and the golden palomino colt sleeps now by the weeping willows where the waggons once stood. His sons, and their colts — all golden palominos — have made our little valley quite famous, and the memory of Indira and Curran Deen lingers as fresh as the morning.

Second Growth

Helen Wilson

When Greta Tavistock was sixteen she went for a walk one night late in summer, along the river to her cousins' place. She took a short cut through the Skoglies' vineyard, remembering how her brother Vernon had made a joke of the whole thing, selling part of their property to the immigrant family to pay off his own indebtedness incurred as racing car driver and playboy generally.

"I must say I don't envy you your new neighbours, Father. They say these people have hordes of children. Live off the smell of an oil rag."

She had laughed with him then, especially at the odd-sounding name. She knew now that the Skoglies did not have hordes of children but only three. The eldest was a boy, Petrich, no older than herself. They had no mother. The war had taken her, they had said when questioned, their faces dark and closed.

Greta paused a moment, watching the reflections of white moonlight brilliant on the water. From where she stood, she could not see the wooden cottage the Skoglies had built, but the vineyard stretched all around her, scrupulously tended. She had heard the family was up at dawn, ploughing, planting the vines, tying them up, cincturing, watching the bunches form, scanning the sky for unseasonal rain, examining the grapes for signs of black spot or other diseases. How carefully they looked after them. Her brothers used to laugh, averting their eyes from their own neglected acres.

At first she had joined them, but, watching the newcomers at work, from behind her own boundary hedge, she'd found herself thinking: It's as though they love the vines and know each bunch by name. And wondered how it would be to feel that. Then she would shrug and try to forget them.

Now, as she walked, her eyes noted the enormous bunches

of black grapes. Each grape was nearly the size of a plum. She fingered one. It came loose in her hand: smooth, luscious, and covered with a kind of pearly bloom which may have been dew or a slight touch of early frost. She licked the cool skin with the tip of her tongue. Then her mouth watered and she took the grape between her teeth. As she crushed it, the juice flowed like nectar and a drop trickled down her chin.

Not room temperature, she thought, but moon temperature; and laughed with sudden abandon.

She looked up and there was Petrich watching her.

He did not speak, just stood there, an untidy, hulking shadow among his vines. He wore a drab, open-necked shirt and trousers that hung frayed below his knees. His dark hair was jagged too, across the paleness of his forehead. A flash of white showed where his shirt opened across his broad chest.

Still he did not speak.

"Your grapes looked so perfect . . . " she stammered. "I couldn't resist tasting. I hope you don't mind?"

He stared at her in silence for so long she grew more nervous and began to move away.

"Don't go." His accent was heavy, but he spoke far better English than the others.

She paused and half-turned.

He moved a step closer.

"Your hair is a flame. In my country the women are dark . . . Many times I watch you as I work in the vineyards when you pass along the road. Your hair is fire, even in the sun."

She could think of nothing to say.

"I must go . . . my cousins will be expecting me." Then, in a rush of girlish snobbery for which she instantly despised herself: "Once my family owned all this land for twenty miles along the river."

"Twenty miles?" He was amazed. "My father has only these few acres. We are all very happy . . . proud."

"But you can't make a living on so little!" she exclaimed with youthful candour.

"Back home we had only half an acre. On rock. We had to carry up the earth in baskets to build the terraces. Everywhere a vine would cling, we built it up."

Half an acre. As big as the area they called their "home" paddock, which contained a tennis court and a pretence of a kitchen garden. Half an acre.

"Your grapes are marvellous," she told him, wiping her mouth with the back of her hand.

"You are welcome." He spoke the words awkwardly, seriously, as though he'd learnt them from a travel phrase book. She felt fruition in the crumbling furrows under her feet, in the rows of vines with their burden of grapes gleaming as the shafts of moonlight discovered them. All the blood in her body seemed to race along her veins as he came nearer, picked an even larger grape and held it to her lips.

"Taste," he told her.

She opened her lips and felt the skin-smooth grape, cold and nectar-sweet, against her teeth. She stared up into his dark eyes and the moonlight was caught in them, too. Or was it the stars, with their sharp, bright, twinkling points?

She could smell the earth on him and the sweat of the day's work, and the juice of the grape trickling down her chin.

Then she was running, running over the uneven ground, without a backward look.

She'd never spoken to him again. Now and then she had glimpsed him among his vines, working, always working; while she and her brothers drove their cars into the city and their father grew too old and weak to be bothered with the running of his property.

When she was twenty she went overseas with some friends, and it was while she was away her father died.

"He left us nothing but debts," wrote her brother Vernon. "To get in the clear we decided to sell the old place. We knew you couldn't care less and it will give you some ready cash to keep you in your old age."

It was not until then that she realized how much she had cared for the home where she'd grown up. But her brother had been right . . . Selling it was the only sensible thing to do. She wrote briefly, and after a long while received an equally brief reply:

"You'll never guess who bought the old place, Greta! The Skoglies! Paid cash, too. Trust those peasants always to have a pretty sum tied up in an old stocking somewhere . . . "

And months later: "Went out to pick up some of my gear. The Skoglies have moved in . . . and I mean moved in. They've turned the side veranda into a car port for their old runabout and tractor. And, just what you'd expect, they've cut down the oaks. The old man swore he needed the ground to plant more vines. What d'you know about that! What peasants! Don't come back, Greta. It'd break your heart. I remember how you loved the oaks."

Yet she had come back, years later. True, she had loved the oaks, but she'd done nothing to keep them. None of them had. But to cut them down . . . just for a few miserable vines! She had to look at the desecration, just to satisfy herself, to feed her waning hate for the Skoglies who had done this thing. Then she would never come again.

So now she turned the last bend in the road from where she'd always first glimpsed the mellow brick walls of the old homestead between the great oaks. She stopped the car.

There were no oaks. But there were other trees, tall lemon-scented gums nearly as big as the oaks, with their silver-pink limbs as smooth as a girl's: up, up to the foliage whose leaves never left the tree bare, but always tossed against the blue sky, veiling its naked beauty from the sun. This was their country, their land and they knew it in the fierce pride of their heritage.

Greta Tavistock sat still, looking, unaware that tears were running down her cheeks; unaware that a tall thickset man had turned out of the vineyard and was coming towards her.

"You are sad because of the oaks?" Peter Skoglie asked without preamble. Not waiting for a reply he went on: "You must forgive my father. Remember, once he had only half an acre from which to feed his family."

It was as though the years had never been.

"Yes," she said, winking away the tears. "Half an acre of rock."

A smile lit the big man's sombre face.

"I knew you would be sad. So when he had gone. I planted the gum trees. It is good you have seen them."

"They're lovely," she heard herself saying: and, though it was mid-afternoon, she felt as though it were moonlight

again and the blood was racing through her veins. Although
the homestead looked different, it was neat and clean, yet
the imprint of an alien hand was upon it. Beyond it the once
bedraggled vines reached up nearly the height of a man, not
this man she thought; and the furrows ran neat and straight,
without a weed showing, nor a gap in the rows. There was a
new drying shed, with sultanas and currants on wire racks
and the smell of fermenting grapes everywhere.

"Your father is dead?" she asked to change the subject.

"Ten years ago. The vines were stricken with phylloxera
— it was too much for him. He refused to pull them out; and
shot himself. My sister is married. My brother found there
were easier ways of earning a living." He smiled faintly.

"I guess he was right." Greta wrinkled her forehead,
thinking back over the years. "I remember my own brother
was always complaining about not enough rain, rain at the
wrong time, too much rain . . . or frost . . . or black spot.
And too much hard work."

They both laughed.

"If you hold on," observed Petrich quietly, "things come
round your way. When phylloxera struck our vines, my
father thought we were finished. After his death, I took out
all the old European vines and replanted with young
American stock grafted vines. My countrymen told me I was
crazy. The first five years . . . " he paused and shrugged,
his face grim. "But after that, things were good for me."

"You've changed," she wondered, looking at him. "When
you first came to settle here, I was afraid. You looked like
people from another world."

"That was true. From a world of war and riot, of back-
breaking work and never enough to eat. A world you people
do not know."

She spoke swiftly. "How could we know — so far away
from the world? But when I went to Europe, the Mediterranean which I had only read of as a glittering playground for
the rich . . . I saw the little vineyards perched on the
mountain sides, terrace on terrace, just like you said. And I
was ashamed."

"People judge harshly when they do not know. Always it
is so. But would you like to see around? The property has

changed, too. It is now fifty acres. My cousins help me work it. Gradually I am specializing. On that ten acres of un-blended red clay I grow my Shiraz. You must try some later. The bouquet is to be remembered — almond, cedar, flower perfume and berry all combining. Some things you cannot explain . . . only experience."

They turned into a vineyard so orderly that it looked regimented. She listened half in a trance, as he explained they were passing rows of Black Shiraz, Cabernet Sauvignon, White Hermitage, Marsanne . . . how had this peasant boy become an expert?

He smiled down at her, guessing her thoughts.

"I saved. I went to night school. One can do a lot in sixteen years. Once a year I visited some famous winery. There was one, in a valley . . . two homes on the edge of a lake . . . an old cellar. I told myself: one day I shall have this too, with little boys sailing their boats on the water and . . . "

"You are married then?" she asked quickly. Then turned away.

"No." His sombre face lit. "I waited. I knew you would come. But now you must see my cellar. I carted big slabs of slate from an abandoned winery and made fermenting tanks myself. That tower . . . " he looked embarrassed . . . "it is what you would call an affectation . . . a folly. One such I saw in another State — it made me think of some of the for-gotten little castles in my own homeland. But I was foolish. You cannot transplant one country to another! Nor should you wish to. One day I shall pull it down."

"Oh, no. Please leave it there. I like it . . . "

"So?"

They went together into the large cellars where the wine was racked into oak storage casks from ten gallons upwards. There was a lovely musty wine and wood smell and the place was dim and cool.

The man gestured towards the casks.

"My father was a craftsman . . . I persuaded him to make casks and leave the pruning to me. His hand was too heavy. Some men are born pruners: there has to be a special feeling. But see . . . there are your oaks. They are not chopped up and burned as you expected."

Greta's face lit up. She crossed the floor and ran her fingers lightly over the sides of one of the thousand gallon giants.

"How beautiful . . . " Her voice was low and husky.

He went to a small recessed cupboard and took from it a bottle of wine and two glasses. With concentration he poured in each a portion of Black Shiraz, a lovely dark red, shading almost into purple.

She took the glass and raised it to her lips. The exquisite bouquet was like incense. She turned to the man watching.

"To the oaks," she said and they drank.

Outside the avenue of trees swayed towards each other, whispering and rustling as the breeze came up from the river.

Hostages

Fay Zwicky

I think I began to hate when I was twelve. Consciously, I mean. The war was then in its fourth year, there was no chocolate and my father was still away in Borneo. I barely knew him. Till then I had learnt to admire what my mother believed to be admirable. Striving to please with ascetic rigour, I practised scales and read Greek myths. Morality hinged on hours of piano practice achieved or neglected. I knew no evil. The uncommon neutrality of my existence as a musical child in wartime was secured in a world neither good nor malevolent. My place among men was given. Did I have feelings? I was not ready to admit them for there seemed to be rules governing their revelation which I either could not or would not grasp. Nameless, passionless, and without daring I repressed deepest candour. But *tout comprendre c'est tout pardonner*; what was once self-indulgence is now permissible revelation. Why, then, should shame crimp the edge of my reflection so many years after the event?

It all started with the weekly visit to our house of a German refugee piano teacher, Sophie Lindauer-Grunberg. Poor fat sentimental Sophie, grateful recipient of my mother's pity. I was to be her first Australian pupil.

"But why me?"

"Because she needs help. She has nothing and you, thank God, have everything. She's been a very fine musician in her own country. You have to understand that this is someone who has lost everything. Yes, you can roll your eyes. *Everything*, I said. Something I hope, please God, will never happen to you. So you'll be nice to her and pay attention to what she says. I've told Mr Grover he lives too far away for me to go on taking you to lessons twice a week."

Suddenly dull and bumbling Mr Grover in his music room smelling of tobacco and hair oil seemed like my last contact with the outside world. I was to be corralled into the tight, airless circle of maternal philanthropy.

The day of my first lesson a hot north wind was tearing at the huge gum in front of the house. Blinds and curtains were drawn against the promised heat. The house stood girded like an island under siege. My younger brother and sister had gone swimming. I watched them go, screwing up my eyes with the beginnings of a headache, envying their laughter and the way they tore sprigs off the lantana plants lining the driveway. I awaited my teacher, a recalcitrant hostage. The rooms were generous and high-ceilinged but I prowled about, tight-lipped, seeking yet more room. A deep nerve of anger throbbed in me and I prayed that she would not come. But she came. Slowly up the brick path in the heat. I watched her from the window, measuring her heavy step with my uneasy breath. Then my mother's voice greeting her in the hallway, high-pitched and over-articulated as if her listener were deaf, a standard affectation of hers with foreign visitors. "Terrible day . . . trouble finding the house . . . Helen looking forward so much . . . " I ran to the bathroom and turned on the tap hard. I just let it run, catching sight of my face in the mirror above the basin.

Could I be called pretty? Brown hair hanging long on either side of high cheekbones, the hint of a powerful nose to come, a chin too long, cold grey eyes, wide mouth, fresh colour. No, not pretty. No heroine either. A wave of self-pity compensated me for what I saw and tears filled my eyes. Why me? Because she has to have pupils. Am I such a prize? No, but a Jew who has everything. "Be thankful you were born in this wonderful country." My mother's voice sounded loud in my ears. "They're making them into lampshades over there." I had laughed but shrank from the grotesque absurdity of the statement. Why the dramatics? All I remember is the enveloping anger directed at everything my life had been and was. I wanted to be left alone but didn't know how or where to begin. "She has lost her whole family. Taken away and shot before her eyes . . . " So? Now she has me.

My mother and Miss Grunberg were talking about me as I stood in the doorway. My own hands were clammy as I moved forward to the outstretched unfamiliar gesture. Hers were small, fat and very white, surprisingly small for such a tall, heavily built woman, like soft snuggling grubs. She herself looked like some swollen, pale grub smiling widely and kindly, a spinster of nearly sixty. Her little eyes gleamed through thick, round spectacles. On the skin beneath her eyes tiny bluish vessels spread their nets.

"So here is *unsere liebe Helene*!"

I raised my eyebrows insolently as the girls did at school after one of my own ill-judged observations. It was essential to the code governing the treatment of victims. But this time I had the upper hand and didn't know how to handle my advantage. The cobbles of Köln and Cracow rang hollow under my boots. The light from the pink shaded lamp fell on my new teacher. The wind blew in sharp gusts outside.

"Helen, this is Miss Grunberg." My mother with a sharp look in my direction. "I've been telling her about the work you've done so far with Mr Grover. Miss Grunberg would like you to have another book of studies." .

"Perhaps you will play *ein Stück* for me. Liszt perhaps?" She nodded ponderously at our Bechstein grand that suddenly took on the semblance of some monstrous piece of abstract statuary, out of all proportion to the scale of the room. "Lord no. I've never done him." I fell into uncharacteristic breeziness. "I'm not really in practice. Hardly anything going at the moment and I'm pretty stale on the stuff Grover had me on for the exams." Deliberately fast, consciously idiomatic, enjoying, yes, *enjoying* the strain of comprehension on my victim's round, perpetually smiling face. "You can *still* play those Debussy 'Arabesques'," said my mother, her neck flushed. "I put the music on the piano," and she gave me yet another warning look.

I opened the lid noisily and sat down with elaborate movements, shifting the metronome a few inches to the right, altering the position of the stand, bending to examine my feet fumbling between the pedals. The "Arabesques" moved perfunctorily. I kept my face impassive, looked rigidly ahead at the music which I didn't see. Even during the section I liked in the second piece, a part where normally I would lean back a little and smile. I had begun to learn how not to please. But the process of self-annihilation involved the destruction of others. *Tout pardonner* did I say?

Miss Grunberg arranged with my mother to return the following week at the same time. "Why are you behaving like this?" asked my mother, red and angry with me after she had left in a taxi. The young blond driver had tapped his foot noisily on the brick path as Miss Grunberg profusely repeated her gratitude to my mother for the privilege of teaching her talented daughter. Moving rapidly away from them I conversed with him, broadening my vowels like sharks' teeth on the subject of the noon temperature. I was desperate that the coveted outside world and its tranquil normality should recognize that I was in no way linked with the heavy foreign accent involved in demonstrative leave-taking on our front lawn.

"Behaving like what?"

"You know what I mean. You behaved abominably to that poor woman."

"I played for her, didn't I?" She came closer to me with a vengeful mouth.

"You could call it that. I don't know what's got into you lately. You used to be such a good child. Now you know the answers to everything. A walking miracle! What terrible things have we done, your father and I, that you should behave like a pig to a woman like that? We've given you everything. *Everything!* And because I'm good to an unfortunate refugee who needs help wherever she can find it, you have to behave like that! I'm sorry for you, *really* sorry for you!"

"Spare your sympathy for the poor reffos!" The taxi driver's word burst savagely out of my mouth. She flew at me and slapped me across the face with her outstretched hand.

"One thing I do know," she was trembling with rage, "the one thing I'm sure of is that I've been too good to you. We've given you too much. You're spoilt rotten! And *one* day, my girl, one day you too may be old and unwanted and . . ."

"A lampshade perhaps? So what." I shook with guilt and fear at the enormity of what I'd said, terrified of the holocaust I'd shaken loose and my mother's twisted mouth. But the revolution didn't get under way either that day

or that year. The heroine lacked (should one say it?) courage.
Sealed trains are more comforting than the unknown wastes
of the steppes. The following week Miss Grunberg toiled up
our front path and I sat down to the new course of Moscheles
studies and a movement of a Mozart concerto. *Her* music.
Scored heavily in red pencil, the loved and hated language
dotted with emotional exclamation marks. Her life's work
put out for my ruthless inspection. She moved her chair
closer to my stool to alter the position of my right hand.
"Finger *rund, Kleine*, always *rund*. Hold always the wrist
supple, *liebe Helene.*" I shrank from the alien endearment
and her sour breath but curved my fingers, tight and deliberate. Her smell hung over me, a static haze in the dry air.
Musty, pungent and stale, the last faint reminder of an airless
Munich apartment house. Her dress, of cheap silky fabric,
rustled when she moved her heavy body. Breathing laboriously
she tried to explain to me what I should do with the Mozart.
She couldn't get used to the heat of the new country and was
beginning to find walking difficult. But I didn't practise
between her visits and gave only spasmodic attention to her
gentle directions. I was shutting myself off from words and
from music, beginning a long course in alienation. I seldom
looked my mother in the eye in those days. I quarrelled
bitterly with my sister, ignored my brother.

About six months after my lessons with Miss Grunberg
started I was not much further advanced. I spent a lot of time
reading in my room or just looking out of the window at the
garden which was now bare. Squalls lashed the gumtree and
drove the leaves from the weeping elm skittering across the
grass. Miss Grunberg now had several pupils amongst the
children of the Jewish community and even one or two
gentiles from the neighbouring school. She lived in a very
poorly furnished flat in a run-down outer suburb. She still
travelled to her pupils' homes. Her breathing had become
very short in the last few weeks. Inattentive and isolated as I
was, I had noticed that she was even paler than usual.

My mother one day told me with some rancour how well
the Lapin girl was doing with the piano. "She never had
your talent but what a worker! She's going to give a recital
in the Assembly Hall next month." I merely shrugged. The

boots of the conqueror were no picnic. She was welcome to them. "And while I'm about it, I've decided to tell Miss Grunberg not to come any more. I don't feel there's much point as you seem quite determined to do as little with music as possible. I've done all *I* can. At least she's on her feet now." On her feet! Oh God! But I replied, "That's all right with me" in as neutral a voice as I could summon.

But that night I ground my face into the covers of my bed, no longer a place of warmth and security but a burial trench. At the mercy of my dreams appeared Sophie Lindauer-Grunberg, pale as brick dust. Her face wasting, crumbling to ash, blasted by the force of my terrible youth. And, waking in fright, I mourned for the first time my innocent victim and our shared fate.

A Slipper for Adriana

Joan M. Bean

The front door of the two-storey terrace house stood open, propped in place by the black cat doorstop Mickey's mother had bought at the last fete. He clattered into the dim coolness of the hallway and chucked his schoolcase into his room as he passed on the way to the kitchen.

Molly Donnelly selected another apple and continued grating the fruit as the boy perched on the high stool. Her body wobbled like a large floral jelly and her mane of permed blonde hair flopped up and down in time with the rhythmic movements of her hands. Mickey grinned at her and pounced on the apple cores. She wiped her hands on her dress and took a tin from the drawer next to the sink.

"I want you to go to the chows and get four pieces of bream and some chips."

"Okay." The boy grudgingly took the money. He wiped his forehead. Molly noticed and smiled.

"All right. Buy yourself a drink if you're that hot. Only don't take all day. Your Dad's comin' home early and we're goin' to the trots."

She gave him a push and a playful slap on the behind. Sure in a good mood, Mickey thought. He skidded along the hall, discarding his sweat-dampened shirt and footwear as he went.

Summer pressed the smell of wool and tar and industry heavily down on Ultimo as Mickey turned into the street again. The narrow thoroughfare hunched its shoulders against Harris Street and its flanks slid in a steep dive towards Wentworth Park.

Mickey paused and gazed raptly at Adriana's house. It stood out like a pink and green and lemon frosted cake in a row of brown, flaking buns. The boy thought it was a terrific house. He could see no reason for his father's surly comments about wogs mucking up the street with their weird colour schemes.

Mickey was not quite sure what wogs were, but he knew they came from queer places like Italy and Greece. Adriana didn't seem very different from the other kids, except for the fact that her mother cooked food with an erky smell. Sometimes Mickey wondered if his Dad liked anyone much, even Mum.

He bought the fish and chips and went to the milk bar. For a moment he weakened as he stared into the deep freeze unit with its array of iced goodies. With a sigh of renunciation he turned to the machine that dispensed miniature plastic gifts of dice, slippers, goblets and other charms, each enclosed in a tiny transparent plastic bubble that you could open with a twist of the hand. He put his coin in the slot and the machine dropped a slipper into his hand. Outside the shop he admired the bauble.

"Howya, Gutless!" Mickey jumped as Ecker Wright's hand fell heavily onto his shoulder. "Got any cash?"

"Nah. Jest spent it on me old man's tea."

Mickey trembled. He wished he did have some money. Ecker forced him against the wall and rifled the pockets of his shorts. The older boy was much taller and he was very proud of the faint dark fuzz above his upper lip. He wanted to be a pug and he got in a bit of practice every now and then on the smaller boys. Mickey had felt those solid fists more than once.

"Gis a few chips then."

Ecker grabbed the parcel. Mickey followed him into the lane, whinging. Ecker carefully unwrapped the chips and scooped out a handful. The smell was too much. Mickey's righteous anger waned.

"Gimme some too, Ecker." The older boy complied, then he re-wrapped the parcel, making sure every crease was in the right place and the two perched on a garbage can and ate their illegal booty with relish.

As Mickey rounded the corner again he drew in his breath and held it until he nearly exploded. Adriana was coming through the plastic strip curtain on the milk bar doorway. The boy forgot the clang of passing trucks and buses. He stood as though impaled on the iron railing of the house next to the shop, one skinny leg tucked stork-like against the other, as the dark-haired girl approached.

Adriana smiled at him and her honey-tan face shone with pleasure. She bent forward against the weight of an old stroller carrying a fat baby in the seat and a hump of groceries on the hood. Another plump little boy clung to the side of the stroller, waddling and protesting at the pace.

"Hi, Adriana," Mickey croaked, hoping to sound offhand.

"Hello, Mickey."

The girl's voice was soft and her look so bright and unself-conscious that he lowered his head in confusion. He noticed a blister on the hot asphalt and he worried it with his toe until a burst of tar oozed out. He started to write Adriana's initials with it and a hundred nerves chased their tails around in his stomach. He felt queer, really queer.

"Are you going swimming tomorrow?" Adriana asked. Mickey looked all hot and red.

"Uh — Yeah. Might." His fingers tightened on the plastic bubble. I like you, Adriana. The words roared around in his head, but they got no further.

"See ya tomorrer then. Here." Mickey thrust the bubble into Adriana's hand and was around the corner and halfway home before the little girl recovered from her surprise.

Taking the slipper from its covering, she turned it this way and that and the anodized gilding put on a brave show, glinting in the sunlight. Adriana smiled dreamily. She slipped the gift into the pocket of her shift and there was a promise of womanhood in the swing of her hips as she moved off.

Mickey thumped the parcel on the table and Molly stared at him appraisingly. "Let me smell your breath."

She seized him and he closed his lips tightly against the treacherous smell of potatoes and vinegar.

"You been into them chips again, haven't you?"

The boy squirmed, waiting for the blow that would knock him silly. Instead, his mother released him. Her face had softened. The lines around her eyes did not look so deep and a shy smile nudged the disillusionment from the corners of her mouth. Molly ratted through the contents of the old stained dresser and extracted a photograph. Mickey recognized his mother. Only just, though. The wiry man in the sailor's rig was his father, but he didn't look much like that now.

Molly put her arm around her son.

"You know what today is, Mick? Our wedding anniversary, your Dad's and mine. They took that picture at the Katoomba Lookout when we was on our honeymoon."

She was twenty years removed from him, her eyes on misty blue valleys, a young girl clutching a mountain devil doll in one hand and a brand new, excitingly aggressive husband with the other.

Mickey shifted uncomfortably, his body stiff against the encircling arm. He was used to his mother's sudden anger and her brusque gestures of affection, quickly withdrawn as though she was ashamed of her weakness. She was different today and he didn't know what to make of it. Mumbling an excuse, he escaped to the sitting room and the more predictable world of the television spacemen.

Molly watched him go with an expression of yearning on her tired face, then she took the newspaper and a stub of pencil and began making her selections for the trots. Later she glanced at the clock.

"Hey, Mickey. Hop up to the pub and tell your Dad his tea's ready. I don't know. He promised he'd be home early today . . ."

Mickey did not wait to hear the end of his mother's complaint. He paused outside the fawn and green facade of the hotel with its advertisements of burly footballers preferring special brands of DA or Bitter. Gathering courage, he sidled into the bar, ducking under bare arms and dodging frothing mugs in transit.

Bill Donnelly fronted the bar counter in a school of ten mates. A barricade of glasses separated the drinkers from the barmaid. Mickey came up for air near Donnelly's stomach, which lapped over his belt in a generous wave. His father's face was florid above the hairy chest. As the child delivered his message to the chorus of good-natured ribbing from the school Donnelly's face darkened. Mouthing an oath, he sent Mickey sprawling. The boy got out in a hurry.

Molly was dressed to go out by the time Donnelly lumbered home. The reek of stale beer beat him in. Mickey backed apprehensively as his father's bulk filled the doorway. The fat-blurred contours of his face were ugly, menacing.

Stolidly, Molly placed his food on the table. The fish and chips had shrivelled and the peas were hard, dark marbles.

"You stupid bitch! What's the idea of makin' a fool of me in front of me mates? Sendin' the kid t' drag me home. Me!" He thumped his chest in outrage.

"It's our anniversary, Bill. I wouldn't of done it but for that. You said . . . "

"I'll teach you to keep tabs on me!"

Donnelly unleashed a backhander that slammed his wife against the sink. Molly righted herself, eyes blazing. She picked the plate up and let him have it. Donnelly blocked it with his forearm and food sprayed in all directions. Mickey crawled under the table, slipping on the squashed chips, and edged his way to the door. As he bolted, the sounds of abuse and breaking crockery followed him.

With his heart pounding furiously, he reached the demolition site and squatted down amongst the ruins to catch his breath. Only a few walls remained of the row of terraces that had stood there, chequered by the coloured geometrical shapes that had been rooms and stairways. They looked sad, like people caught without all of their clothes on. One of the walls reminded Mickey of his own house and a chill ran through him.

He had learned to ride out the storms, but he knew that one of these days he would get home to find Mum splattered all over the place. Like Mrs Carney had been when old Carney chased her down the front steps and bashed her over the head with a hammer before anyone could stop him. They said she had a boy friend, but Mickey found that hard to believe. She was as old as his Mum.

The boy heard the sound of voices and the thump of a football. It was Ecker and his cronies. Feeling safe after the friendly episode of the chips, Mickey emerged to join the rough and tumble.

"Hey, look who's comin'. It's one of them Eyetie kids. Get outa sight," Ecker hissed and the boys ducked behind the walls.

Mickey went cold. Adriana was taking a shortcut across

the lot. This time she carried the baby. Concentrating on her
footwork, she had not seen the boys.

Mickey crouched next to Ecker, wondering what he was
going to do. There was a look of anticipation on the older
boy's face that he did not like. Ecker held his hand up like
a general and the troops leapt out, surrounding the girl.

"Wog, Wog."

"How about some spag, Ag!"

Adriana panicked. She tried to run, but at every turn she
met a barrage of jeers and grasping hands. Twisting away
from Ecker, she fell heavily, bumping the baby. It screamed
in fear. Mickey stood at the back of the group, paralyzed and
shaking as a heavy weight bore down on him, preventing the
forward movement he wanted to make. He felt the sweat
running down the insides of his arms.

Ecker tried to pull the girl to her feet. The flimsy shift
ripped at the shoulder and Adriana screamed hysterically.
Ecker dropped his hand and uneasily motioned to the boys
to stand back. They had quietened, taking the cue from their
leader. Adriana's shocked stare focused on Mickey. He saw
the depth of the hurt in her eyes and he stood scuffing his
foot against a stone, not daring to look up again.

"Now look here, Sis. We were just havin' a bit of fun. It
was a joke, see?" Ecker was scared they'd gone too far, but
he wasn't going to let this little spag eater know that. "If
your old woman asks what happened you tell her you fell
over. Understand?" Ecker injected a lot of venom into his
voice.

Adriana hugged the baby. She looked up at the ring of
hard young faces and decided that the big one meant what he
had said. She nodded voicelessly. The circle broke. Adriana
rose without looking at Mickey and started towards the
street, limping on one injured leg and stumbling on the
rubble. Mickey ran after her. She heard him coming and
turned. Fumbling in her pocket, she found the gift he had
given her. Her voice was a wail and he didn't understand a
word she said as she hurled the thing at him.

The plastic bubble broke open on impact and the silver
slipper fell down between some broken bricks and was lost.
Mickey did not look for it nor did he follow Adriana this

time. When she was well ahead he made his own way home.

He knocked on the closed front door, but there was no answer. He tried the sitting room window. It gave and he climbed in.

"Mum."

The boy walked slowly to the kitchen, his feet squeaking on the lino in the unaccustomed quietness. The room was a mess. Broken crockery littered the sink. Drawers had been pulled out and their contents carelessly stuffed back in. Mickey's throat constricted as he saw the blood-smudged rag that protruded from the pedal bin. He raced upstairs to his parents' bedroom and tore the wardrobe door open. His mother's best handbag and his father's sports coat and trousers were missing. Bill Donnelly's working clothes made an untidy heap on the bed.

The boy sagged with relief. They must have made it up. Again. For a while, anyway. He looked around the house, but there was no note for him. He guessed they had not even thought about him before they had gone out.

Mickey wandered into the sitting room. Inside his chest was a great wad of pain. He picked the television programme up, then put it down again without reading it. The set stared at him, a grey uncomforting rectangle of nothing.

Mickey thought about Adriana and how he'd been too yellow to stop Ecker from knocking her around. He wondered if she would go to the pool tomorrow. He knew that he would not. Then the boy lay down and cried his shame and loneliness into the musty cushion of the settee, and it grew dark outside.

"The Black"

Michael George Smith

She sits in the bus shelter squinting along the quivering black ribbon of bitumen, grumpily searching out the bus. A little apart from her along the bench, a woman fretfully pushes a stroller, her baby noisily dribbling back and forth. The old woman looks strange to the young mother. She feels a little uncomfortable near her. She is impatient for the bus. It will ease the tension. Barely noticing the young woman, the old one sits silent, her chubby fingers pushing at a gold band. It is very hot.

The shelter, four slabs of prefabricated concrete spattered haphazardly with stones — the "natural" look — sits precariously functional by the roadside. It does not give much relief. It does not stop the wind. It seems out of place here, in this flat land. There is a hot Northerly coming down from the Centre, funnelled down unimpeded along the Flinders Ranges, blustery and relentless. It whips hot into their faces in fitful spasms. Overhead an oppressive sun glares down, unremitting in a dazzle of translucent blue sky. There always seems to be more sky here. The air is thick with the weight of it. It seems inescapable.

The hills behind them are low, the land before flat, formless, covered in low, red-brick houses mindlessly repeating themselves into the distance. The wheat fields are slipping quietly under fresh outcrops of suburban sprawl. There is a hiss of sprinklers.

From beneath her scarf, a stream of sweat discovers a path among the deep-carved creases of the old woman's face and trickles downward. She is having difficulty breathing in this heat. She is wearing the black; scarf, jumper, blouse, skirt, shoes and stockings, all black, clinging oppressively to her old body. She, resigned, stubbornly clings to them. It is the way. All her days now wear the same cloth, will do so because they must. It has always been so. It is witness to her meaning.

A memory flickers into mind. Seems all now is memory, or simply habit. The days merely pass as background; cluttering trivialities. Costa had always hated the black. He would say of the old women of home who surrendered unquestioning that they were already dead, mere wizened kernels wrapped in funereal mantles of memory. They showed no care for life. They wore their black like stigmata, cocoons of silent faith in eternal bondage. They seemed almost malevolent in the intensity of their self-imposed confines, malicious and gossiping, as if resentful of living; of the living. Costa was for living. The old ways only stifled. He would have a new life far from these calcified shells of blackness that seemed to deny life. He would educate himself and leave behind the old ways. In Australia, he would say, life could be different. There were no old ways and no demands on the living by the dead. There all were for life — new ways and a new start. They could *be* somebody. The world was changing. He would have his family change with it.

There had been many in black after the war. So many. The women, the young with the old, who were left slowly moved towards their dead. So it must be. It had always been so. Change had come and taken away their centres. Now, there were only husks of black.

He had even made a fuss when she had gone into black for her mother, her now long dead, long unseen mother. She had died in the village she had been born in, had never left, would never leave. Her daughter had not seen her die. She felt cheated. She felt guilty for having let her mother die so far away, unseen. Costa said he was sorry but then she was old and must die some time. He had respected her (had really half feared the old woman, sternly in black even then, when he had first asked for her daughter's hand, so long ago), had cared about the old woman for his wife's sake. But he would not have the black. It made him uncomfortable.

The daughter had wept for months, had wept often since; would suddenly stop doing her chores and sob uncontrollably to herself. Her husband would seem so heartless. She was afraid for him, his disrespect was almost blasphemous. Her mother had died, unseen, so very far from her. She *must* be mourned properly, as was her right, could he not see? It was always so, had always been so.

But then he was her husband. The wife had taken off the black after a few months, had clung to it long enough for decency, still black inside. For Costa's sake. Now she was in black again. Had been for five years. Would be till death. For Costa. No one, nothing could change that. There could be no more changing now.

The old woman takes her handkerchief and wipes the sweat from her eyes. Everything around is very bright, the glare almost unbearable. Her old eyes blink quickly. Near her, the young mother, grumpy, wipes her fretful child's face. She sees the mother turn her face towards her. The old woman quickly looks away. She does not want to talk. There is no one to talk to now.

The bus appears out of the haze, seeming to float out of a distantly shimmering pool hovering indistinct above the middle distance of road. Black smoke coughs from its side as it lurches down through gears towards them. The bright blue and white painted body gives a deceptive promise of relief. Inside, the heat is stifling.

The bus squeals to a halt and concertina doors slap back mechanically. The driver takes the old woman's fare as he watches the mother fussily lift her baby from the collapsing stroller. As an afterthought, he steps out of his seat to help. The old woman shuffles along the aisle to a vacant seat a little apart from the other passengers and lowers herself heavily into the faded red vinyl seat. It is burning hot. She squirms about to get comfortable.

She clambers uncertainly onto the donkey and laughs. She is becoming a woman. Costa holds the head of the animal as she mounts, then leads it forward a few paces. She sways precariously and giggles nervously at her feat. Costa reaches up for a firm, olive-skinned arm and steadies her. They are to be married.

Above them, clinging to the dusty track that climbs

quickly into the bare-boned mountains, the village seems to laugh with her. The village is only small, maybe thirty houses all told, with the golden dome of a small white church crouching a little apart, farther up the track. This land is full of churches. It wears its faith conspicuously. The main town of the island is a dozen miles away, just along the coast. The island is not very large.

Some friends stand about, joking with Costa and his betrothed and the old donkey. From dark windows piercing the smooth, bleach-white face of a nearby house, a couple of young women, brown hair falling into soft brown eyes, lean forward to see and to laugh. They laugh at their little sister, so fragile, perched on the donkey. There is no mocking in their laughter. They laugh with her. Below them, an old woman in the doorway looks on, frowning. It is not decent. Costa is laughing. He knows he has the daughter's heart and he is happy with love and youth and confidence. The mother looks on at the couple, resigned and wrapped in black. She knows that she is overshadowed now, but she also knows she is not displaced, can never be displaced. A mother has the right. Still she frowns. Her husband has been dead some months.

All the buildings are white, bleached, as if they are mere natural extensions of the bare white rock that insinuates itself through the thin soil. The bones of this country jut out everywhere. It is an old country, as old as time. Perhaps Time began with it, a child of the bargain made between Sun and Earth, when Sun and Earth were still gods in this land. Now merely sun and earth. Perhaps. Occasional red-tiled roofs casually break up the mass of whiteness all around, like speckles of blood on chalk. Everything here seems to exist as if by some immortal habit, instilling it with an inspirent, unconscious ease. There is the comfortability born of time-lessness, of having always been.

The sun has known this land long. The great arc of blue overhead, flecked with tissues of white filament as though the air has lightly broken off pieces of some distant mountain top, seems to reach down, protective of its ancient lover. So long have these two caressed, sun and earth, that, like the lazy Cavefish, secure in its cavern darkness, the land has slowly slipped off its mantle of earth to receive the familiar sun. There is no longer need for covering, for the blushing discretion of young lovers, no need for the screen of soil, grass or trees. The cloak of mortal clay slips slowly, unheeded, into the soft warmth of surrounding sea. Earth lies in supine indifference secure in blue water. She will die with the sun. That is their contract, made before Time. They are in harmony.

The land is poor, trees tenaciously clinging to the soil. The people accept its poverty, assured by a consoling Church that trust will be rewarded. The trust seems justified. They will always be poor but there is always just enough to eat. That is all they expect. There is none of the aspiration of the past, when men of this land led the world. The Lord provides and the people are humble.

It is hot; a light, moist heat. There is a breeze mounting from the sea. The sea is never very far away in Greece. Islands pierce the sky-blue reflection of sea as silently as clouds. Sky, sea, land and sun have long ago made their peace. They are as one. The doors of the houses seem to heave a sigh of relief as they open to the breeze. Silver fingers ripple through the deep green of olive trees and there is a smell of blossom. The land seems asleep, has slept a thousand years, becoming a single, static frame of light and white. Only the half-forgotten ruins scattered amongst docile flocks of sheep attest to any former interest in the world. The land no longer seems to care, content to slumber in the warm, secure sun, lulled by the soft rolling swish of windmills. Its time has passed.

Far off, on the mainland and beyond, another war is beginning. The face of Europe is changing again, convulsing in reaction to the speed of change. The island is still peaceful. It will not escape the force of change. The signs are already there, come to the island as the Romans had, as the Turks had done before. The island would survive, as it had always survived. It would be poorer still.

The men are joking with Costa. They are friends or they are relatives. Everyone is a friend or a relative in the village. Except perhaps the old man, Stanopoules. He is from Kithira, another island further to the east. He is the wealthiest man in the village, perhaps the whole island, and a recluse. He wants no friends. They cost money. He is accepted, butt of cruel jokes about his miserliness. No Greek will have another Greek for his master. Still, he is harmless. He keeps to himself.

There is a new schoolmaster from the mainland. He is a communist and he would prepare the island for the fight to come, for the "Liberation". The elders of the village distrust him. They do not like his talk against the King and the Church. But some, the younger men, listen, gather in the night in the little classroom and whisper. They would be Patriots, would fight for their land.

In the town, Italian soldiers have arrived. Not many, but some. To "protect" the island. The teacher must now teach Italian in the school. Mussolini has ordered it. The old men resent the Italians as they resent all outsiders. They silently put up with them. At least they are not Turks. There are still Turks in Greece, but they are no longer masters. They keep to themselves. The Italians will be thrown out in their turn.

The young ones are learning from the Italians. They are learning that the world has left them behind. They hear stories of new ways, the new politics and tales of wars in Eritrea, of incredible atrocities, of barbarians. They want the Italians out, but they will listen to the stories. And they bring money to the island. Some of the young women find them handsome. The island seems to be awakening from a long, deep sleep. More young men are gathering at night with the schoolmaster.

Perched on the donkey, she takes no notice of the world. It is far away and it is near, in this young man, Costa, and in her family. The world may be changing but right now there is love and there is laughter. The donkey is getting grumpy and is refusing to move. The game is over. Costa reaches up and lowers Irini from the animal's back. He is a proud man, proud of his love, of his strength and proud to be Greek. He is ambitious. He would give his bride more than this simple village life. He is a reader, wants perhaps to go one day to the mainland to study. He has seen films of life in America. He dreams of leaving the poverty of the village.

She only dreams of him, the man who will be her husband. As it was meant to be. She had always been his, had been since they were children. Time and God would make them one. He would be somebody in the village and she would be his proud wife. Dust rises around the donkey's grey legs. Small white clouds.

The bus is noisy and uncomfortable. The seats feel clammy with sweat. Even with the windows open, the bus seems stifling, the wind's hot breath pushing into the old woman's face without the slightest indication of any relief. It is almost spiteful in its incessance. Still, she thinks, better open than closed. It is so dry. She looks silently out of the window at the passing houses.

Some dust is being spun up into filmy red fronds in the haze of paddocks that lie behind the houses. The houses here are all red; red bricks, red tiles, as red as the earth, all almost identical as they sit in their segregated little squares. The sun has already burnt away most of last winter's lawns in an apparently willful denial of fruitfulness — the sun's age-old promise. Instead, the sprinklers slap impotent across red mud as yellowing survivors of lawn tenaciously grip the spreading red dirt by spindly tendrils of drying roots.

The sun has always been here. The land is stark and uncomfortable, burnt a dusty ochre. There has never been any giving, sun to earth, the sun a cruel master to the struggling earth, dust-smothered. Life is merely tolerated. The sun's fire has scourged this land through ten thousand years till even the trees seem more red than green, leaves, a mass of dried-out dun khaki, seem held up in supplication by long, bony, flaking fingers that split out of long, gaunt white arms. The sun disregards the gift and stares on, oblivious; unflinching, unforgiving. It hangs in the unblinking eye of sky, fierce and crackling. Even the air seems to jangle with the tension, flicking about in hot rushes away from the light, quivering into melting distances that turn to illusory water. Cicadas, hidden, drone into the night.

The wind is shaking the drooping heads of the trees. They seem tired of the effort of rising up. There are little explosions of bright crimson fire splashed through the trees like so many drops of paint, flowers with spine-like petals couched in hard brown nuts, tightly gripping a hopeful future of trees. There is a dust haze hanging on the horizon. Perhaps there will be a dust storm. That might at least break this awful heat. Most probably not.

Some believe that there were no gods in this land. There are old ones who know who are hidden away to die. The young ones deny the tales, vague superstitions. The gods, if they ever existed, were long ago bulldozed under supermarket carparks. The old woman knows nothing of the old ways of this land. She does not want to know. There is nothing here. She only knows her own land, only wants to know her own ways. There is nothing here, for her.

The baby has decided it has had enough and erupts in a violent wail of frustrated rage. It rages against a universe it does not comprehend, that will not pay attention and stop this annoying heat. The universe begins to rock the baby jerkily, irritable. Mother Universe has had enough too, without having to put up with this. The old woman thinks the young one a bad mother.

Two women across the aisle complain to themselves about the heat, droning into each other's faces. It's all these rockets, they upset the atmosphere. The old woman only vaguely comprehends their chatter, suspicious that it might be about her. "You must learn to speak English now, girl," Costa had prodded. "You are in a new land now and you must learn to speak its language."

"I am born Greek and I shall die a Greek," she had said, eyes flashing defiance. Stubborn, she stared into Costa's thick moustache. He still wore it as they did on the island, never really becoming the cosmopolitan he thought he could be.

"And so you will be always a Greek, as I am and always will be. But we are in Australia now and so we must live by the ways of these people, become one with them. The old ways are behind us now. We must become Australians and begin again."

He too had learned, from the Italians, then the Germans and finally the Allies that Greece had left behind, that because it had forgotten the world the world had rushed in and tried to take it for itself — for Italy, for Germany, like the Turks had. He was too proud to accept any foreign master, had been in the Resistance. But he was also too proud to be left behind. He wanted a better life for his wife, for his family, than a poor, worn-out Greece could give. His brother had gone to America and wrote to him of his two cars. He knew nothing of Australia, except that some parts had vineyards and had a climate like Greece. He knew a little of vines from his father's piece of land. And it might be easier to get established in Australia. America was so expensive. His brother's letters told him so. In Australia he might start a new life that would be more than a little cottage with a few goats and these old ways, the women in black. He would have more than that for his family. His sons (he would have sons) would have a future, away from the dying and the poverty. There was so much poverty now the war was done.

She had tried to learn English, had tried for Costa. She could speak well enough. She could talk to shopkeepers, the baker. Maybe occasionally the neighbour, about their children. No respect, not like Greek children. No need to speak to anyone else. They had no opinions that could interest her. She only half comprehended now, had never grasped the abstractions. There was no more use for her than half-forgotten English. No need to speak at all really since Costa had died. Only now and then, on the special days, when she would make the trek to the City by train, to go to the church. And then she only spoke Greek, as she lit a candle for Costa. She kept to herself even then. There was no one there of her island. That made a difference.

Costa had never really been able to adjust either, though he had worked hard. His English was too heavily accented and though there were none of the old ways of his own land here, there were ways that pushed him aside from the people he had thought would welcome him. There was prejudice in the land as deep as his own against Turks, of Germans, only now he was the minority. There were no other Greeks in the factory or the suburb in which he lived. With no papers he could never really do much more than factory work and there were the children to feed. They had a small bungalow, just like all the others around the suburb, and he kept a couple of goats in the paddock behind it. Once arrived, he had neither the money nor the knowledge to get to the vineyards. He had a vine in his garden, and a few vegetables and fruit trees which kept him busy. But it wasn't what he had expected. The land was hot and dry. It didn't seem to care at all. There were some friends at work but no one close. His sons had English friends. They eventually followed their ways. He felt left behind, but could not change. He followed the ways he knew. He never really felt Australian.

She did not really like her neighbours. They did not seem decent. They were not Christians, not Orthodox. She mistrusted them.

They thought her strange. A little black beetle of a woman.

She still had relatives in Greece. They were poor. They wrote when they had something to say and she would reply, wishing she could find the money to go home. The letters were fewer since her mother had died. She would probably never see her island before she died. She would often cry to herself over this. She would die far from home, without a witness, like her mother. And no Costa. Her sons lived interstate, had lives and wives of their own. They loved her and would visit occasionally, but they resented her in little ways and were glad to get back to their own lives. They had become Australians, their friends outweighing the influence to be Greeks. She was sad that they seemed so ashamed of their origins. Away from her, they were proud of her. She tended to smother them. They would have liked one day to send her back. They knew that it was what she wanted. But they also knew that she would never leave their father. And he was here. He was finally part of Australia. It all seemed a little pathetic, but that was their mother — a mind of her own.

The sun flashes a hundred little suns around her, piercingly bright in the chrome of bus seats, passing cars and windows. The reflections make her eyes water. The black bitumen seems to grow soft. In the distance it dissolves altogether into the shimmering mirage that hovers above the road. An illusion of cool relief. The sun often plays tricks with this land, taking away by an abundance of giving. There is smoke rising far off in the Ranges. The old woman wishes for the relief of a cool breeze off the sea. The rims of her eyes are red.

The taverna is full of people. The room is singing and shouting as the men drink mastika. The young men are dancing, intense, concentrating on the subtleties of their step, their arms outstretched like wings, fingers snapping, feet stamping out the rhythm of the bouzoukia. The old men shout out approval or instructions on the *right* way to do it. They smoke Turkish tobacco, thick and aromatic, as they sip their ouzos. The village is gathered to celebrate the wedding of Costa to Irini.

The war is still far off. Soon it will overwhelm everything.

The church had seemed bathed in gold, a warm comfortable yellowness of light drifting down from the stained glass portraits of Christ and various saints who clustered into the windows above as if for a better look. The gold and silver inlays of the icons winked reflected suns into the whispers of smoky incense that seemed to carry with them the prayers and songs of generations, mingled with the drones of a small dark man perched in a box to the left of the couple, reading catechisms from a heavily jewelled book before him. Long white candles, held by children, were festooned with white ribbons. The priest was dressed in a heavily embroidered cassock, with a great silver crucifix nestling beneath his full beard. It is the traditional manner. Even the smallest church in Greece has treasures. The people give what they do not need and the church displays their faith in opulence.

Irini wears the crown of white blossom in her thick, brown hair, tied by a fragile cord of ribbon and flowers to the crown nestled incongruously in Costa's black hair. His face is very serious, his moustache waxed in the old way and his high, stiff collar cutting into the painfully close-shaved pink of his neck. They kneel before the altar as the priest chants over them in heavy, luxurious tones. His voice is soothing, lost in his beard. Irini is blissful.

The stern faces of the host admiring the windows seem to have softened. A trick of the light. She looks at Costa, this stranger she has known all her life. She is giving herself to him now, before God, for life, for love. He seems different but he is the same. He is ambitious. He is her husband, to love and obey, till death.

Her name is Irini. It means Peace. It is more. She carries his name. A new beginning. The wife of Costa. He will *be* somebody.

Her old brown eyes blink, watery, beneath the black cowl of scarf drawn tight over the old woman's hair. She takes the handkerchief clenched in her hand and wipes the moisture from her eyes. The hair, barely visible beneath the scarf, is steel-grey, not yet white. Her face is deeply creased, with the beginnings of a web of smaller connecting creases that will soon become a permanent veil across the once young face. There is still some resilience in the skin, struggling against inevitable collapse. She is merely a shrivelled kernel of a self, what remains when the substance is removed. Costa had always wanted life to go on after death, hated the denial of life in those left behind. He could never see, could never understand the secret candle, always alight, the old women carried about in their black. Now she bears his death, defiant of the ways around her, proud of the witness she bears so conspicuously in the perpetuity of black. It is her sign that her love is eternal. It has always been the way. It is as it should be.

Her eyes lower to scan the hands crossed in her lap. They are chubby and arthritic, covered in the blotches of years in the hot sun. Her skin is olive, distinctly Mediterranean. The rings of her undying marriage are wedged firmly in the flesh of her fingers. They have never left her hand. They will go with her to dust.

The bus lurches to a halt and she lifts her heavy black form from the sticky seat and shuffles down the aisle. She feels a little nauseous from the diesel fumes and the suffocating heat. She has never got used to buses, any more than to the heat.

The shopping centre is all concrete and glass and plastic.

People mill about in groups or in silence to the drone of over-head piped music. She bustles about her business quite alone. She knows a few faces, but no one to whom she has any-thing to say. She keeps to herself. Her people are gone from her. Even her sons. As if already dead. As if *she* were already dead.

"Why did we come here, so very far away? It is so hot and dusty. There is no green here, no softness. There are no other Greeks. Who will I have to talk to? Who will be my friend? Why did we have to leave home? I will never see my mother again, never see my home, I know it. I do not like this place, Costa. The people, they stare. Why did we come?"

"It will be all right, Irini. It is just a little different here, that's all. We can have a new life here without the wars and the superstitions, without the old, dead ways. People like you for what you are here. They give you a new start. We will have a good life here, you'll see. I wanted you to have all I could give. I wanted a new life for us. I brought us so we could be happier. I wanted you to be happy".

A couple of children playing begin to chant, dancing around the old woman in black, meaningless taunts from lips that do not yet comprehend the spite in the words. It's just a game, with words they have heard the grownups use. The old woman looks so odd, absurd. A disgusting old black beetle of a woman. Quickly bored and not a little scared at the old woman's scowling, they run off to new adventures.

The old woman frowns. It is not proper, these children, have they got no homes? They must have bad parents. A good, Orthodox Greek boy or girl would never behave like these little ruffians. In Greece, a child has the proper respect. In my land, there is . . .

She forgets the children and carries on with her shopping. She is oblivious to the other shoppers. She carries on as if by habit. There is no resistance. Only the longing, the long withering towards his death. Her sun has gone out. She is faithful to their bargain. The flesh is slowly slipping away from life. Merely the cold, wornout husk of the black signi-fying the night Costa left behind.

Smoko

Ray Wood

The sudden shriek of the siren split through the throbbing noise of the factory floor, cleaving through a hundred headaches.

Smoko!

Greg, robot-like after three hours and countless hundred repetitions at his machine, switched off the power and switched on his mind.

He echoed the sigh of the settling hydraulics and mingled with the men in oil-stained overalls who were slinking to their rest areas. All around him he saw men with blank expressions, delving in lockers for cigarettes, sandwiches and racing papers which they carried with little conversation and less enthusiasm to various dingy corners.

Greg wandered to one area where a group of men were perched on old packing cases. A card game was already in progress: tattered cards were slapped down with oaths and old jokes on an upended forty-four gallon drum.

One of the group noticed him: "G'day. New, encha?"

Greg started explaining how he'd just started, how he'd left his small bush town to find more money in the city.

The other cut him short with an "Anyhow, I'm Jacko and this is Perce and that's Davo . . . " and a hurried round of introductions of which Greg caught few and remembered fewer. He felt slightly uneasy. It was a different world, coming from his familiar three-man workshop in a town where a wander down the street meant a dozen conversations. He glanced around the endless rows of drab green machines.

"Big place this, isn't it?" he said, more to make conversation than anything.

"Yeah," said Jacko. "Big bloody dump. Half the bloody machines are unsafe. Still, can't make too much of it —

plenty of poor bastards out on the dole queue waiting to take our place and the foreman'd be happy to get rid of any of us given half a chance."

Greg looked puzzled.

"Pays him to keep up a good turnover, see," explained Jacko. "Then we don't get too united, don't start getting militant. Still, there's plenty of us been here for years. Long-termers you might call us, with no time off for good behaviour."

While Greg and the others laughed dutifully at Jacko's joke, another man called out: "Got a team yet?"

"Sorry?"

"Got a team yet. Gotta have a team if you work here. Everybody's got a team. Couldn't have a smoko without talking about teams.

"Course, I'm lucky, I follow the real footballers — you'll come and barrack for my lot if you've got any sense."

Immediately a dozen voices broke in with various colorful descriptions of the geriatric and paraplegic qualities of the teams supported by the others. Greg sensed it was an often-repeated discussion, with stock phrases used to avoid the need for thinking up fresh conversation during the brief reprieve from the throbbing, vibrating, mind-numbing machinery.

"Bloody football," Jacko's voice cut through the others. "All you lot can ever talk about."

"Well, at least with a match you can see a result," said the man pointed out as Perce, a small wrinkle-faced man who had stayed silent until then. "Beats this bloody life. Working day in, day out. No end in sight. Start with the siren, eat with the siren, pee with the siren, go home with the siren. Bloody machines going all day so you can't even think. No wonder a bloke goes to the footy — he can see something different, something happening, have a good yell and see a result at the end of it."

From the look of the others, Greg gathered this was a rare occasion, a fresh line of discussion.

"I know what Perce means," said another man, spitting out bits of a chunky cheese sandwich. "Fair drives a bloke crazy working here. Don't know what you're making, just churning out bits of metal."

"Bloody bosses don't care," cut in another worker. "We're just like the little bits of metal to them. Units of production. They use us as a buffer — if times are good they take us on, if they muck things up they lay us off."

Perce returned to the discussion: "At least we've got work most of the time. Plenty of poor sods out in the streets haven't worked for years."

"Yeah," said another man. He stood up as though to lend emphasis to his remarks, at the same time thumping down his mug with a force that splashed tea on to the cards. "My lad's just turned twenty and still hasn't seen a job. And you know why? 'Cos of people like you!"

"Whaddya mean?" asked Perce, red spots appearing in his factory-sallow cheeks.

"You bloody know what I mean," said the newcomer to the conversation. "Your missus goes out to work. You've got a nice color telly and that boat you go out fishing on. And my kid's out of work — and the bloke next door. While you take in two incomes. You lot make me sick."

Again a dozen arguments broke out at once. Greg sat, bewildered, while the theories flowed. He could tell the arguments were emotional rather than rational — those with working wives had all the counter-arguments to those without.

Jacko, who evidently saw himself as some sort of leader, tried to restore amity by changing the subject.

"No good arguing among ourselves," he said loudly. "Might all be out of a job this time next month."

His comments had the desired effect. The others stopped squabbling and looked silently at him.

"Whaddya mean?" asked Perce.

"Well, I've heard the firm's being taken over," said Jacko. His attempt to look grave in keeping with the nature of his message was almost overcome by his pride in being the centre of attention, bearer of a new rumor.

"My boy's got a mate who goes with a girl whose Dad's in the accounts section here and he says there's talk of some other firm buying the people who own this place — and you know what happens to blokes like us when that sort of thing goes on."

"Who owns this place now, anyway?" asked Perce.

"Don't really know," said Jacko. "Last time they changed the letter-heading it was some fancy name. In the small print it mentioned a company. Apparently one of the shop stewards tried to look it up but found it was mostly owned by other companies and it got too hard for him — bloke at the place where you look things up got a bit shirty anyway because he was in scungey working clothes and made the place look untidy."

"Don't they tell you these things?" Greg asked innocently. He looked bewildered when the others laughed, though he could tell the laughter reflected bitterness at a situation, not derision of him.

"Tell us," said Jacko. "Tell us! That's a good'un. It breaks their bloody hearts to have to pay us, leave alone tell us anything."

"Remember that consultation committee thing they set up a few years back," said Perce. The others made sneering comments.

Greg asked: "What was that."

"First thing we knew was when notices appeared round the place saying they had set up a consultation committee to involve the workers. Some bloody consultation — didn't even consult us in the first place."

Perce took a long swig of tea from his chipped and cracked mug.

"Well, some of the blokes thought it was a trick, something to undermine the union or get more work out of us or something. Anyway, we decided to give it a go. Old Joe Buckley was our bloke on the committee — bloke who got killed when the boiler door blew off last year. Still see the marks on the wall. It was in the papers. Only time in his whole life he did anything to get his name in the papers and he wasn't there to see it.

"Anyway, he'd noticed there was this big stockpile building up in the out stores so he asked them if they were planning to lay people off. 'No', they said.

"Next week, stockpile was bigger. Same question, same answer — no layoffs.

"Third week, could hardly move for bloody stockpile. All round the place, crates everywhere. All the garages were used and they piled stuff up in the paddock next door. Old Joe asked them again about the situation. 'Don't worry,' they told him. So he came back and told us we were safe. Know what happened?"

He paused dramatically.

"What", asked Greg.

"Next day — next bloody day — they put off three hundred of us. Didn't have the guts to make announcement or anything. Just put notes in the pay packets so the blokes found out when it was too late to do anything.

"Anyway, after that the consultation committee rather fell apart, you might say."

Perce finished his tea with a dramatic fourish, tilting the mug back and banging it down on the oildrum. The card game had been forgotten as the workers crowded round to back up Perce's story, nodding and shaking their heads in chorus to emphasize his points.

"But couldn't the union do anything?" Greg asked.

Again voices broke out, using well-practised arguments and counter-arguments.

"Bloody union," said Perce. "Top officials are all busy trying to get into parliament and haven't got time for us, the organizers all spend their time in the Industrial Commission and the shop steward's only interested in studying Marx at night school."

Seeing a heated argument was about to break out on Perce's views, Greg got in quickly: "But surely there are laws and things."

"Course there are," said Perce. "But the laws are not on the side of the workers, are they? And if they are meant to help us, nobody obeys them. Look — see that drum there."

He pointed at the upended forty-four gallon drum which served as card table and resting place for their battered mugs and flasks.

"See that label?"

Greg felt rather silly as he twisted his neck to read the

upside-down label. He tried to pronounce the multi-syllable chemical name and faltered.

"What is it?"

"Exactly," said Perce as if Greg had made his point for him. "What is it? They brought it out for use in some of the processes. Blokes found it helped keep the machinery clean so they started using it.

"Then they started coming out in blisters. Got worse — bloody agony for some of the blokes. Eventually they twigged — it was this chemical wasn't it? Apparently it should only be used with gloves. Did they tell us that? Did they issue gloves? No bloody way."

Greg persisted: "But isn't that illegal? What about the Department? . . . "

"Department," snorted Perce while others chuckled. "Bloody Department. Well, for starters they've got so much work and so few inspectors they only get round here about once every ten years. Then the management usually hears they're coming and gets the place cleaned up until they're gone. Even if they can find something wrong they can't do much — some 'order' or a piddly fine which doesn't mean anything to a firm like this — they'll just sack somebody and pay the fine with his wages instead."

Greg felt slightly sick. He felt he'd grown up suddenly. It had all been so simple back home, where everybody knew everybody and there wasn't a manager or owner who was not in the same sports team or service club as at least some of his workers. "So what happened?"

"Oh, we got the union in," said Perce. "But the firm said they weren't to blame and the makers said it wasn't their fault and the union lawyer said it would be hard to prove and the union didn't have the funds for a long test case with the money those bastard lawyers earn so it all petered out. The blisters went — from the hands, anyway. Still a few blistered minds around."

Jacko evidently felt he had been out of the limelight too long and stuck out his chest in prelude to a statement.

"What made me sick was the foreman's attitude," said Jacko. "Remember him, old Eight-fingered Eddie. One of the old school. Said we were a lot of bleeding pansies. Weren't in the industry until you'd lost at least a finger."

"Is he still here," asked Greg.

"No, he got his in the end," said Jacko. "Tried to clear a jam on one of the big machines without switching it off. Ended up in little bits all round the shed. Served the bastard right."

"Course, I blame the wogs," said a burly, bucolic man who had been silent until then.

"Here we go again," muttered Perce for Greg to hear.

"Yeah, we'd have a strong union if it wasn't for all them dumb wogs they bring in," said the burly man. He looked round as though expecting a challenge.

"Too stupid, that's their trouble. Don't understand unions. Last time there were layoffs half the silly buggers went and asked for their union fees back — thought they'd been paying into a credit union. Can't speak English proper, that's their trouble. Shouldn't let them in unless they speak English."

Nobody countered him; the murmurs seemed to reflect some agreement and some opposition and a general disinclination towards debate. Once again, it was Greg who played the straight man.

"What about teaching them?" he asked the dogmatic speaker.

It was Jacko, however, who answered. "We all said that once. After all, most of them seem good blokes once you get to know them. But the firm wouldn't pay for any lessons. The union tried to get a course going but most of them wouldn't go because it was too far away and anyway they had to get home because Mama had a night shift so they had to look after the kids. Bloody firm of course was too mean to let them off for lessons during the day. Costs them a packet in compo, though, every time one of 'em loses a finger or something through not being able to read instructions."

"Can't they just translate things," Greg inquired.

The burly man took up his tirade. "That's the bloody trouble. Firm did that once. Put round pamphlets in all those wog languages — turned out most of them couldn't even read their own language."

"But don't they have a leader or someone among them who . . . ?"

"They're even worse," said Perce. "One of their blokes got elected shop steward. First of all there was trouble 'cos he started looking after his own. He always backed his own people in a dispute against the others and we nearly ended up with bloody tribal wars. Then it turned out he wasn't even looking after his own people. Ripping them off, he was. Taking about twenty dollars a week off each of them telling them it was union fees, put the fear of God into them that he could get them the sack at any time, and translated everything his own way to twist it to suit himself."

Jacko spoke up again: "Personally, I feel sorry for them. Poor bastards come all this way, leave everything behind, come to a strange country, can't speak the language."

The fat man grabbed his chance. "Then they should bloody well learn," he crowed. "And they should stop congregating together and mix with proper people and eat proper food."

"How many languages do you speak?" Greg asked quietly.

Jacko chortled. "He's right you know." He told the fat man. "Who was it who was moaning about his holiday overseas and how the natives didn't speak bloody English properly and he couldn't get a decent steak. Who was it, then?"

"Yeah," Perce joined in. "And I don't blame 'em sticking together. If I went to a foreign place I'd stick with people I knew. Look at that film on telly the other night about Aussies in London with their own bloody pubs and whatnot — and that's in a place where they speak the same lingo. Well, almost."

The big man subsided into mutterings as others took up the theme. It was as though Greg's initially diffident challenge had released pent-up feelings.

"Some of 'em come straight from tiny little places to the big city," said Perce. "Imagine coming from some Greek version of Whoop-Whoop, where you know everyone and a traffic jam's when two donkeys come down the road at the same time. Then come to a place like this."

"That's true," — Jacko couldn't allow himself to be left out of any argument, especially if people were swaying one way. "I've heard some of them haven't hardly seen a town of a thousand people before. Then they get flung here in a factory with more than five thousand. No wonder they go bananas."

"I heard of one woman over in the other block who was found bawling her eyes out in a corner," said Perce. "Turned out she started that morning and got lost going from the personnel office to her workplace. Broke down in the end. They had to ask all round till they found somebody who spoke her language. Bloke took her home — and the bastards docked his pay for the time he was out."

"Bloody personnel office," said Jacko. "Personnel, pig's arse. Don't think of us as persons. Just names on a filing card, that's what we are. Wonder they don't bring in a law making us all use numbers instead of names to make it easier for their computer.

"Now take young Greg here. Did they fill you in on conditions and things when you joined?"

"Not much. They gave me a form for the social club and told me which shed to report to."

"Typical," said Jacko. "Bloody typical. Got a locker — no, thought not. Bloody factory fodder, that's all we are to them. Don't even allocate a bloke a locker. Bet if you was one of them smart-arsed clerks starting work in the office, bloke with no apprenticeship or nothing they'd have bloody escorted you to your bloody desk and issued you with your own rubber plant and all."

Laughing, Greg moved to the empty locker Jacko pointed out to him. Rust patched the dull green like dried blood on a jungle floor, under a layer of Penthouse centrefolds. The shelf had long since broken, the hooks had gone. On the floor lay an archaeological layer of debris, souvenirs of past occupants. Greg gathered up cigarette packets and old racing papers, a well-thumbed sex magazine and sundry festering sandwich wrappers. In the corner he spotted a dogeared old paperback. It was in a foreign language.

"That's this then," he enquired casually "Someone been brushing up for their long service leave trip?"

The others fell quiet. Strangely quiet, almost guiltily silent.

"Must have been Old Reffo's," muttered Perce.

"Who's Old Reffo?"

Perce shuffled uneasily. None of the others answered. Greg looked round and eventually Perce said: "Well, it was a long time ago now. Forgotten about it, really.

"Old Reffo had that locker at one time. We called him Old Reffo because he was in that lot of refugees they brought in after the war and nobody could make out his real name. S'pose we couldn't even call him Old Reffo now or Al Grassby would be after us."

Nobody laughed.

"Anyway, he had this thick accent and nobody could understand him. Not that anybody tried much. Fair bit of prejudice then against foreigners."

Greg looked at Jacko and the fat man quickly. No irony seemed intended.

"Anyhow," Perce went on. "He kept himself to himself. Good at his machine but never one of us, if you know what I mean. Never came down the pub. Didn't even follow a team. Just sat on his own at smoko. Sometimes he read them books in his own language. Often he'd just sit and do calculations. We all reckoned he was half nuts. Sat there, face like a bloody bulldog, never smiled, scribbling away.

"Then it all came to a head. Had a row with the foreman one day. Real bastard we had then — makes this bloke look like a bloody fairy. Anyhow, it all started when Old Reffo tried to tell him something, some modification to the machine or something.

"Foreman started getting impatient because he couldn't really understand him. Then he told him just to shut up and get on with his work. Real bloody ding-dong in the end. Foreman carrying on, yelling and swearing, telling him he was a stupid refugee bastard and lucky to be allowed in let alone have a job."

"Told him he was paid to work, not think," Jacko supplemented.

"Yeah," agreed Perce. "Still, they all use that one. If I had a dollar for every time I'd heard that I wouldn't need to work. Anyhow, you could see that it hit Old Reffo hard. Didn't say anything, mind. Never did. Just got on with his machine. But he — well, he sort of . . . sagged.

"Next day, didn't turn up. Day after, neither. Personnel

people ended up sending round to his place. Done himself in, he had. Gas oven job. It was poisonous in those days. Before natural gas.

"Anyway, when they cleared up his flat they found his papers. Not newspapers like, papers from universities and things. Turned out he had more degrees than a bloody thermometer. And he'd just been scraping a living in this shit-hole. Worse in those days, too. Not as many Acts and things."

Jacko paused, his sense of the dramatic again working at least time-and-a-half.

"But you know what was really funny?" he asked Greg. "Not funny, comical, like, but funny strange."

"What?"

"Turned out he'd only designed the bloody machine, back in his own country. Shit-hot expert he was in the old days. No wonder he could make suggestions. Trouble was in all the mess after the war he couldn't prove his qualifications and immigration was up to here with reffos claiming they were doctors and so on.

"Glad to get a job, he was. Here! Had to stay alive. Till the bloody foreman killed him."

They were all silent, in a silence of embarrassment rather than reverence for the dead or remorse at the tale.

The fat man broke the silence by noisily slurping his tea.

"Strewth," said Perce. "You always sound like bathwater going down the bloody plughole."

It was not very funny, but they all laughed, from relief.

At that moment a newcomer to the group waddled over — an immense, whale-like man who flopped onto a packing case and only just drowned its protesting creak with his wheezing sigh. From the ribald greetings, Greg learned that Arthur was the name of the workmate, whose bulky frame was almost grotesque from a diet of beer and telly interspersed with fish'n'chips and fast foods. Further jokes indicated that Arthur was a bachelor who looked after himself, badly, backed slow race horses, and revelled in the sole glory of being a cause of bantering bad humor.

The jokes were old, almost hallowed by tradition. Today, however, there were obvious signs of fresh emphasis for Greg's benefit.

"See yer've got yer gorgonzola shirt on," said Perce, nodding at the ripped and hole-spattered grubby blue singlet wrinkled over Arthur's enormous belly and framed by the gape of his grubby overalls.

They all laughed as though it were a new joke, presumably to convince Greg it was.

"Get it," Perce nudged Greg. "So many 'oles it looks like a gorgonzola cheese," he explained in case Greg, being a bush bloke, didn't grasp the subtleties of suburban sophistication.

"Gruyere," said Greg.

"Yer what," said Perce.

"Gruyere," Greg repeated. "It's gruyere cheese which has the holes, not gorgonzola."

They all looked at him. He realized he had offended an unwritten code: some faces registered suspicion of a superior knowledge, others resented that he had smart-arsed a change into their ritual routine ribaldry.

Jacko broke the ice which was rapidly forming. "Gruyere — don't know where it grew but if that belly of Arthur's grows much more it'll be falling over 'is bloody knees" — and for the second time that smoko there was a burst of laughter heavily tinged with relief.

The laughter faded as the siren shrilled again. Faces changed, as though in Pavlovian reaction to a signal to stop smiling and thinking and living.

"Smoko over," somebody muttered. Cards and papers and teamugs were put away. Men began scuffling back to their machines, their animation drained by the succubus siren.

As Greg headed for his bay, Jacko caught up with him. "Anyhow mate," he said, "Welcome to the gang. We're not a bad bunch of blokes when you get to know us. You'll soon learn the lurks and perks. Beats being on the dole, anyway.

"Tell you what, why dontcha come to the footy with me on Saturday?"

He punched Greg lightly on the shoulder, bestowing the knighthood of the shopfloor and the pub and the terrace on a Saturday arvo.

"After all, you're one of us now, mate."

Greg looked round at the long rows of men, suddenly

anonymous, switching on their machines and switching off their minds for another bout of endless repetitions making things they didn't know for people they didn't know in a world that didn't know them.

"Thanks," he said, tonelessly. "Thanks."

Middle Eastern Questions

Nancy Keesing

Whether or not he had guessed she would never know, and since 1974 when it happened, and through the wars in Lebanon, the question grew in significance and quality of distress.

The ordered taxi was slow in coming. She waited, fuming, not because she would be late since, these days, she always ordered a cab for a good half-hour earlier than ought to be necessary, but impatient at inefficiency. Impatient with herself, too, because she felt it should be possible to put to some use the time one wasted in waiting, but was always too restless to do anything other than prowl. If she was ready for an expected taxi, visitor or arrival of that sort she couldn't even force herself to read.

She set her suitcases outside the front door, then returned to the house to check, compulsively, that doors and windows were all locked, the stove switched off. She stood by a window facing up the leafy lane and peered through heavy shrubs in the next-door garden towards the road. There was no sign of a cab.

She opened the door of the hall cupboard and stood at its long mirror, adjusting a scarf, worn like a cravat inside the collar of her green tweed coat. A single hair floated above the well-sprayed surface of thick, still reddish hair; she patted it down and, when it drifted free again, tweaked it out. She decided that she really didn't look to be nearly fifty, and then, with dissatisfaction, that she did. Angry at looking nearly fifty she closed the door and strode with consciously lithe, long strides — because the walk gives away one's age, and she dreaded the careful, fostered gait of the elderly — to the garden path, and saw a glitter of garish yellow duco through trees. It had arrived. No. It overshot the entrance of the narrow lane, and had to reverse while she dashed back to pull shut and check the door behind her, and carry the suitcase down steps to the gate.

Exasperated, she now wished that, after all, the taxi had not come. Then she would have been forced to drive herself to the airport, which might have been preferable despite the awkwardness of having to carry luggage from parking station to terminal lounge. But at least she would have avoided the inevitability of yet another taxi driver's marvellous excuses.

This one pulled up, glanced at the suitcases, and jumped out of the car to open the boot. A stocky, swarthy man, as short as she was tall, and as crouched as she straight; and quite appallingly cheerful. "My God," she thought, "a monkey."

"My-a God," he cried, as she settled herself on the front seat beside him, which she forced herself to do, as a rule, because she so loathed the conversations of drivers, consequently feeling guilty and aware of intellectual snobbishness as one of her besetting sins, "My-a God, I nearly do not find you. Nice quiet little lyne though. On the radio, they tell me Map 46, F7. They-a wrong. Always I check my own map. Here," he thrust a dog-eared volume towards her as he reversed up the lane, "you-a look for yourself." So pleased with himself that it was impossible to express annoyance at the delay.

She pretended to scrutinize the map, and agreed that "they" were wrong. All the "theys" who are always wrong, and all the garrulous taxi drivers who are always right. Know-alls about everything under the sun. Half an hour of the company of this simian. To prove himself a conversationalist, he switched off his two-way radio.

"You want-a overseas terminal?" he asked.

"No, domestic, ANA." If he expected her to explain two large, much and internationally labelled suitcases, she did not intend to oblige.

"Ah," he sighed, and turned to smile fetchingly, displaying nut brown, and gleaming golden teeth. "And I think to myself: this-a lovely lydy and her nice ports, she goes overseas, so lucky."

Three choices now: impossible silence; ridiculous explanations of reasons for, and duration of, visit to Melbourne, or predictable enquiry.

Despising banality she asked:

"Which country do you come from?" Glancing at his fleshy, rounded nose and full lips, she awaited one of the several possible answers that would be as predictable as her question. Wonderful if he should answer as the enquiry deserved with inventive Greenland or Alaska. He said:

"Lebanon, lydy. But twenty-three years I been in Australia."

"Have you ever been back home for a visit?"

Oh yes. Yes indeed. He has. Only last year he spent six months in Beirut, staying with his mother.

"How lovely. She was well?" How odiously gracious-lady could one sound?

"Well!" She feared, groundlessly, that he would take his hands from the wheel but he was a careful driver with none of the swoops and sudden sickening dashes of so many of his colleagues. Nor was he in competition with everything else on the road. Nor critical of any other car, truck or bike. The golden smile sufficed. She continued to look at his hands, though. Spiky black hairs bristled as far as the first joints of his stubby fingers. The yellowish nails, she noticed, were cut straight and kept very clean.

"Well! She-a well all right. Like a young girl. Like one-a my sisters. She-a beautiful. She-a thin. She-a black hair. Beautiful." His rasping voice was warm.

Her questions now elicited five brothers and six sisters, all remaining in Lebanon, and that he was the only one of his family to migrate. Also that he had never married.

"Freedom. I like-a freedom. Why I give up-a freedom? You tell me!" She cannot. Nor what he is free for. To travel in Australia, perhaps? No! When he first arrived he had to work, for two years, on an engineering project in the country and he hated living there, though the work was not bad.

"But then I come for Sydney. Big city. Nice big city. I always lived in a city. Beirut, she was my home town. I now live-a Sydney twenty-three years."

"A beautiful city," she said, meaning Sydney.

"Was beautiful. Not now." He said, meaning Beirut.

"Could be beautiful now, but — pah — the big powers, big countries, big politics, no one knows what goes on. No one . . . " But he is a taxi driver, so he knows, and his passenger will be made to know.

Desperately she tried to think of some topic to turn the conversation and could not, so she offered him a cigarette which he took with a "thank you lydy" and lit when the next red light halted traffic. She also lit a cigarette — the nearest available substitute for shared salt.

"No one knows," he blew smoke savagely, "not in Austrylia or anywhere else."

This is the point, she thought, where I really ought to tell him. It is somehow unfair, and even indecent, to allow him to go on. If I don't, or can't, tell him, then I must change the subject. But how? To what? Too late.

"I tell you. Last year, last September, near where I live-a Beirut with my mother, the Israels' planes, they bomb a school. Seventy-four little children playing in yard. Mostly killed. Like-a that school there," but he didn't take his hand from the wheel to point it out, and she glanced from the wrong side of the car to a row of 1920-ish brick cottages, neatly kept with tiny gardens, painted wooden porches and shiny little windows like pursed lips.

"Frightful," she said.

"Why those Israels do that?" His voice was aggrieved but not aggressive. "I tell you. You ask America. You ask Russia. Ask those big countries. Why those big countries not leave everyone else alone? Why those Englands take Palestine and say-a that Abba Eban: you-a Premier and that yankee Golda Meir: you-a Prime Minister? And I tell you. No one knows-a nothing. Nothing is what they tell us. Listen. Every day that six months in Beirut, I get-a *Sydney Morning Herald* sent-a me air mail. And I tell you there-a nothing told in this country about seventy-four little children at all."

His face was expressionless, his eyes fixed on traffic.

"Why-a we not told? They not want us-a know. Why those Israels do that? Big politics. Jewses and Arabs good friends-a thousand years, eh? Brothers, eh?"

She really ought to tell him, but said something weak like: "Oh yes."

All her life she had disliked being close to squat, swarthy people with greasy, large-pored skin, rounded features and dark, oppressed eyes. All her life had resisted the unreasoning, unreasonable, unsuitable prejudice. Once, as a girl, she'd allowed a man like that to take her out a few times. He was a nice fellow, intelligent and good. But it was no use. When they danced together the very feel of him made her shudder; his black, oily hair at the level of her chin was torture; squeamish horror choked her throat at the pressure of his reticent, fat fingers on her back.

She feared and despised these reactions. She held passionate beliefs — that appearance counted for much less than character and ability, that race should count for nothing. Irrational repugnance aside, she would have married anyone. She always felt wretched when belief and passion were so easily dispelled by arcane and unwished-for emotions. She also perceived these dreaded and dreadful emotions as another side of her own vanity, her pride in being slim and tall and vigorous and straight-spined.

During their silence the driver glared morosely at a container truck inching the narrow road ahead. He made no stupid attempts to overtake it. He was a patient, excellent driver. She should think herself fortunate.

The truck turned off at a corner. The Lebanese accelerated and said, matter-of-factly:

"In Beirut last year, every Sunday, I spend ten dollars. Not a rich man, but I spend ten dollars, and I carry-a big bag to one of those Palestine camps. You know how-a children live there? In rags. In ten inches-a mud. I take food. I take-a chips. I-a not mind for adults, you know. But children — I crazy about children. Beautiful children, so happy-a see me every Sunday."

It came into her mind to say that, free as he said he liked to be, he wore chains, like everyone else. Instead she replied:

"How very good of you."

"Look, I tell you. Arab countries, we got all-a oil. America short-a oil. We stop oil-a America. America stop. Just so. Stop. So, one day, we have to do that."

She contemplated asking about that oil. About the inequalities of wealth in Middle Eastern countries. About sheiks with millions, and refugees who were no longer refugees, in stinking mud and rags. About his ten dollars every Sunday.

But it was impossible to pursue those questions unless she could, in return, offer her own disclosure.

One safe question, though.

"You speak French too, I suppose?"

"French, Arabic, English. In-a Lebanon school you-a learn them all. Now. When I-a school, only Arabic and French. I learn English in-a war. We like Austrylians in-a war. Lot-a Austrylians in Beirut. Nice blokes. Americans — pah! Lot-a Americans in Beirut. You know, no one speak-a them damn Yanks. No one. But Austrylians — in our home, all-a time. So nice, so friendly, so you-as-good-as-me-mate. You know?"

"And that is why you came to Australia?"

"So now I speak English all-a time. In Austrylia. This last month, I don't like even-a think French. My brother-in-law makes me very sad. Six weeks ago, in Paris, he die. He go-a Paris for a medical conference. He-a doctor. Only twenty-eight, and he drop dead. He wore himself out. Looking after those seventy-four children, he burst his heart."

"How frightful." How banal.

"So now," he straightened himself in his seat, "I speak English only. All-a time." After a very brief silence he said:

"I tell you. I had a very good friend. Ever since I came-a Sydney. Austrylian lydy. Old woman, you'd say; name-a Shirl. Every Sunday a dinner at her house. Her son my good friend too. And what you think? In her will, she give me that house. Her son live in-a country and now I live in that house. Big plyce. Nice yard — big. Kids next door-a me kick-a football in my yard. Welcome, any time. You know what. Those kids are Jewses. Their father, that Jew, my good friend. We talk. I tell him what I tell you, but we good friends. His wife, when they come-a my house, she cleans it sometimes like-a mirror and I say, now I got-a house like-a mirror, not like my house at all."

He laughs.

"Do you cook for yourself?" They were close to the airport now. Three minutes of food talk should see them safely arrived.

"Nah! Not cook. Good cafes. But I tell you what, now."
Remorseless.

"Last week in my cab I pick up-a lydy. Lydy like you.
Lovely fair hair. Nice dress. Nice house. She want to know
what country I come from, and I tell her and she says she is
a Jew and she says, how Arabs be so wicked-a God's choosen
people? On-a on she goes. I say-a her: 'Lydy, Arabs and
Jewses are brothers, I-a not hate Jewses.' But she goes on-a
on about them Israels. I-a not supposed-a answer her, you
know? Taxi rules, see. Not-a say anything back. By cripes, I
got-a hold my mouth. On-a on. God's choosen! You know?
When we get-a Bellevue Hill to the address she wants, I so
angry I-a shake. I let-a open-a own door and then I say: 'You
know why people hate Jewses? Because-a Jewses like you!'
What you think-a that, lydy?"

She thought he was absolutely right. Perhaps absolutely
percipient. Now, entering the entrance of the airport, she
should at least and at last tell him that she was, herself, a
Jew. But he had drawn up at the Terminal and was making
a great business of reading the meter. So she told him
nothing, but added a generous tip, for which he thanked her
warmly. He jumped out of the cab to lift the two heavy suitcases from the boot, and set them carefully, side by side, on
the pavement. She looked down at his bushy black hair,
his hunched shoulders. On his feet he seemed older than
when he crouched over the steering wheel.

"Thanks very much," she said.

"Thank *you,* lydy," he answered gravely. She met his
sombre, nearly black, gaze.

Whether or not he had guessed she would never know.

Before the Day Goes

Peter Goldsworthy

Frank walked through the early morning darkness of the shop, unlocked the front door, and carried out the newspaper banners.

For the last time, he thought. *For the last bloody time.*

Outside, the day was pulling itself slowly together — the sky blue and cold, the first sunlight splintering through the gums across the road. He filled his lungs with the coldness, then slowly exhaled, the breath vanishing a few centimetres from his nose.

To be leaving on a day like this. He smiled to himself, with the luxury of regret.

The town huddled along the highway in each direction — little more than an aisle of pubs and petrol pumps, he'd often thought. An oasis of beer and oil in the wheat.

Nothing else in the place was moving — or only the couple of flies that bumped sluggishly at his face. He brushed them easily aside — intruders in a morning that was his alone, that might have been created for no other purpose.

Then he walked back into the shop, lit the kero primus, put the kettle on and started peeling potatoes.

There was little else to be done in the mornings — the customers were still in bed. But it was his favourite time — an hour or two of peace that not even the drudgery of potato peeling could spoil. For his fingers would quickly find a rhythm of their own, the bucket between his legs would fill itself, and his mind was free to roam . . .

A truck revved suddenly in the back lane, then a clattering of cans.

Currie, the abo nightman, he guessed — and slammed the back door before the stink could penetrate.

The abo was supposed to have his truck out of town by dawn, or at least downwind from town by dawn, but it was bugger the council regulations as far as Currie was concerned. Let them find someone else to pick up their shit if they wanted it done in the secrecy of night — he preferred to sleep.

Frank remembered the morning a few years before when they'd ambushed the abo on his morning rounds. Bluey Horton, Jimmy Fisher and himself — the three of them might still have been at school, but were old enough to know how to treat a boong.

They had sneaked out before breakfast that morning, and hidden themselves — and their loaded airguns — in the bushes down by the Murphys'.

"Because the Murphys have ten kids, worm!" Bluey had explained. "Their shit-can's a real brimmer by the end of the week!"

As usual, the whole thing was Bluey's idea — and as usual, he was right. Currie was actually staggering as he came out the side gate with the can on his shoulder.

They waited till he was halfway to the truck, stranded in the middle of the road, then let him have it. The first slug missed completely, the second pinged harmlessly off the can, but Frank's, more through luck than aim, caught him on the knee and down he went. And over went the can on top of him — a thick tide of sludge.

"Don't worry, Currie!" Bluey yelled back as they ran. "It's September! You're due for a bath anyway!"

The abo tried vainly to catch them, squelching clumsily across the road in his boots and leather apron — but they were already gone. Vanishing before him like smoke, like warm breath on a winter morning.

"Francesco! Open the bloody door, eh? *Presto, presto!*"

Frank had been dreaming — he dropped his potato knife, and unlocked the back door.

"*Scusi*, Cesare. It was the stink — the *merda.*"

His uncle pushed irritably past, both arms wrapped around a crate of greens.

"You bloody always dreaming," he snorted.

Outside, his father was pulling more crates off the back of the truck, and Frank went to help.

"*Ciao*, Papa."

"*Ciao, nino.* How's business?"

It was the same question his father always asked — and would keep on asking until he died, Frank realized. For life in the new country might have been good — a shop, a market block, a new brick house — but never quite good enough not to worry.

"*Non c'e male,*" Frank answered, as he always answered — and with the ritual over, and the truck emptied, the two older men were soon driving away. Back to breakfast in the father's house, then a day of plastering in the uncle's house next door.

Spaghetti Street, the locals had started calling that corner of town. For if the new houses were too big to be ignored, they could at least be found ugly.

And they were, Frank knew — ugly brick boxes, ostentatiously festooned with wrought iron, *terrazzo* and marble veneer. *Dago* ugly. A third block was reserved next door for him — but the thistles that covered it could sprout into rain forest for all he cared — he would never be living there.

They had discussed it again only the Friday night before.

"It's time you settled," his father said, "I will write to the city — to friends, *calabresi.* This Australian girl — OK for now, but not for later. Too lazy to work, too *pigro* — so skinny, she might snap!"

He laughed at his joke, then abruptly stopped and looked Frank in the eye.

"Mark well these words that I tell you, *nino.*"

"Fuck these words that you tell me," Frank wanted to say as he walked out the door.

But his anger was soon forgotten — because Friday night was drive-in night, and Val was waiting to be collected. And Val might be skinny, but she wouldn't snap. She worked hard in the back seat every Friday night, and she hadn't snapped yet.

"Yoohoo! Anybody in!"

He must have been dreaming again — someone was calling from the front of the shop, but he hadn't heard the door.

"Coming!"

His first customer had her back turned as he walked in — a broad plump back that could have belonged to any one of a hundred town matrons. But didn't.

"What'll it be, Mrs Horton?"

"A sandwich loaf, thanks Frankie," she said, turning her face to him — a face that could also have belonged to any one of a hundred, he thought. The reddened cheeks, the bleached country eyes . . .

What was it his father used to say? A country town contains the whole world? Or was it the other way round? *Tutto il mondo è un paese.*

He liked to pretend he'd forgotten the meaning of the old words sometimes — even to Mamma, who had no English. Soon, of course, he could forget their meaning — as soon as he'd left the family that spoke them.

For it was their country town, not his. Their *paese*. Their shop, their market block, their squat brick boxes at the far end of Spaghetti Street.

"Hurry, will you Frankie?" Mrs Horton interrupted. "I haven't got all day!"

"One sandwich loaf," he said, and wrapped it.

There was more to the world than was contained in this country town, he was sure.

They had lived in that other world once — but only briefly, and he'd been too young to remember. A few images still stuck in his mind — a crowded cabin, a corner of swaying deck that always stank of vomit.

And then later, an equally crowded cabin on land. The migrants' camp, the *ostello*.

"The doghole, they mean!" Mamma had moaned — but at least there was room to stretch their legs. And trees to fall out of, and a patch of grass to kick balls across.

Although that was small consolation for the absence of his father, who had started vanishing from his life for weeks on end, it sometimes seemed. And Uncle Cesare too.

"The shifts," Mamma would whisper when he asked. "The morning shifts at the brickworks, the afternoon shifts at the Holdens . . . "

The two men would leave the cabin before he woke each morning, and return home only after he was asleep at night. He might have forgotten his father existed altogether, if it weren't for the giggling that sometimes woke him in the dark. And the thrashing of sheets.

How long had those endless shifts lasted? Frank couldn't properly remember — a childhood, an eternity. But finally there came a morning that he *could* remember — the first morning they didn't go to work. The morning they were sitting around the table when he went out to play after breakfast, and still sitting there when he came back in for lunch. Smoking their thick brown cigarettes, and burning their throats with *grappa*.

And even when they did finally leave, it was only for an hour or two. A wild tooting announced their return, and Frank rushed outside to join the crowd that had gathered. For they were displaying the fruits of all their labour — Cesare sitting proudly behind the wheel of an enormous red van, and his father towing a trailer-house behind his ancient Ford.

"*Santa Pazienza!*" Mamma exclaimed. "They will take us for gypsies! For *mendicanti!*"

And perhaps she was right. Next morning they drove out of the city — a long cavalcade of people and possessions. A circus, Frank thought delightedly, sitting high in the red van next to Cesare and watching the trailer-house sway across the winding road in front.

For at first they were crossing the hills — the narrow mountain wall around the city. Driving up steep valleys and across swollen creeks, through orchards of almond and fruit, and slopes of thin fat-uddered cattle.

La bella campagna, according to Cesare, but Frank was too nauseous for beauty. The dipping and curving of the road had made him giddy, and twice the red van was forced to suddenly stop.

"A rough crossing, *nino?*" Cesare teased him as he sputtered into the roadside bushes.

But at last the turbulence in the earth passed, and they drove down across a narrow plain to the river.

"The only river?" Cesare informed him. "The only river in the whole thirsty country!"

And they stopped by the river, and washed themselves, and ate. And drove over a bridge, and on into the wheat country beyond — deeper and deeper into the wheat until the yellow fields had vanished in the blackness of night, and the trailer-house in front finally stopped.

And his father stepped out, and examined the town that surrounded them.

And decided.

They peddled fish and chips from the red van at first — but only at first.

"Work fit only for Greeks!" his father would curse each morning, as he gutted and filleted the *pesci.* The same *pesci* he drove a hundred and fifty kilometres to the coast to fetch each Friday.

They rented a corner of asphalt from the local service station for the red van, and a corner of the showground for the trailer-house. It was cramped — but no more cramped than the *ostello.* Or even the ship. And before long they were offered a real house.

It was a Friday night, Frank remembered, that Bluey Horton's dad, the stationmaster, mentioned the disused fettlers' cottage down by the tracks. His parcel of butterfish was warm in his hands — he was feeling generous.

"Nominal rental, Mr Panozzi," he smiled. "We can't have the place lying empty."

So suddenly they were no longer gypsies — and wouldn't be Greek *pescivendori* for much longer either, if his father could help it.

For he had found the block he wanted a kilometre out of town. A kilometre downwind from town — the same block the abo Currie had been emptying his cans on to for years. The council let it go for a song, and before the end of that first year a bore had been sunk, a glasshouse built, and the windows of the red van filled with other things besides the stink of *pesci*. Soft globes of tomato, heavy melons, corn like thick thighs.

"Whatever is your secret, Mr Panozzi?" the ladies would ask as they queued outside the van.

And his father would laugh — the thick gypsy laugh he knew they wanted to hear.

"Just wash the veg careful, *signore*!"

Frank was older then, and could remember those first months in the town as if it were yesterday. And perhaps it was only yesterday — the years between seemed to have vanished overnight.

Years spent learning the new vocabulary — holding the words in the back of his mouth, and keeping the flies out of the front. And years spent learning other vocabularies — how to play foot with the awkward shaped balls, how to trap and skin rabbits, how to do the draw-back . . . and how to use his fists on the abos, the seemingly endless tribe of Curries of every shape and size and shade of black.

"Jesus! How many of them are there?" Bluey whispered to him one weekend, as they lay on their bellies in the cemetery peering into the backyard of the Curries' house.

If house was the word for a tin shed surrounded by heaps of old tyres, yellowing newspaper, broken glass . . .

"It's not a house!" Bluey said, remembering an opinion his mother had expressed. "It's a bloody chook-shed!"

But Frank didn't really care — the sun was hot, the marble slab beneath him cool, and he could have slept there all day.

And probably would have, too, if Bluey hadn't taken his

shanghai out, and started slinging ball-bearings on to the abos' roof.

And they had to leave in a hurry.

Come here before the day goes.

Frank had been at school for years before The Sign went up in the window of the General Emporium. But although he could read the words perfectly, he couldn't understand them — and neither could he understand the anger they produced in his father.

"Day go, day go!" the abos shouted across the schoolyard for a week or two. But quickly tired of it when the words had no effect on Frank.

And words proved of no more value to the Emporium. For it was a war of prices, not words — and as everyone in town knew, the dagos' were cheaper. And were still cheaper, even after building their new shop.

It took a whole summer to finish, Frank remembered — a summer of family slavery. Even Sergio — his other uncle — arrived from the city to help, and was paid at family rates — bed, board, and nightly *grappa*.

There was something that had drawn him immediately to Sergio — a kind of carefree joy, a love of life that he hadn't come across before. At least, not in adults.

Most of the time his uncle didn't work too hard, but when he did things happened with effortless ease. Footings would suddenly be poured, roofing timbers cut, bricks thrown almost carelessly into perfect mortared rows.

And then there was his talk. During his smokos — Sergio had innumerable smokos — he would rock back on his heels in the shade, dunk pieces of bread in a mug of wine and talk. Sergio could talk for almost as long as Frank could listen — of life in the city, of cards and clubs and money, of feasting and dancing and loving . . .

And above all, of his *professione*. Of playing the foot. His uncle did nothing else during winter, as far as Frank could gather, except play the foot. Then in summer, when there was no foot to play, he just drifted. A few weeks bricklaying with a brother here, a month fruitpicking with a cousin there. "*Vagabondo!*" Cesare would chide him — but tenderly. For Sergio was their youngest, their little *giovane*. And the older brothers were more than a little envious, Frank sensed — just as he himself was envious.

Especially when summer was over, and the shop was built, and the vagabond had gone. And taken the red van with him, that they needed no longer. Like a gypsy.

That same summer the Emporium closed, Frank remembered. And The Sign in its window vanished overnight — painted over in the same shade of grey that Cesare had used on the roof of the new shop.

And Frank finally understood.

"They're cutting their own throats, the dagos," he overheard Bluey's mum on the phone one day. "They can't even live on the prices they charge — all packed into one house like a mob of abos. Still, who's arguing . . .?"

But somehow they did live — and even Mrs Horton had to admit they were more than a mob of abos. For next summer Sergio returned, and between smokos a new house began to raise itself at the far end of town. And no sooner was its roof nailed down than the foundations of another were poured next door — a house for Cesare, and his wife arriving soon from Italy.

"Next year we build a *palazzo* for you, eh Francesco *mio*?" Sergio would tease. "And the lucky *signorina!*"

But it wasn't a joke to Frank — it seemed all too likely. And after his house, another for little Angelo. And then Maria, and Carla, and Cesare's children when they came, and . . .

"Spaghetti Street!" he shouted loudest and first at school, to show the others — just as he always shouted boong first. And just as it was his boot that felled the sports teacher during football training, and his crazy falsetto that ruined the chorus on Gilbert and Sullivan night and the entire opera degenerated into a giggling, squeaking farce.

Frank got his end in first, too — with Val Murphy in the

back seat of Bluey's Customline. It was the first verified root for any of them — unless the story about Bluey in the cemetery with one of the Currie girls was true. But Bluey, of course, always denied that one — and with the help of his fists, if necessary.

Frank was also the first to leave school — although that wasn't all his own idea. The headmaster, a Gilbert and Sullivan fan, had more than a little to do with it.

But soon they had all left — Val working in Goldsbrough Mort's, Bluey Horton humping wheat bags at the silo, Jimmy Fisher covering himself with grease at the service station.

And it was good at first — the new freedom. The money jingling, sometimes even crinkling, in their pockets, Friday nights gathering together at the drive-in, Saturdays at football and dance, and Sundays anywhere. Frankie and Val, Jimmy and his girl Sharon, and Bluey, always the chauffeur and odd one out.

And the one who tired of the routine first, Frank recalled. They had driven right through to the coast the Sunday Bluey first mentioned it, and were lying on the sand boozing.

"I'm just going to clear out one day," he suddenly said, as if the immensity of ocean around him had given him ideas. "I'm not wasting the rest of my life in a dump like that. Blink and you'd miss it . . . "

Only Frank was listening — Jimmy and Sharon had vanished into the sandhills, and Val was halfway round the beach to the point, dragging her feet through the shallows.

"What about it, Frankie?" Bluey went on. "The city, I mean."

He was half-pissed, Frank realized — the only time he meant what he said.

"Any day," Bluey said. "I'll come for you, Frankie. I'll take you with me . . . "

It was the wedding that finally decided him, Bluey said.

The sight of Jimmy Fisher scrubbed clean for once in his life, and somehow wedged into a suit. And Sharon next to

him, her face as white as her dress with the exertion of
sucking in her swollen belly.

Even Bluey had dug out a suit from somewhere for the
wedding — and looked dressed to kill, Val said.

"Dressed to kill all right!" he complained, loosening
his collar. "Dressed to bloody strangle!"

He told Frank during the toasts, when the two of them
had sneaked outside to pinch the wheels from the bride-
groom's car.

"Friday," he whispered. "Around lunchtime. Three toots
on the horn, and you either come with me — or stay . . ."

"Val might come too," Frank said — but more as a
question.

"You're cunt-struck," Bluey sneered. "Plenty more of
those in the city!"

They wiped the grease from their hands, adjusted the
nooses of their collars, and walked back into the reception.

"Friday!" Bluey reminded him.

"Second breakfast, Francesco *mio*!"

He'd been wandering again — Mamma had arrived with
lunch, and to mind the shop while he ate it. Or ate them —
the same peanut butter sandwiches he'd eaten every lunchtime for the last ten years. Ever since that first week at
school, when Bluey had grabbed the smoked fish out of his
bag, and run waving them around the yard.

"*Grazie.*"

He pushed through the back door and squatted in his usual
spot, back to the wall — the same section of wall he'd laid
himself the previous summer when they extended the shop.

The noon sun poured its warmth down over him, and even
the bricks behind him were warm — a solid reservoir of
warmth. He ate drowsily, chewing slow mouthfuls and
pushing them down his throat.

He was still eating when the Customline pulled up in the
back lane, and tooted three times — and he didn't stop
eating. His suitcase was packed and hidden among the crates,
but suddenly he couldn't seem to move.

Suddenly the world had pressed in around him — Mamma in the shop, his father and Cesare up the road, Val in her office across the street . . . even the sun shining above, and the warm bricks in the wall behind.

Bluey shouted, but Frank only shook his head — and then the car was gone, spinning its wheels and spitting gravel against the tin fence as it went.

The city could wait, Frank decided. There wasn't any hurry — no hurry at all.

Brief Notes on the Authors

LEONID TRETT was born in Estonia in 1905. He had a legal education and works now as a publicist and essayist. He has also written imaginative literature, in both Estonian and English. A number of works in the latter language are still awaiting publication.

ANDRÁS DEZSERY was born in Hungary in 1920. He has extensive experience as a publisher, author and journalist in both Hungary and Australia. He is the founder of Dezsery Ethnic Publications in Adelaide (1975) which has published: two works by himself — *Neighbours* (1980), a collection of short stories, and *The Amphibian* (1981), a novel — *English and Other Than English. Anthology in Community Languages* (1979) and seven books by ethnic writers in the original languages.

IRMGARD DUHS was born in 1939 in Striegau, Silesia. In post-war Germany she grew up in a village near Frankfurt am Main where she also attended high school and teacher's college. She immigrated to Australia in 1968, working first in factories and later as a teacher in govenment and private schools. In the early 1970s she spent two years in England and remarried. She now lives at Mt Tamborine, Queensland, and devotes her time to writing.

MARIA NOVAK was born in Hungary in 1922. She has worked as a nurse in Australia and has written poems and stories in both English and Hungarian.

HEINZ NONVEILLER emigrated from Austria at sixteen and within a relatively short time began writing in English. He has had a number of stories published in Australia, some of which have been broadcast by the ABC.

PINO BOSI was born in 1933 in a town ceded to Yugoslavia after 1945. His family immigrated to Australia in 1951. In 1970, after an active career in Journalism, he turned to freelance writing and has since written for a wide range of Italian and Australian magazines, and television and radio. He has also published six books and had one of his plays staged in Adelaide. He has been active in the sphere of multiculturalism and is about to publish *Who's Afraid of the Ethnic Wolf*.

VASSO KALAMARAS settled in Western Australia in 1951. She began writing in the early 50s and has published widely in both Greece and Australia, including: two bilingual volumes of poetry, a volume of poetry in Greek, a book of bilingual short stories (from which the stories in the present collection are taken) and a play, *The Breadtrap*, premiered in Melbourne in 1981. She lives in Perth and teaches Modern Greek at Perth Technical College.

UGO ROTELLINI was born in Italy and came to Australia with his parents at the age of five. He has worked in a variety of jobs, more recently as a social worker with the Department of Immigration and Ethnic Affairs. He has only recently begun to write for publication and has had several poems and short stories published in various magazines and newspapers.

VIC CARUSO was born in Italy in 1949 and settled with his family in Melbourne in 1956. He has worked as a journalist and was chief of staff with the *Australian's* Melbourne office. Since 1979 he has been a television reporter.

JUDAH WATEN was born in Odessa, Russia, in 1911, and immigrated with his family to Western Australia in 1914. He now lives in Melbourne and has established a firm, longstanding reputation as a major novelist, story writer and cultural activist.

ZENY GILES was born in Sydney in 1937 of Greek parents. She now lives in Newcastle and has in recent years published several stories, some of which have already appeared in a number of anthologies. Her story "The Economies of Mourning" won first prize in the Melbourne *Age* short story competition in 1980.

MORRIS LURIE was born in Melbourne in 1938, to which city he returned in 1973 following seven years abroad. He has published four novels, four collections of stories, three collections of reportage, three books for children, and a volume of plays. His stories have appeared in the US in *The New Yorker*, and in *Telegraph Sunday Magazine*. He has been widely translated and anthologized, and broadcast on the BBC.

NICHOLAS ATHANASOU was born in Perth and grew up in Sydney where he completed a medical degree. He has begun writing only recently and has to date had a number of stories published in: *inprint. The Short Story Magazine.*

ANGELO LOUKAKIS was born of Greek parents in 1951 in Sydney. He has a Master's degree in English from Sydney University and has been involved in multicultural education. A volume of his short stories (*For the Patriarch*) was published by the University of Queensland Press (1981).

GWEN KELLY was born in Sydney and has lived for the last twenty-seven years in Armidale, NSW, where her recently retired husband was a Classics Professor. She has written prose for publication since the 1950s, including four novels, the most recent being *Always Afternoon* (Collins, 1981). Her short stories can be found in numerous magazines and anthologies (including a German collection of Australian short stories). She has won the Lawson award for prose at the Grenfell Festival four times and the Melbourne *Sun Herald* short story award in 1980. From 1974-76 she held a Senior Literary Fellowship from the Literature Board of the Australia Council.

TOM HUNGERFORD was born in Perth in 1915. He began a long, continuous career in journalism in 1932, except for five years' active service in the Second World War. He has had numerous stories published in various anthologies, both in Australia and abroad. He has been an active short story editor for the Fellowship of Australian Writers and is currently a foundation member of the Western Australian Literary Fund Committee and Film Library Committee.

JOE WRIGHT is a farmer near Scone in New South Wales. He has taken up writing relatively recently and draws, for his subjects, on his considerable experience of life in the bush. His story "Indira" won the *Woman's Day* fiction competition in 1973. Since then he has published numerous stories in various newspapers, magazines and anthologies.

HELEN WILSON, as the daughter of a mining engineer, spent many years in the Western Australian outback, especially the goldfields. This is reflected in many of her stories and in her novels, *The Mulga Trees* and *Bring Back the Hour*. Many of her stories have appeared in overseas journals and have been broadcast by the BBC and the ABC. "Second Growth" is one of these, having first appeared in *Fair Lady*, in South Africa. Mrs Wilson has travelled extensively and now lives in Manly, NSW, where she has been actively connected with literary societies, having been a member of the Committee of Management of the Australian Society of Authors for five years. In 1980 she was awarded the Order of Australia Medal for services to Literature.

FAY ZWICKY was born in 1933 in Melbourne where she was educated and began to write both stories and poetry. She now lives in Perth and, apart from writing, is involved in the teaching of literature at the University of WA. A collection of her poetry, *Kaddish*, was published by the University of Queensland Press in 1982.

JOAN BEAN was born in Dubbo, NSW. She attended school in Sydney and has done tertiary study in both Victoria and NSW, graduating with a BA in English Literature at the University of Sydney in 1980. Apart from freelance writing she has worked as a textile designer, social worker, draftswoman and editorial assistant. In addition to short stories she has published several poems and two television plays.

MICHAEL SMITH was born in Greece (Rhodes) of a British father and Greek mother. Most of his early life was spent in England before his immigration to Australia, still at a relatively young age. He is a graduate of Adelaide University and particularly interested in rock music, a subject on which he has published in several Australian magazines.

RAY WOOD was born in the UK in 1943 and, after working in Fleet Street and the BBC, migrated to South Australia in 1973, subsequently working for the ABC and the South Australian Government. "Smoko" was his first serious attempt at fiction writing. His sympathy and empathy for ethnic migrants was aroused by personal experience of the traumas of migrating compounded by a visit to Japan when "being unable to read even the simplest sign I began to comprehend just how much more savage the experience must be for somebody from a small Greek village". He has also won awards for television scriptwriting and poetry.

NANCY KEESING A.M. was born in Sydney in 1923; her parents' families had settled in New Zealand and Australia in the 1840's and 1850's. She has had a career of more than thirty years as a poet, critic and writer of fiction and as a person closely involved with writers' affairs (including a period as Chairman of the Literature Board). She has published four volumes of poetry and is represented in numerous poetry anthologies. As well as editing numerous historical and literary anthologies, she has published three volumes of literary criticism, two children's novels, a biography and memoirs. She is presently Chairman of the NSW Committee of the National Book Council.

PETER GOLDSWORTHY was born at Minlaton, South Australia, in 1951. He spent the earlier part of his life in various other South Australian towns and finished his schooling in Darwin. He graduated in medicine from the University of Adelaide in 1974 and currently practises part-time. A collection of his short stories, entitled *Archipelagoes*, and a volume of his poetry, *Readings from Ecclesiastes*, were published by Angus and Robertson in 1982. He is married to a fellow graduate and has three children. "Before the Day Goes" won the 1980 Premio Bancarella Literary Award, organized by the Italian Festival of Victoria.